SAVAGE SUNDAY

Look for these exciting Western series from bestselling authors
WILLIAM W. JOHNSTONE
and **J. A. JOHNSTONE**

The Mountain Man
Preacher: The First Mountain Man
Luke Jensen: Bounty Hunter
Those Jensen Boys!
The Jensen Brand
MacCallister
The Red Ryan Westerns
Perley Gates
Have Brides, Will Travel
Will Tanner, Deputy U.S. Marshal
Shotgun Johnny
The Chuckwagon Trail
The Jackals
The Slash and Pecos Westerns
The Texas Moonshiners
Stoneface Finnegan Westerns
Ben Savage: Saloon Ranger
The Buck Trammel Westerns
The Death and Texas Westerns
The Hunter Buchanon Westerns

AVAILABLE FROM PINNACLE BOOKS

SAVAGE SUNDAY

A DUFF MACCALLISTER WESTERN

WILLIAM W. JOHNSTONE

AND J. A. JOHNSTONE

PINNACLE BOOKS

Kensington Publishing Corp.

www.kensingtonbooks.com

PINNACLE BOOKS are published by

Kensington Publishing Corp.
119 West 40th Street
New York, NY 10018

PUBLISHER'S NOTE
Following the death of William W. Johnstone, the Johnstone family is working with a carefully selected writer to organize and complete Mr. Johnstone's outlines and many unfinished manuscripts to create additional novels in all of his series like The Last Gunfighter, Mountain Man, and Eagles, among others. This novel was inspired by Mr. Johnstone's superb storytelling.

ISBN-13: 978-0-7860-4753-6
ISBN-10: 0-7860-4753-4

First Pinnacle paperback printing: June 2021

10 9 8 7 6 5 4 3 2 1

Printed in the United States of America

Electronic edition:

ISBN-13: 978-0-7860-4754-3 (e-book)
ISBN-10: 0-7860-4754-2 (e-book)

Chapter One

Wyoming Territory

Duff MacCallister sat on his horse, Sky, with Bear Creek behind him, watching as Elmer Gleason, Wang Chow, and two other cowboys worked to round up the cattle he would be taking to market. Duff, who had arrived in America some time ago, had been a cattleman in Scotland. The cattle he raised were Black Angus, and he had introduced the breed to Wyoming.

Elmer, who was his foreman, came riding over to him. "You ain't moved in so long, I didn't know but what you was a statue someone put up here," he teased.

"Sure now, 'n what would be the need of my moving when there's a good man handling things?" Duff asked.

Elmer smiled. "I'm a good man all right, 'n I'm glad you could see it."

"I was talking about Wang."

"Wang Chow? Why, that heathen wouldn't know the difference betwixt a cow 'n goat iffen I wasn't here to tell him."

Duff knew that Elmer calling the Chinaman a heathen was all in jest, for though he often used that sobriquet when referring to Wang Chow, the two men were actually very close friends.

"Perhaps Wang is a good man because you made him a good man," Duff suggested.

"Yeah, now, that's the truth of it," Elmer replied.

"What's the count?" Duff asked.

"We've got four hunnert 'n twenty rounded up so far," Elmer said. "I cipher that out to figure we'll need eighty more before we have the full gather. We'll have 'em all in before dark, so's we can leave first thing tomorrah mornin'."

"I've scheduled two special trains with fifteen cattle cars each, for the shipping of the cattle. One will be here at eleven, and the other at twelve. You'll have to see to the loading. The lass 'n I will be for taking the ten o'clock passenger train so we'll be in Cheyenne before the cattle arrive."

"So, Miss Meagan is goin' with you, is she?"

"Aye, 'tis a trip she's been looking forward to."

Elmer chuckled. "No more 'n you, I'm bettin'."

"Sure 'n 'tis a smart fellow you are," Duff replied with a laugh.

"Well, don't you be worryin' none 'bout them cows, on account of me 'n Wang will get the trains loaded," Elmer said.

Cabin, five miles west of Cheyenne, Wyoming Territory

The cabin had been abandoned when the four men found it, and it showed the disrepair from being a long time empty, with broken windows and missing doors. The only improvement they had made was to get the stove back in working order.

Bart Jenkins used his hat to protect his hand as he lifted the coffeepot off that same stove and poured coffee into his tin cup. There were three others around the stove. Moe Conyers, a cowboy who had been fired from the last three ranches where he had worked. Slim Gardner, whose honest work had been minimal, from teamster to mopping the floors in a saloon. The third was a black man, and nobody knew much about his background, nor did they even know his name. He identified himself as Black Liberty, but Jenkins was almost certain that wasn't his real name.

"How much money are we talking about?" Slim asked.

"It's hard to tell," Bart said. "It's a bank. How much money is in a bank?"

"I don't know," Moe said. "I ain't never robbed me no bank before. I mean, you can get yourself shot holdin' up a bank."

"You won't be holdin' up the bank," Bart said. "Neither you, nor Black Lib."

"What? Why not? You ain't leavin' us out, are you?"

"No," Bart answered. "I've got a job for both of you. Black, they's a saloon in Hillsdale called the Hog Waller in the town, 'n right acrost the street from it is Sikes Hardware Store. They's a bench in front of that store, 'n that's where I'm goin' to want you to be, 'cause you can tie your horse off right there. Don't worry none 'bout bein' colored. They's two, maybe three families of colored people in town, so nobody will pay you no never mind. You sit there while Moe goes into the saloon.

"Moe, what you're goin' to do when you go into the saloon is commence a-shootin' up the place, but you better watch out for the bartender on account of he's likely to have him a shotgun under the bar.

"Don't stay long enough for anyone to shoot back, then you run outta the saloon, climb up on your horse, 'n ride outta town, headin' north. They's only the sheriff 'n one deputy in town. Soon as they hear the shootin', they'll more 'n likely come a-runnin' after you.

"Black, soon as you see the two lawmen chasin' after Moe, you get on your horse 'n chase after them. Moe, after you've come out of town a little ways, find yourself a rock to get behind, 'n wait for 'em. With Black comin' up behind 'em, you'll have the sheriff 'n his deputy caught betwixt the two of you 'n you can ambush 'em. Oughta take no more 'n you two to shoot the sheriff 'n his deputy. While you two is takin' care o' them, me 'n Slim will ride in 'n rob the bank. Won't have no problem with it, cause the sheriff and deputy will more 'n likely be dead by then. Ever'one else will still be thinkin' 'bout the shootin' that happened in the saloon.

"We'll meet back at the cabin, but ride aroun' a lot so's to throw anyone that might be a-chasin' you off track. Don't be a-leadin' 'em to the cabin. That way we'll always have a place to hide out," Bart said.

"What time we goin' to do this tomorrah?" Moe asked.

"Right after noon. That way there'll be some customers in the saloon, but not likely so many as to cause you any problems when you commence to shootin' the place up."

"Damn if that ain't about the best damned idee I've ever heard," Moe said.

Chugwater, Wyoming Territory

Biff Johnson, owner and proprietor of the Fiddler's Green Saloon, was opening a little earlier than he did on most days. He had told Duff he would be there when they came into town this morning. As he reached for the coffeepot, he knocked something from the shelf, and reaching down, he retrieved the pennant. Holding the pennant in his hand for a moment, as if studying it. It was a symbol of his past, a thirty-three inch by twenty-seven inch, swallow-tailed flag of the kind that had been hand-stitched by New York City seamstresses during the Civil War. It featured a field of thirteen red and white alternating stripes and a blue canton with thirty-five stenciled gilt stars, forming a circle within a circle, plus four more stars, one in each corner of the canton.

As the former Sergeant Major Benjamin Franklin Johnson held the flag, Custer's last battle came to him with a clarity and intensity as great as it was on the day it happened.

June 25, 1876

Custer had already detached Benteen's Battalion, as well as the trains, then he continued north, along with Reno's Battalion. When they reached the South Fork of the Little Bighorn River, he held up his hand and stopped the column. "Major Reno!"

Reno came to the front, saluted, and reported to Custer.

"Major, I want you to take your three companies across the river and attack the village from the south. Maintain pressure against them. I will go a little farther north, cross the river, and attack from the other side." Custer smiled. "This way we will have the devils between us."

"Sir, do you think it is wise to split your command?" Reno asked.

"Major, you will do as I have ordered," Custer said firmly.

"Yes, sir," Reno said with a salute then rode to the back of the column to give orders to his battalion.

"Sergeant Major Johnson!" Custer called after Reno left.

"Yes, sir?" Biff answered.

"I want you to detach yourself from Captain Keogh, and go with Major Reno."

"But, sir, I would rather be with my own troops."

"I know you would, Sergeant Major, and I would rather have you with us, but Reno is untried. I would feel better knowing that you were with him."

"Yes, sir," Biff replied, the disappointment obvious in his voice.

Custer continued toward the village, while Reno, as ordered, pressed against the bottom end of the village where the Hunkpapa Lakota were located.

After his first engagement with the Indians, Reno dismounted his men and had them form a skirmish line.

"Sir, the colonel ordered us to attack the village," Biff said. "We aren't attacking, we're defending. We're cavalry, sir, we should stay mounted."

"When you get your own command, Sergeant Major, you can make the decisions," Reno replied in a high-pitched, frightened voice. "But you aren't in command, are you? I am. Now form a skirmish line like I told you to."

"We won't be able to sustain a skirmish line," Biff said.

"Do as I tell you, Sergeant Major!" Reno ordered.

"Yes, sir."

The result of Reno's incompetent leadership was exactly as Biff had predicted. Because Reno's troops lost their mobility, the Indians were able to maneuver around the skirmish line. What was supposed to be an attack became first a defense line, then, as Reno couldn't hold it, he ordered his men to fall back toward the river, where their defense was even less effective. As the fighting intensified, he lost his nerve and ordered a retreat.

Reno completely abandoned his men, thinking only of his own safety. Instead of an orderly retreat, it became a rout. Many of his men did not make it across the river, where Biff, Lieutenant Tom Weir, and a couple of the other officers finally managed to establish a defense.

When Benteen arrived, Biff thought their units would merge then move forward to relieve the pressure on Custer. There, he saw the body of First Sergeant Frank Varden, Biff's closest friend in the regiment, and he felt a particular loss seeing Frank lying among the many wounded and dead. Biff dismounted and kneeled next to his friend.

"Biff, when me 'n you get out of the army, what do you say we open us up a saloon?"

"Sounds good to me," Biff replied. "What'll we call it? Johnson and Varden?"

"Nah, we'll give it a good name. We'll call it Fiddler's Green."

"My friend," Biff said quietly. "You're at Fiddler's Green now. Save a place for me. I'll be along one of these days."

As he turned over First Sergeant Varden's body, he found a guidon Varden had tucked into his shirt.

* * *

"This guidon," Biff said quietly in the saloon, looking at the one he was holding in his hand. As he put the swallow-tailed flag back in its place, the memories of that battle faded away, sight and sound, tone and tint.

He had opened his saloon and, as Varden had suggested, he called it Fiddler's Green. Cavalry legend has it that anyone who has ever served as a cavalryman will, after they die, stop by Fiddler's Green—a shady glen where the grass is good and a nearby stream of cool water provides for the horses. There, cavalrymen from all wars and generations will drink beer, chew tobacco, smoke their pipes, and visit. They will regale one another with tales of derring-do until that last syllable of recorded time, at which moment they will bid each other a last good-bye before departing for their final and eternal destination.

The front door opened and four people walked in—Duff, Meagan Parker, Elmer, and Wang.

"You mean the sheriff ain't closed this place as a health hazard yet?" Elmer called out.

"I've got my rats and roaches trained," Biff replied. "They run away and hide anytime a sheriff's deputy comes in here."

"Now, you see there, Wang? If roaches can be taught, why I bet even you could larn somethin'," Elmer teased.

"If I am walking with two other men, each of them will serve as my teacher. I will pick out the good points of the one and imitate them, and the bad points of the other and correct them in myself," Wang replied.

"That's one o' them things that heathen feller, Confusion, is always sayin' ain't it?"

"Confucius," Wang corrected.

"Well, hell, ain't that what I done just said?"

Meagan laughed. "Elmer, I suggest that you stop now before you get yourself in any deeper."

"Yeah, well, I was goin' to stop anyhow. I thought we come in here for a drink.

"Use my table," Biff invited.

Chapter Two

Duff, Meagan, Elmer, and Wang sat at Biff's private table having a drink. There had been a time when a few of the customers had questioned Wang Chow's right to be in Fiddler's Green, but Biff had let them know, in no uncertain terms, that Wang would always be welcome. And because Fiddler's Green was a particularly nice saloon, no stigma was ever attached to a woman being there. Meagan felt quite comfortable in the environment.

"Listen, if you happen to see one of them silver hatbands, I'd like you to buy it for me," Elmer said. "I can give you some money for it now, or you can just tell me how much it costs, 'n I'll pay you when you get back. I think one o' them silver hatbands would make me look just real elegant."

"Elegant, you say. Aren't you displaying a bit of vanity there, Elmer?" Meagan asked, a little laugh showing that she was teasing.

"Well, here's the thing, Miss Meagan. If I don't brag on myself, who will? You know Duff ain't goin' to do it, 'n the heathen here, why he don't even know what braggin' is."

Meagan laughed. "You do have a point. I'll look for it, for you, Elmer. I'm going to be doing quite a bit of shopping for my store."

"Thank you, ma'am," Elmer said.

"What about you, Wang? What could we be getting for you from the big city?" Duff asked.

"I want nothing."

"How long do you think you'll be gone?" Biff asked.

"Two or three days," Duff said. "You heard the lass. She wants to tarry a bit, 'n I'll be there with her until she's done."

"There's no need for you to stay with me, Duff. I can get home by myself," Meagan said.

"Ha, you don't understand, Miss Meagan. He ain't worried none 'bout you gettin' back by your ownself. He's worried 'bout him gettin' back by his ownself," Elmer said, and the others laughed.

Meagan glanced toward the clock. "The train is due within the next half hour. Don't you think it might be a good idea to go down to the depot now?"

"Aye," Duff replied. "I'll be for wantin' to check on the cattle one more time before we leave, so now's a good time to do it."

"Have a good trip, and don't be doing anything I wouldn't do," Biff said as they stood from the table to leave.

"Damn, Biff, you've just told 'em they can do anything they want to do, 'cause just what is it that you wouldn't do?" Elmer teased.

* * *

At that same moment, one mile west of Chugwater, Lou Martell, a man of some disrepute, and three others, just as disreputable, were breaking camp.

"You sure this fella we're lookin' for is in Chugwater?" Deekus Carlotti asked.

"I read about 'im in a newspaper that picked up a story from the *Chugwater Defender*. It said a Chinaman named Wang Chow worked for a rancher here, by the name of Duff MacCallister. 'N this Chinaman come from China, so you know it's the selfsame one."

Carlotti laughed. "Well hell, don't all Chinamen come from China?"

"Did you come from Italy?" Martell asked.

"What? No, I was borned in Arkansas."

"Yeah? Well most of the Chinamans here was borned here, too. But this here Wang Chow was borned in China, 'n he kilt some important people there. Now China has put out a reward of a hunnert thousand dollars to anyone who can bring him in, or kill 'im."

"Hey, Martell, if we capture this Chinaman, we won't have to be a-takin' 'im all the way back to China, will we?"

"No, they's these fellas in San Francisco called the Dongs, or somethin' like that. If we can get 'im to them Dongs . . ."

"I think it is *Tong*," Gabe Kellis said.

"Yeah, the Tong. Anyway, all we got to do is prove to the Tong that he's been kilt. We can do that by takin' his head back to 'em, 'n when we do that, they'll give us twenty-five thousand dollars," Martell said.

"Wait, I thought you said this here Chinaman was worth a hunnert thousand dollars." The protest came from a man named Emmet Willard.

"It's only a hunnert thousand dollars if we take his head all the way to China," Martell replied. "Do you really want to do that? Anyhow, when's the last time you ever had twenty-five thousand dollars?"

"I ain't never had me no twenty-five thousand dollars."

"Well, all we got to do to get it is kill us a Chinaman. 'N just how hard do you think that will be?"

"Here's what I'm worried about, though," Carlotti said. "If we just up 'n kill 'im, what about the sheriff? Ain't we liable to have to deal with him on account of we murdered someone?"

"We don't need to be a-worryin' none 'bout no sheriff," Martell said. He held up a piece of paper. "This here paper is a reward from China. All we have to do is show the sheriff this paper."

"How's the sheriff goin' to read it, if it's in Chinese?" Carlotti asked.

"It's in Chinese 'n it's also in American," Martell said.

Kellis laughed. "There ain't no such thing as an American language."

"What the hell do you think we're talkin' in now, if it ain't American?" Martell asked.

"English," Kellis said. "We're talkin' *English*."

"Hmm. I allus thought that was the same thing," Martell said. "All right, boys, put out the fire. We're a-fixin' to go into town, 'n make us a lot o' money."

* * *

As Duff, Meagan, Elmer, and Wang walked toward the depot, they could smell the closely packed cattle from Sky Meadow and hear the almost human bawling cries they were making because the change in their environment made them anxious. Five hundred head of Black Angus cattle had been crowded into the loading pens at the Chugwater Depot.

Duff had sold the cattle to a Kansas City cattle broker, who would take delivery of and pay for them in Cheyenne. The recently built railroad from Ft. Laramie to Cheyenne took its route took through Chugwater. What used to be a two-day hard drive of the cattle had been reduced to a little more than two hours.

The railroad would have put a caboose on one of the leased trains, and he and Meagan could have ridden for no additional cost had he wanted, but he'd passed on the offer. He wanted to be in Cheyenne before the leased trains arrived so he could see to their distribution there. He wasn't worried about leaving the cattle behind. Elmer and Wang, two of his best men and closest friends, were remaining. Duff was confident they would see to the shipment of the cattle.

"Elmer, as soon as you get the beasties loaded, you and Wang can be for taking a little time off while Meagan and I see to the business in Cheyenne."

"Now, just what do you think me 'n this heathen can find to do while you two is gone?" Elmer asked.

"Well, I don't know what you two might find to do,

but perhaps Vi Winslow and Mae Lin would have a suggestion," Duff replied with a smile.

"Oh, yeah. I forgot about them," Elmer said.

"Elmer, you wouldn't want me to tell Vi that you had forgotten about her, would you?" Meagan teased.

"No, now, there ain't no call for you to go 'n do nothin' like that," Elmer protested. "She might not never let me have no more o' them pies she bakes."

Vi Winslow owned Vi's Pies, a small, but one of the more successful businesses in Chugwater. She was an attractive widow in her early forties who had shown an interest in Elmer, and that interest was reciprocated.

"Train comes." Wang didn't engage in banter, not because he was aloof, but because English was a second language to him.

"What train? I don't hear no train," Elmer challenged.

"Train comes," Wang repeated. "Look." He pointed north.

There, barely discernable, was a thin ribbon of smoke.

"Oh, yeah. Well sure. I mean if you're talkin' about *that* train, now that you mention it, I see it, too," Elmer replied. "I just didn't know which train you were talking about."

Half an hour later, with good-byes said and final instructions given, Duff and Meagan boarded the train, then took a seat in the day coach, all they would require for a trip less than two hours.

Meagan wasn't traveling with Duff only because they were friends, though indeed their relationship was quite close. Like Elmer, she was a partner in ownership of the cattle that were being sold, so even if their personal relationship hadn't been close, she had every right to represent her interest.

"Duff, do you think Elmer and Vi will ever get married?"

Duff chuckled. "I'd not be for knowin' that, lass, and you have to admit that Elmer is a cantankerous old chancer."

"'N here you are speakin' with a wee bit o' the unfathomable Scottish talk. What would chancer be?" Meagan asked, perfectly mimicking Duff's Scottish brogue.

"Bha mi a 'smaoineachadh gu robh thu ag ionnsachadh a' chànain," Duff said in Scottish-Gaelic.

"Tha mi ag ionnsachadh a 'chànain," Meagan said, getting exactly the roll and lilt in her response. Then she repeated in English, "I *am* learning the language."

Duff laughed. "Sure now lass, 'n your words make me think I'm back in the heather again. Chancer means that Elmer has a wee bit o' the chicanery about him. But even so, 'tis a good man he is."

"You're lucky, no, *we're* lucky to have two such"—she paused, searching for the right word—"remarkable men as friends."

"Aye, lass, we are indeed."

Shortly after the train left the station, Duff thought about the woman sitting beside him. Back in Scotland there had been Skye McGregor, the woman he had planned to marry. But on the very day before they were to wed, she was murdered by a dishonest sheriff, and that had caused Duff to seek revenge. His success in exacting vengeance forced him to leave Scotland, thus accounting for his presence in America.

He'd thought he would never meet another woman to fill his heart as Skye had done, but to his surprise, Meagan had done just that. Feeling her so close and breathing in her perfume, he could almost believe she was the only woman he had ever felt that way about.

Chapter Three

After Elmer had seen the train off, he glanced up at the clock. "We got us an hour until the first one o' them two trains Duff ordered will get here. That's just about time enough to have us a piece of pie. You want to come with me?"

"You go. I think it would be better if I stay here and wait for the train," Wang said.

"Uh-huh. You're sure you ain't plannin' on stealin' them cows soon as I'm gone?"

"I have thought about this," Wang said, going along with the tease. "But I do not think I can do this by myself."

"Well, there you go then," Elmer said. "There ain't no need for me to be a-stayin' here to keep an eye on you. I'm goin' to go have me a piece of pie, but I'll be back before the first train gets here."

"Please tell *zhāng nüshì* Vi of my good wish for her," Wang said.

"I'll do that, but don't you be goin' after my woman. You got one of your own," Elmer said, smiling to ameliorate his words.

Vi's Pies was quite busy when Elmer arrived, so he just ordered a piece of apple pie. Then, sitting at a corner table by himself, he had time to think, and he thought of the events of his life that had brought him to this place and this time.

He had a background of experiences that far predated his arrival in Chugwater and his employment at Sky Meadow. It could be said that he was, more than most men, the sum total of all his experiences.

During the Civil War, Elmer had ridden with Quantrill's irregulars. After the war was over some of the men who had ridden with Quantrill and who had nothing to come back to continued just as they had before. Jesse and Frank James were such men, and for a short while Elmer had been a member of the James Gang, but in a fortuitous bit of timing, he left the gang just before their infamous and disastrous Northfield Raid. Going west, he lived with the Indians for a while, then, drifting even farther west, he signed on to the crew of a merchant ship at San Francisco.

For five years Elmer sailed the seas, visiting exotic ports of call from the South Sea Islands, to India, the Philippines, Japan, and China, rising in rating from an able-bodied seaman to bosun's mate. His thoughts turned to his time aboard the *Eliza Jane*.

July 10, 1872, at sea

Most of the sailors on board were recent additions to the crew. They were fifteen days out of Sofala, Mozambique, when Elmer learned they were planning a mutiny. He went to the captain with the information.

"How many are there?" Captain Chambers asked.

"They's at least fifteen of 'em," Elmer replied. "I don't know, maybe even as many as twenty."

"That's more than half the crew," Captain Chambers said. "Lord help us, we'll never be able to stand them off."

"Yeah, but they ain't none of 'em will have guns," Elmer said. "I will have a gun."

"But you are just one man," the captain said, his voice laced with concern.

"I'll have a gun," Elmer repeated.

It was three days later before the mutineers decided to put their plan in action. As chief boatswain, Elmer was on the quarterdeck with Captain Chambers and the helmsman.

Twenty of the crew approached the quarterdeck. Most were armed with belaying pins. A few even had knives.

"You folks up on the quarterdeck, come on down," one of the sailors called out. "We're takin' over this ship."

"You're the leader of this mutiny, are you, Larrabee?" Elmer asked.

"Yeah, I'm the leader. Step aside so we can get to the cap'n, 'n you won't be hurt none," Larrabee answered.

"You got this all planned out, have you? So tell me, Larrabee, are you a-plannin' on bein' the new captain?"

Larrabee smiled. "Someone will have to do it."

"We've already got a captain."

"Yeah? Well, we're about to take care of that."

"I tell you what. All of y'all who'll just back away now 'n go on back about your business, ain't likely to get hurt. But if any of you so much as put one foot on the ladder you're goin' to be hurt, 'n hurt bad. Mostly, you're goin' to be kilt."

"Let's go, men!" Larrabee shouted as he started up the steps toward the quarterdeck.

Elmer pulled a sawed-off shotgun from behind the binnacle and fired both barrels at the men who had answered Larrabee's call. At that range, the eighteen thirty-caliber balls of the two barrels of 10-gauge, double-ought shot threw out an absolute kill pattern of three yards. Larrabee and five other men were cut down by the blast.

So shocked were the other mutineers that, for just a moment, they stared at the bloody carnage of what, but seconds earlier, had been living co-mutineers.

That hesitation allowed Elmer to reload the sawed-off shotgun. "Anyone else want to try?"

The remaining fourteen men gave Elmer no reply and withdrew meekly.

After leaving the sea, Elmer spent some time in Afghanistan, where, as a mercenary, he had been fighting for the Afghans against the British. He knew that Duff fought for the British, serving with the Black Watch Regiment, but Elmer was glad that Duff hadn't been in Afghanistan. Elmer didn't like to think he and Duff would have ever been enemies. That was part of Elmer's history, and it couldn't be changed.

Although he'd finished his pie, his thoughts turned to Afghanistan.

October 5, 1879, Badakhshan province of Afghanistan

It was raining hard as Elmer waited on the Khyber Pass Road in the shadow of the Hindu Kush Mountains. He had information that a British pay officer would be coming this way, accompanied by a small guard detail. Elmer's men were hidden in the rocks completely out of sight, whereas the British soldiers and the stagecoach were on the road in plain view.

As the pay detail approached, Elmer held his hand up, prepared to give the signal but held back when, unexpectedly, the British officer in charge of the guard rode to the front, stopped, then looked down the road. A captain, he sent two of his soldiers on ahead.

Elmer turned in his saddle to make certain his men were well concealed and motioned for Sajadi to get out of sight. At his signal, the Afghanis slipped back behind the rocks.

If the advance guard had been more observant, the British captain might have been forewarned. One of the boulders had been prepared to be rolled down upon the trail, and the path between it and the road had been cleared of rocks and natural elevations that might impede the deployment of the boulder. But the Brits gave no more than a cursory glance ahead.

It was obvious that the soldiers were miserable in the cold rain that ran down their shakos and dripped under the collars of their soaked red jackets, making them miserable and less attentive than they should have been. Their scouts ahead of the detail were perfunctory at best, then they rode back at a quick trot through the narrow, muddiest part of the road to report that all was well.

The captain sat on his horse for a long moment, as if trying to decide whether or not he should trust the report.

"Come on, Brit," Elmer whispered under his breath. "They told you it was clear. What are you waiting for?"

Finally, the British officer gave the order to proceed.

With a sigh of relief, Elmer waved once, and Sajadi returned to his position by the boulder that had been freed to roll easily. Elmer stood by, watching the coach and the escort detail continue ahead, waiting until all were fully committed.

Choosing the exact moment, he brought his hand down and heard two sharp reports as a sledgehammer took out the wedges holding the big rock back. With crunching and loud popping sounds, the boulder started down, reaching the middle of the muddy road with the crashing thunder of an artillery barrage. At the same time the boulder blocked the path of the coach, Elmer and his men moved out onto the road behind the Brits and fired several shots into the air.

"You're surrounded!" Elmer shouted, urging his horse onto the road from behind the boulders alongside it. He leveled his pistol at the soldiers. "Throw down your guns and put up your hands."

"Mercenaries!" one of the soldiers shouted, and he threw down his rifle. The other soldiers, perhaps taking their cue from him, threw their weapons down as well. Only the British captain refused the order. He brought his pistol up, pointed it at Elmer, then pulled the trigger.

Elmer saw the cylinder turn and heard the hammer click, but the cartridge misfired.

Elmer aimed at the officer. "Drop your gun, Captain! Do it now! Don't make me kill you!"

The captain lowered his pistol, then let it drop into the mud. "Good Lord! That accent. Are you a Yank?"

"Don't be callin' me a Yankee, damn you. I fought agin' them damn Yankees for four years."

"You are! You are an American! What are you doing fighting on the side of the savages?"

"They're payin' me. You ain't. Now, I want all you boys to get down offen them horses," Elmer ordered.

Grumbling, the men got down, and a couple of Elmer's men, all of whom were Afghanis, began gathering up the horses.

"You're stealing our horses?" the British officer asked.

"It ain't called stealin,' sonny," Elmer explained. "It's called confiscating enemy assets. You're the enemy of these boys, and these here horses are assets. And, speaking of assets, I'll take the money satchel."

"What makes you think we are carrying money?"

"Because you are delivering the payroll." Elmer chuckled. "But I'll bet you didn't know you were delivering the payroll to my boys." He pointed his pistol at the captain. "Now tell the pay officer inside the coach to throw out the money satchel, or I'll shoot you dead."

"Leftenant Davencourt, please, deliver the satchel," the captain called.

A canvas bag was tossed out through the coach window. Sajadi retrieved it, then using his Khyber sword, whacked off the top part of the bag. He let out a little chortle, then reached down inside to pick up a handful of gold coins. He showed the gold coins to a round of cheers, then he dropped them back into the bag.

"You're making a big mistake, mister," the captain said. "That money belongs to Her Majesty."

"Does it now?" Elmer asked sarcastically. "Well, I'll just bet the old bag has a lot more where this came from."

At that moment, Elmer saw the end of a pistol poke out from the passenger window. He fired at the stagecoach, not to hit whoever was inside, but merely to get his attention.

"Get out of the coach, now, friend," Elmer ordered, "or the next time I'll shoot to kill."

The coach door opened, and the pay officer stepped down. He was an overweight man, wearing a red jacket with white lapels. He swore angrily. "You bloody Yank!"

"I done told this other feller, I ain't no damn Yankee," Elmer said.

His men had loaded all the money into two other sacks and tied the necks of the sacks together, then handed them to Elmer. He laid them across his saddle in such a way as to allow one bag to hang down on each side of the horse.

"Captain, would you and your boys be so kind as to shuck out of them clothes right now?" Elmer asked.

"Shuck out?" the captain replied, not understanding the term.

"Take 'em off," Elmer said. "All of you. Take off your clothes. Strip down to your long johns."

"Now, just a damn minute, sir," a sergeant said. "I have no intention of taking off my clothes."

Elmer lifted his pistol. "Get out of them."

Grumbling and protesting, the soldiers began undressing. A few moments later, all of them, including the captain and the pay officer, were standing in the mud in their long johns. This was in accordance with the plan, since Elmer believed that a lack of clothing and horses would preclude any chase. The two men Elmer had assigned to pick up the uniforms did so.

"Look at these here officers, men," Elmer said. "Without them fancy uniforms and all that brass and braid, they don't look all that highfalutin, do they?"

"You bloody knave. You've no right to demean our officers like that."

Elmer recognized the man who spoke as one who, a moment earlier, had been wearing the stripes of a sergeant.

"You are a good man, Sergeant," he said with what to the sergeant and the other British soldiers, seemed to be a surprising amount of respect. He turned to the driver. "Unhitch the team."

"What's the reason for that?" the driver asked.

"No reason," Elmer replied. "I just want to keep you folks busy for a few minutes after we're gone, that's all. It'll take you that long to get back into harness. By then we'll be gone. Oh, and you'll find your clothes in a big heap about a mile down the road."

Elmer returned to the States after his time in Afghanistan, and he wound up in New Mexico for a while, then from New Mexico he drifted up to Wyoming, and that's where he and Duff met.

Duff discovered him when he found Elmer living in an old, abandoned mine on property Duff had just acquired.

Elmer had located a new vein of gold in the mine, but except for a few nuggets, had been unable to capitalize on it, so he was living a hand-to-mouth existence in the mine, unshaved and dressed only in skins.

Because the mine was on the property Duff had just filed upon, everything Elmer had taken from the mine actually belonged to Duff, and while Duff had every right to drive Elmer off, he didn't. He offered Elmer a one-half partnership in the mine. The legitimacy of that partnership enabled Elmer to abandon his hermit-like conditions, and he built a cabin near Duff's house on the ranch.

The partnership had paid off handsomely for both of them. Elmer was Duff's foreman and closest friend. And Duff's half of the proceeds from the mine had built Sky Meadow into one of the most productive ranches in Wyoming. The gold had long since played out, but Elmer had an interest, not in the ranch itself, but a 20 percent interest in whatever the ranch earned.

Wang Chow also had an interesting background. He was an ordained Buddhist monk, trained in martial arts at the Shaolin Temple in Mount Song of Henan Province, China. He was expelled from the order when he used his skills to kill the men who had murdered his family. When a death decree was issued against him, he came to America as an ordinary worker.

When Duff discovered him, he was sitting on a horse with a noose around his neck. He had been sentenced, not by the court, but by a group of vigilantes. His crime was riding in a surrey with a white woman. There was no untoward connection between Wang and the woman. He was merely riding with her.

As a result of Duff's rescue, the Chinaman had committed himself to Duff from that moment on. Wang never used a gun, but he didn't have to. So far, his martial arts skills had served him well.

He was totally unaware that the Dowager Empress Ci Xi had, through the Tong in America, placed a reward of one hundred thousand dollars for proof that Wang had been killed.

Chapter Four

"Fiddler's Green? What the hell kind o' name is that for a saloon?" Deekus asked. "You think they'll have some fiddler a-wearin' green, 'n just fiddlin' away?" He held his arms out and began moving one of them back and forth as if he were using a bow.

The others laughed.

"It don't make no difference what the name of the saloon is," Lou said. "Saloons is where you can always find out stuff. We'll go to the saloon 'n make out like we're friends of Wang Chow, like we knowed him before. All we gotta do is ask the bartender where at it is that we can find Wang Chow, 'n most likely he'll know."

"Hey, reckon we could get us a beer there before we go off chasin' this here Chinaman?" Gabe asked.

"Yeah," Deekus added. "The thing is, if we get to drinkin' us a couple of beers or so, 'n make out like we're just real friendly with folks, most special the bartender, looks to me like he'd be more likely to tell us what we need to know."

"I don't see no reason why we couldn't have us a

beer or two," Lou said. "It might be good to warsh down some o' the trail dust."

"You're tellin' me," Willard said. "I got me so much dust in my mouth that I could plant me a field of cotton."

"Corn," Gabe said.

"What?"

"You cain't grow cotton up here. It's too far north. You'll have to grow corn."

The other three men laughed.

"What's the name of this place again?" Deekus asked.

"Fiddler's Green," Lou said. "I think that's Chugwater just ahead there."

"Damn, I'm already tastin' the beer," Gabe said.

"I'm already spendin' the reward money," Deekus said.

After Elmer and Wang had gotten the cattle loaded onto the two trains, they decided to have a drink at Fiddler's Green Saloon before going back out to the ranch.

"Did you get the cattle loaded?" Biff asked.

Fiddler's Green was practically a museum to the Seventh Cavalry in general, and to Custer's last battle, in particular. The walls were decorated with regimental flags and troop pennants, with arrows, lances, pistols, and carbines picked up from more than a dozen engagements. Biff also had General Custer's hat. He gave thoughts back to that day.

August 4, 1876, Monroe, Michigan

Sergeant Major Biff Johnson was in full dress uniform complete with the medal of honor he had won at the

Battle of Sailor's Creek. As soon as he stepped down from the train, he escorted General Custer's widow into the depot building, then left her there while he made arrangements for a carriage to take her home.

Half an hour later, with the task done, he saluted Libby to take his leave of her.

"Sergeant Major, wait a moment, please," Libby called out to him. She went into another room for a moment, then returned, carrying a hat. "This was the general's favorite hat. I would like for you to have it."

"I thank you ma'am," Biff said. "I will treat this hat with honor."

That hat and the pennant he had taken from Varden's body had the highest position of honor of all his artifacts in Fiddler's Green Saloon.

"Here it is," Lou Martell said as he and three other men approached the little town. "This is Chugwater."

"How do you know?" Deekus Carlotti asked.

"Don't you see what the sign says?" Martell said.

"You know I can't read."

"Willard, tell 'im what the sign says."

"It says Chugwater, population six hunnert 'n twelve," Emmet Willard said, proudly displaying his ability to read.

"Are you sure this here town is where the Chinaman lives?" Gabe Kellis asked.

"That's what we was told."

"'N all we got to do is kill 'im,'n prove to this feller Tong that we done that?" Gabe continued.

"That's all we got to do," Lou said.

"But this Tong feller is in San Francisco, ain't he? That's a long way to go," Willard said.

"We can go to San Francisco by train. Yeah, it's a long way to go, but it's worth it for twenty-five thousand dollars." Martell said.

"I don't figure the railroad is goin' to let us just bring somebody's head on board," Carlotti said. "Don't you think they're likely to raise a ruckus about it?"

"We'll have his head in a sack. There won't nobody even know what it is we're carryin'."

"What if it gets to stinkin'?" Doolin asked.

"Iffen it's just the head, it won't get to stinkin' like it would iffen it was his whole body," Martell said assuredly.

"Are you sure someone in the saloon will be able to tell us where he is?" Kellis asked.

"Well, there's that saloon we was told about just ahead," Martell explained. "People that goes into saloons most o' the time knows just about ever'one that's in town, 'n there can't be that many Chinamen."

The four men looped their reins around the hitching rail, then pushed their way in through the batwing doors. They stopped just as soon as they stepped inside.

"Lou, lookie there. There's a Chinaman at that table back there."

"Yeah," Martel said. "I see 'im."

Elmer saw the four men come in, and decided they were either just passing through or were new to Chugwater, because he had never seen them before. All four of the men were wearing guns in holsters that were low and tied down. They looked like gunfighters.

The four looked around the room and spoke among themselves for a moment.

Martell pointed to Wang and called out, "Hey, you! Are you the chink that's named Wang Chow?"

"I am called Wang Chow," he replied, showing no reaction to the pejorative sobriquet.

Drawing his pistol, Martell pointed it at Wang. "You got a price on your head, chink."

"What the hell are you talkin' about?" Elmer asked. "There's no paper out on Wang. You've got the wrong man."

The man with the gun smiled and shook his head. "Uh-uh, I ain't talkin' 'bout no 'Merican reward. This here reward comes from some Chinaman, 'n it's for one hunnert thousand dollars."

"What Chinaman would that be?" Elmer was aware of the conditions that had forced Wang to flee China.

"All I got to do is get him to some Chinaman named Tong in San Francisco, and we'll get the money," Martell explained.

"Tong is not a person, and I don't wish to return," Wang said.

"What do you mean, Tong isn't a person? He is, too. He's the one that's put out the reward on you. And it don't matter none whether you go back or not. We're goin' to get paid whether we get you back alive, or whether we have to kill you. If we can prove you're dead, we'll still get paid."

"I do not wish to return," Wang repeated.

"All right. If that's the way you want it." The gunman raised his pistol and cocked it, but that was as far as he got.

To the shock of everyone in the room, Wang put his hand on the table, then did a somersault over the table. Out of the somersault, he was but a few feet in front of the startled Martell. Wang pivoted around on his left leg and smashed his right leg into the would-be gunman's face, and Martell went down.

"What the hell?" Kellis shouted. "Shoot 'im! Shoot the crazy chink!"

None of the other four had drawn their guns, having depended upon Martell, the self-appointed leader of the group, to handle the situation. Kellis made a grab for his pistol but was stopped when Wang drove the heel of his hand onto the outlaw's chin with such force that Kellis joined Martell on the floor. Deekus Carlotti and Emmet Willard were taken down by simultaneous blows from the knife edge of Wang's hands when he whipped out both arms, catching the men unaware.

Elmer joined Wang, and the two of them picked up Martell and Kellis's guns from the floor. Neither Carlotti nor Willard had managed to draw, so their guns were still holstered. Once he had all four pistols, Elmer removed the cylinders from the pistols, then he and Wang returned to their table and waited for the four men to regain consciousness.

After a few minutes they began moving around, then, groggily, got back to their feet.

"What . . . what happened?" Martell asked.

"You fell down," Elmer said.

The others in the saloon who had witnessed the action laughed.

"Yeah," one of them said. "The four of you were so clumsy you just tripped over yourselves."

"You!" Martell said, pointing to Wang. "You did this?"

"Yes," Wang replied.

"Why don't you boys put your guns back in the holsters and get on out of here?" Elmer nodded to the four pistols on a nearby table.

"To hell we'll put 'em back in our holsters!" Carlotti grabbed one of the guns, pointed it at Wang, and pulled the trigger. He was rewarded with a click and nothing more. In surprise, he held the gun up and looked at it. "Hey! Hey, this gun ain't got no cylinders."

"I've got 'em," Elmer said.

"What the hell are you doin' with 'em?"

"Right now, I'm keepin' you boys alive," Elmer said. "Though I don't have no idea why I should be doin' it."

"Mister, if you don't give us those cylinders, we're goin' to wipe the floor with you," Martell said.

Elmer chuckled. "Yeah, you did such a fine job of it before."

Martell put his hand to his cheek, which was already showing the bruise, and he was quiet for a moment. "How long are you plannin' on keepin' 'em?" he asked with less belligerency.

"You can pick 'em up at the police station in Cheyenne," Elmer said.

"Cheyenne? That's more 'n fifty miles from here!"

"Yeah, ain't it?" Elmer said.

Martell and the other three men glared at Elmer and Wang.

"This ain't the end of it," Martell said.

"No, I don't reckon it is," Elmer replied.

With angry and sullen looks on their faces, but with no alternative, the four men left Fiddler's Green.

"Whooee, that was pure somethin' to watch!" said Bob Guthrie, one of patrons. "Biff, why don't you give Elmer 'n Wang another drink, on me?"

"Why, thank you, Mr. Guthrie," Elmer replied.

Two hours later, after the second of the two chartered trains were loaded, the conductor went over to talk to Elmer. "Here's your bill of lading, five hundred cows."

"Thanks, Pete," Elmer said. He and Pete had met shortly after the train arrived and collectively had seen to the loading of the cars. "Pete, do me a favor, will you? When you get to Cheyenne, give this box to Duff MacCallister. These here animals is most his, so you won't have no trouble a-findin' 'im."

"All right," Pete replied, reaching for the box without question.

Elmer had put the four pistol cylinders into the box, along with a letter explaining the strange package.

Some miles away from Cheyenne at that moment, Bart Jenkins and the men with him were putting their planned bank robbery into effect. Black Liberty rode into town first, and he could feel the eyes of everyone in town staring at him. He was pretty sure they were looking at him because of his color, but he was used to that and didn't give it a second thought. Seeing the bench in front of Sikes Hardware Store and the hitching rack very close, he rode over, dismounted, wrapped his reins around the hitching rack, then took a seat on the bench.

"What are you doin', just a-sittin' there?" a man asked.

Black Lib glared at him, but didn't answer. His glare was so intimidating that no response was needed.

"No problem or nothin'," the man said. "I was just a-wonderin', is all." He hurried off, frightened by his brief encounter with the muscular black man who was sitting in front of Sikes Hardware Store.

As Black Lib sat there, his mind drifted back to a time seven months earlier. Then, he had been known as Julius Jackson, and he was a corporal in the Tenth Cavalry of Colored Troops, though everyone referred to them as buffalo soldiers.

Normally the arms room was closed and locked, but Corporal Julius Jackson had managed to acquire a key. He was using his access to the arms room to steal guns and sell them to the Indians, just a few rifles or pistols at a time.

He was picking out the weapons he could use, selecting ones that he knew were unassigned. He had three 45-caliber Model 1873 Springfield carbines and three 45-caliber Colt Single Action Army Model 1873 revolvers set aside.

"What the hell are you doing in here?" a loud voice called.

Startled, Jackson looked up to see the first sergeant. "I was, uh, taking inventory, First Sergeant."

"Inventory, my foot. Someone has been sellin' army weapons to the Injuns, 'n I knowed damn well it was you that was doin' it," First Sergeant Hawkins said. Ten years older than Jackson, Hawkins was a veteran of the USCT, the United States Colored Troops of the Civil War. After the war he had stayed in the army and was one of the longest-serving soldiers of the Tenth Cavalry.

Although the Tenth Cavalry was composed of black soldiers and black noncommissioned officers, such as Sergeant Hawkins, all the officers of the regiment were white.

"Come on, we're goin' to see the cap'n," Hawkins said.

"You got no call to do that, First Sergeant. I told you, I was just countin' 'em is all," Jackson said.

"No you wasn't. You was fixin' to steal 'em." Hawkins had his pistol drawn, and he made a little motion with it, indicating that Jackson should go with him.

"How we goin' to get out of here?" Jackson asked. "You closed and locked the door to the arms room."

Hawkins glanced toward the door, which was exactly what Jackson wanted him to do. Holding a bayonet in his hand, Jackson stabbed Hawkins in the neck when his attention was momentarily diverted. The first sergeant collapsed without making a sound.

Jackson deserted the army that same day, and because

he would no longer be able to use the name Julius Jackson, he took on the alias Black Liberty, or Black Lib.

Seeing Moe come riding into town, Black Lib let his memories slip away and got ready to carry out his role in what was to come.

Chapter Five

Moe dismounted in front of the Hog Waller saloon, drew his pistol, then pushed through the batwing doors and stepped inside. Four men were playing poker, two bar girls were sitting together at another table, one man was standing at the bar, and the bartender was leaning against the wall behind the bar with his arms folded across his chest.

The two bar girls looked up at Moe with practiced welcoming smiles.

The bartender looked toward him as well. The bored expression on the bartender's face turned to a look of fear when he saw the pistol pointed toward him. "What the hell? Is this a holdup?" he called out in alarm.

"No," Moe replied. "This is a killin'." He pulled the trigger and saw the bullet hole appear in the bartender's chest.

The two bar girls screamed as Moe then turned his gun toward the customer who was standing at the far end of the bar and shot him. Then he shot one of the bar girls. The four men sitting at the poker table dived to the floor, and the remaining bargirl just stood there, too frightened to move. Moe started to shoot her as well, but decided against it and left the saloon. He got on his horse and rode out of town at a gallop.

"What is it?" someone out in the street shouted.

"What's happening?" another yelled.

"There must be a gunfight goin' on in the saloon!" still another declared.

Most of the people on the street who'd heard the shooting, including those who called out in shock and confusion, reacted by running into nearby buildings to get out of the line of possible fire. Black Lib remained calmly seated on the bench, waiting for his cue.

No more than a few minutes after Moe left town, the sheriff and two deputies galloped after him. Black Lib was surprised to see two deputies; Bart had said there would be only one. But it didn't matter. He had a job to do, so he mounted and followed the sheriff and his deputies north, out of town.

Bart and Slim were less than a mile south of town when they heard the shooting.

"That's it. That must be Moe shootin' up the saloon. Let's get this taken care of." Bart dug his spurs into his horse's side, and his horse leaped forward so quickly that a surprised Slim was left behind for a moment and had to hurry to catch up.

When they rode into town, they could see the turmoil and agitation of the town's citizens. Many were gathered around the front of the Hog Waller Saloon, while almost as many had gathered at the north end of town, looking in the direction that the shooter had taken, and the sheriff and his two deputies had taken after them.

Nobody noticed the two riders who dismounted in front of the bank. Bart and Slim went inside. Two bank tellers and one customer were there conducting their business.

"Were you outside? What was that shooting about?" one of the two bank tellers asked the lone customer.

"It come from the saloon," the bank customer said. "I heard tell that the feller doin' the shootin' kilt the bartender, one of the customers, Alex Ward, 'n one o' the bar girls. Don't know her name. Then he got on his horse 'n galloped out of town, headin' north."

"Kilt the bartender?"

"Yeah, that's what they're sayin'."

"Damn, Muley's got a wife 'n two kids. Wonder why he didn't use the shotgun?"

"I don't reckon he had time."

"Sheriff Twitty go after him?"

"Yeah, him 'n both deputies."

"Damn, what will happen next?"

"A bank robbery will happen next, gentlemen," Bart said at that moment, pulling his pistol.

The startled men in the bank looked around. Two men were holding pistols.

"Teller, if you would, please, empty your cash drawer, then open the vault and empty it as well," Bart said, indicating the nearest teller.

"I can empty my cash drawer, but I can't open the vault. It's locked, 'n I don't know the combination."

"Then you ain't worth nothin' to us, are you?" Bart pulled the trigger, and blood, brain, and bone detritus exploded from the side of the teller's head.

"My God, you shot Fred!" the other man said.

Bart turned his gun toward the man who had just shouted. "What is your name?" Bart asked.

"Rudy. Rudy McVey," the frightened man said.

"Well, Mr. McVey, you have two choices," Bart said. "You can open the vault for us and live, or you can refuse the way Fred did. If you refuse, I'll kill you and just take what money you have in the cash drawer."

With hands shaking so badly he could barely control them, McVey worked the combination, then pulled the door open. "There."

"Thanks," Bart replied as he pulled the trigger.

"What'd you do that for?" the bank customer asked. "Rudy done what you told him to do."

"I'm afraid Mr. McVey might be able to give the law a good description of us."

"Well, hell, I can—"

"Yes, you could do that, couldn't you?" Bart shot the customer, as well.

Bart and Slim ran from the bank with Bart holding the cloth bag into which the money had been stuffed.

"Hey!" They heard someone shout. "I just heard some shootin' in the bank, 'n them two fellers come runnin' out! I think the bank's been robbed!"

They rode at a gallop, their getaway uncontested. Everyone in town had been distracted by what had happened in the saloon, and nobody was mounted.

Two miles north of town, Sheriff Twitty, unaware that the bank had been robbed, stopped and held up his hand.

"What are you doin', Sheriff? Ain't we goin' after 'im?" one of the deputies asked.

"I don't know," Twitty replied. "I tell you the truth, I don't feel good about this. Somethin' is funny about it."

"What do you mean?"

"Why would someone just go into a saloon 'n start shootin'?"

"I don't know why."

"It could be that he was just wantin' to draw us out of town, into a trap. They might be settin' an ambush for us."

"They? There was only one shooter."

"Yeah, but I don't expect there's really only one. And why would he be doin' that? I got a feelin' somethin' is goin' on in town. We'd better get back there."

Black Lib was surprised to see the sheriff and his deputies riding back toward him. He had not yet drawn his Winchester, nor was he holding a pistol in his hand.

"Hold up there, mister," the sheriff called out to him. "What's a colored man doin' out here?"

"I saw the three of you chasing out after that man that shot up the saloon, and I figured I'd help you. You know, in case there was a reward or somethin'."

"Far as I know, there ain't no reward. We don't even know who it is," the sheriff said. "And even if there was, we wouldn't be sharin' it with you."

"Because I'm a colored man?" Black Lib asked stridently.

"Bein' black don't have nothin' to do with it. It's just that I wouldn't share it with nobody other 'n my deputies."

Black Lib watched the sheriff and his deputies go on back into town, then he continued up the trail until he reached the spot where they had planned to have the ambush. He rode forward slowly, not wanting Moe mistaking him for the lawmen. "Moe? Moe, it's me. Black Liberty."

"Yeah, I see you, Black Lib. What happened? Why didn't the sheriff 'n his deputies come after me?"

"They started out after you, but for some reason they give up."

Moe came out from behind the rocks where he had been waiting. "I hope there was time enough to rob the bank. Come on, let's get back to the cabin."

Once they returned to the cabin, Bart looked at the money spread out on the table. "Eight hunnert dollars," he said disgustedly. "Who the hell would expect a bank not to have no more money than eight hunnert dollars?"

"Well, Hillsdale most likely ain't got much more 'n a hunnert or so people," Slim said. "You wouldn't expect it to have too much money."

"They's three less people now," Moe said with a giggle. "Woulda been six less, iffen the sheriff 'n his two deputies hadn't turned coward on us."

"There is six less," Slim said. "We kilt the two bank tellers and the feller that was in there."

"Eight hunnert dollars," Bart said again. "Hell, that warn't hardly worth it."

Cheyenne, Wyoming Territory

The man known to all as "Lonesome John" stood at the end of the bar in the Red Bull Saloon, nursing a bottle of beer. He effused a strong odor, the by-product of his occupation, mucking out the stalls at J.C. Abney's Livery. No one had ever asked him to stand alone. He had made his own decision to do so because he was, by choice, a loner. His hair was long and unkempt, and his beard, which came down to his chest, was scraggly.

"Want another beer, Lonesome?" the bartender asked.

John held up his glass which was half full. "I'm still nursing this one," he said.

"Nursin' it ain't goin' to make that glass get 'ny fuller," the bartender joked.

"No, but on the other hand, buying another beer will make my purse smaller," John replied. "Besides, I have applied a very strict limit upon the amount of liquor I imbibe. Alcoholism was hard enough for me to escape. I have no wish to fall back into that morass."

"Suit yourself," the bartender replied, returning to the other customers who were standing at the bar. The truth was, the bartender had no idea what John had just said.

John stared at his glass, but he wasn't seeing beer. He was seeing the face of Cynthia Louise.

What am I doing here?

If he could go back to St. Louis, he was sure he could put his life together again.

Go back? How the hell am I going to go back with only four dollars to my name?

The whistle of the approaching train interrupted his reverie. Mr. Abney had asked him to go to the depot to meet the train and check on an express package he was expecting. John tossed down the rest of his beer and walked across the street to the depot.

On board the train

The front door of the car opened, and a gray-haired man wearing a blue uniform stepped into the passenger car. This, Meagan knew, was the conductor.

"Cheyenne," he called out. As he passed through the car, he kept repeating his announcement. "Cheyenne, we're coming into Cheyenne."

"We're here," Meagan said, but she realized that Duff hadn't heard her. He was asleep. She cleared her throat. "We're here," she said again, not raising her voice. "Are you going to sleep all day?" Meagan teased, laying her hand on his shoulder.

Duff made a harrumphing sound and sat up in his seat. "I'm nae asleep, lass."

"Why didn't you answer the conductor when he spoke to you then?" she asked.

"The conductor spoke to me? What did he say?"

Meagan laughed. "He said we're coming into Cheyenne."

"Aye, I heard that."

Meagan laughed again. "Of course, you did. All I can say is, I wish I could sleep like that. You can go to sleep anywhere, anytime, at the drop of a hat."

"You can credit that to my time in the Black Watch,

Third Battalion, Royal Regiment of Scotland," Duff said. "Sure 'n you learn to sleep when you can."

"Yes, well don't go back to sleep now. We are coming into Cheyenne."

"You dinnae have cause to be for worrying. I'm awake now."

Chapter Six

The Union Pacific Depot in Cheyenne was built by the architectural firm of Van Brunt and Howe of Kansas City. The two-story Romanesque depot was not only Cheyenne's largest, it was also its most impressive structure, with a tower in the center of the building that could be seen from anywhere in Cheyenne. The depot was large enough to afford desk space for businesses that, while not part of the railroad, had operations directly related to the railroad.

As soon as Duff and Meagan stepped down from the train, they saw to their luggage. That taken care of, they looked up Abner Pugh, who represented the Kansas Cattle Brokerage Firm at one of the businesses with a desk in the office building part of the depot. Several other businesses were represented in the building as well, including an express desk that handled shipments other than those sent by the US Mail.

As Duff and Meagan walked by the express desk, they couldn't help but notice the odor that, cocoon like, hung around a man who was standing there. The man needed a shave, a haircut, and, most of all, a bath and clean clothes. Meagan wasn't sure she had ever seen a more disheveled man.

"Yes, sir, Mr. MacCallister," Abner Pugh said, responding to Duff's greeting. "I received your telegram, and I'll be most happy to buy your beeves. We're always in the market for Black Angus cattle, and to be honest, I have no idea why many more cattlemen haven't taken to raising Black Angus."

"Ah, you know how 'tis, Mr. Pugh. People are slow to leave something that is familiar to them."

"They're going to have to learn pretty fast," Pugh replied. "Angus and Herefords are bringing top price in the markets, but it's hard to get a plug nickel for longhorns."

Lonesome John was listening to the conversation between Pugh and Duff.

"I'm sorry, Lonesome," Tom Dunaway said. "You'll have to tell J.C. that his package didn't arrive today."

"All right, thanks." John didn't know the man Abner Pugh had called MacCallister, but from what he had overheard, he could perceive that MacCallister was a wealthy man. As he contemplated that information, an idea came to him.

It had been almost two years since he'd left St. Louis, and he was sure that if he could go back, he would able to straighten things out. But the train ticket would cost twenty-seven dollars, and so far, he hadn't been able to save that much money. He needed about fifty dollars to buy the ticket, get some new clothes, and find a place to stay in St. Louis while he began the program of recovering his life.

MacCallister might just be the solution to his problem.

John hated the idea of stealing from anyone, but his situation had grown more desperate each day. When he was a heavy drinker, he had been able to drown his situation in alcohol. But by a supreme effort, he was sober, and acutely aware of the depths to which he had fallen. Still he believed that staying drunk made matters worse.

Duff had only a peripheral awareness of the disheveled man who had been standing in front of the next desk. With their business concluded, he turned toward Meagan. "Lass, and would you be for wanting to take a meal at the Cheyenne Cattlemen's Club?"

"Cattlemen's club?" Meagan replied. "Do they not realize there are women in the cattle business? They may not let me in."

Duff chuckled at the suggestion. "Don't you be for worryin', lass, they'll let you in. You've my word on that."

"So what you are saying is, that even though I am a cattle owner, the only way I can get in is as your guest?"

"I . . . uh," Duff started, but his comment was interrupted by a lilting laugh.

"I am teasing you, Duff. I would love to take our meal at the Cattlemen's Club."

Waiting outside in the corral area, in position to see MacCallister leave the office, John stepped back behind one of the holding pens so as not to be seen. He watched as MacCallister and the woman walked toward the holding pens, and he positioned himself to confront them. He pulled his gun and waited nervously. He had never used the gun except for taking a few shots in target practice.

"I want you a-wearin' that gun at all times," J.C. Abney had told him. "Havin' all them horses in one place here in the livery makes 'em an invitin' target for horse thieves."

John was about to use his pistol for the first time, not in the lawful defense of the animals in his charge, but as an outlaw. As he stood there waiting, he could feel his stomach fluttering. He didn't know if his nervous condition was driven by fear or a visceral reaction to his violating his promise to use the gun only to oppose the commission of a crime. It didn't matter, he was committed. He had no choice but to carry it out.

Totally unaware that they were being stalked, Duff and Meagan walked out into the holding pen area to make arrangements for their cattle when they were due to arrive later that same day.

"'Tis not big enough for them to be held for any length of time," Duff observed, "but the creatures will nae be here for too long."

As they started toward the Cattlemen's Club, they walked through the narrow lanes between the pens. Just ahead of them John suddenly stepped into the path, pointing a pistol at Duff and Meagan. Duff recognized him as the man who had been standing near them back in the broker's office.

"Stop right there!" John said in a loud voice. "I'll be relieving you of any money you may have on your person."

"Tell me, lad, what makes you think we are carrying any money?"

"You did come here to sell your cattle, didn't you?"

"Aye, but I haven't sold them yet," Duff said.

"Perhaps not, but I'm quite sure you have enough money to defray any expenses you may incur as you are waiting for the payment, and I'm afraid that, due to the circumstances of my current situation, the amount of money you are carrying makes little difference to me. I'll just ask you to hand over any money you have."

"'N would you be for tellin' me why I might want to do that?"

"What do you mean, why? Do you not see that I'm holding a gun on you? The threat of being shot should be ample incentive for you to choose money over injury and possible death."

"Aye, 'tis easy to see why you might think that. But I should tell you that I am skilled in the art of rapid extraction of my pistol, and once it is engaged, I never miss my shot. So 'tis askin' you I am, to put away your pistol before such a thing is needed."

The man confronting them looked confused. "What did you say?"

"He said if you don't put your gun away, he will shoot you," Meagan said in a voice that exhibited absolutely no apprehension.

"I know what he said. I'm just surprised that he would say such a thing when I obviously have the advantage of holding my pistol in my hand, while his gun is still in its holster."

Duff drew his pistol and fired, his bullet striking the would-be assailant in his gun hand.

With a cry of pain, John dropped the gun and put his

left hand over the wound to his right hand. "Damn, that wasn't an idle threat, was it?"

"'Tis not a deep wound, 'n 'tis thinkin' I am, that the bullet will nae cause you any permanent problem, but 'twould be best if you would see a doctor."

"I'm afraid that I am too deficient of funds to see a doctor."

Duff took out a twenty-dollar bill and handed it to the man who, but a few moments earlier, had tried to hold him up. "Here. 'Tis enough for you to see a doctor 'n maybe get yourself a meal," Duff said.

"Mister, I don't understand you. I just tried to rob you, and now you are giving me money of your own free will?"

"What would be your name?" Duff asked.

The man laughed. "Under the circumstances, I would be foolish to tell you who I am, wouldn't I? Why should I tell you my name just so you can report me to the police?"

"I've nae intention of reporting you to the police, lad. 'Twas a friendly request is all."

Despite the situation, the man smiled and held up his hand. "Friendly, you say? Tell me, do you have a habit of shooting your friends in the hand?"

"Nae, but my friends don't have a habit of attempting to rob me."

"Touché." The would-be robber sighed. "My name is John, though I have been given the sobriquet of Lonesome John. I'm not disposed to give you my last name at the moment. I have covered my family name with nothing but shame."

"John it is then. John, 'twould be best if you would be for tellin' the doctor that you shot yourself in the hand. There's nae need for any to know that you were tryin' to rob me."

"Am I to take it that your generosity extends to you not taking me to the police?"

"There's nae need for me to be doin' that. You didn't rob me."

"You're right. I didn't, did I? Though the difference between actual and attempted robbery would seem small. Apparently, I have failed in yet another endeavor."

John held the twenty-dollar bill out toward Duff. "Mr. MacCallister, I can't take this money. I did nothing to earn it."

Meagan laughed out loud. "John, a moment ago you were ready to take our money at the point of a gun. Do you consider that earning it?"

John chuckled as well. "I will grant you, that is rather convoluted reasoning. Therefore, I will take the money, and you have my undying gratitude." He looked down at his wounded hand. "I suppose I had better get over to the doctor's office. Damn if I didn't do a dumb thing like shooting myself in the hand."

Meagan chuckled softly as the man who called himself John hurried off. "I do believe that our new friend John is the most articulate robber I've ever met."

"Aye, 'twas his competency with the language that led me to give him twenty dollars, thus violating the code of the parsimonious Scotsman."

"I swear to you, Mr. Duff MacCallister, you are the most unique man I have ever known."

"And would you be for thinkin' that's a good thing?" Duff asked.

Meagan put both hands on his arm and pulled him closer to her. "Aye, lad, 'tis a very good thing," she said, responding in his own brogue.

Chapter Seven

Cabin outside Cheyenne

The four men had occupied the cabin for over a month and had, out of boredom as much as anything else, made several improvements. The door had been rehung and the windows repaired, not with glass as there was no glass available, but with boards to cover the holes.

At the moment, Black Lib was sitting on the floor with his Springfield carbine spread out in pieces before him.

"Damn, Black Lib, I ain't never seen no one clean their guns as much as you do," Moe said. "Is that somethin' you learnt whilest you was in the colored army?"

"It wasn't a colored army. It was a colored regiment, the Tenth Cavalry, which is a part of the US Army."

"Black Lib deserted," Slim Gardner said with a laugh. "When his company come up agin' some Injuns, why ole Black Lib here, ran away

"I don't have nothin' against no Injuns," Black Lib said as he ran a cleaning rod through the barrel of his Springfield. He had not told any of them, not even Bart, that killing First Sergeant Hawkins was the real reason for his desertion.

"I wonder," Moe Conyers said, "if we was to get ketched up by the law, would you go to prison with us or would you be put in some army prison?"

"Whether he goes to army prison or not, he won't be with us," Bart said. "I done three years in prison, 'n didn't see no colored folks there. They got their own prisons."

"That's right," Black Lib said with a smile. "Our prisons have soft beds 'n chairs, 'n we ain't locked in our cells except at nighttime. Durin' the day we can visit, play cards or checkers. We've got our own saloon, too, 'n once a week, they let soiled doves come in, 'n we can spend the night with 'em, if we want to."

"What?" Slim asked, literally shouting the word.

Black Lib laughed.

"He's foolin' with you, Slim," Bart said.

"Yeah?" Slim glared at Black Lib. "I don't like being fooled, you black son of a—"

Slim's sentence was interrupted by a threatening glare from Black Lib.

Slim forced a laugh. "What I mean to say is, you got me good."

Cheyenne

John had overcome the feeling of being embarrassed because he had taken the money from the very man he had tried to rob. Well aware of the threat of gangrene, he decided that going to the doctor was well worth the expense and used that money to visit Dr. Urban's office, which was located upstairs over the barbershop.

The bullet had gone all the way through his hand, and the torn pieces of his shirt that he had poked into both the entry and the exit holes had just about stemmed the flow of blood. The twenty-dollar bill he had been given brought his personal wealth up to twenty-three dollars. He would need only four more dollars to have the price of a ticket to St. Louis, but that wouldn't be enough. The trip to St. Louis would take forty-eight hours, and he would have to eat somewhere along the way. And even the money he had was about to be decreased by five dollars, the cost of his medical treatment.

Dr. Urban looked at John's damaged hand. "You're lucky," he told John. "It's a ridge cut between your thumb and your index finger. It won't take long to heal, but you must keep it very clean to prevent sepsis. When it does heal, you should have full use of your thumb and your index finger."

"Thank you, Doctor. That's good to know."

"And you say you shot yourself in the hand?"

"Yes, it was damn fool thing for me to do, I admit."

Dr. Urban chuckled. "You're a big boy. You should know to be careful when you play with guns."

"Oh, I will in the future," John said. The medical expense of five dollars brought his personal fortune to eighteen dollars, which was the most money he had had in a long time.

He worked at the livery. The owner, J.C. Abney, gave him ten dollars a month to muck out the stalls and a place to live, which was actually just a walled-off corner of the loft. Almost all of his salary was used for food, thus making it very difficult for him to save anything.

John looked at the bandage on his hand. He was sure

he could still muck out the stalls, but he was going to have to be careful to keep it clean.

Duff was greeted warmly by the maître d' when he and Meagan arrived at the Cheyenne Cattlemen's Club. He'd been there many times before and had a persona that was most memorable.

"Mr. MacCallister, it is so good to see you again. Are you just visiting our fair city or have you brought more cattle?"

"Good afternoon, Mr. Sanders. 'Tis cattle I have brought. And Miss Parker, as well." He nodded toward Meagan.

"Duff, did you mean to include me with the cattle?" she teased.

Duff chuckled. "Nae, for none of the cattle have as sharp a tongue as you."

"A sharp tongue means a sharp mind," Meagan replied.

"Lass, you've a wit about you that is so sharp it could cut paper," Duff replied with a little self-deprecating laugh.

Duff turned his attention back to Sanders. "Miss Parker isn't sure she will be welcome here as she is a cattle woman, 'n the name is the cattlemen's club."

"Ah, Miss Parker, not to worry, a beautiful lady like yourself is always welcome."

"So, I'm welcome because of how I look and not because I own cattle? Would a homely cattlewoman be just as welcome?"

"I . . . uh . . ." Sanders stammered, not certain how to handle the question.

Duff laughed. "The lass is just having a wee bit o' fun with you. Dinnae be for paying her any mind."

"To be sure," Sanders said, the relief showing on his face. "This way. I have a nice table by the window for you." He led them through the dining room then held out his arm inviting them to the table he had selected.

"What are you going to do with the money you make from the sale?" Duff asked her when they were seated and Sanders had returned to the front.

"I'm going to remodel my store and order new stock."

She owned Meagan's Dress Emporium, which was one of the most successful business operations in all of Chugwater. She also owned several head of cattle that were intermingled with Duff's herd. Originally her participation in the ranch had been the result of a loan she had made to Duff, but when he attempted to pay her back, she said she would rather him consider it as her investment in cattle. Ever since that time, as cattle were sold or bought, Meagan was a 10 percent participant.

As the good women of Chugwater liked to explain to anyone who might ask about their relationship, Meagan and Duff were courting. It had been an extended courtship. Meagan wasn't ready to give up her dress shop and move out to Sky Meadow, and Duff didn't want to move in to Chugwater. Though they had never finalized their relationship by way of marriage vows, the affection they felt for each other was none the weaker for any lack of documentation.

Later that same afternoon

There was an hour between the two trains Duff had hired. The first having already arrived, Duff and Meagan waited in the depot for the second. As they had done with the first one, they would observe the off-loading of their cattle.

"Here comes a train," Meagan said. "I wonder if it is ours."

"I would expect that it is," Duff said.

As the train grew closer, his expectation was proven to be correct. They watched the engine pass, then the long line of stock cars. Finally, the train came to a complete halt.

One of the freight train crewmen walked toward Duff carrying a box. "I'm the conductor of this train. Would you be Duff MacCallister?"

"Aye. You are nae be for telling me that there was some trouble with the cattle now, would you?"

The conductor chuckled. "No, we had no problems at all. But a gentleman by the name of Elmer Gleason asked that I deliver this box to you."

"Very well. I thank you."

"No problem," the conductor said before turning back to supervise the off-loading of the cattle.

"What is it?" Meagan asked.

"Upon my word, 'tis four revolver cylinders," Duff said, surprised by the contents of the box.

"Why on earth would Elmer send you four pistol cylinders?"

"I'm sure this letter will tell us." Duff read the letter, then chuckled.

Duff,

These here 4 cilenders come from the guns of some no-counts. After Wang taken care of em I got these out of their guns and I told em they could get em at the police station in Cheyenne.

Duff handed the letter to Meagan, and she, too, chuckled after reading it. "It looks like we will be visiting the police station."

Once the cattle were counted by the broker's men, and in the holding pens, they went back into the office to see Abner Pugh.

"Five hundred head safely arrived and counted. Here you are, Mr. MacCallister," Pugh said, counting out the money. "At seventy-five dollars per head, it comes out to thirty-seven thousand, five hundred dollars."

"And your share, lass, is three thousand seven hundred and fifty dollars," Duff said, counting out the money.

From the cattle broker's office to the Cheyenne Cattleman's Bank and Trust was a walk of but a couple of blocks down Sixteenth Street, but as they would be passing the police station before reaching the bank, they stopped there first.

The first man Duff saw was the desk sergeant. The policeman was wearing a pith helmet and heavy sideburns that came down the side of his face then hooked around to connect by way the full moustache.

"Could you be for helping us?" Duff asked.

"Yes, sir, I'm Sergeant Creech. What can I do for you?"

"'Tis a favor I'm asking of you," Duff said, opening the box to show the policemen the four revolver cylinders. "There may be some men calling for them."

"Who?" the confused policeman asked.

"I'm nae able to tell you that, for I dinnae know. But who would come here to ask for them, other than the people that lost them?"

"I'll be damned. Revolver cylinders seem to me to be funny things to lose, and not one, but four of them," Sergeant Creech said. "Howsoever, if someone shows up asking for 'em, I'll turn these things over to 'em."

"You have my thanks."

"And who might you be?" the police officer asked.

"MacCallister. Duff MacCallister."

"Duff MacCallister? Are you the one who owns the big ranch up near Chugwater?"

"Aye, I have a ranch there."

The expression on the police officer's face brightened. He stuck his hand across the desk. "I've heard of you Mr. MacCallister, and I'm that pleased to meet you." He held out the four cylinders. "And don't you be a-worryin' none 'bout these things. If someone shows up askin' for 'em, well I'll turn these things right over to 'em."

"You have my thanks," Duff said.

Chapter Eight

The bank was but a few more buildings down the street, and once there, Meagan and Duff were greeted by Joel Prescott, a tall, prematurely gray-haired, distinguished-looking man, whose blue eyes reflected his intelligence. He was not only the president of the bank but also Duff's friend, the friendship having developed from Duff's frequent visits to the bank.

"Well, Duff MacCallister, I see you have abandoned the paradise of Sky Meadow to come visit the wicked city," Prescott teased.

"Aye, for there is business to be done."

"And would that business have anything to do with the bank or is this just a courtesy visit?"

"'Tis business with the bank, for we have just sold five hundred head of cattle to Mr. Pugh, 'n I'll be wanting to make a deposit of twenty-five thousand two hundred fifty dollars to my account, and seven thousand dollars to Elmer Gleason's account. Also, I'll be holding back one thousand dollars in cash from my account, and five hundred from Mr. Gleason's account."

"My, my, Mr. MacCallister, that brings your account

up to a little over sixty-five thousand dollars. You may be interested to know that that makes you one of our largest depositors," Prescott said. "And oddly enough, Mr. Gleason, with an account of just over twenty thousand is also in the upper tier of depositors. And you, Miss Parker, will you be making a deposit as well?"

"No, I have some business to take care of back in Chugwater, so I am going to make my deposit there."

"Mr. Kendrick," Prescott called.

A rather smallish man with a receding hairline and an oversized nose above a thin-lipped mouth came into the room in response to Prescott call. His glasses had slipped down, and he slid them back up his nose. "Yes, sir, Mr. Prescott?"

"See to this deposit and bring Mr. MacCallister two deposit receipts, one for himself, and one for Mr. Gleason, would you please?"

"I'd be glad to," Kendrick replied.

"I don't know what I would do without Eli," Joel said after Eli left. "He graduated from West Point, one year behind me. When I arrived I took over the company he was commanding. Above his rank, I made him my executive officer. And he is the best executive officer I have ever had, whether in the army or civilian life."

"'Tis a good thing to have good men working with you." Duff thought of Elmer and Wang."

"Yes, with me, rather than for me. That's exactly how I would describe him. By the way, speaking of Eli, he is to be our guest tonight, as Nettie and I celebrate our anniversary. And, if I may presume upon our friendship, I wonder if you and Miss Parker would do me the honor of coming to my house tonight to help us celebrate our wedding anniversary?"

"I would feel like an outsider among your guests," Duff replied.

"You wouldn't be an outsider, for Eli would be our only other guest," Joel said with a chuckle. "We had planned to have only Eli to celebrate with us, but when one of the bank's largest depositors happens to be in town, it would be foolish of me not to extend the invitation."

"And rude of me not to accept," Duff said. "Aye, Mr. Prescott, we will be there."

Joel Prescott watched as Duff and Meagan left the bank. He knew that Duff had been an officer in the Black Watch Regiment, and he knew all about the Black Watch, for he had studied them while in West Point.

Most of Joel Prescott's customers knew little about his time in the army, and even less about his time at the US Military Academy. Graduating tenth in a class of forty-two, he just missed getting a commission in the engineer corps. He had a choice between serving in the infantry or in the finance corps. He chose the finance corps, and as a finance officer, he missed all the military operations against the Indians. He served for three years at Jefferson Barracks in St. Louis, then at Fort Laramie, where he met, fell in love with, and married Nettie Lindell, whose father, Colonel Michael Lindell, was his commanding officer.

Fort Laramie, two years before

"You know, don't you, Captain Prescott, that without any kind of military action in your background, that you will most likely be stuck in grade for the rest of your career. If you would like, I could see to it that you get such exposure."

"I appreciate the offer, Colonel, but I am considering submitting my resignation."

"What? Leave the army?"

"It is as you said, sir, without any experience in the field against the Indians, I will never go higher in rank than captain. On the other hand, I have been in contact with someone who wishes to use my financial experience to back me in founding a bank in Cheyenne."

For a moment, Colonel Lindell looked stunned, then he smiled and extended his hand. "I think perhaps you have made a good move, Joel. And although Nettie has been on an army post for her entire life, I'm certain that she will quickly take to being the wife of a leading citizen in the community. And as the president of a bank, that's exactly what you will be."

"Thank you, Colonel," said a relieved Joel Prescott. "I was hoping that you would see it that way."

"You're leaving the army, sir?" Lieutenant Kendrick asked, after Joel told him of his plans. "May I ask why?"

"An opportunity has presented itself to me in Cheyenne," Joel explained. "The Denver Bank and Trust has offered to back me in building and opening a bank in Cheyenne."

"You mean opening a brand-new bank?" Eli asked.

"Yes, they have a branch there now, but they want to close it, which will give us an opportunity to take some or all of their depositors."

"Why would the Denver Bank and Trust be willing to do such a thing?" Eli asked.

"They want a presence there, but they don't want the trouble of maintaining a branch. I have promised to work with them to the extent that my bank will, in essence, be their branch."

"What a marvelous opportunity!" Eli said, enthused by the concept.

"Lieutenant Kendrick, you have been the best executive officer I have ever had. I know it would be asking a lot of you, but I wonder if you would consider submitting your own resignation and coming with me."

Eli hesitated for no more than a moment, then with a broad grin, he nodded. "Yes, sir, Captain. I would love to."

Joel shook his head. "Not captain and lieutenant. Now it is Joel and Eli.

The first six months had been difficult, but when the Denver Annex Bank closed, Joel got nearly all of their depositors. And Eli was every bit as good a vice president as he had been an executive officer.

"I couldn't help but overhear the invitation you gave to Mr. MacCallister and the young lady to celebrate your anniversary," Eli Kendrick said. "I'm glad you did. Something as important as an anniversary shouldn't be celebrated alone."

"What do you mean alone, Eli? You have already agreed to be there as well," Joel said.

"Yes, but the dynamics have changed," Eli said. "When it was just the three of us, there was an intimacy to it. We have been together so long that it was almost as if I were your brother, or maybe even Nettie's brother. Though, I confess that I didn't think of her as a sister when she was Nettie Lindell and I danced with her at the Commander's ball."

Joel smiled. "I am not unaware, Eli, that you were my rival."

"I was never really in the running," Eli said. "You know that, I know that, and so does Nettie. But, yes, I will be at the dinner tonight."

Joel smiled. "Thank you, I'll be glad to see you there, and I know that Nettie will. You and I are her connection to the army life she had always known."

After their business with the bank was taken care of, Duff and Meagan secured adjoining rooms in the Inter-ocean Hotel on the northwest corner of Sixteenth Street and Capital Avenue. The hotel was housed in a large three-story building that was as impressive as anything Duff had seen for the short while he'd lived in New York. The hotel could brag of having had such famous guests as Ulysses Grant, Charles Dickens, Mark Twain, and at the moment, Edwin Booth, though neither Duff, nor Meagan had seen him.

It had been Meagan's suggestion that they spend some time in Cheyenne. It was considerably larger than Chug-water, and she wanted the opportunity to buy a few things that simply weren't available in the smaller city. And, because they would be going back by train, she wasn't limited as to the number of things she would buy.

At the Myers Dry Goods store, she bought several bolts of fabric—velvet, chiffon, crepe, and silk—that would be used to make dresses for sale in her shop. Al-though she was quite a good seamstress, her business was so successful she was able to hire others to help make the dresses, most of which were her own designs.

While Meagan was shopping, Duff went to the telegraph office to send a message to Elmer.

Having accepted Joel Prescott's invitation to dinner, Duff and Meagan took a hack to his house that evening. They were greeted by an attractive woman who, Meagan supposed, must be in her early forties.

"Joel told me that Mr. MacCallister had a lady friend. I'm Nettie Prescott, and you are?" she asked Meagan.

"I'm Meagan Parker, and I thank you, Mrs. Prescott, for the invitation"—Meagan chuckled—"though I know it was Mr. Prescott who actually invited us. I hope we aren't too much of an intrusion."

"His invitation is mine, my dear, and please call me Nettie. Duff has been here many times and is always welcome, and that makes you welcome, as well."

"You are most gracious, Nettie," Meagan replied. "And I do hope you will call me Meagan."

"Oh, my, what a beautiful dress," Nettie said gushingly. "The lavender brings out the blue in your eyes. Wherever did you find it?"

"I have a dress shop in Chugwater," Meagan replied. "I designed and made this myself."

"Oh, what a magnificent talent that is."

Once inside, they were aware of the aroma of beef being roasted, as their cook was finishing the last details of the meal.

"Please," Nettie said. "Joel and Eli are having drinks in the parlor."

"Welcome, Duff, and Meagan," Joel called out when they reached the door. "You'll find Scotch, brandy, and wine on the sideboard in the dining room. Help yourself."

"Scotch, you say? 'Tis a foine man who would greet a Scottish guest with Scotch," Duff said with a broad smile.

"So tell me, Duff, do you miss Scotland?" Nettie asked when Duff and Meagan returned with their drinks, Scotch for Duff and wine for Meagan.

"Aye, I do miss some things about it—my friends, my farm, the countryside," Duff replied. "But I've made new friends here, I have a ranch, 'n 'tis beautiful country around Chugwater. 'N I feel if I went back to Scotland, I would miss this place even more than I miss Scotland now."

Meagan reached over to touch Duff's hand.

A rather plump woman with gray hair piled on her head and wearing an apron appeared in the doorway between the parlor and the dining room. "Mr. and Mrs. Prescott and guests, dinner is ready," she said.

"Thank you, Jimmie Mae," Nettie replied.

During dinner, Duff asked Joel Prescott about his background. "'N would ye be for tellin' us how you came to Wyoming?"

"The army sent me to Ft. Laramie, where I served as a finance officer. I met this beautiful young lady, who just happened to be the daughter of my commanding officer, and I married her, thinking it would get me in good with the colonel."

Meagan laughed. "Surely, that's not the only reason you married her."

Joel smiled at Nettie, then took her hand. "Well, maybe

it isn't the only reason. Anyway, I left the army soon after, came here to Cheyenne, and with a couple of investors, started the Cheyenne Cattleman's Bank." Joel glanced over at Eli. "And I don't kid myself that I have done it alone. Eli was with me at Fort Laramie, and I talked him into leaving the army, as well. I don't think the average citizen would understand the significance of that. Like me, Eli was a graduate of the academy, and as an officer in the regular army, he had a secure future ahead of him. But he gave all that up to join me in this risky venture."

Joel and Eli lifted their glasses toward one another.

"Meagan, have you enjoyed your visit to Cheyenne?" Nettie asked.

"Yes, very much," Meagan replied. "I've managed to get a lot of shopping done, though I must confess that our visit here started with a situation that could easily have gotten out of hand."

"Oh?"

Meagan told of their encounter with the man who'd identified himself only as John. "I must say, however, that he seems to have a remarkable vocabulary."

"You are talking about the one they call Lonesome John," Joel said. "He works at the livery, mucking out stables."

"You know him then," Meagan said.

"Yes, and I must say I am very surprised that he attempted to rob you. I would never have thought that of him. And don't be misled by his appearance. He is much more than he seems."

"I suspected that," Meagan said. "What do you know of him? I mean, for someone as articulate as he is, to present such a disheveled appearance, there must be some story."

Joel shook his head. "That would be for John to say."

After dinner, they went back into the parlor, where Eli entertained them by playing the piano.

"Why, I've never heard Chopin's Nocturne Number Nine played more beautifully," Meagan said. "You play as well as any professional pianist I've ever heard."

"Thank you, Miss Parker," Eli replied. "I did consider it, but my father secured an appointment to West Point and insisted I give up music and become an army officer."

"We know Duff's background," Nettie said after Eli played a piece by Beethoven. "What is your background, Meagan? I'm sure you weren't born in Chugwater." She laughed. "I doubt that anyone was born in Chugwater."

"I was born in Memphis, where my father had a riverboat business. During the war, his boats were either sunk or confiscated. After the war he got a job as a boat captain going up and down the Mississippi River. My mother was a good seamstress, and with my father being gone so often, she taught me."

"Well, if that dress you're wearing is any indication of your skill as a seamstress, you mother taught you very well."

"Thank you. You are most kind."

"I'm glad we accepted Joel's invitation," Meagan said after they left the Prescott home that evening. "Nettie is a delightful person, and you and Joel and Eli seemed to get along quite well."

"Aye, Joel is not only my banker, he is also my friend.

I've seen Eli in the bank, of course, 'n we have always exchanged pleasantries, but tonight is the first time I've ever spent any time around him."

"I can see why Joel would want him as a friend. He is intelligent, honest, and engaging. What more would someone want in a friend?"

"I can think of nothing more, and you have made an accurate appraisal of him."

Having a drink at the Red Bull later that evening, part of Eli wished he had not accepted Joel's invitation. It wasn't that he didn't enjoy himself. He had, very much so. Eli was still attracted to Nettie Prescott, and had been since she was Nettie Lindell. Part of the reason he had agreed to leave the army and come to Cheyenne with Joel was so he could be around Nettie, but he had never let on to her. He considered himself too much of a gentleman to make his feelings known to the wife of his boss.

Eli drank alone, then started back toward the bank even though it was closed. As the vice president, he had some work that needed to be done, work he had not been able to get to earlier in the day.

As Eli was unlocking the door, Police Lieutenant Kirby happened by.

"Working late, are you?" Kirby asked.

"You know what they say, Dan. A busy man's work is never done," Eli replied. "Won't you come in and have a cup of coffee with me? It was made this morning, but all I have to do is heat it up, and that won't take long. The fire in the little stove was well banked."

"Thanks for the invitation, Eli. I believe I will."

"How are things going?" Eli asked, once they were in the bank and settled.

"Things are going pretty well, considering the fact that I'm going to have to deal with a man by the name of Bart Jenkins."

"Who's Bart Jenkins?"

"He's an outlaw. That's the only way I can put it."

"Is he going to be difficult?"

"No more than any other outlaw, I guess. But I'm wearing this badge, and dealing with people like Bart Jenkins is what I do all the time."

Chapter Nine

Chugwater

Elmer and Wang were putting a new roof on the smokehouse when Elmer saw a lone rider coming down the long, dedicated road to Sky Meadow.

"I wonder what that feller wants?" Elmer said.

Wang looked in the direction pointed out by Elmer. "He comes to bring telegram."

"What? Now just how the hell do you know that?"

"He wears the hat of one who delivers telegrams," Wang said.

"Oh, yeah, I knowed that," Elmer said. "I was just testin' you to see if you knowed it, too." He climbed down from the smokehouse roof and walked out to meet delivery boy. "You got somethin' for me?"

"Are you Mr. Gleason?"

"Yeah, that's me."

The boy didn't dismount but held the yellow envelope down for Elmer. Elmer took the envelope, then tipped the boy a quarter.

"Thank you, Mr. Gleason," he said with an appreciative smile.

Elmer watched the boy ride away then opened the envelope to read the telegram.

POLICE HAVE PISTOL CYLINDERS STOP
INTERESTED IN STORY STOP $7000
DEPOSITED PLUS $500 CASH STOP
$500 BONUS FOR WANG STOP STAY OUT
OF TROUBLE STOP
DUFF

"Here now, what do you think of this, Wang?" Elmer asked after reading the telegram. "Duff is givin' you a five-hunnert-dollar bonus, though for the life of me, I don't see why. You ain't done nothin' to earn it."

"Perhaps it is because I seed and manage the pastures, I control the weeds, I take care of gathering the hay, I build and repair fences, I shovel snow, I chop wood, and I keep the irrigation canals clean," Wang said.

"Oh, well yeah, if you want to count that," Elmer said with a little laugh. "What do you say we go spend some of our money at Fiddler's Green? Let's see if we can get in 'n out without you beatin' someone up."

Cheyenne

If Duff had been by himself, he probably would have gone back to Chugwater the next day, as his business was concluded. But he remained in Cheyenne because Meagan asked to stay just a little longer.

"I've still got some shopping to do, and," she added with a conspiratorial smile, "*Macbeth* is playing at the Cheyenne Opera House. I have bought tickets for us. The eminent actor Edwin Booth is playing the title role."

"*Macbeth* is a good play," Duff said.

"You know *Macbeth*?" Meagan asked.

Duff smiled. "What Scotsman doesn't know *Macbeth*?" He began speaking, projecting as if on stage.

"To-morrow, and to-morrow, and to-morrow,
Creeps in this petty pace from day to day,
To the last syllable of recorded time,
And all our yesterdays have lighted fools
The way to dusty death. Out, out, brief candle!
Life's but a walking shadow, a poor player
That struts and frets his hour upon the stage
And then is heard no more: It is a tale
Told by an idiot, full of sound and fury,
Signifying nothing."

Meagan laughed and clapped her hands appreciatively. "Oh, you do know it. I thought you might. I hope you don't mind seeing it again."

"Nae, why should I mind? You can listen to music more than once, so watching a good play more than once is nae different."

"Thank you for agreeing to go to the play. I was afraid I might have to find some way to bribe you into going."

"Aye, perhaps it would take a bribe."

Meagan put her hand on his arm and smiled salaciously. "Oh, I had planned on it as a bribe or a reward."

"And just when will I be collecting on this bargain you have made?"

"In time," Meagan promised. "But right now, I have more shopping to do."

"All right, you go ahead and shop. I think I'll spend some time in the Cattlemen's Club."

As Duff walked from the hotel to the club, he saw four men riding down the middle of Sixteenth Street. Though he had no way of knowing, they were the same men to whom belonged the revolver cylinders he had left at the police station earlier.

He also saw Lonesome John carrying a large sack over his shoulder, headed for the livery stable. From the way he was walking and handling the sack, Duff realized it must be heavy.

"Hello, John, would you be for needing help with the bag?"

"Mr. MacCallister. No, thank you, sir. I think I have the task well in hand."

"Speaking of hands, how is yours?"

John chuckled and held out his hand, showing the small bandage. "It was a clean shot you made, Mr. MacCallister, all gun, and little hand. You are quite a marksman."

"I thank you for the compliment, lad."

"No, I'm the one who should be thankful. It was the skillful way you engaged your pistol that stood between a hand barely scratched and one that could be mangled."

"'Tis hoping, I am, that we never find ourselves in a similar situation," Duff said.

John's laugh was self-deprecating. "I have learned my lesson, Mr. MacCallister. I will never again put myself in such a position with anyone."

"'Tis good that you take it in such a way."

"Yes, sir," John replied. He patted the heavy sack on his shoulder. "I'd better get to the stable with these oats. I've a lot of hungry horses as my guests."

The four men who had ridden by MacCallister without particular notice were Lou Martell, Gabe Kellis, Deekus Carlotti, and Emmet Willard. They had come to Cheyenne to retrieve the cylinders to their pistols.

"Say, Lou, do you think the police will give us back them cylinders that the Chinaman took offen us?" Carlotti asked.

"Yeah, I been wonderin' 'bout that, too," Kellis said.

"Don't worry bout it. I got it all figured out," Martell said.

"What? How you goin' to get 'em back?"

"You just let me handle that," Martell said.

"I hope you got it figured out, 'cause right up there's the police station, 'n these guns ain't worth a bucket of mud when they don't have no cylinders in 'em," Willard said.

The four men dismounted in front of the police station, then went inside. A police sergeant looked up at them, surprised to see so many come in at the same time.

"What can I do for you gentlemen?" he asked.

"They's supposed to be four pistol cylinders here for us," Martell said.

"What makes you think that?"

"My name is Roy Carter. I own a small spread up near Bordeaux. I had a man workin' for me by the name of Smith, but I fired the no 'count. Somehow, he got a-holt of the cylinder from my pistol 'n from three others. He left me a note sayin' we could pick 'em at the police station here in Cheyenne. Now, are they here, or was he a-lyin' to me?"

The police sergeant chuckled. "They're here all right. I have to tell you, some of us have been wondering why they showed up here. Wait for a minute 'n I'll get 'em for you."

Five minutes later, with the cylinders back in their pistols, Martell and the others left the police station. Shortly thereafter, he and the other three men were riding north on the Walbach road just north of Cheyenne. They had no particular sense of purpose or destination.

"Lou, we got to get us some money," Carlotti said. "I ain't hardly got enough to buy more 'n a couple o' beers."

"Yeah, I thought we was sposed to get twenty-five thousand dollars for capturin' or killin' that Chinaman," Kellis said. "Only we didn't get no money on account of we didn't do it."

"You want to go back and try again?" Martell asked.

"Hell no. If you're goin' back after that chink, you can go without me," Willard said. "I don't want nothin' no more to do with 'im."

"Yeah, well you don't have to worry none about that, 'cause we ain't goin' after him again," Martell said.

"All right, but we need to come up with some other way to get us some money," Carlotti said.

"You say that like I could just—" Martell stopped in midsentence and smiled. "Boys, here comes our bank."

"What do you mean, here comes our bank?"

"There's a stagecoach comin' up the road. We're goin' to rob it."

"It prob'ly ain't carryin' no money," Kellis said. "Most o' the money shipments goes by train now."

"How much money do you have?" Martell asked.

"I don't know. Two, maybe three dollars."

"I'm damn sure the stagecoach is carryin' more money than that."

"How do we do it?" Willard asked.

"The coach is comin' this way, we'll just ride up the road real casual like, 'n when we actual meet up with the coach, we'll stop it."

It was said of Chance Lane that he was the best driver on the South Wyoming Stage Line, and many said he was probably the best in all of Wyoming. He had a real good touch with the reins and could make a six-horse team respond to his bidding with only the slightest application.

Lane's shotgun guard, Jed Lucas, had just announced that this was his last trip. He was quitting.

"Why are you quitting?"

"I'm quittin' 'cause I get bored just sittin' here, ridin' back 'n forth. It ain't the same with you. You're drivin', 'n that gives you something to do, but I ain't doin' nothin'."

"What else are you goin' to do?" Lane asked. "You got 'ny thing in mind?"

"I thought I'd see iffen maybe I could get me a job on the railroad. Hell, the railroad is goin' ever'where now. I wouldn't be surprised if purty soon there won't be no stagecoaches goin' nowhere."

"Well, they ain't built no railroad to Walbach yet, 'n until they do, they'll be needin' stagecoaches."

"Yeah, I reckon you're right. Hey, Chance, look at them four men comin' toward us. They're all spread out across the road. How come they ain't got out of our way?"

"I don't know. It is some peculiar," Lane said.

Martell and the other three men were spread all the way across the road, effectively blocking the passage of the stagecoach. They continued toward the coach until they could hear the sounds of it approaching, the hoofbeats of six horses, the squeaks and rattles of the coach rocking on the thoroughbrace, and the occasional shouts of the driver.

"Hey, it's got a shotgun guard," Carlotti said. "That's good, ain't it? That means it's carryin' some money."

"It could be."

The four men approached the coach casually, so as not to cause the driver any alarm.

As they came in contact with the coach, Martell called out, "Now!"

At his command, all four men raised their pistols, pointing them at the driver and the shotgun guard.

"Here, what is this?" the driver called.

"What does it look like, mister? It's a holdup," Martell replied.

"The hell you say!" Jed shouted, raising his shotgun.

All four of the stagecoach robbers fired at him, and three of them hit him. One of the bullets plunged into his heart and he was killed instantly.

"What's goin' on out there?" a passenger called out from inside the coach.

Martell fired at the coach, hitting the top of the door. "It ain't nothin' none of you needs to be a-worryin' about," he called back. "You folks just stay in the coach, lessen you're wantin' to be kilt."

"We ain't goin' nowhere," a frightened voice replied from inside.

"Throw down your strongbox," Martell ordered the driver.

"I ain't carryin' no strongbox. All I got is a messenger pouch."

"Throw it down."

"What do you want it for?"

"Don't argue with me, driver, just throw down the damn bag."

The driver threw the canvas bag down.

"All right, you can go now," Martell said.

"You kilt Jed," the driver said.

"Yes, and we'll kill you if you don't get on out of here now," Martell replied.

The driver snapped the whip over the team, the pop as loud as a pistol shot. "Hee-yah!" he called out, and the team jerked ahead. Martell and the other three watched the coach drive away.

"What's in that messenger pouch?" Carlotti asked.

Martell opened the pouch and looked inside. "Damn!"

"What is it?"

"There ain't nothin' here but a bunch o' letters." He held the pouch upside down, dumping the mail. "No money."

"Why was they carryin' a shotgun guard for?" Kellis asked.

"Yeah, 'n why did the damn driver throw down on us, if he didn't have nothin' to guard?" Martell tossed the pouch aside.

When it hit the ground, Carlotti started shooting at it. Kellis began shooting at it as well, then Willard and Martell. They fired several rounds, laughing as the bullets punched holes in the bag, and pushed it around.

"Let's go," Martell said. "It's prob'ly best we don't stay aroun' here no more."

"What are we goin' to do for money?" Carlotti asked.

"I don't know. We'll come up with somethin'. Just give me some time to think about it," Martell said. "But the first thing I'm goin' to do is find me a saloon 'n have a drink."

"Yeah, sounds like a pretty good idea to me," Kellis said, "but where will we go? We can't go back into Cheyenne. Not now, 'cause that's where the stagecoach was a-headin'."

"Lookie there," Carlotti said, pointing to a sign on the side of the road—HILLSDALE, 8 MILES. "Why don't we go there?"

"That sounds about as good as anyplace else," Martell said.

Chapter Ten

Just under an hour later, the four men dismounted in front of the Sundown Saloon, pushed through swinging batwing doors, then stepped up to the bar. It wasn't any cooler in the saloon, but at least it gave them a respite from the sun they had been riding in for the last two days.

Martell took his beer, then turned around so his back was to the bar and began looking around. It was no different from any other saloon he had been in. The main room, deeper than it was wide, held a scattering of tables, most occupied. Three percentage girls were working the tables. A scarred, upright piano was at the rear of the saloon, though nobody was playing it.

"Hey, what the hell?" Carlotti asked. "There's a colored man back there. He ain't got no business bein' in—"

"Hold it, Carlotti," Martell said, holding out his hand. "I know that fella."

"You know the colored man?"

"No, but I know one of the men with him. Me 'n him has did some business together." With a big smile on his face, and carrying his beer with him, Martell went over to the table.

Two of the men looked up toward him, the expressions on their faces showing irritation at being disturbed.

The man Martell knew stood up with a broad smile on his face. "Lou Martell," he said, extending his hand.

"Hello, Bart."

"Boys, this is Lou Martell," Bart said. "Me 'n him done us a couple of jobs together. Lou, this here is Moe Conyers, that's Slim Gardner."

"This colored man with you?" Martell asked.

"Yeah, he is, 'n he's a pretty good man, too. I don't know what his real name is, but he's callin' hisself Black Lib."

"Black Lib?"

"Actually, Mr. Martell, the name is Black Liberty, but I will answer to Black Lib."

"That your real name?"

"I don't see no need for nobody to know my real name, seein' as I'm gettin' along just fine as Black Lib."

Martell nodded. "That's good enough for me. Bart, these here is my pards." He motioned the other three over to join him and pointed them out as he called their names. "The big 'un there is Deekus Carlotti. The ugly one with the scar on his face is Gabe Kellis. Emmet Willard is the scrawny one, but don't let him bein' sort of scrawny like that give you no wrong ideas, 'cause he's fast as greased lightnin', 'n kin shoot a flea offen the hind leg of a dog from fifty feet away."

"What are you doin' in Hillsdale?" Bart asked.

"Well, truth is, I come lookin' for you. I told my boys you was the best there ever was at findin' ways to make money, 'n I was hopin' you might have a job we could do."

Bart stroked his chin. "Is that a fact?"

"Well, yeah, but if them boys you got with you is enough, I reckon we can find somethin' on our own."

"No, now wait a minute," Bart said, holding up his hand. "It may just be that havin' twice as many men might make a job a little easier."

"Yeah, 'n it would mean we got to split the money eight ways, too," Moe said.

"Don't you be worryin' none about that," Bart said. "With twice as many men, our jobs could be a lot bigger than anything we've done so far so that even a eight-way split will give us more money."

"Yeah, I guess that's right," Conyers said.

"All right, Lou, if you 'n your pards wants to join up with us, how 'bout you come along with us to a cabin we got nearby?"

"Sounds good to me," Martell said, without seeking the affirmation of any of his men.

He and his men joined the others for one beer then followed Bart and his men out of town.

"We goin' toward Cheyenne? 'Cause if you are, me 'n the others had better go someplace else," asked Martell.

"What's wrong with goin' to Cheyenne?" Bart asked.

"We held up a stagecoach 'n kilt the guard. All we got for it was a bag full of mail, but I figure the driver 'n the passengers has prob'ly told ever'one in Cheyenne about it. Told who we was."

"You mean they knew you?" Bart asked, surprised by Lou's comment.

"No, but they prob'ly told ever'one what we looked

like, 'n we was just in Cheyenne before, so that's how they could find out."

Bart chuckled. "Well, never you mind about that. Right now we're goin' to a cabin that we've got. It's outside Cheyenne, by maybe eight or nine miles."

Deekus Carlotti came riding up alongside Lou. "Hey, are we goin' to stop 'n eat some'ers? Me 'n the others is gettin' some hungry."

The question had been directed toward Lou, but Bart answered. "We ain't that far from the cabin now, 'n we got eats there."

Carlotti nodded, then dropped back behind the two leaders.

The men reached the cabin within ten more minutes. Bart had been calling it a cabin, but it was bigger and better constructed than Lou had anticipated. He would have called it a house. There was also a stable for the horses.

"Damn, Bart. This is quite a layout you got here," Lou said.

"Better than sleeping on the dirt," Bart replied.

"Or under it," Lou joked.

Bart laughed.

Once inside, Slim Gardner began frying some bacon, then he fried some cornbread in the bacon drippings. That and a couple of cans of beans made up the meal.

There was no table, so the men took their meals seated on the floor.

"So, tell me, Bart, have you got any jobs lined up?" Lou asked.

"I'm talking with someone about a job now, a big job,

I mean a really big job, and if it comes through, it will mean more money than any of us have ever seen before."

"What is the job?" Lou asked.

Bart shook his head. "I'd rather not say. I don't want to jinx it."

Lou chuckled. "Well, if it is as big as you say, we sure as hell don't want it jinxed."

Cheyenne

"Kirby, did you hear that the stagecoach was held up and the shotgun guard killed?" Chief Peach asked.

"I heard some folks talkin' about it, yes."

"I'd like for you to go down to the stagecoach depot and talk to the driver, then locate and interview the passengers who were on board."

"Chief, why is that any of our concern? It happened outside the city limits, and that means outside our jurisdiction. Seems to me that would be the job of the sheriff, or at least one of his deputies. But I'll do it if you ask me."

Chief Peach laughed. "Hell, Dan, I thought I just did."

Kirby walked down to the depot where he found the driver, Chance Lane, talking to Ken Proffer, the depot manager.

Lane looked around as Kirby came in. "Where the hell were you when we needed you?".

"Lane, you know damn well that the police don't have any jurisdiction outside of town. Tell me what happened."

"We were stopped by four men, 'n they shot Jed without so much as a fare-thee-well. Shot 'im dead, they did.

He's down at the undertaker's now. Ponder has already come got 'im."

"How much money did they get?"

"Hell, that's just it," Lane said. "All the hell they got was the mailbag, and there sure as hell warn't no money in there unless a couple of 'em had a few dollars or somethin'."

"Did you get a good look at them?" Kirby asked.

"Yeah, I got a real good look at 'em. They wasn't even wearin' no masks or nothin'."

"Thanks," Kirby said.

A few minutes later he dropped a paper on the chief's desk. "Here's a description of the ones that held up the stagecoach."

Peach picked it up and studied it for a moment. "Creech, would you come in here, please?" he called.

A moment later, the desk sergeant stepped into Chief Peach's office. "You need somethin', Chief?"

"Tack this up on the wall, 'n tell ever'one to have a good look at it and keep an eye open to see if they see anyone who matches these descriptions."

Creech looked at the descriptions for a moment. "I'll be damned. These are the same ones."

"Same ones? What are you talking about, same ones?" Kirby asked.

"You 'member I told you about them four men who come in here to get the cylinders for their pistols? The leader said his name was Roy Carter, and he owned a ranch near Bordeaux. They was three men with 'im, 'n they all fit these descriptions."

"Thanks, Sergeant. If you would, please, send someone

down to Sheriff Twitty's office and tell him or one of his deputies to take look around Bordeaux for a ranch owned by a man named Roy Carter. Like as not, that's not his real name, and he doesn't own a ranch near Bordeaux, but it wouldn't hurt to check."

"All right, Chief. I'll get right on it."

Chapter Eleven

While Meagan continued her shopping, Duff remained in the Cheyenne Cattlemen's Club, visiting with other cattlemen and playing in a low-stakes poker game.

"MacCallister, I'm told that you raise Angus," said Drury Vaughan, one of the cattlemen. "Has it been profitable for you?"

"Aye, very profitable."

"I must say that when I switched from longhorns to Herefords, I considered Angus. I'm too invested in Herefords to make the move into Angus now. But switchin' to Herefords has been a good move for me."

"I like longhorns," one of the other cattlemen said. "Hell, those critters damn near take care of themselves."

"You're right, Glen," Drury said. "But if it comes down to a degree of profit or ease of raising them, I prefer profit."

"There's something to what you're saying," Glen replied. "The price of longhorns has dropped so much I'm damn near giving them away now."

"Did you men hear about the stagecoach holdup?" Ray Kelly asked.

"I'll take one card," Drury said, then to Kelly, "How much money did they get?"

"That's just it. They didn't get nothin' at all, but they kilt Jed Lucas."

"Damn," Drury said. "Jed was a good man. I thought he had retired already. What was he doing on that coach?"

"They're saying it would have been his last ride," Kelly said.

"I don't mean to be callous or anything, but it was his last ride," Drury said.

"Yeah, well I hope they find them that done it, is all I got to say.

"Gentlemen, show your cards," Kelly said.

Duff's three eights were beaten by Drury's full house.

"Well, lads 'tis time for me to go." Duff stood up then. "But 'twas an enjoyable couple of hours I spent with you."

"G'bye, Duff," Drury said as he raked in the pot, which consisted of four dollars and seventy-five cents.

The other players bade him good-bye as well, and with a slight wave, Duff departed the table.

Meagan joined Duff for lunch at the Cattlemen's Club. "Have you enjoyed visiting with all the cattlemen?" she asked with a mocking smile.

"Aye, but I enjoy my time more with a cattlewoman."

Meagan laughed. "Well, you can always go shopping with me."

To Meagan's surprise, Duff accepted her invitation.

* * *

That night Duff and Meagan attended the performance of *Macbeth* at the Cheyenne Opera House. The auditorium would hold 360 people, and Meagan didn't see an empty seat when they showed their tickets and went inside.

The theater was a showpiece of elegance, including a large chandelier in the lobby, carved woodwork, and a grand staircase to the balcony. The curtain opened and the audience grew quiet.

Very soon, Meagan was drawn into the story that follows a brave Scottish general named Macbeth, who receives a prophecy from a trio of witches that one day he will become King of Scotland. Consumed by ambition and spurred to action by his wife, Macbeth murders King Duncan and takes the Scottish throne for himself. He is then racked with guilt and paranoia.

As Meagan had pointed out earlier, the player of the title role, and the person who had drawn the large audience, was Edwin Booth. He had worked hard to overcome the stigma his brother had brought to the family name. Over time, talent and perseverance enabled him to win back the following he had enjoyed before that April night when his brother, John Wilkes Booth, used a derringer pistol to put a ball in the back of President Lincoln's head.

When Edwin made his first entrance, the audience applauded loudly. For just a moment, he broke the "fourth wall" and made a slight bow of appreciation for his reception then turned to the stage.

MACBETH: So foul and fair a day I have not seen.

FIRST WITCH: All hail, Macbeth! hail to thee, thane of Glamis!

Meagan was held spellbound by the actors as they blocked their positions on the stage and delivered their dialogue. She followed the play act by act in her program, until she saw that they were in the fifth and final act.

The audience drew tense with excitement and anticipation as they realized the play was coming to its conclusion. Macbeth and Macduff were poised for their climactic fight.

MACBETH: I bear a charmed life, which must not yield,
    To one of woman born.
MACDUFF: Despair thy charm;
    And let the angel whom thou still hast served
    Tell thee, Macduff was from his mother's womb
    Untimely ripp'd.
MACBETH: Lay on, Macduff,
And damn'd be him that first cries, "Hold, enough!"
*(*MACBETH *falls before the sword of* MACDUFF.*)*

The curtain closed shortly after Macbeth was killed, and the audience applauded loudly as the players returned to take their bows. The applause was loudest for Edwin Booth.

"Oh, that was wonderful!" Meagan said. "And wasn't Edwin Booth magnificent?"

"Would you be for making me jealous, now?"

"What? No, of course not."

Duff laughed. "'Tis but a joke, lass."

"But he is a very handsome man," Meagan teased.

After the final curtain, Duff and Meagan returned to the Interocean Hotel, but before going up to bed, they decided to have a glass of wine and a piece of cake. They were the only ones in the dining room at that hour, and they were enjoying their conversation when another hotel guest come into the room. They were surprised to see that it was Edwin Booth.

He looked around the room for a moment, saw Duff and Meagan, then smiled and approached their table. "I say there, please excuse the intrusion, but I find it most uncomfortable to sit at a table by myself. I wonder if I could join you?"

"Aye, 'twould be a pleasure to have your company."

"Thank you very much," Booth said taking his seat at the table. He extended his hand to Duff. "I'm Edwin Booth."

"Yes, we saw you at the theater tonight," Meagan said. "I thought your performance was brilliant."

"What a nice thing for you to say to me," Edwin replied. "And who might you be?"

"I'm Meagan Parker, and this is my friend, Duff MacCallister."

"MacCallister, you say? Interesting. By coincidence I happen to know some theater people by that same name. They are brother and sister, I believe."

"Aye, they would be my cousins, Andrew and Roseanne MacCallister," Duff said.

The smile grew large on Booth's face. "Yes, that is them! Well now, isn't this a fortuitous meeting? I shall enjoy my evening repast all the more, knowing that I am in good company. Do you see your cousins much?"

"Not as often as I would like."

"I shall speak of our meeting when next your cousins and I meet."

"It would be good of you to do so."

"Booth, you treasonous monster, what are you doing in Cheyenne? You should have been hung along with the others who conspired with your no-account brother." The loud challenge came from a man who had just stepped into the dining room. He was a big man with wide shoulders and no neck. He walked up to the table and stared down at Booth for a moment, then his gaze took in Duff and Meagan. "Do you know who you are sitting with? You are sitting with the man who kilt the president."

"Oh, is that so?" Duff asked. "'N here I was under the impression that the foul deed was done, not by this gentleman, but by his brother."

"What difference does it make? A Booth is a Booth, 'n I intend to rid the world of them, here and now." The man raised his hand high, and Duff saw for the first time that he was holding a knife.

While his hand was raised so, it presented the soft part of his stomach to Duff, who flattened his hand, then drove the tips of his fingers deep into the man's solar plexus, knocking the breath from him. Stunned, paralyzed, and gasping hard to recover his breath, the big man dropped his knife and stood there with his eyes and mouth opened wide, looking toward Duff.

"You'll be recoverin' your breath in a moment, but not your knife. I'll be keeping that, and I'll be taking this moment to appeal to you. 'Tis sure I am that you know this Mr. Booth had nothing to do with the death of the president. I'll be for asking you to leave this room now, and once you do, this unpleasantness will be over. But if you come back in here, I will shoot you dead. Do you understand me?"

The man, still gasping for breath, nodded his head then turned and walked away.

"Thank you, Mr. MacCallister. Something like this has happened to me quite a few times since my brother performed what must be the most perfidious act in the history of our republic. It hasn't happened in quite a while, though, so I was rather hoping it had passed. I see that it has not."

"There may be other incidents," Duff said. "But I think you'll nae be bothered by that unfriendly gentleman again."

Booth laughed. "I rather think not."

Their conversation continued for another hour or so as Duff and Booth exchanged stories about Andrew and Roseanne, some of which had them laughing. It was not until midnight that they took leave of each other then went to their rooms.

It had been a long and tiring day for Duff, and he fell asleep rather quickly.

The cabin

"The Bank of Laramie," Bart said.

"Laramie? That's a dangerous town," Martell said. "Hell, vigilantes have hung fifteen maybe twenty people there in the last ten years or so."

"That's why we're going there," Bart said.

"What? Bart, that don't hardly make no sense a-tall," Martell replied.

"Yeah, it does. It makes a lot of sense. All them lynchin's

has drove all the outlaws out of town, 'n folks has put lots of their money in the bank 'cause they think it's safe. But with eight men, we can damn near take the town over."

"Yeah." A broad smile spread across Martell's face. "Yeah, that's right, ain't it?"

"Robbin' the bank in Laramie will give us some operatin' money until we do our job with the bank in Cheyenne," Bart said.

"Whoa now, hold it, hold it," Martell said, holding up his hands. "Cheyenne's a lot bigger 'n Laramie, besides which they got a pretty big police force there. Even with eight of us, it would be awful dangerous for us to try 'n rob that bank."

"We aren't going to hold up the bank," Bart said.

"What do you mean we ain't goin' to hold up the bank? Ain't that what you just said?" Moe asked.

"Not exactly. It's, uh—"

"Bart, whyn't you let me tell it to 'im?" Black Liberty said, looking up from the stick he was carving with the Bowie knife he always carried. "Mr. Martell, Bart's figured out a way for us to take the money from the bank without ever havin' to be there."

"How are we going to take the money without being there?"

"There ain't no need for any of us to be worryin' none about it. If all of us just do what Bart tells us to do, whenever it is that he tells us to do it, why then everything will work out just fine," Black Lib said.

"You ain't nothin' but a colored man. Who the hell are you to tell me what to do?" Martell asked.

"I'm a colored man who's smart enough to know what Bart is talkin' about."

"I ain't goin' to stand here 'n let no nig . . . uh, colored man tell me what to do. Hell, I'm better 'n you or any colored man there ever was."

Black pointed his knife at Martell. "Maybe you'd like to prove just how much better 'n me you is."

"If you mean gettin' into a knife fight with you, no. I ain't a-goin' to do that."

Black Lib returned to his whittling. "Well now, it could maybe be that you're smarter 'n I thought you was."

Martell thought about shooting Black Lib, but he was one of Bart's men, and because of that, he enjoyed Bart's protection. With a frustrated sigh, Martell stepped outside.

A few minutes later, Bart stepped outside to talk to him. "You all right?"

"Bart, why you got someone like that uppity black with you anyhow? He thinks he is as good as a white man. What do you know about him?"

"Truth to tell, I don't know all that much about Black Liberty, only that he had once been a buffalo soldier, and that he deserted. I also got me a pretty strong suspicion that somewhere in his past, he musta murdered someone, 'n maybe that's how come he wound up leaving the army, or maybe that's why he joined it in the first place."

"That don't say nothin' 'bout why you got 'im workin' with you."

"He ain't never done nothin' to cause me to want to get shed of 'im."

"Yeah, well, I don't like it. But if it's all right with you, then I reckon it'll have to be all right with me."

"I thought you might see my side of it," Bart said, speaking in a way that was dismissive of the subject.

"I'm curious as to what it is you've got set up in the bank in Cheyenne?"

"I haven't told anybody about it yet, 'n I'd rather not. If it doesn't work, the fewer people who know about it, the better everything is. And if it does work, it'll be good for all of us."

"All right," Martell said with a nod. "We're just joinin' you, so far as I'm concerned whatever you get will be the same as found money to us."

Chapter Twelve

It wasn't unusual for Bart Jenkins to keep his own counsel, so keeping quiet about any specific plans he might have for the Cattlemen's Bank of Cheyenne wasn't out of character for him. He also had his own background story that he had not shared with anyone.

Three years earlier

Bart Jenkins, whose real name was Will Hawkins, was a shotgun guard for the Western Arizona Stage Line. He stood in front of the stage depot in the small town of Cactus Needle, Arizona Territory. He watched as the three passengers, all men, got into the coach. The driver, Merlin Proffer, came walking down from the bank, carrying a satchel.

"How much money are we carryin' today?" Hawkins asked.

"That ain't none o' your business," Proffer replied.

Hawkins and Proffer didn't get along very well. In fact, Proffer had asked to be assigned another shotgun guard, but none of the other drivers wanted to ride with Hawkins, either.

The money Hawkins asked about was being transferred to a bank in Yuma.

Hawkins climbed up into the high seat and was joined by the driver, who used his whip to make a loud pop over the six-horse team. The coach rolled quickly down the street, then out of town.

“Nice day for a drive, ain’t it?” Hawkins asked.

“I have to have you ride with me. I don’t need to talk with you,” Proffer growled.

Hawkins steamed over it for about three hours. They had driven about fifteen miles since leaving Cactus Needle, which meant they were about three miles from Yuma.

And that was when he got the idea.

Pulling his pistol, Hawkins shot the unsuspecting driver in the temple, then, grabbing the reins, he pulled the team to a halt.

“Hey, what’s goin’ on up there?” one of the passengers called.

“I expect you folks better step outta the stage,” Hawkins said as he climbed down with his pistol in one hand and the shotgun in the other.

Two of the men looked like drummers, both of them overweight. The third man was about Hawkins’s size, and he was dressed as a cowboy.

“What did we stop for?” one of the drummers asked.

“So I could do this,” Hawkins said, shooting the one who asked. Even as the other two men were calling out in alarm, Hawkins shot them as well. Then, he shot the cowboy in the face with the shotgun so that even his closest friend wouldn't be able to identify him.

Hawkins took the cowboy's clothes, then dressed the cowboy in his clothes. Taking the money—a little over five hundred dollars—from the case, he walked the rest of the way to Yuma, where he boarded the train for Phoenix.

Arriving there, he took a hotel room using the name Bart Jenkins as his new name. He got the name from two businesses he had seen on the street—Bart Ebersole Hardware and Joseph Jenkins Apothecary.

Three days later, Bart Jenkins, as he thought of himself, read the headlines in the Phoenix Herald.

CACTUS NEEDLE COACH ROBBED

Driver, Shotgun Messenger, Two Passengers Slain

The story went on to give the names of the driver, Merlin Proffer, the shotgun guard, Will Hawkins, and two passengers—Wendel Hayes and Clyde Driscoll, both salesmen. The third passenger, Frank Emerson, a cowboy, was missing, and believed to be the culprit.

Bart smiled when he read the story. He had gotten away with the money and nobody was looking for him because he was dead. They were looking for Frank Emerson.

Not too long after that, Bart met Lou Martell in the Sundown Saloon in Flagstaff. The two men hit it off, and over the next few months robbed isolated grocery stores and trading posts. After killing a sheriff and his deputy, Bart and Martell split up.

* * *

Meeting him in the Sundown Saloon in Hillsdale, so far from where they'd met, and so long after they had parted, was quite a surprise to him.

Cheyenne

For Duff and Meagan, the day proved to be as busy as the previous one. Meagan did more shopping to buy some additional items for her store. Duff went with her, not wishing to spend another day trying to make conversation with the other cattlemen who were habitués of the club.

"I think I'll buy something for Elmer and Wang," Duff said.

"Yes, good idea. I'll get something for Vi and Mae Lin," Meagan offered.

It didn't take him long to complete his shopping. He looked for, and found, the silver hatband Elmer had requested, then he bought a pair of gloves for each of them. The selection was easy. Anyone working on a ranch always needed a good pair of leather gloves.

Meagan spent the rest of the day looking for something for Vi and Mae Lin. She wanted to get them something nice, but also unique. She got a gemstone facial roller for Mae Win, who had, Meagan thought, beautiful, blemish-free skin. The clerk assured Meagan that a regimen of using these gemstone facial rollers would keep her skin beautiful.

Vi was a little more difficult to choose for. Meagan finally settled on something called a split-decision pie pan, which would allow Vi to bake two pies on the same pan. They would be perfect for Vi's Pies, and Meagan actually bought four of them.

That night they had dinner at the Cheyenne Cattleman's Club, then attended an opera at McDaniel's Theater.

After a long and busy day, they welcomed the bed that night, and though they had two rooms, they used only one.

The next morning Joel Prescott kissed his wife good-bye, then walked out to step into the cab which, by arrangement, was there to pick him up at eight o'clock every weekday morning.

"Good morning, Mr. Prescott," Leo Kelly, the driver said.

"Good morning, Mr. Kelly. I hope you had a good night," Prescott replied.

"Yes, sir, I did. Thank you." Kelly snapped the reins against the horse to put the cab in motion.

Prescott waved and called out to pedestrians as the cab passed over the cobblestoned Seventeenth Street, the horse's hooves making a hollow clopping sound.

He thought about his position in the bank. His opting to leave the army had been a wise decision. A captain lived fairly well in an army environment, but as president and principal stockholder of the Cattlemen's Bank of Cheyenne, he was giving Nettie a much more fulfilling life than she had ever known during her association with the army.

The cab stopped in front of the bank, and Prescott climbed down.

"I'll be here at four o'clock this afternoon to take you back home," the cabdriver said.

"Thank you, Mister Kelly."

When Prescott started to put his key in the front door, he was surprised to see that it was already unlocked. He figured Eli must have arrived earlier than normal, and though Prescott had told him to never leave the door unlocked when it wasn't business hours, Eli had done so more than once.

"Eli?" he called as he stepped inside and locked the door behind him. "Eli, I've told you to keep the door locked if we aren't open."

Prescott got no answer.

"Eli, are you here?"

He still got no answer, and that was even worse. Not only was the bank unlocked, it was unlocked with nobody there.

Prescott went into his office and sat, waiting from Eli to arrive. Something bothered him. As he thought about the accounts being moved, which had the effect of leaving the bank completely out of funds, he wondered how he would be able to face his customers. He wished Eli was there. Eli had been his closest friend for quite some time. Joel would share some of his concerns with him. But Joel was alone, and having to deal with acute depression.

It was normal for Prescott and Kendrick to arrive at 8 A.M., which was one hour before the bank opened, but when Kendrick arrived it was fifteen minutes past eight.

"Joel?" he called. "Joel, I'm sorry I'm a little late, but I had some personal business to take care of. Do you have anything you want—" He stopped midsentence. He had just stepped into the president's office and saw Joel's body lying on the floor.

Blood had pooled onto the floor from the head wound. Kendrick didn't have to make a further check; he knew that the bank president was dead.

Hurrying to the front door, he opened it and called out to the first passerby he saw. "Please, go to the police station as quickly as you can and tell Chief Peach that Mr. Prescott has been killed."

"Prescott? Ain't he the bank president?"

"Yes, please, hurry."

Kendrick paced back and forth in the main room of the bank, waiting for the police to arrive. A couple of times he went back into Prescott's office to have another look at him.

He had left the front door unlocked, and hearing it open, he hurried to the front of the bank.

"Kendrick, what's this I hear about Mr. Prescott being killed?" Chief Peach asked. Lieutenant Kirby was with him.

"It's true, Chief. He's in his office, dead."

"What happened to him?"

"I don't know. I was about fifteen minutes late this morning, and when I went in to Joel's office to explain my absence, I found him like, well, come into his office with me and see for yourself."

Kendrick led the two police officers into Joel's office

and pointed to the body on the floor. "I found him like this."

Chief Harold Peach knelt down for a closer examination and saw a piece of paper sticking out from beneath Joel Prescott's body. He pulled it out, then looked up at Kendrick. "Did you know this note was here?"

Kendrick shook his head. "No, sir, Chief. I didn't know anything about it. I was so upset that I didn't stay in here very long."

Harold Peach read the note, then shook his head. "I'll be damned."

Lonesome John was currying a horse in the livery barn when two men who stabled their horses permanently with Abney came to get their horses. They didn't need John to get their horses for them.

"Can you believe it?" one of the men said. "I had a hunnert 'n ten dollars there, 'n now it's all gone."

"Yeah, I lost near a hunnert my ownself, 'n folks all over town has lost money. Some of the businessmen have lost five, ten, maybe even fifteen thousand dollars."

"It's goin' to take awhile for the town to recover from all that."

"What I don't understand is why he took all that money, then kilt hisself."

"Who knows? He always was sort of a strange man in my book."

The other man laughed. "Hell, Adam, Joel Prescott was rich. All rich folks is kinda strange."

"What are you two men talking about?" John asked.

"You mean you ain't heard? That banker feller, Joel Prescott stoled all the money from the bank, then shot hisself."

"Joel is dead?" John asked, shocked by the news.

"Deader 'n a doornail," one of the two men replied with a chuckle.

They had their horses saddled and rode off, leaving behind a distraught Lonesome John.

He pinched the bridge of his nose, then stepped over to one of the stall walls and stood there for a long moment. What the two who had just left didn't realize was that Lonesome John, the stable hand, and Joel Prescott, the wealthy banker, were very good friends. John felt the loss deeply.

He closed his eyes, and he was at Sportsman's Park in St. Louis, attending a Brown Stockings baseball game. The batter popped up the pitch, and it came backward, into the stands.

Joel reached and caught the ball, snatching it out of the air with one hand. "Did you see that?" he asked, proud of his move.

"George McManus was watching," John teased, talking about the manager of the baseball team. "I think he wants to sign you up to play for him."

Four years after that happy event, the man known in Cheyenne as Lonesome John stood against the wall lamenting the death of the only friend he had in town. Those who gave him the news intimated that Joel had committed suicide. You never know what's in a person's soul, but John couldn't make himself believe that Joel Prescott took his own life.

Chapter Thirteen

With all of their business in Cheyenne completed, Duff and Meagan were at the depot waiting for the train that would take them back to Chugwater. Meagan was chatting about seeing *Macbeth* and the opera *Aida*, as well as their chance meeting with Edwin Booth.

"I can't wait to tell Vi and all my friends," she said. "Why, they will be just pea green with envy that we actually shared a table with a famous actor like Edwin Booth. And of course, with all the material I got, I'm going to be very busy designing new—" Meagan stopped in midsentence.

"Oh, Duff, listen," she said in awestruck voice.

"What is it, Meagan?"

"One of those men just said that Mr. Prescott was dead."

Duff stepped over to the two men who were carrying on the conversation. "Please forgive the interruption, gentlemen, but did you just say that Joel Prescott is dead?"

"Yes, he took all the money from the bank, then kilt hisself."

"Why would he kill himself if he took all the money?" Duff asked.

"Hell, who knows why that crazy man done what he done?"

"What is it?" Meagan asked when Duff returned to where she was waiting for him. "What happened?"

"Those men just said that Joel embezzled all the money from the bank, then took his own life. I have to go to the bank to see what this is all about."

"We'll both go," Meagan said.

"There's nae need for you to be going."

"I'm going with you," Meagan said resolutely.

"All right," Duff agreed, without offering any further argument.

They walked down to the bank, where they found it crowded with depositors anxious to find out what happened to their money.

One of the men was jerking on the locked door. "Open up!" he shouted. "Open the damn door to this bank! You got no right to keep it closed." He jerked on the door again. "Open this door, or we'll kick it down!"

"Every cent I've got 'n the world is in that bank," said one of the other anxious depositors. "I have bills to pay and a payroll to meet."

"Where is our money? What happened to it?" another angry depositor shouted.

They weren't the only ones expressing their anger and concern. At least two dozen more were all shouting at the same time.

"Open the damn door!"

Eli Kendrick stepped out of the bank and held his hands up. "People, I know you are all upset, but please be quiet and let me speak to you." He spoke loudly enough to be heard.

"Who the hell are you, mister?" asked one the men in the angry crowd.

"I'm Eli Kendrick, the vice president of this bank." He paused for a moment then added, "Although technically, I suppose I would be the president, now that poor Mr. Prescott is gone."

"What the hell happened to our money, Kendrick?" someone yelled angrily. "Did Prescott steal all the money, then commit suicide?"

"People, please, just be patient for a while and give us time to deal with this."

"You don't need to deal with this. You need to deal with us!" somebody shouted. "You give us our money now, or we're going to tear you apart, limb from limb!"

"Gentlemen, I'm for thinking you dinnae want to do such a thing," Duff called out, stepping up to the front of the crowd just before it got out of hand.

"Who the hell are you?" someone called.

"My name is Duff MacCallister, and like all of you, I have money in this bank." He paused for a moment. "That is, I did have money in this bank."

"I would like to point out to the rest of you that Mr. MacCallister has more money in this bank than any other depositor," Kendrick said.

"If you got that much money in here, what are you doing protecting Kendrick?" someone called out.

"Attacking Mr. Kendrick will nae solve anything. Leave the man be so he can go about his business of findin' out what happened to our money."

Reluctantly, but with no other choice, the crowd of angry depositors dispersed. That left only Duff, Meagan, and Kendrick.

"Thank you, Mr. MacCallister, for defusing what could have become a most explosive situation," Kendrick said. "I appreciate you coming to my defense. At least you understand that I'm as much in the dark here as anyone else. And seeing as you are one of our largest depositors, perhaps I owe you a little more. Please, come in and we'll talk about it."

When Duff and Meagan stepped into the bank, they saw Harold Peach, chief of the Cheyenne Police Department.

"Mr. MacCallister," Chief Peach said, "what are you doing here?"

"Chief, Mr. MacCallister is one of our largest depositors. If we can satisfy him as to what happened, that might help with the others."

"All right," Chief Peach said. "What can we do for you, Mr. MacCallister?"

"I understand that you think he shot himself?"

"There's no thinking to it. That's exactly what he done," Chief Peach said.

"Mr. Kendrick, did Joel keep a gun in the bank?"

"Yes, he was quite proud of the fact that he was a graduate of West Point and was a captain when he left the army. He was quite proficient in the use of pistols."

"What kind of pistol was it?" Duff asked.

"It was a Colt model pistol. A .45 millimeter and it is standard issue in the army. Prescott must have brought it with him. No doubt it's the same one he carried when he was in the army. 'N that's the one he used to kill hisself."

"How do you know he committed suicide?"

"He told us he committed suicide," Peach said.

"What?" Duff asked.

"He left a note," Chief Peach explained.

"I wonder if you would you be for letting me see the note?"

"The note is part of a police investigation. Why should I let you see it?"

"Chief Peach, Mr. MacCallister and Joel were good friends," Kendrick said. "I don't see what harm it would do to let him see the note."

"All right. It's down at the police station. Come along with me 'n I'll show it to you. Would you like to come along with us, Kendrick?" Chief Peach asked.

"No, I . . . uh that is, I would like to come with you, but I feel that it is incumbent upon me, not only as Joel's business partner, but also as his very good friend, to call upon Mrs. Prescott. She has no family here, no one to comfort her. I'm sure she would like to hear a sympathetic voice."

"All right, yes, I think that would be a very good idea," Peach said. "Just because that worthless husband of hers turned out to be such a crook, there's no need for us to take it out on her. I've always thought of her as a very gracious lady. Yes, by all means, drop by and see her."

Duff and Meagan walked with Chief Peach down to the police station. Unlike the sheriffs' and city marshals' offices Duff was used to, the police station was considerably larger and there were half a dozen desks, a couple of which had policemen sitting behind them.

"Lieutenant Kirby," Chief Peach called when they stepped into the station.

"Yes, Chief?" Kirby was a big man, over six feet tall and weighing over 200 pounds. His head was completely bald and somewhat bullet shaped. His thick neck and bullish shoulders gave him the appearance of having been carved from one solid block of granite.

"Get the suicide note Prescott left, then bring it into my office so we can show it to MacCallister."

"Why do you think we should do that, Chief? I mean being as how this is an ongoing investigation."

"Just show him the note, Dan. Don't make this more difficult than it already is."

"Yes, sir."

Duff and Meagan followed Peach into his office, where he took off his hat, then sat in the cushioned chair behind his desk, settling down with a long, self-suffering sigh. "It's been a busy morning. Sit, sit," he offered pointing to two more chairs in the relatively large office.

Meagan sat, but Duff remained standing. A moment later Kirby came into the chief's office and handed a piece of paper to Duff. As he perused the note, he held it in such a way that he and Meagan could read both read it at the same time.

I embezzled all the money, and lost it in bad investments. I have failed those who put their trust in me. I cannot face all the people I have betrayed. Please forgive me.—Joel Prescott

Duff handed the note back to Kirby. "Chief, I thank you for taking us into your confidence."

"You're quite welcome. I'm just sorry this happened."

"Tell me what did happen," Duff said. "I mean for at least, as far as you know."

"It's pretty simple, really," the chief said. "Apparently, he held a gun to his head and pulled the trigger. It was before banking hours and he was the only one there. Kendrick says that when he arrived for work this morning, he went into Joel's office and saw him lying on the floor."

"On the floor, you say? And here now, he must have been standing when he shot himself. 'N tell me Chief, would you not be for thinking now, that that is a wee strange? Most people are sitting down when they kill themselves."

"Yes, I suppose that is how most people kill themselves," Chief Peach said. "But it's obvious that Joel was standing."

"Standing or sitting, it doesn't make any difference how he killed himself. He took all the bank's money then shot himself," Kirby said. "It's right there in the note."

"How is Mr. Prescott's wife doing?" Meagan asked.

"I'm the one who told her Prescott shot himself. She didn't take it very well, as you might expect," Kirby said.

"Is that the way you told her?" Meagan asked.

"Yeah, why not? That's what happened."

"You might have found some way to soften the blow."

"My job is to provide facts, not comfort her. That's a job for preachers and priests, and the like."

* * *

Half a dozen angry depositors were standing in front of the Prescott house when Eli arrived to pay his respects. He started toward the front porch.

"There ain't no need in you a-goin' up to the door," said one of the men standing out front. "She ain't a-talkin' to nobody."

Disregarding all the people standing in front of the house, Eli stepped up to the door and knocked. "Nettie, it's me, Eli."

A moment later, Jimmie Mae, the maid, opened the door. "Come on in, Mr. Kendrick. Mrs. Prescott is in the parlor."

"Thank you." Stepping into the parlor, he saw Nettie sitting in an overstuffed chair in the corner, holding a handkerchief to her eyes. "Nettie, I'm so sorry this happened," he said in as comforting a voice as he could manage.

"Hello, Eli," she greeted. "Thank you for coming."

"How are you doing?"

"Not very well," she replied with a subdued sob.

Eli shook his head. "Nor am I. This is almost too much for me to accept. I mean that Joel would take his own life without any regard for what it would do to you, or to me, his best friend. On top of that, he caused the bank to collapse, which hurt all the depositors who depended on us. Now you and I are forced to apologize for the failure of the bank, and the wrongdoing of the man in which I had absolute trust. I never would have believed he would do anything like this."

"Oh, Eli, do you think . . . I mean, do you actually believe Joel defrauded the bank and killed himself like they are saying?" Nettie asked, her voice cracking in her grief.

Eli sighed before he answered. "I don't know if it is true, but the evidence of it being true is incontrovertible, and I feel somewhat to blame for it."

"You feel some guilt? How so?"

"Nettie, let me ask you this. Had he been acting strangely around you?"

"What? No, not at all. Why would you even ask such a thing?"

"That he was able to cover it up is a testament to how much he loved you. At work, he couldn't hold it all in. He was very depressed, and I knew that he was in some trouble. I tried to get him to talk to me about it, but he wouldn't do it. I had no idea his depression was this severe. I should have tried harder to get through to him. That's what I meant when I said I bear some of the blame. Now it looks as if he took the money, hoping to use it to pay off his personal debts. As it turned out, he was unable to do so, and because there was some honor remaining in him, he committed suicide."

"But, that can't be true, Eli. We have no personal debts."

"Could there be debts that you know nothing about?" Eli asked.

"I . . . I don't know," Nettie admitted in a small voice. She was quiet for a moment, then she looked up at Eli. "Eli, just how much money was taken?"

"I'm afraid every cent in the bank was taken," Eli replied. "Two hundred and twenty-three thousand dollars."

"Oh, God in heaven," Nettie said, again breaking down in tears.

"I'm sorry, Nettie. I'm so sorry. "I'll leave now, but I want you to understand that I will be here for you, anytime you need me."

"Thank you, Eli. That is so nice of you."

He walked over to her and she stood to let him embrace her. Eli held the embrace for a long moment, then with a nod of his head, he left.

At police headquarters

"That's a lot of money. Don't you wonder why someone would take that money, then commit suicide?" Duff asked.

"I'll tell you why. He was crazy, that's why," Lieutenant Kirby said. "Big banker, wearing a suit, and thinking he was better than everyone else. Turns out, he wasn't."

"I'm just having a hard time thinking that Joel killed himself," Duff said. "I may look around a wee bit."

"Look around all you want," Chief Peach said. "To me, it's an open-and-shut case."

As soon as they left the police station and could talk, Meagan spoke up. "Duff, when we had dinner with Mr. and Mrs. Prescott, he didn't seem depressed to me. Did he to you?"

"Nae, but some are able to cover their depression with a false cheerfulness."

"But could he maintain that false cheerfulness as long as they're saying Mr. Prescott did?"

"It would be hard to do," Duff admitted.

"And here's another thing. Did you notice anything queer about that note?"

"In what way?"

"It wasn't written in cursive. It was printed."

"'Tis nae so odd. For some, their cursive is hard to read. I would think that if it be a suicide note, you would want everyone to be able to read it."

"That's true. But what if someone else wrote the note, and they wanted to write it in such a way that nobody else would be able to recognize the handwriting?"

Her words stopped Duff in his tracks. "Faith 'n begorra, lass, 'tis a good point you have made. Let's go speak with Mrs. Prescott."

"Yes, we should call upon her, if for no other reason, then to extend our condolences," Meagan agreed.

"Aye," Duff replied.

When Duff and Meagan arrived at the Prescott house, the crowd of people outside had grown larger. Some had come out of a genuine concern for the widow's well-being, but any expression of sympathy was overcome by the voiced objections of those who had come to let her know how displeased they were with her husband. Two men had started their own dialogue.

"Are you telling me that nobody has any idea what he did with the money?" the man asked sharply.

"I don't know," the other answered.

"Well, if anybody knows, it'll be his wife, and I plan to get it out of her."

Duff interrupted confrontation. "Mister, I'll be askin' you to leave the poor lady alone now."

"Who the hell are you to tell me what to do?"

"I'm the man that'll be throwin' you out on your backside if you don't leave now."

The belligerent one took a look at the muscular build of the man who had challenged him, and realizing that he could only come out on the bottom of any actual physical confrontation between them, withdrew meekly.

"I'll be for asking the rest of you to leave now," Duff said.

With groans of discontent, the more belligerent members of the group were herded away by those whose presence outside the house had no hostile intent. After the protestors were gone, Duff knocked on the door.

It was answered by Jimmie Mae, who, when she saw who it was, smiled in relief. "Come on in, Mr. MacCallister, Miss Parker," she invited.

A moment later Duff and Meagan were face-to-face with Nettie Prescott.

"Thank you for running the others away, Mr. MacCallister and Meagan," she said as she wiped her tears with a handkerchief. "It is so good of you to come."

Once inside they saw Eli Kendrick standing in the parlor.

"It is good of you to come, Mr. MacCallister," Kendrick said.

"Kendrick," Duff said.

Nettie saw Meagan looking at Kendrick, and she made the introduction. "Miss Parker, this is Eli Kendrick. He was Joel's very good friend. Mine too, actually, and the vice president of the bank."

Meagan acknowledged Kendrick with a nod of her

head, then she turned her attention back to Nettie. "Nettie, I'm so sorry for your loss."

"Mrs. Prescott, did the police share the note with you?" Duff asked.

"I didn't actually see the note, but I know that he didn't commit suicide."

"But you seem to think that he did, I believe?" Duff said to Kendrick.

"Yes, I know it is difficult for Nettie, uh, that is, Mrs. Prescott, and indeed for all of us who cared so deeply for Joel to accept that he committed suicide. Unfortunately, to me, that fact seems inescapable."

"Nettie, why are you so certain that he didn't?" Meagan asked.

"We had a very happy marriage. We were very close, and we had no secrets from each other. He could start a sentence, and I would finish it. When you are that close to someone, you know them inside out. I know that he didn't take one dollar from the bank, and I know that not in a million years would Joel kill himself."

"And you say you didn't see the suicide note?" Duff asked.

Nettie shook her head. "I didn't want to see it."

"Nettie, when your husband wrote a letter or made an entry into a journal or something, did he write in cursive or did he print?" Meagan asked.

"Oh, heavens, I never saw him print anything. Why, Joel had beautiful penmanship. Excuse me, but why would you ask such a thing?"

"Because the suicide note was printed," Duff said.

"That proves it!" Nettie said, dogmatically. "Joel would

never commit suicide, and if he did, he would not have printed a suicide note. Mr. MacCallister, someone else took the money, then killed Joel to make it appear as if he did it."

Nettie turned her attention to Eli. "Eli, Joel was your friend, and you worked with him. Surely you know that he never printed."

"I have to admit that seeing the note printed out, rather than written in cursive, did give me pause," Eli replied. "It wasn't enough for me to question whether or not he was the author of the note, but now that I think about it, perhaps I am having second thoughts."

"Thank you for that," Nettie said, looking gratefully toward Eli.

"With both of you thinking Joel dinnae write the note, that's enough to make me think he dinnae kill hisself."

"If he didn't kill himself, than someone killed him," Meagan suggested.

"Aye, but by itself, the note is nae proof enough for the police," Duff said. "If you would like, I'll look into the matter for you to see what I can find out."

"Yes, please do. It won't bring my husband back, but I'll not have Joel's name smeared."

"Aye, 'n 'twould be good to find out what happened to the money, as well."

"The money, yes," Kendrick said. "Believe me, as an officer of the bank, I would very much like to know what happened to the money. I am having to deal with a lot of angry depositors. Please do what you can, Mr. MacCallister, to find out what actually happened."

* * *

"Duff, do you believe Nettie? Do you think Joel didn't commit suicide?" Meagan asked after they left the Prescott house.

"I do believe her, but I want to have a look at the body."

Chapter Fourteen

"Oh, I'm afraid the body is not ready for viewing yet," said Loomis Ponder, the mortician.

"Mr. Ponder, I would just like to see him, if you dinnae mind. Joel Prescott was a friend of mine, and as I am but visiting your fair city, I dinnae know if I will be able to make the viewing. If you haven't gotten the body prepared, it will nae make a difference to me."

"All right," Ponder relented with a sigh. "Come on into the back room."

The body of Joel Prescott was lying on the embalming table. Prescott was not a very big man, and under these circumstances he looked even smaller.

The bullet wound, cleaned now, was just above his left eye. There was also a bruise on the left side of his face.

"What is this?" Duff asked, pointing to the bruise.

"That is the reason I didn't want you to see him yet," Ponder said. "Before a body is to be viewed, I like to remove all sources of wounds. I will close the bullet hole with wax and cover it and the bruise with powder and paint."

"How do you suppose he got that bruise?"

"Heavens, there is no way of knowing that. It probably has nothing to do with the wound. He may have had it for some time."

"No," Duff said. "I saw him just yesterday, and there was no bruise."

"When I recovered the body, it was lying on the floor," Ponder said. "Perhaps the bruise on the side of his head is the result of the fall."

Meagan was waiting out front and when Duff came from the embalming room, he put his arm on her arm and gently led her outside. "You and Nettie are right," Duff said. "l dinnae believe there is any possible way that Joel killed himself."

Duff told her about the bruise on the side of Joel's face, and about the position of the entry wound of the bullet. "It is here, above his left eye. That would seem to me to be a most awkward position for a suicide shot." He made a pistol of his hand and forefinger, then held it up, awkwardly, to his left eye.

"So, what are we going to do now?" Meagan asked.

"You can go back to Chugwater, but I think I'm going to surrender my ticket and take another room at the Interocean Hotel."

"If you stay here, I'm going stay here as well," Meagan insisted.

They returned to the depot, and Duff stepped up to the ticket counter. "We would like to surrender our return tickets. We'll be staying in your fair city for a while longer."

"Do you want a refund or a later ticket?" the clerk asked.

"I dinnae know when we'll be going back, so we'll be for taking a refund."

The clerk took the two tickets, then handed them a full refund. "We look forward to doing business with you again."

Returning to the Interocean Hotel, Duff and Meagan were able to reclaim the same rooms they had before. They took their luggage back upstairs, then Meagan went to Duff's room.

"What do we do now?" she asked.

"I'm going to see the governor," he said.

"You're going to see the governor? Whatever for?"

"I'll be for asking a favor from him," Duff said without being more specific. "In the meantime, I think you should send a telegram to Elmer and Wang and tell them we're going to be delayed."

"Should I tell them why?"

"I would nae tell them yet. Let me see what we can find out, first."

"All right. You go see the governor, and I'll send the telegram. Meet for lunch, where?"

"We can meet here."

Capitol building

Duff stood at a window, looking south. There was a considerable amount of traffic on the street and the walks on either side were crowded with pedestrians doing business with the many stores that fronted Capitol Street.

At the far end of the street, he could see the Union

Pacific Depot, its dome towering above all. He knew Meagan was there, sending a telegram to Elmer and Wang. They would be wondering about the delay, but Duff didn't want the telegrapher to know anything about his plans. It wasn't that he didn't trust the telegrapher, but he thought it better to be safe, than sorry.

"Mr. MacCallister?" the clerk said.

"Aye," Duff replied, turning away from the window.

"Governor Warren will see you now."

"Thank you."

The clerk led Duff into the governor's office. Governor Warren was a rather frail-looking man in his mid-sixties. He had white hair and a white moustache that appeared to come directly from his nostrils and sweep down to either side of his mouth. His frail appearance, however, belied his history. During the Civil War, Governor Warren had been a noncommissioned officer for the Union Army. At the Battle of Port Hudson, his entire platoon was wiped out by Rebel artillery. Despite a severe scalp wound and overwhelming odds, Sergeant Warren managed to sneak through the lines and destroy the enemy cannon that had wreaked so much havoc against the Union troops. For this, he was awarded the Medal of Honor, and that medal now occupied a frame on his wall.

The governor was wearing rimless glasses, and he looked up as Duff approached his desk.

"'Tis thanking you I am, Governor, for granting me an audience," Duff said.

"Would you be the same MacCallister who owns

Sky Meadow Ranch in Laramie County?" the governor asked.

"Aye," Duff responded, wondering why the governor would ask that.

"Dan Norton speaks very highly of you."

Duff smiled. "We are lucky to have a barrister as foine a man as Dan Norton, 'n 'tis not only a skilled lawyer, he is a good man."

"What can I do for you, Mr. MacCallister?"

"You have heard about the collapse of the Cattlemen's Bank and the apparent suicide of Mr. Prescott?"

"Yes, of course. But you said apparent suicide. Are you saying that Prescott didn't commit suicide?"

"I do have my doubts."

"I must say that it surprised me as well," Governor Warren said. "I knew Joel Prescott quite well, and I would never have expected someone like him to commit suicide. You asked to see me. Has it something to do with this?"

"Aye, that is the reason. Governor Warren, if Joel Prescott dinnae commit suicide, that means someone killed him, and he, or they, would also be responsible for the missing money."

"That makes sense," Governor Warren replied. "But why have you come to see me about that? Wouldn't it be better for you to go to the police?"

"Aye, 'n I have done so. But 'tis a special request I would ask of you."

"And what would that request be?"

"I would like to investigate this myself, to see what I can find. And in order to do that, I will need some authority."

"Authority?"

"Aye. I would like for you to appoint me as a marshal of the Territory of Wyoming."

"Oh, I'm afraid I don't have any money in the budget authorized to pay for such a position."

"I'll nae be for wanting any money, Governor. All I want is the legal authority to investigate this happening."

Governor Warren stroked his chin for a moment. "No salary, you say?"

"Aye, 'tis nae need for a salary."

Governor Warren smiled, then nodded. "All right. I'll draw up a warrant appointing you as a territorial police officer, working exclusively for the governor. That will give you authority over any policeman, deputy, or sheriff in the entire territory."

"Thank you, Governor. I appreciate that."

"As I said, Mr. MacCallister, I knew and liked Joel Prescott. If you can find proof that he did not embezzle money from the bank, I think it would be of some comfort to Mrs. Prescott and to all of us who considered him a friend."

After Duff left Governor Warren's office, he walked from the capitol building back to the police office.

"What do you want, MacCallister?" Lieutenant Kirby asked. "I can tell you right now we're not going to be investigating Prescott's suicide. The bank money is gone, Prescott is dead, he left a suicide note. This case is closed."

"I would like to speak to Chief Peach," Duff said.

"I told you this case is closed, and I'm not going to bother the chief because you lost some money when Prescott swindled the bank. You aren't the only one who lost money. A lot of other people lost money, as well."

"I dinnae want to do this, Leftenant, but I'm ordering you to summon Chief Peach."

"You're what?" Kirby said explosively. His face turned red with anger. "What the hell do you mean you are ordering me to summon Chief Peach?"

"I have the governor's warrant as a special officer of the Territory of Wyoming with authority over all city police and county sheriff departments. That gives me the authority to order you to summon Chief Peach."

"I've never heard of such a—"

"It's all right, Lieutenant," Chief Peach said, having come from his office to investigate Kirby's shouting. "Come in, Mr. MacCallister. I'll see you now."

"Thank you, Chief."

"Now, I believe I heard you say something to Kirby about having a warrant from the governor?"

"Aye, 'tis an appointment as territorial marshal."

"May I see the warrant?"

"Aye," Duff said, removing the typed warrant and showing it to the chief.

OFFICE OF THE GOVERNOR,
TERRITORY OF WYOMING

To Whom It May Concern:

Know all by these presents that I, Francis E. Warren, Governor of the Territory of Wyoming by appointment of President Chester Arthur, do hereby appoint Duff MacCallister of Laramie County as a special territory police officer with authority over every police and sheriff's department within the Territory of Wyoming.

By my hand and seal:
Francis E. Warren
Governor, Territory of Wyoming

"What can I do for you, Mister—uh, what is your title? How do I address you?"

"I have nae title. Mister will do."

"All right, Mr. MacCallister. What do you want from me?"

"At the moment, I dinnae need anything from you," Duff replied. "I will be looking into this suicide to see if I can find out what happened. I'm just showing this so that you will ken that I'm nae interfering."

Chief Peach nodded. "All right. I'll let my men know so they won't interfere with your investigation. But it seems very much an open-and-shut case to me. It's just like the note said, Prescott embezzled the money, lost it all, then, in disgrace, he killed himself."

"How did it go with the governor?" Meagan asked when Duff returned to meet her for lunch at the Interocean Hotel."

"It went well. He gave me the appointment that I asked for."

"Can you deputize others to help?"

"Why do you ask?"

"I would think that Elmer and Wang might be helpful."

Duff nodded his head. "Aye, lass, 'tis a good thought. Did you send the telegram saying we would be delayed?"

"I did."

"Good. Then I'll be for sending them another telegram, asking them to join us."

The cabin

"Rob a train?" Bart asked.

"Yeah, it's been done before," Lou said. "Actually, it's been done lots of times."

"I'd think that robbing a stagecoach would be a lot easier," Bart said.

"How much money did you get from your last stagecoach holdup?" Lou asked.

"You know damn well I didn't get 'ny money. All we got was a packet of letters."

"Uh-huh, and there's a reason for that," Lou said. "Most money shipments go by train now. When a stagecoach does carry a strongbox it's doin' it for one bank, where railroads do it for three or four banks. Plus, most folks who ride on a train has got money, so we may as well rob them, too."

"How we goin' to stop a train?" Bart asked. "If you ain't noticed, them things is made of iron, 'n a bullet won't go through 'em."

"We won't have to stop the train," Lou said. "It'll stop itself."

"What do you mean, it'll stop itself?"

"They's one of them big water tanks about ten miles south of Cheyenne. All the trains has to stop there. We'll just wait on one of 'em."

"Yeah," Bart said. "Yeah, that's a real good idea. Hell, there cain't be that much to it. Actually, oncet you get it stopped, it's prob'ly easier to rob a train than it is a stagecoach. Trains don't have no shotgun guard on 'em."

"Why are we doin' this anyway?" Carlotti asked. "I thought we were sposed to be robbin' the bank in Laramie. We know banks has got money. We don't know that the train does."

"Right now we need to raise a little operating money," Bart said. "If we hit the train and the bank in Laramie, we'll be able to wait for that money we'll be getting from the bank in Cheyenne."

"Yeah, what about that money in Cheyenne? You've mentioned it before. I mean, just how much money are we talkin' about?" Lou asked.

"A little over two hunnert thousand dollars," Bart replied with a smile. "Our share will be one hunnert thousand."

"When are we goin' to do this?"

"It's already been done," Bart said.

"What do you mean, it's already been done?" Martell asked. "You mean the money has already been took from the bank?"

"Yes."

"Well, to hell with tryin' to rob a train or this bank in Laramie. Seems to me if we've already got a hunnert thousand dollars, that would be enough to make anybody happy," Martell said with a broad smile on his face.

"Yeah, well we ain't got it worked out just yet how it is we're sposed to get our share," Bart said. "That's why we got to do these other jobs first."

"Who done it? Who robbed the bank?" Martell asked.

"Yeah, that's what I'd like to know, too," Carlotti said. "Who took this here money we're sposed to be getting."

"There ain't no need for nobody to know that just yet," Bart said. "When it comes time for us to do our part, then you'll know."

"That's another thing," Conyers said. "Just what is it we're sposed to do that will cause us be able to get our share?"

"I'll tell you when the time comes," Bart said.

Chapter Fifteen

Cheyenne

After Duff sent the telegram to Elmer and Wang, he turned to Meagan. "I think I'll go back down to the police station."

"To ask for their help? I thought that was why you sent for Elmer and Wang."

"Aye, 'tis why I sent for Elmer and Wang. I just need to ask a few more questions is all."

"Do you mind if I go with you?"

"Nae, I dinnae mind."

Returning to the police station, they saw one of the policemen interrogating a prisoner whose wrists were handcuffed.

"Yes, sir, Mr. MacCallister. What can I do for you?" asked Sergeant Creech, the desk sergeant.

"Could we be for having a talk with Chief Peach? Duff asked.

"No, on account of the chief ain't here, right now," Creech answered. "You can talk to Lieutenant Kirby, though. He's in charge when the chief ain't here."

"That will do," Duff said.

Sergeant Creech escorted Duff and Meagan through the labyrinth of halls until they reached an office toward the back of the building. Kirby had his own office, and he looked up from his desk when the three entered. He looked first at Duff, then at Meagan, his eyes lingering long enough to make her feel a bit self-conscious about it. Then he turned his attention back to Creech.

"What are you doing here, Creech?" Kirby asked in a gruff voice.

"Lieutenant, these people was wantin' to talk to the chief, but seein' as he ain't here, I figured you could talk to 'em," Creech said.

"Yes, come on in," Kirby invited. His voice was low and rumbling, as befitting his appearance. "You've already been here once, haven't you MacCallister? What are you doing back so soon?"

"I have further evidence that Joel Prescott didn't commit suicide," Duff said.

For just a moment Kirby stroked his chin and stared at Duff. "Why would you say such a thing, seeing as the money is gone, and we have a suicide note?"

"Aye, but 'tis a phony suicide note. I've also examined the body 'n 'tis not the wounds of a man that committed suicide."

"Do you mind telling me how you came to these conclusions?"

"Well, for one thing the note is printed, 'n according to Mrs. Prescott, her husband had a good hand for writing and never printed. But mostly 'tis the wounds." Duff held his hand in the shape of a pistol, then lifted it to his head. "A person who commits suicide by gun shoots himself here"—Duff touched his finger to his temple—"or here." He put the finger in his mouth.

"But," he said, taking his hand away. "Joel's wound was here." He put his finger above his left eye. "He was right-handed, and would have had to reach across his face, then turn his hand around in a very awkward position to shoot himself above the left eye. Why would he hold the pistol in such a way? In addition, he had a bruise here, on the side of his face, as if someone hit him there."

"I'll look into it," Kirby said.

"Nae, I'll be looking into it. I just came by to let the chief know what I'm doing, so he'll keep people like you away from the investigation."

"What the hell are you saying?" Kirby asked angrily. "You've got no right to keep me from doing my duty."

"You may recall, Leftenant, I have a warrant from the governor," Duff said. "That gives me the right."

Kirby glared at him for a moment longer, anger apparent on his face. "All right. You've told me. Now get out of my office."

"Is it just my imagination or does Lieutenant, or Leftenant as you call him, Kirby not like you?" Meagan asked with a little chuckle as they were walking back to the hotel from the police station.

Duff laughed as well. "It is nae just your imagination, for 'tis my thinking that the angry leftenant is nae a friend of mine."

"I also get the idea Lieutenant Kirby is so convinced Mr. Prescott committed suicide that he isn't interested in any other possibility."

"Aye, lass, for that is the same thing I'm thinking."

"So, what are we going to do?"

"I'm going to start at the beginning," Duff said. "Let's go down to the bank. I want to speak with Mr. Kendrick again."

The front door of the bank was locked, but Duff pounded on the door loud enough and long enough that eventually Kendrick came to the door and opened it.

"Ah, Mr. MacCallister, and to what do I owe the honor of your visit? Excuse me for being so late to respond to your knock, but I wasn't really sure who was out here. Also, I'm sure you understand that the bank is closed."

"I've nae come for to do business with the bank," Duff said. "I've come to investigate the murder of Joel Prescott."

"Murder?" Kendrick gasped. "I admit that this whole scenario, Joel embezzling the funds and then committing suicide, seems most unlikely. But have you come to the conclusion that Joel was actually murdered?"

"Mrs. Prescott does nae believe Joel wrote the note. And you said yourself that you had never seen Joel print anything."

"That's true, I never did see him print anything."

"You found the body, did you?" Duff asked.

"Yes." Kendrick shuddered. "I have to confess that it was the most awful thing I have ever experienced, finding my closest friend on the floor like that, his head lying in a pool of blood."

"Where was he?"

Kendrick led Duff and Meagan to a private office, then pointed. "He was lying right there."

"What time was this?"

"It was about eight fifteen."

"Eight fifteen? But the bank doesn't open until nine."

"Yes, but Joel and I always arrive an hour early."

"You were here then. Did you hear the shot?"

"No, uh, I came in about fifteen minutes later than I normally do. That's when I found him. If I had been here and realized what Joel had in mind, I'm sure I could have talked him out of it. Even though I'm convinced Joel shot himself, I'm open to believing someone killed him, and if I had been here, perhaps I could have stopped it, or at least my presence may have prevented it."

"Was the door locked or unlocked when you came in?"

"It was locked."

"How many keys are there to the door?"

"Two. I have one, and of course, Joel had one."

"And yet, whoever killed him had access to the bank."

"Oh, that's right! I hadn't thought of that," Kendrick replied. "As much as I hate to admit it, the fact that the bank was locked when I arrived, does bring us back to the strong suggestion that he did commit suicide, doesn't it?"

"Aye, thank you," Duff said. With a nod, he indicated to Meagan that they could leave.

"Mr. MacCallister?" Kendrick called.

Duff looked back toward him.

"If there is anything I can do to help you in your investigation, please don't hesitate to call upon me. Joel and I served in the army together. He was the commanding officer, and I was his executive officer, and when he left the army to start the bank, he invited me to come with him. If he didn't commit suicide, I want to see whoever did kill him pay for his crime."

"Thanks," Duff replied.

Chugwater

Elmer and Wang were in Fiddler's Green saloon.

"They cain't nobody beat me in a-throwin' horseshoes," Elmer was saying. "Why iffen they was to be a world championship horseshoe throwin' contest, I'd win."

"He who speaks without modesty will find it difficult to make his words good," Wang said.

Elmer wagged his finger at Wang. "No, now don't you go spoutin' off some of that Chinese stuff you're always sayin'. I'm just tellin' you that I'm the best they is, that's all. 'N it ain't braggin', iffen it's a fact."

"Hey, you! Chinaman!" someone shouted. "What the hell are you doin' in here?"

Elmer looked toward the man who was shouting, but didn't recognize him. That didn't surprise him. Everyone who lived in Chugwater or on any of the adjacent ranches knew Wang.

"Bartender," the loudmouth shouted toward the man who was standing behind the bar with arms crossed. The stranger didn't realize the man was more than just a bartender. He was also the owner.

"Can I help you, mister?" Biff asked.

"How come you to let a Chinaman in here to stink up the place?"

"Wang, I'm going to quit going anywhere with you. Hell, seems like ever' time we turn aroun' someone has a bone to pick with you," Elmer said.

"I will not fight him," Wang said.

"I don't believe I've seen you in here before," Biff said. "What's your name, cowboy?"

"The name is Turk, but most folks call me Turkey."

"I don't doubt it. What can I do for you, Mr. Turkey?"

"That Chinamen sittin' over there don't have no business in here. I think you ought to throw 'im out."

"See, listen to that feller, Wang. You sure seem to bring a lot of hostile folks down on us. I don't know why me 'n you is friends like we are."

"I do not want a friend who smiles when I smile and who weeps when I weep, for my shadow in the pool can do better than that," Wang said.

"Is that another one of them things this Confusion feller said?"

"When one who is wise speaks, one who is smart listens."

"Well?" Turkey said loudly, still talking to Biff. "Are you goin' to throw that Chinaman out, or what?"

"How about if you throw him out for me?"

Turkey grinned. "You're damn right I will."

As he started toward the table, those in the saloon who knew Wang smiled in anticipation of the show they were about to see. Wang and Elmer sat engaged in their own conversation as if unaware of the man approaching.

"Hey you, Chinaman," Turkey said when he reached the table. "You got no business bein' in here, so if you don't get out, I'll be throwin' you out."

"The man of courage acts before he speaks. The coward speaks before he acts," Wang replied.

"What the hell did you just say? Did you just call me a coward, you slant-eyed chink?"

Elmer chuckled. "You know, I think he did."

"Stand up! Stand up! I'm about to throw you out of here!"

"I will not fight," Wang said.

Turkey smiled. "Good. That'll make it a lot easier for me to throw you outta here. Now, stand up!"

Wang stood, then walked a few feet away from the table. "When anger rises, think of the consequences."

"Yeah? Well think of this," Turkey said in a loud and aggressive voice. He swung in a sweeping right cross.

Wang didn't raise his hands to fight back or even to ward off the blow. In a move that was barely discernable, he leaned back and let Turkey's fist slide by without contact.

Turkey had put so much energy into the swing that it threw him off balance. Wang could have easily taken advantage of it, but he didn't.Turkey straightened up then tried a left cross, again easily dodged by Wang.

Changing his tactics, Turkey began throwing jabs, left and right, while Wang, without once raising his hands in defense, simply leaned left or right at the last second to that Turkey continued to miss. After a full minute of missed swings, he stopped, then leaned over with his hands on his knees, breathing hard.

Still breathing in audible gasps, he stood up and stared at Elmer and Wang for a long moment. Then, his wind recovered, he straightened, smiled, and looked directly at Wang. "I'll tell you this. You're about the damndest feller I ever seen." He extended his hand in the offer of a handshake.

Wang accepted it.

"Friend?" Elmer said. "Suppose you step up to the bar there, and have a beer on me."

"Thanks," Turkey said. "I believe I will."

At that moment Biff came up to them. "The drinks are on the house, for everyone."

The customers cheered.

Biff was carrying a two-by-four piece of wood. "Turkey, let me show you what might have happened if Wang had decided to hit back."

Biff held out the two-by-four and Wang, bringing the knife edge of his hand down, easily broke the board.

"Damn," Turkey said in awe. He looked at Wang. "I'm sure as hell glad I didn't make you mad."

The others in the saloon laughed.

"Mr. Gleason?"

Elmer looked up to see the Western Union messenger.

"Yeah?"

"This is for you, sir," the boy said, handing Elmer the yellow page.

ALL FUNDS IN CATTLEMEN'S BANK
STOLEN STOP COME TO CHEYENNE WITH
MOUNTS STOP
DUFF

Elmer read it, then folded it, and put it into his pocket. "Wang, we're going to Cheyenne. Duff needs us."

At ten o'clock that same evening, Elmer and Wang stood on the depot platform as the train pulled into the station, its headlamp throwing a long beam before it. The train stopped with a hiss of steam, a squeal of brakes, and the clanging of couplings transferring the stopping action along the entire length of the cars.

The telegram had asked Elmer to bring the horses, so he watched to make certain the four mounts were loaded onto the attached stock car before he got on the train. Wang had boarded earlier and was sitting quietly in the car.

"I hope we find the crook that stole our money," Elmer said when he took a seat beside Wang.

Chapter Sixteen

"You know what? They ought to sell beer on trains," Elmer said.

"It is good that they do not," Wang replied.

"Yeah, you might be right. The train ought not to sell beer, but I believe if some enterprisin' feller was to get on 'n start sellin' beer his ownself, why, he would make a lot of money."

"If someone gets drunk on a train, there is no place for him to go," Wang said. "He would disturb others."

"Hell, there ain't no need to be a-worryin' none about that, on account of you can't hardly drink enough beer to get drunk."

Bart Jenkins, Lou Martell, and the six other men with them were waiting at a railroad water tower that railroaders knew as Tower Number Fifteen, counting down from Ft. Laramie.

"Does ever'one know what it is that they're goin' to do?" Martell asked.

"Yeah," Moe Conyers said. "I'm goin' to be in the engine, keepin' a gun on the engineer 'n the fireman."

The men were camped out next to the railroad where it crossed Little Horse Creek. At the moment, all eight of them were sitting around a small campfire, over which they had made a pot of coffee.

"Should we be having a fire like this?" Conyers asked.

"Why not?" Martell asked.

"Well, won't the people on the train see the fire?"

Martell laughed. "The train has to stop for water, so it don't make no difference whether there's a little campfire here, or not."

"Oh, yeah, I guess you're right, aren't you?"

Black Lib, who had been up on the berm standing between the tracks, came back down to the campsite.

"How does it look up there, Black?" Bart asked. "See any sign of the train yet?"

"No sign of the train yet."

The men heard the sound of a distant whistle.

"Here it comes," Bart said. "Ever'one get ready."

The train they were waiting on was heading south on the Fort Laramie and Cheyenne Railroad. It roared through the night, a symphony of sight and sound. Red and orange sparks glittered from within the billowing plume of smoke that was darker than the moonlit sky. Clouds of steam escaped from the drive cylinders, then drifted back in iridescent tendrils to dissipate before they reached the rear of the engine. The passenger cars were marked by a long line of luminous windows, glowing like a string of lanterns.

The ninety-three passengers on the train included Elmer and Wang, who were going to Cheyenne in response to Duff's summons. In the stock car ahead were four horses, their own plus Duff's horse Sky and Meagan's horse Mollie.

At the moment, Wang was sleeping. Elmer had turned down the gimbal lantern that was nearest his seat so he could look through the window without seeing his own reflection. At the moment he was looking at the moon's reflections on the rocks and trees.

In a way, sitting quietly, staring out at the dark, reminded him of the long hours of night watch on board the *Eliza Jane* when he could see the white tops of waves, illuminated by moonlight, standing out sharply against the dark ocean. At such times he, the starboard watch, and the helmsman would be the only ones awake. Those periods of watch tended to relax his very soul, and though Elmer lacked the ability to articulate the feeling, he inherently felt at one with the spread of stars overhead.

Although there was no water to see, often there were long periods of uninterrupted desert land that gave the illusion of the ocean. And of course, the stars were overhead.

His ruminations were brought to an end when the train stopped. It didn't arouse any curiosity, because he knew it had to be a water stop.

He could see some men outside, and for a moment he wondered what they were doing, then he got a very clear idea of what was going on. They were there to rob the train. "I'll be damned," he said.

"What do you see?" Wang asked.

"I think we are being robbed." Elmer pulled his pistol and held it close beside him, waiting to see what would happen next. He didn't have to wait but a short time before someone burst into the car from the front door.

The train robber was wearing a bandanna tied across the bottom half of his face, and he was holding a pistol, which he pointed toward the passengers. "Everybody stay seated!" He was holding a sack in his left hand, which he gave to the passenger in the front seat. "Gents, I want you to drop your wallets into the sack. Ladies, if you got 'ny jewelry, why that would be appreciated, too."

"Look here, what gives you the right to—"

"This gives me the right," the train robber said, turning his gun toward the man in the front.

Another gunman came on board to join the first. "How is everything going?"

"Nothing I can't handle. Is everything under control out there?"

"Yeah," the second gunman answered. "We've got the engineer covered, and we're disconnecting the rest of the train from behind the express car."

"How will I know when you're pullin' the express car away? I mean, what if you fellas leave and I don't know you're gone? I'll be stuck back here."

"We'll blow the whistle before we go."

"There ain't no need for you two to be a-worrying about that. You two ain't a-goin' nowhere," Elmer said.

"What? Who said that?"

"I did," Elmer replied. "Both of you, drop your guns."

"The hell we will!" the first gunman shouted as he

fired at Elmer. The bullet smashed through the window beside Elmer's seat.

Elmer returned fire, shooting two times. Both of the bandits went down.

During the gunfire, women screamed and men shouted. As the car filled with the gun smoke of the three discharges, Elmer and Wang scooted out through the back door. Elmer jumped from the steps down to the ground, then fell and rolled out into the darkness. Wang climbed up onto the roof of the car and started running forward.

"Gabe, Deekus? What the hell's goin' on in there?" someone shouted from alongside the track. "What was the shootin' about?"

"Gabe and Deekus?" Elmer called. "Was that them two fellers' names?" He was concealed by the darkness, but in the dim light that spilled through the car windows, he could see the man who was calling out at Gabe and Deekus.

"What do you mean *was* their names?" the bandit asked.

"I reckon it still is their names, only the reason I said was is 'cause they won't be usin' them names no more. I done kilt both of 'em. Now drop your gun and put your hands up, or I'll kill you, too," Elmer called out to him. "I've got you covered."

"I'll be damned if I will!" Realizing he was in a patch of light, the train robber moved into the shadow to fire at the voice from the darkness.

He may have thought he would be shielded by moving out of the light, but the two-foot-wide muzzle flash of his pistol showed Wang exactly where he was, and Wang leaped down from the roof of the car, suddenly materializing like an apparition from hell.

"Ahh!" the outlaw called out in fright. He turned his pistol toward the ghost, but before he could pull the trigger, Wang brought the knife edge of his hand down, breaking the man's wrist and causing him to drop the gun. He cried out in pain.

Elmer stood up then, and moved along the side of the train to join Wang and his prisoner. One of the passengers poked his head out to see what was going on.

"Get back inside!" Elmer shouted gruffly.

The passenger jerked his head back inside quickly.

About thirty feet back from Slim Gardner, Black Lib, whose dark clothes and dark skin had made him invisible in the night, watched the interplay between Gardner and the man who had leaped down from the top of the train. He thought about shooting at them, but there were two of them to his one, and, they had Slim with them. In the darkness, Black couldn't be sure if he could shoot without hitting his partner.

Turning, he hurried to the front of the train, where Bart, Martell, and Willard were trying to figure out how to get through the closed doors and into the express car.

"Kellis 'n Carlotti is both dead," Black Lib said. "'N Gardner's been captured."

"What? Who the hell is doin' that?" Bart asked.

"I don't know, but looked to me like half the people on that car are fightin' back."

"What are we goin' to do, Bart?" Emmet Willard asked.

"I think we need to get outta here," Bart said.

"And leave the money?" Martell asked.

"We've done got two kilt 'n one captured," Bart said. "I think we need to get outta here while we can."

Elmer and Wang were in the express car with the prisoner.

"Are you a-takin' me to jail?" the prisoner asked.

"We ain't takin' you to a picnic," Elmer answered.

"You ain't goin' to be able to keep me, you know," the prisoner said.

"Go ahead. Jump out of the car," Elmer said. "I would really like to see that."

"Ain't no need for me to be a-jumpin' out of the car. Bart 'n the others will come break me out of jail."

"Who's Bart?"

"He's got a gang that most controls this entire county."

The cabin

The five remaining men of what Bart was calling the Bart Jenkins Gang rode up to the little cabin that sat in the dark before them.

"Get your horses took care of, 'n we'll meet inside," he said.

After saddles had been removed and the horses tied to an improvised hitching rail, the men, who had not spoken since leaving the point of the failed train holdup, gathered in the little cabin. Bart lit a lantern, and they all sat in the flickering light, sharing the last two bottles of whiskey.

"Well, that sure as hell didn't work out, did it?" Conyers asked.

"What I would like to know is who the hell was it that done all that?" Willard asked.

"Ain't no sense in a-cryin' over spilt milk," Bart said.

"What spilt milk is it that you're a-talkin' about?" Conyers asked.

"It means what just happened, happened, and there ain't nothin' we can do about it," Black Lib explained.

"Yeah," Bart said.

"Bart, we've lost three men, now. Have you thunk on that?" Martell asked.

"You think I don't know?" Bart replied.

"Well, I was just commentin' on it, is all," Martell said.

"What do we do now?" Moe Conyers asked.

"We're goin' to take the bank in Laramie," Bart said.

"Wait a minute. We just now tried to hold up a train, 'n didn't get away with no money at all. What makes you think holdin' up a bank will be any difference from holdin' up a train?" Martell asked.

"The bank ain't a-goin' nowhere," Bart said. "Ain't no need to stop it, 'cause it's already there."

Martell smiled. "Yeah, it is, ain't it?"

"What I want to know is, will we get as much there as we'll be gettin' from the money that has already been took from the bank in Cheyenne?" Conyers asked.

"Prob'ly not, but have you ever heard the old sayin', 'a bird in hand is worth two in the bush'?"

"Yeah, I've heard it," Willard said. "But I never could figure out what it meant."

"The money from the bank in Cheyenne is the two

birds in the bush," Black Lib said. "Money in the Bank of Laramie is the bird in hand."

"I still don't know what that means," Willard said.

"I think it means we're goin' to rob the bank in Laramie," Martell said, without further attempt at explanation.

Chapter Seventeen

Cheyenne

The other side of midnight Duff was sitting on a wooden bench just outside the depot. He had no suspects in mind, but he was absolutely convinced that Joel Prescott had not killed himself. He had asked Elmer and Wang to come, because he knew he could use their skills. Elmer was good with a gun, if it came to that, and he had an innate common sense that let him see when things weren't as they were supposed to be. Wang didn't use a gun, but with his martial arts skills, he didn't need one. He also had a keen analytical mind. Both men would be an asset in his investigation into what actually happened.

"Train's a-comin'," someone called, and Duff looked north to see the headlamp.

When the train rolled to a stop, he was waiting trackside and saw Elmer and Wang step down from the express car. A third man was with them, and for a moment Duff thought perhaps they had made an acquaintance during the trip down, then he saw that the man with them was walking with his hands tied behind his back.

"Hello, Elmer, Wang," Duff said. "Who is your friend?

"This one ain't no friend of mine," Elmer said. "Him 'n some others tried to hold up the train."

"How many?"

"Don't know how many they was, but they's three less, on account of this man 'n the two that is lyin' dead up in the baggage car. I kilt them two, 'n Wang captured this one. The rest of 'em—I don't know how many they was—got away."

"Did you bring the horses?" Duff asked.

"Yeah, they're in the stock car."

"All right. You two take care of the horses. J.C. Abney's Livery is just a few doors down. While you're doing that, I'll take this man down to the police station. When you're done, meet me in the lobby of the Interocean Hotel and I'll get you checked in."

Duff took his prisoner inside the police station. Lieutenant Kirby was watch commander. He was sitting at his desk, arms folded across his chest, and sound asleep.

"Leftenant Kirby, I have a prisoner for you," Duff said.

Kirby opened his eyes, took in the situation, then glared up at Duff. "Who the hell are you to bring a prisoner to me?" he asked in a gruff voice, obviously displeased at having been awakened. "You got no right to be bringin' me a prisoner."

"Have you forgotten that I am a territorial marshal with a commission from the governor's office?" Duff asked.

"Oh, yeah, I forgot about that. All right. What did this man do?"

"He and several others tried to hold up the train. Due to a couple of my friends who were on the train, the robbery attempt was unsuccessful. Most of them got away, but this man was captured and two were killed."

"Two of 'em kilt, you say?"

"Aye. Their bodies are down at the depot, right now."

"All right. Let me get Gardner here in jail, then I'll wake up Ponder, 'n tell 'im he has business."

"How do you know?" Duff asked.

"How do I know? How do I know what?"

"How do you know this man's name? Neither Elmer nor Wang could get it from him, 'n I couldn't, either."

Kirby paused for a moment before he answered. "He's been in jail before, 'n I remember him. He runs with the Jenkins gang. They have a hideout somewhere around here, but seein' as we can't leave the city to look for 'em, there don't nobody know where it's at."

Leaving his prisoner behind at the police station, Duff walked back down to the Interocean hotel, wondering if Elmer and Wang would be there yet. When he went into the hotel, he saw the two of them sitting in the lobby.

"Meagan come to sit with us while you was gone," Elmer said.

"I had to," Meagan said with a little chuckle. "Otherwise, two disreputable characters like you would frighten the night clerk."

"Come on. Let's get you checked in," Duff suggested.

Laramie, Wyoming Territory, two days later

Bart Jenkins, Lou Martell, Black Lib, Moe Conyers, and Emmet Willard rode up to the front of the Bank of Laramie at five minutes after nine in the morning. Bart, Martell, and Black Lib dismounted and went into the bank. Moe Conyers and Emmet Willard remained outside to hold the three horses.

The bank was empty except for a lone teller who looked up and greeted them with a smile. "Good morning, gentlemen, and congratulations, we just opened not more than a few minutes ago and you are our first customers. I'll be right with you as soon as I take care of a few things."

"You'll be right with us now. We are robbing the bank, so I want you to open the vault." Bart made a motion toward the vault with his pistol.

"Oh, gentlemen, I'm afraid I can't do that now," the teller said.

"What do you mean, you can't do that now?"

"The vault is on a time lock, and it can't be opened until ten o'clock."

"What do you mean it can't be opened until ten? The bank opens at nine."

"Oh, indeed it does, and we have some funds in our teller's drawer which are normally sufficient for our very early customers. If there is a demand for more money, they will just have to wait until ten o'clock."

"Open the damn vault!" Bart shouted.

"Sir, I explained to you that it cannot be opened until ten. You could have a seat and wait until then, I suppose."

Bart growled in frustration. "You say you've got some money in the teller's drawer?"

"Yes, enough operating funds to get us by until we can open the vault."

Bart looked over at Black Lib, who was carrying a cloth sack. "Give him the sack. You, teller, put into the sack, all the money you have in that drawer."

"Yes, sir. I'm sorry it didn't work out better for you," the teller said in the same bright voice he used with all his customers.

With the sack only about one-fourth full, Bart and the others left the bank, then rode out of town quickly, but not at a gallop that would raise the attention of the citizens of the town.

"Six hunnert dollars," Martell said. "That's just a little over one hunnert dollars apiece. Bart, when are we going to get the money that's already been took from the bank in Cheyenne?"

"Right now," Bart said resolutely. "I'm goin' to town right now to see the feller I'm sposed to see."

Bart met his contact on the banks of the Minnehaha Lagoon. "I know you've got the money. Now, what is it I have to do to get my share?"

"I need you to take care of someone."

"Take care of someone? What do you mean?"

"His name is Duff MacCallister. He's asking too many questions."

"Does it matter how I stop him?" Bart asked.

"No. I want him stopped, and I don't care how you do it."

"When do I get the money?"

"You'll get the money as soon as MacCallister is no longer a problem."

"All right. Where can I find 'im?"

"I know he goes to the Red Bull Saloon from time to time."

"All right. You just have the money ready, 'n I'll take care of MacCallister for you."

Cheyenne

"Duff MacCallister? What do you want with him?" the bartender asked.

"I cowboyed some down in Texas with a feller by the name of Duff MacCallister, 'n I was just wantin' to see if this here one is the same one," Bart said. "I was told that he comes in here sometimes. I just wanted to see what he looks like, is all.

"Well, as it so happens, he is here, right now," the bartender replied. "That would be him sittin' at the table back there with the woman 'n them other two. Mr. MacCallister is the one that's sittin' closest to the piano."

Bart looked where the bartender pointed, then shook his head. "No sir, that ain't the same one I knowed, so I won't be goin' back there 'n botherin' 'im none. I was just wantin' to see if it was the same one, is all. I hope I didn't bother you none, askin' you the question. By the way, I'll take two beers."

"It warn't no bother a-tall." The bartender filled two

mugs and set them on the bar in front of Bart. "Besides which, I've always figured that helpin' out my customers when I could was a part of my job."

"'N you done it real good, too," Bart said. Taking the two filled beer mugs, he started toward a table that had already been claimed by Lou Martell.

Martell was staring at the same table the bartender had just pointed out. "That's him."

"I thought you said you didn't know MacCallister," Bart said.

"I don't know 'im."

"Then what do you mean, that's him?"

"I don't know who MacCallister is, but the feller I'm talkin' about, is that Chinaman. His name is Wang Chow," Martell said in a voice that was bitter, despite having been quietly spoken.

"How do you know that Chinaman?" Bart asked.

"When I was in San Francisco a couple o' months ago, I heard that some Chinaman by the name of Tong was willin' to give twenty-five thousand dollars to anyone who would capture Wang Chow." Martell grinned. "Or kill 'im," he added.

Bart laughed. "Tong ain't the name of a Chinaman. The Tong is a lot of Chinamen. A gang. How did you know where to find the Chinaman you was lookin' for?"

"We was told we could find 'im in Chugwater, 'n sure 'nuff, when we got there, he was just sittin' there in a saloon like as if he owned the place. Same as he's doin' here. 'N that sort of scrunched-up face you see sittin' by him was there, too. I never did find out what his name was."

"Hmm. They must be friends with MacCallister seein' as they're sittin' with him. The Tong is willin' to give twenty-five thousand dollars for the Chinaman, you say?"

"Yeah, that's what I was told."

"Well, that's good to know. It might wind up that when we take care of MacCallister, we could also get twenty-five thousand from the Tong for the Chinaman. What'd you say his name was?"

"His name is Wang Chow, but I tell you true, he ain't someone you want to mess with. I ain't never seen no one who can fight like he can."

"I wonder how good he is at dodgin' bullets?"

"I don't know. We never got the chancet to shoot at 'im."

"When we're ready, we'll shoot all three of 'em. MacCallister, the Chinaman, and that old cowboy that's sittin' with 'em."

"Duff, you mind them cylinders we sent you?" Elmer said.

Duff chuckled. "Aye, 'tis not easy to forget getting a package containing four revolver cylinders."

"You see them two men at that table over there? The one right next to the post?"

"I see them."

"Well, that feller on the left is one of the ones we took the cylinders from. I wonder what he's doin' here?"

"Well, don't you suppose he might have come to pick up his cylinder? You did tell them that you would leave them at the police station, here, didn't you?"

"Yeah, that's what I told 'em all right."

"He's been staring at us," Meagan said.

"Given the way Wang handled them, I suppose he would be looking," Duff said. "I can't imagine he would be wanting another visit with our friend."

Chapter Eighteen

John wasn't sure when he came up with the idea of calling on the widow of Joel Prescott. He had never met her but felt a connection to her through his friendship with Joel. He did know, though, that he couldn't call on her looking like he did.

As he worried about that, he saw what might be a solution to his concern. It was Max's Barbershop, and the sign out front read HAIRCUT, SHAVE, BATHS.

John got a sudden idea. He had enough money remaining from what MacCallister had given him to be able to take advantage of the opportunity before him and stepped inside. The barber was sitting in his own barber chair reading a newspaper.

"I would like a haircut, shave, and bath," John said.

"You might want to take your bath first," the barber suggested.

John saw the reflection of himself in the mirror, and nodded. "Yes." He went into the bathing room and saw a pair of pants and a shirt hanging on a hook. He stepped back out to speak to the barber. "Some pants and a shirt are hanging in there."

"Yes, they belonged to a fella who was here a couple of weeks ago. He had just bought some new clothes, and he left his old ones here."

"Do you think it would be all right if I took them?"

"In your case, mister, I think it would be more than all right. I think you'd be doing a favor to anyone you happen to be standing around."

John suffered the insult quietly then stepped down into the bathtub, being careful to keep his bandaged hand dry.

After the bath and the change of clothes, he returned to the barber chair. "I feel half-human now." He put his hand to his hair, then to his beard. "Do you think you might make look whole human?"

The barber chuckled. "Get into the chair, Lonesome John, and let's see what we can do."

John wasn't surprised that the barber recognized him. The barber kept a horse and buggy at the livery.

The John who exited the barbershop half an hour later was clean shaven and had his hair well trimmed. He was wearing the pants and shirt he had taken, only to keep from putting the dirty clothes back on. Actually, inside a suitcase in his little loft-room back at the livery, unworn for over two years, was a dark gray suit, a white shirt, a collar, and a tie.

As John put on the suit, he was amazed at the sense of self-worth it gave him. He no longer felt like a dreg of society, a creature to be scorned and ignored except when some interaction was necessary. He was a man, confident and equal to any other.

To test his theory, he went into the Red Bull Saloon and stepped up to the bar.

"Yes, sir, what will it be?" the bartender asked.

"I'll have a beer."

"One beer coming up," the bartender said, holding an empty mug under the spout of the beer keg. "I don't believe I've seen you before. Are you just passing through town, or have you come to stay?" the bartender asked as he placed the full mug in front of John.

"I haven't decided," John replied, pleased that he hadn't been recognized.

Fifteen minutes later, he was satisfied that nobody who knew Lonesome John would recognize the person standing on the front porch of the Prescott home. Nor would anyone connect him with the unwashed, ill-kept, and odiferous denizen of the livery stable.

Although he had never officially met Joel Prescott's wife before, he had seen her, so he knew that the woman who answered the door wasn't Nettie Prescott.

"Yes, sir?" the woman said.

"I'm an old friend of Joel's. I'm here to pay a sympathy call on Mrs. Prescott. Is she at home, and is she receiving?"

"Yes, sir, please come on in to the parlor, and I'll fetch her for you."

"Thank you."

John stepped into the parlor. As he waited, he stood by the fireplace, looking at the photo of Joel and Nettie Prescott.

"Yes, sir, may I help you?" a well-modulated voice said from behind John.

There was also a huskiness to the voice, no doubt,

John thought, brought on by long periods of crying. He turned toward the voice and saw a beautiful woman standing there, dressed all in black.

He made a slight bow. "Mrs. Prescott, I have come to offer my condolences. Joel was quite an exceptional man."

"You called him Joel. Did you know my husband?" Nettie got a questioning expression on her face and she tilted her head sideway, to demonstrate her confusion.

"Yes, ma'am. I knew him quite well, and I'm happy to say that I counted him as a friend."

"Sir, you will excuse my perplexity, I'm sure, but how is it that you say you are my husband's friend, yet I have never met you? Who are you?"

"The name is Cunningham, ma'am. John Jacob Cunningham." John felt no hesitancy about giving Nettie his real name. That name wasn't known by anyone who lived in Cheyenne.

"Mr. Cunningham, how did you know my husband?"

"Oh, I met him when he was an army captain, stationed at Jefferson Barracks in St. Louis."

Nettie smiled. "Oh, yes, he was at Jefferson Barracks before he came to Ft. Laramie. So, then you and Joel were in the army together?"

"No, ma'am. I'm sorry. I didn't intend to give you that impression. Joel was an army captain, I was a civilian, but we shared a love for baseball."

"Tell me what baseball team Joel followed."

John smiled. "That's easy. In fact, that's how I met him in the first place. We would often see each other when we went to Sportsman's Park to watch the St. Louis Brown

Stockings play their games. Later, of course, the Brown Stockings changed their name to the St. Louis Browns. Neither I nor Joel changed our allegiance, and we continued to follow the same team, even though their name changed.

"At first, we knew each other only as devotees of the game of baseball, but our friendship grew rather quickly and we began to meet on social occasions. He would be my guest at my club, and I would just as frequently, be his guest at the officers' club. I was saddened when Captain Prescott was posted to Fort Laramie, way out in Wyoming."

Nettie's smile grew broader. "That's where I met him. Now, I know for sure that you knew him. Other than Eli, who had been his executive officer at Ft. Laramie, there are very few who knew that Joel had been an army officer, fewer who knew that he had been posted at Jefferson Barracks, and even fewer who knew of his love of baseball. How did you hear that my husband was deceased?"

"A gentleman of Joel's stature doesn't die without it becoming well known."

"I guess that's true," Nettie said. "Mr. Cunningham, it is nearly dinnertime. I wonder if it would be too presumptuous of me to invite you to dine with me. You can tell me more about the relationship between you and Joel."

"It wouldn't be presumptuous of you at all to invite me, Mrs. Prescott. But I'm afraid it would be most presumptuous of me to accept."

"Oh, nonsense. Why would you say such a thing?"

"Because, dear lady, you are still in mourning, and I'm sailing under false colors."

Again, Nettie's expression was one of confusion. "You mean, you didn't know my husband? You and Joel weren't friends?"

"We were friends all right. Very good friends when we were in St Louis. And, I'm pleased to say that that friendship was renewed when we met again, here in Cheyenne. And nothing could be more evident of that friendship than the fact that he kept my secret."

"Your secret?"

"Yes, ma'am. The false colors I was referring to is that you already know me. You just haven't made the connection yet. You may know me as the poor wretch everyone calls Lonesome John."

Nettie gasped, and covered her open mouth with her hand. "You? You are Lonesome John?"

"Your confusion stems from the fact that you have never seen me except in a most disheveled condition. Tonight, I made a specific effort to clean up and make myself presentable before meeting you."

"I can understand that. I mean your occupation would, uh, not allow you much opportunity to keep clean," Nettie said.

John shook his head. "No ma'am, I'm not going to allow myself the false luxury of blaming my condition on the fact that I am a livery stable employee. I'm afraid that my sloth is of my own making."

Nettie was quiet for a moment as if contemplating what she had just learned. Then, once again, a comfortable smile crossed her face. "It doesn't matter. You are certainly presentable now, and as long as you were Joel's friend, you are my friend, as well. Please, Mr. Cunningham, won't you take dinner with me?"

"Mrs. Prescott, I would be delighted to have dinner with you."

"Please, call me Nettie."

"I don't believe for a minute that Joel committed suicide," Nettie said over the dinner table once the banker's demise became the subject of their conversation."

"Nor do I," John said. "Such a thing wasn't part of Joel's psychological makeup."

Nettie put her fork down and stared across the table at John. "Who are you?

"I'm sorry. Do you not believe that Joel and were friends?"

"Oh, indeed I do believe you were friends, you know too much about him that wasn't generally known. But you aren't—I mean, surely you haven't always been a stable hand."

"It's honest work," John replied defensively. "I find no shame in honest work."

Nettie reached across the table and put her hand on his, and for the first time since arriving, John was aware of her as a woman, rather than just the widow of his friend.

"Please, I didn't mean that as a demeaning comment," she said. "I meant no offense."

"I'm sorry I reacted as I did," John said. "And I take no offense from your words. You are right. I haven't always been a stable hand. But I . . . I just don't feel like talking about it right now. I hope you understand."

"I do understand," Nettie said. Again, the smile. "Perhaps you can tell me at some future meeting."

It was John's time to smile. Her remark suggested there would be some future meeting between them, and he found that to be a very encouraging thought. "Yes, once I am comfortable with sharing some of my sordid past, I would be glad to tell you."

"You . . . you aren't a wanted criminal, are you?" Nettie asked, her face reflecting her apprehension.

"No, please put yourself at ease on that score. My fall from grace, I'm afraid, was of my own making."

She paused for a moment of contemplation, then the expression of concern was replaced by a trusting smile. "You will be coming to Joel's funeral, won't you?"

"I wouldn't want to intrude."

"Nonsense, you wouldn't be intruding. And it's quite possible there wouldn't be enough people there for your presence to be considered an intrusion. I'm afraid my poor husband is not very popular now. The entire town believes that he stole all the money from the bank."

"I am one hundred percent convinced that he neither embezzled funds from the bank nor did he commit suicide. I would be honored to attend his funeral."

"It will be at St. Mark's Episcopal Church, tomorrow afternoon," Nettie said.

"Thank you for the invitation," John replied.

"John . . . Do you mind if I call you John?"

"No, of course not."

"John, you know that if he didn't embezzle the funds, someone else did, and if he didn't commit suicide, that means someone killed him."

"Yes, perhaps the police are looking into it."

Nettie shook her head. "I don't think so. They, like everyone else in town, are convinced that Joel did take the money and then killed himself."

"I have a feeling that the truth will come out. Don't ask me how I know, for it is only a premonition, but it is a very strong premonition."

They visited for a while longer, then John announced that he must leave. Nettie walked to the front door with him and he took both her hands in his.

"Thank you so much for coming, John." She smiled. "I do hope to see you at the funeral."

"I will be there," John promised.

"Under the circumstances, most of my encounters with the people from town have been unpleasant. It is bad enough that I have lost my husband, but to have such scurrilous attacks against him is more than I can take. Your visit tonight was like a cool drink of water."

John squeezed her hands lightly. "I will see you tomorrow afternoon."

Chapter Nineteen

"A thousand dollars, just for killin' one man?" Sy Harrigan asked.

"Actually, they's three of 'em," Bart said. "Well, four, if you count the woman."

"I ain't a-goin' to shoot no woman. 'N iffen I have to shoot the other two, it'll cost you extry."

"Yeah, well if you shoot the one I want you to shoot, like as not the other ones will leave town."

"Who's the feller you want me to shoot?"

"His name is MacCallister. Duff MacCallister. You ever heard of 'im?"

"Yeah, ain't he some rich rancher or somethin'?"

"That's the one."

"What for do you want 'im kilt?" Harrigan asked.

"Why does that make any difference to you? I'm payin' you a thousand dollars to kill 'im. That's all that should matter."

"How come you nor none of your men don't kill 'im?"

"He knows who we are, 'n we prob'ly can't get close enough to 'im to kill 'im."

"Make it fifteen hunnert dollars, 'n I'll do it."

"You said you would take a thousand."

"I know, but now I'm thinkin' maybe I might need a couple others to help me out. This way I can give 'em two hunnert 'n fifty dollars apiece."

"All right," Bart agreed. "But you don't get nothin' till you kill 'im."

"Let me ask you this, Jenkins. How do I know you've even got the money?"

"I don't have the money, but I will have it after my, uh, business is taken care of."

"Yeah, well, you better. 'Cause if I don't get the fifteen hunnert dollars for killin' MacCallister, I'll kill you for nothin'. Now, where will I find MacCallister?"

"More 'n likely, you'll find 'im in the Red Bull. He's a big man, 'n he's some kind of a foreigner, 'cause he don't talk English real good."

"And you say there will be two other men with him?"

"More 'n likely. One of 'em is an old man with a wrinkled face 'n white hair. But don't let him bein' old fool you, 'cause he's real good with a gun. The other man is a Chinaman."

"A Chinaman, you say?"

"Yes, 'n don't get too close to 'im," Bart said, recalling what Lou had told him about their encounter with him.

"I won't get no closer 'n takes to shoot 'im."

"And a woman."

"What's the woman look like?"

"She's a real purty woman, but you don't need no description of her. If you see a woman with MacCallister, more 'n likely it'll be this 'n."

"I ain't worried none about the woman, but them other

two men might be a problem. It'll cost you extry to kill them."

"I'm already giving you five hunnert dollars more."

"Actually, you ain't give me nothin', yet. You said I was goin' to have to wait till your business is done. If I have to wait, and I have to kill them two that'll be with 'im, then I want another five hunnert. It'll cost you two thousand dollars."

Bart sighed. "All right. Two thousand."

Harrigan smiled. "They are as good as dead."

As Bart had suggested, Duff was in the Red Bull Saloon. At the moment, he was playing cards in a little alcove in the back of the saloon. None of the men playing cards with him fit the description Jenkins had given Harrigan, and he wondered where they were.

Elmer was having a drink at the Cowboy's Haven Saloon, and Wang Chow was at Lu Chang's Chinese Restaurant. All three had the same objective—to see if they could find any information that would support their strong belief that Joel Prescott had not committed suicide.

"So, you're a Wyoming territorial marshal, are you?" asked Hodge Deckert, one of the cardplayers at Duff's table.

"Aye, with a governor's warrant," Duff said.

"I don't know as I've ever heard of a territorial marshal. A US Marshal, 'n a town marshal, yeah, but I ain't never heard of no territorial marshal. I didn't know that we had none of them."

"I'm the only one," Duff replied without further

amplification. Examining his hand, he saw that he had a pair of aces, so he discarded three, hoping the draw would improve his hand.

Deckert was the dealer, and he discarded only one card.

"Damn, Hodge, you hopin' to draw five of a kind, are you?" one of the other players asked, to laughter around the table.

"Say, MacCallister, I heard that you lost a lot o' money when Prescott took all of it, then shot hisself," said a player named Carson.

"I don't believe he shot hisself," Deckert said.

"What? Well, what the hell makes you think that?" Toomey asked.

"Well think about it, Toomey. They say he took over two hunnert thousand dollars from the bank. If you took that much money, would you then just turn right aroun' 'n shoot yourself?"

"Maybe he felt bad about it," Toomey said.

"If he felt bad about it, all he woulda had to do was put the money back, and no one would be any the wiser."

Toomey was quiet for a moment before he replied. "Yeah, now that I think about it, that don't make a lot of sense."

"If Prescott dinnae shoot himself, would you be for having an idea who did shoot him?" Duff asked.

"If I was thinkin' on it, 'n if it warn't Prescott what shot his ownself, I'd say that it's more 'n likely that feller works down to the livery done it. The one they call Lonesome John," Deckert said.

"Lonesome John? 'N would you be for tellin' me why

you would be for thinking such a thing?" Duff asked, surprised by Deckert's guess.

"I've seen 'em talkin' there in the stable. I don't know what they was talkin' about, but I'm sure it was more than just about takin' care of Abney's team 'n surrey. I sorta figure that Lonesome John was tryin' to make friends with Prescott, 'n maybe tried to borry some money, only when Prescott wouldn't give it to him, why Lonesome John shot 'im."

"Yeah well, if Lonesome John is the one that done it, why is he still here? You'd think with all that money, he'd be run away some'ers else by now," Toomey said.

"Which is why I don't think Lonesome John's the one that done it," Carson said. "I still think Prescott shot hisself. Besides which, they found that note on 'im, don't forget. 'N in the note he says his ownself that it was him that shot hisself."

Harrigan, who had come into the saloon a few minutes earlier, ordered a drink then walked to the back of the saloon to look around into the little alcove where the card game was being played. He stood there, sipping his drink for a while, watching the game until he was pretty sure which player was his target.

"Well now, Mr. Duff MacCallister, you don't look all that tough to me," he said under his breath.

The cards weren't running that well for Duff, but he wasn't in the game to win money. He was in the game to glean whatever information he could. By hedging his bets, maximizing his good hands, and minimizing his bad, he was able to stay in the game for some time. He didn't win anything, but his losses were minimal. His biggest loss, though, was that he wasn't able to pick up any useful information.

When the game was over, Duff told the others good night, then walked just two buildings down the street to the Interocean Hotel and up to Meagan's room. He tapped on the door. "Meagan, if you nae be asleep, would you be for opening the door?"

"Who's there?" Meagan asked.

"Lassie, do you nae know—"

The door was opened before he finished his comment. Meagan stood there in a housecoat, laughing at him. "Sure now, Duff MacCallister, 'n with your brogue so deep, would you be for thinking that I would nae be knowing who was calling out to me?" she asked, mimicking Duff's brogue perfectly.

"Would it be all right if I came in?" Duff asked.

"No, I think I would rather stand here in the doorway so that anyone walking down the hallway could see me in a housecoat talking to a man. It would make good conversation over the breakfast table tomorrow morning." She stepped back. "Come in," she invited.

"Have you heard from either Elmer or Wang tonight?" Duff asked.

Meagan shook her head. "I haven't heard from either one of them. They are either out or they've come back to their rooms without me knowing. How was your outing? Did you find anything?"

"Not really. One of the players suggested that it might be Lonesome John."

"Oh, surely it wasn't him," Meagan said. "Why would he do such a thing?

"Dinnae forget, he did try to rob us," Duff pointed out.

"Yes, but even you broke down and gave him twenty dollars. I don't know why John is working in the livery stable, but you can tell from his language that he is a very well-educated man. Besides, if he did it, why is he still working in the livery stable? Why didn't he take the money and run?"

"But 'tis as you say. There is more to our livery stable attendant than meets the eye," Duff said.

"Or," Meagan suggested, "Kendrick could have killed Mr. Prescott but remained behind to throw people off."

"Aye, 'tis a wise thought," Duff said.

Harrigan had followed Duff back to the hotel, then hurried across the street and climbed up into the hayloft of a barn that belonged to McKnight and Keaton Freighting Service. He had planned it all along when, earlier in the day, he had checked the register to see which room Duff was in. He actually had two adjacent rooms, and Harrigan had no idea which room it would be, but from the angle he enjoyed from the loft, he could see into both rooms. One room was dark, and one room was light, and as he watched, the light grew brighter.

"Would you like the window up to catch the night breeze?" Duff asked.

"Yes, thank you. That would be quite pleasant," Meagan replied.

Duff turned the key to make the lantern brighter and

walked over to the window to adjust it. He saw a sudden flash of light in the hayloft across the street, knew it was a muzzle flash even before he heard the gun report, and pulled away from the window at the precise instant a bullet crashed through the glass of the window, slamming into the wall on the opposite side of the room. Someone was shooting at him!

"Duff!" Meagan shouted.

"Get down, Meagan! Get down on the floor!" He cursed himself for the foolish way he had exposed himself at the window. He should have known better.

Two other shots came on the heels of the first, so close together that Duff knew there had to be three men.

Even before the echo of the first three shots died out, he had started to extinguish the lantern. Then, getting an idea, he set the lighted lantern on a table, away from the window, keeping the room illuminated.

He wished he had his rifle. He could engage them from there, but all he had was his pistol, which meant he would have to go after them.

"What was that?" someone shouted from somewhere in the hotel.

"Gunshots. Sounded like they came from the . . ."

That was as far as the disembodied voice got before another volley of three shots crashed through the window, shattering what was left of the windowpanes.

"Meagan, are you all right?"

"Yes, I'm fine."

"We have to get out of this room. Let's go next door to my room."

"All right," she agreed.

Staying low, the two of them left Meagan's room as more rounds came through the window to slam into the wall.

A few residents of the hotel stood in the hallway, believing it to be safer than to remain in their rooms. For a moment, Duff considered leaving Meagan in the hall, but that might leave her exposed if there was another shooter besides the three.

Duff and Meagan moved into his room, leaving it dark. More shots were fired, but none came through his window.

"Get down behind the bed, and keep it dark in here," Duff said. "As long as the lantern burns in your room, they'll think I'm still in there." He got ready to leave. "Lock the door, 'n let nae one in except me, Elmer, or Wang."

"You're going after them?" Meagan asked.

"Aye."

"Be careful, Duff. I don't know what I would do without you."

He nodded in response, though he realized she could not see him in the dark room. "Nae to worry, lass. I'll be careful."

Hurrying downstairs, he saw the hotel clerk ducking down behind the front desk.

"What is it?" the clerk asked, his voice strained by fear. "Are we getting shot at?"

"Aye. Is there a back door to the hotel?"

"Yes, go right down that hall," the clerk replied, pointing, without getting up.

Duff exited the back door of the hotel, ran down the alley for a short distance, then came up between two buildings, stopping just before he stepped out into the street.

Checking the large opening of the hayloft, he realized that he could cross the street without being seen, unless someone was looking directly at him. He darted across the street and then between two buildings before reaching the alley and hurrying toward McKnight and Keaton's enclosed area where all the wagons were parked. He worked his way through the wagons and slipped into the back of the barn.

Frightened by the shooting, the mules in the stalls were shifting around nervously.

With his pistol drawn, Duff moved toward the front as quietly as he could.

"He ain't shot back none at all," someone said from the loft floor, which was just above Duff.

"Hell, I think we got 'im. I think he's lyin' over there in the hotel, kilt."

"The lantern is still on."

"Yeah, that's why I think we done kilt 'im. You know damn well iffen he was still alive, he woulda put the lantern out by now."

"I tell you what, Morris. If you're so sure we got 'im, why don't you step up to the window there 'n take a look?"

"All right. I will," Morris said.

Duff heard footsteps across the loft floor, and he got into a position where he could look up and see someone standing near the window.

"Hell, I think he's dead," Morris said.

Duff took aim, then fired two times. He saw puffs of dust from where the bullets hit, then a body tumbled through the open loft door, hitting hard and raising dust when it fell onto the street below.

"Hell and damnation!" one of other two voices shouted from above. "He shot Morris!"

"Yeah, but where did the shot come from? Did it come from the winder?"

Duff punched out the two empty shell casings, put in two new bullets, and shot two more times just to keep the shooters' heads down.

"Hey, Harrigan, he's som'ers down below us! Them two bullets come right up through the floor."

Duff had heard two names, Morris and Harrigan. He didn't recognize either name, though he knew Morris was the one he had killed.

"Where is he, Petro, do you see him?"

"No, I don't see 'im, but I know damn well he's come inside."

"What the hell is he, a ghost?" Harrigan asked. "We seen 'im at the winder. How did he get over here?"

Morris, Harrigan, and Petro. Duff knew the names but didn't know the men, and he didn't know why they were trying to kill him.

"Petro!" Harrigan called again. "Do you see him?"

"No," Petro answered.

Duff moved quietly through the barn, looking up at the hayloft just overhead. Suddenly he felt little pieces of hay falling on him and he stopped, realizing someone had to be right over him. Then he heard it, a quiet shuffling of feet. Duff fired twice, straight up, then he heard a groan and a loud thump.

"That's six shots. You're out of bullets," a calm voice said.

Duff looked over to his left to see a man standing openly on the edge of the loft. He was holding a rifle and, inexplicably, he laughed. "I ought to thank you for killin' Morris and Petro like you done. That just leaves more money for me." He raised his rifle to his shoulder, and Duff fired.

"What?" the outlaw gasped in shock, dropping his rifle and clutching the wound in his stomach.

"Six shots, aye," Duff said flatly. "But I replaced the first two."

Harrigan stood there, holding his hand over the wound in his stomach. Duff saw him wobble back and forth a couple of times, then fall from the loft, flipping over so as to land on his back in the dirt below. Duff walked over to look down at him. Harrigan was dead.

"All right. Whoever is in there, come out with your hands up. This is the police."

"I'm coming out, officer. Dinnae be for shooting me," Duff said as he walked out with his hands raised.

Two policemen were standing out in the street, both of them holding guns pointed at him.

"MacCallister?" one of the officers asked.

"Aye, 'tis me."

"Did you shoot these two men?"

"Aye, but there were three of them. You'll find another up in the loft."

"You know 'em?"

"Nae, but I heard their names called out. Harrigan,

Morris, and Petro. Do those names mean anything to either of you?"

"How did you come to kill them?"

"They tried to kill me," Duff answered. "They shot out the window in my room over in the hotel. If you dinnae believe me, you can ask the desk clerk."

"I've no reason not to believe you," one of the police officers said.

Both of them had put away their pistols, and, though the hour was late, several of the townspeople, alerted by the gunshots, were standing in two or three bunches on the street.

"Why were they after you?"

"They were paid to come after me. This one"—he pointed back toward Haggarty's body—"said that by killing Morris and Petro, I had fixed it so he would get more money. I believe the outlaws must have some paper out on me." He chuckled. "I wonder how much I'm worth."

Chapter Twenty

St. Mark's Episcopal Church

Nettie was standing in front of the church with Eli Kendrick. So far the only mourners to show up were Chief Peach, Lieutenant Kirby, Duff, Meagan, and two men who appeared to be with them, though Nettie had never met them.

"Terry, Homer, and Vernon haven't shown up yet," Nettie said, talking about the two bank tellers and the secretary.

"Oh, I'm afraid they won't be here," Eli said.

"Oh? Why not? Why, they've been with the bank from the very beginning."

"I tried to talk them into coming, but they refused."

"You mean you had to try and talk them into coming?" Nettie asked.

"Yes, I thought it would be comforting to you for everyone who had worked with Joel to attend. Then I realized that having them attend, especially with their attitude, would be anything but comforting. I'm sorry. Perhaps I could have ordered them to come."

"No," Nettie said, reaching out to put her hand on his. "You did the right thing, and you are sweet for doing it."

Eli offered his arm to Nettie. "Shall we go in?"

"Uh, no. I need to stay outside for a moment or two."

"I understand," Eli said with a sympathetic smile. "I'll wait here with you."

"No, please, Eli, you go on in. I just need to wait here for a moment longer."

Eli had a look of confusion on his face, but he nodded. "All right. I'll not force you to go in. I know how difficult this is for you. It is difficult for me, too. Joel was my closest friend, but he was your husband. I know the pain must be even more for you."

"Thank you, Eli," Nettie said, squeezing his hand.

He went inside, and Nettie remained out front, studying the approach to the church. Would John come? Nettie wondered. Maybe he is too ashamed of who he is, a stable hand who is universally looked down upon. If that was the case, she could understand it. Showing up for Joel's funeral might well subject him to humiliation.

She smiled. If anyone saw him the way he looked when he called on her, they wouldn't recognize him.

"Oh, I do hope he comes." She spoke that wish aloud, quietly to be sure, but looked around quickly to make certain nobody overheard her.

This is silly, she told herself. *Standing out here hoping he will show up so I can see him again.*

She wanted to sit with him. How in the world could she ever explain holding those thoughts at her husband's funeral?

Just when she was about to go into the church alone,

she saw someone coming up the street. He was too far away for her to recognize his face, but he was wearing the same suit she'd seen him the night before. Yes, it was John!

Nettie felt a quick surge of joy, which was even more quickly put aside by her sense of shame. Joel wasn't even in the ground yet. On the other hand, John was Joel's good friend, so if you looked it that way, there was nothing untoward about being glad that John could be there to celebrate Joel's life.

"Good afternoon, Mrs. Prescott," he said when he reached her."

"It's Nettie, remember?"

"Yes, Nettie."

She offered her arm and John took it, then escorted her into the church.

They were met in the narthex by a church layperson. "Ah, Mrs. Prescott. You can sit anywhere in the sanctuary you wish, but a place has been reserved for you on the very first row. Uh, and will this gentleman be with you?"

John started, "I can—"

"He is with me," Nettie interrupted.

"Very good," the layperson said.

With John holding Nettie's elbow, they walked down the center aisle of the nave. John looked around and saw Duff and Meagan. Two other men were with them, one older looking, and one Chinese. Except for Eli Kendrick, Chief Peach, Lieutenant Kirby, and Loomis Ponder, the undertaker, no one else was in the church.

Kendrick, watching Nettie and John come in together,

had a facial expression that one could almost say was of anger.

They passed the transept, and took a seat in the front row. The casket lay on a catafalque, and though it was closed, Nettie stepped up to it and lay her hand on the shining mahogany wood. "Joel, I know you didn't do this," she said, speaking so quietly that those who saw her lips moving thought she was in prayer. "May the Lord keep you in His arms," she said, then crossed herself.

John stayed back to allow her a moment alone with her husband, and when she crossed herself then turned away, he could see the tears in her eyes. He took her hand and helped her sit down. He felt bad that he didn't have a handkerchief to offer her, but that wasn't necessary. Nettie reached down into the top of her dress and pulled out a lace-bound handkerchief. She dabbed at her eyes, then returned the handkerchief.

Father Nathaniel Sharkey, the priest of St. Mark's, stepped out of the sacristy and moved down to the front of the chancel, then began to read from the Book of Common Prayer.

"'Remember thy servant, Joel Prescott, O Lord, according to the favor which thou bearest unto thy people, and grant that, increasing in knowledge and love of thee, he may go from strength to strength, in the life of perfect service, in thy heavenly kingdom; through Jesus Christ our Lord, who liveth and reigneth with thee and the Holy Ghost, ever, one God, world without end. Amen.'"

The responsive "Amen" was low, due to the paucity of mourners present.

Father Sharkey continued with the Order for Burial.

"'Unto God's gracious mercy and protection we commit you. The Lord bless you and keep you. The Lord make his face to shine upon you, and be gracious unto you. The Lord lift up his countenance upon you, and give you peace, both now and evermore. Amen.'"

He closed the prayer book, then looked over the ten people who had come to the funeral service. "I have read the collects from the Book of Common Prayer, but it was for form only, and I'm afraid it has nothing to do with Joel Prescott. Why do I say that, you may ask. It is no secret that Joel Prescott lies before us as a sinner. We are all sinners, but in the case of Joel Prescott, I fear his sins are without redemption. He embezzled every cent of money that had been placed in his trust. That is very evil. It deprived many of our citizens of their life's holdings."

Sharkey held up his finger. "Had he stopped there, the courts of man would have convicted him, but he could have asked for and received forgiveness from God." He shook his head. "But Mr. Prescott didn't stop there. No, friends, he put a pistol to his head and pulled the trigger. Joel Prescott committed suicide. And there is no redemption from suicide.

"The sin of suicide he committed imperiled his very soul, forfeited heaven, and opted for hell by his own free will and actions. Joel Prescott turned away from God and embraced something else in His place. Suicide is deadly to the mortal life. It is also deadly to the life of grace because it insults the honor of God and injures the soul of the sinner. Suicide is like a malignant tumor. It is lethal to the spiritual life.

"Here endeth the chapel service for this sinner. I'm

afraid we have no pallbearers, and the casket must be carried to the hearse for transportation to the cemetery. I would ask that from the men who are herein present, that six of you would perform this necessary service."

At the cemetery, which was behind the church, the grave had already been opened. There was no catafalque so the closed coffin sat on two sawhorses. The day was dark and dreary, and though it hadn't yet begun to rain, the heavy clouds hung low, pregnant with promise.

A chair had been brought for Nettie, but she preferred to stand and at the graveside she was with Meagan.

Father Sharkey, almost as if angry that he had to conduct the funeral of someone he considered guilty without redemption, addressed Nettie and the few others who had come for the interment. "Because it may rain, the committal will be brief." He opened the Book of Common Prayer, and read from the "Burial of the Dead."

"Unto Almighty God we commend the soul of our brother, Joel, departed and we commit his body to the ground, earth to earth, ashes to ashes, dust to dust, in sure and certain hope of the resurrection unto eternal life. Amen."

Nettie and the others responded with "Amen."

Father Sharkey nodded at Loomis Ponder, and he, in turn, signaled four men to lower the casket by means of ropes.

Nettie watched until the casket was lowered beyond her vision. "Please," she said to Meagan. "I don't want to see anymore."

Meagan put her arm around Nettie's shoulders, then walked her back toward the church, away from the graveyard and its many ghosts.

After the burial, Nettie held a reception in her home, and it was attended by everyone who had attended the funeral, and though neither Sergeant Creech, nor the bank secretary, Vernon Woodward, had attended the funeral, they were there as well.

As the attendees spoke quietly with each other or with Nettie, Duff was standing beside Meagan, and both were drinking coffee. He was looking at the well-dressed man who had sat with Nettie at the funeral and seemed to be helping her with the reception.

"I'll be damned," Duff said quietly. "I've been wondering who that was. It's him."

"Who is him?" Meagan asked. "Who are you talking about?"

"I've been trying to place that man, and I know who it is. It's John. The same man who attempted to rob us."

"What? Are you sure?"

"Aye, look at him. In your mind, give him long hair, an unkempt beard, and dirty clothes. But you don't even have to do that. Look at the bandage on his hand."

"Oh, my!" Meagan gasped. "It is! But what on earth is he doing here?"

Chief Peach, Lieutenant Kirby, and Sergeant Creech came over to speak with Duff.

"How are you coming with your investigation?" Chief Peach asked.

"Not so well, I'm afraid. 'Tis sure I am that Joel didn't

commit suicide, but I've nothing but my own belief, for I've nae evidence to back me up."

"You're wastin' your time, MacCallister," Lieutenant Kirby said. "He took everybody's money then killed himself."

"Leftenant, I'll ask you what I have asked everyone else. Why would Joel steal two hundred thousand dollars, then kill himself? Why didn't he just run away with the money?"

"I don't know. Maybe he felt guilty and couldn't face anyone."

"That makes nae sense. If he felt guilty, he could have just put the money back before it was discovered."

"Who can explain someone like that?" Lieutenant Kirby asked.

"Where is the money?" Meagan asked.

"Yeah, that's what I'd like to know," Kirby said. "Where is the money?"

"Doesn't that make you wonder? The money was in the bank the day before. His suicide note says that he stole the money, then he killed himself. What happened to the money? Where is it now?"

"I don't know. Who does know? He was crazy. That's all I know."

"Kirby, this is not the place to argue about it," Chief Peach said. "We are in his home to give comfort to his widow, not to attack Joel Prescott."

"I was just saying . . ."

"Don't say anything," Chief Peach said more sternly. "If you can be civil about it, let's go tell Mrs. Prescott good-bye, then get back to the station. We still have a town to look after."

The three policemen, including Sergeant Creech, who hadn't said a word during the discussion, left.

Eli Kendrick, who had not approached Nettie during the reception, had been watching the well-dressed man who had sat with her in the church and was standing with her as she greeted those who had come. Eli had no idea who it was. He went over to see Nettie, as much out of curiosity as from his intent to express his condolences.

"Oh, Eli, good," Nettie said when he stepped to her. "I'd like to introduce you to Mr. Cunningham. Mr. Cunningham, this is Eli Kendrick, who was Joel's vice president of the bank."

Eli and John shook hands.

"Are you from here, Mr. Cunningham?" Eli asked. "Excuse me for asking, but I thought I knew all of Joel's friends, and I don't believe we have ever met."

"Mr. Cunningham and Joel were very good friends in St. Louis."

Eli smiled. "Yes, I knew that Joel was in the army at St. Louis. Is that when you met him?"

"Yes," John said without further explanation.

"Well, uh, Vernon and I should get back to the bank." Eli smiled self-deprecatingly. "Even though the bank no longer has money, we still have work to do.

When Eli and Vernon left, only John, Duff, Meagan, Elmer, and Wang remained.

John hadn't left Nettie's side from the time of the funeral, the interment, and the reception. He saw tears well up in her eyes again, but he was ready, handing her a napkin.

"Thank you."

Duff and Meagan went over to speak to her again.

"Nettie, I am so sorry," Meagan said to her. "I wish I had words to comfort you."

"I know. And I very much appreciate your sympathy."

John noticed that Duff had been looking at him, though trying not to be obvious about it.

John smiled. "If you think hard enough, Mr. MacCallister, you will recognize me." He held up his bandaged hand.

"Iongnadh mòr!" Duff, so surprised that he spoke in Scots Gaelic. "Och, mon, so I was right. You are—"

"The contemptable man who attempted, without success, to rob you."

"Aye, but how—?" Duff stopped in midsentence. He wasn't quite clear what question he actually wanted to ask.

"You wish to know why I am here. I know it seems unlikely, but Joel and I were very good friends, and had been for quite a long time. Our friendship began long before my descent into the pitiful creature I have become."

Duff smiled. "If I may use a phrase from my friend, Elmer, 'you clean up nice.'"

Duff and John laughed out loud, their laughter so incongruous to the funeral atmosphere that the others looked over toward them.

Meagan glanced toward Nettie to see if she had been upset by the inappropriate laughter, only to see her smiling.

"Apparently you have recognized Lonesome John," Nettie said.

"You mean he . . . you are . . . ?"

"Yes, ma'am. I am the loathsome creature who made an unsuccessful attempt to rob you."

"But, what are you . . . never mind. I have no right to ask that question," Meagan said.

"As I told Mr. MacCallister, I am here to mourn the loss of someone who, before I fell on difficult times, was a very good friend of mine. And I'm pleased to say that even when he found me in my current, disreputable state, he honored that friendship."

"John and Joel began their friendship in St. Louis," Nettie explained.

"So you knew Joel very well, did you?" Duff asked.

"Yes."

"John, would you be for telling me what you think happened?" Duff asked.

"I don't know what happened, but I am absolutely certain of what didn't happen. Joel did not commit suicide. Such a thing was simply not a part of his psyche."

"Aye, 'n 'tis good to hear you say that, for I believe the same thing."

"Mr. MacCallister has volunteered to look into it," Nettie said.

John shook his head. "That's a noble thought, but I fear the police will look upon that as interference."

Duff pulled out his warrant from the governor and showed it to John. "This gives me authority over any law official in the entire Territory of Wyoming."

John read it quickly, then smiled. "Indeed it does. Good luck," he said as he returned the governor's warrant to Duff.

Chapter Twenty-one

After leaving the reception, John went into the Red Bull Saloon for a drink. Instead of standing at the end of the bar out of shame in the way he looked and smelled, he stepped right up to the middle of the bar and was met immediately by the smiling bartender.

"What can I get you, sir?" the bartender asked.

"Hello, Sam. I think I would like a beer."

Sam got a confused look on his face. "Do I know you?"

"It's been quite a while since I was last here." John didn't consider it a lie. He had come into the saloon shortly after arriving in Cheyenne, and that was before his descent into alcoholism and slovenliness. He'd meant it had been a long time since Jonathan Jacob Cunningham had been there. It was because he looked upon himself as two people—Jonathan Jacob Cunningham, who he was when he'd arrived, and Lonesome John as he had been for most of his time in Cheyenne.

One of the percentage girls smiled and walked up to him, moving her hips provocatively. "Hello, you handsome devil you. Would you like to share a drink with me? And maybe have a short date?"

John smiled. On all his previous visits the girls had stayed as far away from him as they could. "Thank you, Sue, but I'm afraid I'm going to be occupied."

The expression on the girl's face was even more shocked than Sam's had been.

"You . . . you know my name? How is that?"

"Well, you are a very pretty girl. You have no idea how many people you don't know do know your name."

"You mean I'm famous?" Sue asked.

"You might say that," John replied with a smile.

"How about that? I'm famous," Sue said to herself as, with a big smile, she turned away from John.

Eli Kendrick was also in the saloon, sitting alone at a table in the back of the room. About to leave, he saw John come in, watched him for a moment, and saw him turn away the percentage girl. He decided to stop by and talk to him on the way out.

"Mr. Kendrick," John said with a welcoming smile.

"Who are you?"

"Oh, I'm sorry. I thought Nettie introduced us. I'm John Jacob Cunningham, and as the lady said, Joel and I were very good friends."

"From St. Louis, you said."

"Yes."

"You were in the army?"

"Joel was in the army, not me." John smiled again. "But then you know that, of course, for you served in the army with him at Ft. Laramie. No, our relationship was considerably less gallant. We shared a love for baseball."

"That may be so, but you say you knew him in St. Louis. How did you hear about what happened to Joel, and manage to get here in time for the funeral?"

"Oh, it just so happened that I was already here," John replied.

"That was convenient," Eli said, his expression rather flat.

"Yes, I suppose you can say that it was."

"I must get back to the bank. It's amazing how much paperwork I'm having to go through, even with a bankrupted bank."

"I'm glad you were able to come," John said. "I know that Nettie greatly appreciated your visit."

"Look, Mr. Cunningham, I'm not sure what your relationship is with Nettie, but she is very vulnerable right now, and I wouldn't want to see you do anything to hurt her."

"Heavens, why would I want to hurt that dear lady? That's the last thing on my mind."

"Good. Well, as I said, I must get back to the bank. If you're going to be here for a while, I'm sure we will see each other again."

"Yes, I'm sure as well."

Shortly after Kendrick left, John saw J.B. Morrow, publisher of the *Cheyenne Leader*, come into the saloon and order a drink at the bar. He gave a friendly nod toward John.

That's when John got an idea and addressed the publisher. "Mr. Morrow, do you mind if we have a few words?"

"I don't mind at all," Morrow said with a friendly smile. "Would you join me at a table?"

"Yes, thank you," John said.

Morrow got his drink, then the two men walked over to an empty table. "Now, what is it you want to talk about?"

"I would like to apply for a position with your newspaper."

"You would, would you? What is your name?"

"Jonathan Jacob Cunningham."

"What newspaper experience do you have, Mr. Cunningham?"

"I recently worked for Mr. Joseph Pulitzer and the *St. Louis Post-Dispatch*." That wasn't entirely a lie. He had written several articles for the paper, but they were freelance articles.

"That's quite a well-known newspaper. Why did you leave? Were you fired?"

"The newspaper did not fire me, sir. I left St. Louis because of the allure of the West. I didn't want to stagnate in the city of St. Louis, where everything is available with no effort at all. I'll admit that it is coming a little late in my life, but you might say this is my rite of passage. I want to prove myself in a more trying environment. Or, in the argot of many adventurers, I came because I wanted to see the elephant."

Morrow clapped quietly and smiled broadly. "Well, I must say, Mr. Cunningham, you do seem to be able to turn a phrase."

"Sufficient to secure employment?" John asked.

"I'll tell you what, Mr. Cunningham. Why don't you drop by the newspaper office tomorrow morning? I can't make the decision by myself. I'm sure you know that I am only half-owner of the paper. My partner is J.W. Sullivan."

"Thank you, Mr. Morrow. I will be there."

John was excited about the possibility of working for

the newspaper, but he was concerned about what kind of impression he would make. The suit he was wearing was the only one he owned. Most of his clothes were worn and imbued with the permanent odor of horse manure. He needed new clothes, and he needed a place to live. He would lose his loft lodging rights as soon as he quit his job at the livery.

But to get new clothes and a place to live, he needed money. He thought about going to Nettie, but decided against that. He couldn't get a loan from the bank. It had no money to loan.

MacCallister. Yes, that was his only hope. But, where would he find him? John knew that the rancher was staying at the Interocean Hotel, but it was unlikely he would be there in the afternoon.

But Miss Parker might be there. John decided to take a chance of finding Miss Parker at the hotel. He was reasonably certain that she would know how to find MacCallister.

When John reached the Interocean, he stopped for a moment before he went in. It was the most elegant hotel in town, and part of him still felt the humiliation of what he had become and where he lived. But, he told himself, it was the only way out.

Gathering his courage, John walked into the hotel, and was about to step up to the front desk to inquire as to what room Miss Parker was occupying when he saw her sitting in a chair in the lobby, reading a book. He walked through the lobby to talk to her. "Miss Parker?"

Meagan looked up, then smiled. "Mr. Cunningham, isn't it?"

"Yes ma'am." John saw the title of the book. "*A Tale of Two Cities*. An interesting coincidence since I, like Dr. Manette, sometimes feel as if I have been incarcerated for a long time. But I, of course, have no daughter to welcome me."

"You've read this book?"

"Yes, I enjoyed it very much." John chuckled. "I don't know whether to say Charles Dickens is on par with Mark Twain, or Mr. Clemens is on par with Mr. Dickens. They are both wonderful authors."

"Yes, yes they are," Meagan replied enthusiastically.

"Have you read anything by Jane Austen?" John asked.

"No, I haven't."

"You must read *Pride and Prejudice*. I'm sure you will enjoy it."

"You are a most intriguing man, Mr. Cunningham."

"You flatter me," John said.

"I see that you aren't wearing a bandage on your hand."

"I see no reason to wear it anymore. It was nothing but a crease. I don't know whether to say I was lucky or if Mr. MacCallister was lucky for making such a clean shot that the bullet hit much more of my gun than it did me."

"You're the one who's lucky. Duff is the one you tried to rob. Few other men could have shot the gun out of your hand, or would have even tried, for that matter. And even fewer wouldn't have taken you to the police and pressed charges."

"I agree. Miss Parker, could you tell me where I might find Mr. MacCallister?"

"Oh, I'm afraid there's no telling where he might be at the moment. He's investigating the murder of Joel Prescott."

John nodded. "Yes, I'm certain it was a murder."

"Is there anything I can help you with?"

"No, I . . ." John paused, then took a deep breath. "Yes, maybe you could spare me some embarrassment. I want to borrow one hundred dollars from him, but if you believe there is no chance, tell me now, and I won't make a fool of myself by asking."

"What do you want the one hundred dollars for?"

At first he was hesitant to tell her, then realized she couldn't give him an accurate answer as to how MacCallister might react if she didn't have all the information. "Tomorrow morning, I am to meet with Misters Morrow and Sullivan, publishers of the newspaper the *Cheyenne Leader*. It is my intention to resign my job at the livery and take a position with the newspaper. This is the only suit I have, so I would like to have another bath and buy some new clothes. Also, as I will be giving up my employment with the livery, I must find more, uh, suitable quarters."

"What would you do with the newspaper?"

"I would hope to be a writer of some sort, a columnist or a reporter."

Meagan was quiet for a moment, then she smiled and said, "All right."

"By all right, do you mean you think Mr. MacCallister would look with favor upon my request for a loan?"

"No."

John's face fell.

Meagan's smile grew broader. "I mean I will loan you the money."

"You? But why?"

"You do need the money, don't you? And my one hundred dollars is just as good as Duff's one hundred dollars. You might say that I believe in you. Now, do you want the money or not?"

"Yes, Miss Parker. Oh yes," John said enthusiastically. "And please know that my appreciation has no bounds."

"Wait here," Meagan said. "I'll go up to my room and get the money."

John waited nervously until she returned. He felt somewhat self-conscious about borrowing money from a woman, but she had made the offer, and he needed money. He would swallow his pride and accept it.

It took but a moment or two until she returned with currency clutched in her hand.

"Where are you going to buy your new clothes?" Meagan asked.

"To be honest, I don't know. So far, my shopping experience has been limited to the grocery store and the saloon. I'm not even sure where I should go."

"Well, you came to the right place. I've done nothing but shop since we have been here, so I know just about every store in town. I would suggest that you go to Falkoff's. They have a wide line of clothes, and they are reasonable. If you shop carefully, you could probably get at least four outfits for fifty dollars, and a decent suit for thirty dollars. That will leave you one hundred and twenty dollars."

"What?" John gasped.

Meagan smiled. "I'm not sure one hundred dollars is enough, so I'm loaning you two hundred dollars."

"Miss Parker . . . I don't know what to do."

"You could start by taking the money. I'm getting tired of holding my arm out."

John took the money. "Oh, thank you. I shall be eternally grateful, and I will repay you as soon as I can."

At ten o'clock the next morning, John presented himself to a young woman sitting behind the desk in the front of the newspaper office.

"Yes, sir, can I help you?" she asked.

"I would like to see Mr. Morrow and Mr. Sullivan."

The young woman smiled. "You must be Mr. Cunningham."

"Yes," John said, surprised to be recognized.

"I was told to look for you and to take you to their office as soon as you arrived. This way." The young woman led him through the composition and press room to an office occupied by both Morrow and Sullivan. They were engaged in what appeared to be an argument. John assumed Sullivan was the one talking. He had already met Morrow, and Morrow wasn't talking.

"What do you mean the South Pole is a continent?" Sullivan asked. "The South Pole is just like the North Pole. There's nothing there but ice."

"No, the South Pole is a continent. Let's ask Cunningham here. Cunningham, is the South Pole a continent?" Morrow asked.

"If I answer, I fear I might antagonize one of you, and I'm really in no position to do that."

"Speak up, if you know the answer. It won't bother us," Sullivan said, then he smiled. "Especially since I know I'm right."

"Well, uh, Mr. Sullivan, I hate to tell you, but you are wrong. The South Pole is actually Antarctica, a continent. It is fifth in size of the seven continents, larger than Europe or Australia."

Both Morrow and Sullivan got surprised looks on their faces.

"How do you know that?" Sullivan asked.

"I read it once, and it just stuck in my mind," John said.

Sullivan got a broad grin on his face, then he stuck out his hand. "Mr. Cunningham, you are hired."

Chapter Twenty-two

Not yet having acquired new quarters, John lay on his cot in the little room at the edge of the livery loft that evening, staring up into the darkness. He could smell the hay and the horses and their droppings from the stalls below. It was an odor he had gotten used to, so that didn't bother him. He could also hear their shuffling as they moved to get into position for sleep. Most of the time the horses would sleep while standing, but often, if there was room, they would lie down. The stalls were large enough to allow them to do that if they wished.

Noises came from town as well. Somewhere a baby was crying, and a dog was barking, but he didn't know if they were related or not. From the two nearest saloons he could hear conflicting pianos, as well as the occasional high-pitched scream of a woman, followed immediately by her laughter.

As John lay there, he thought of Nettie—thinking of her as "Nettie," and not just as Joel Prescott's widow. He knew he had no right to think of her in any way other than as Joel's widow but couldn't put aside the fact that he felt more alive since meeting her this evening, than he had at any time since leaving St. Louis.

It was true, as John had told her, that he and Joel had become good friends while both were in St. Louis. Sometime later, a series of events caused John to leave St. Louis. He was an emotional wreck when he'd stepped down from the train in Cheyenne. He had a hundred and twenty-six dollars, so he felt no need to look for a job right away.

He should have. He spent most of his time and money in the Red Bull Saloon losing himself in whiskey. He became an alcoholic derelict, letting himself go in appearance and decorum. He stopped bathing, he stopped shaving, he stopped changing clothes; he did nothing but drink until he ran out of money.

Eventually, he sobered up as a matter of necessity. He could no longer afford to drink. Unless he got a job, he also couldn't afford to eat. He had become such a mess, he was not employable by any business that would require him to maintain a sense of decorum and self-respect.

About to give up all hope of finding a job, as a last resort, he applied at the livery.

"What can you do?" J.C. Abney asked.

John shook his head. "I don't know, but someone suggested I try here. I have nothing to lose, as it seems I am unable to function in any societal capacity."

"Then what makes you think you could work here?" J.C. asked.

"I know that the stalls need to be mucked out, and I am certainly capable of shoveling feces."

J.C. laughed. "You mean if I hired you to shovel manure, you would be all right with that?"

"I may have too much experience, but I think I could handle such a position."

"All right. Get yourself a shovel and start working. You are hired."

As he lay in bed in his loft quarters for the last night, he thought of the time he had spent working in the stable, and though it had been humbling work, he couldn't help but be thankful to Mr. Abney for giving him the job. After all, it had kept him from becoming a beggar on the street. In the final analysis, any legitimate employment was more honorable than begging.

But that was all behind him now. He had been hired by the newspaper, and it was work more in keeping with his intelligence and, he was sure, would enable him to regain his pride.

"You have been a good employee, Mr. Prescott," Abney said, when John submitted his resignation. "I know that when you came here, you had your own devils to deal with, but you never let that interfere with your work. And while I hate to lose you, I'm glad for you. I've no doubt but that you will be a very good newspaperman."

John had very little to do to move out of the loft the next morning. He had only the suitcase to move. But his last morning, he felt obligated to Mr. Abney and the horses in his care to feed them and rub down those that needed it. While he was in one of the stalls, he heard two men talking. On the other side of the stall wall, they were unaware of his close proximity and felt free to speak, even though they were speaking quietly.

"Ever since MacCallister got that warrant from the government, he has been a pain in the rear, poking around, lording it over everybody. I'm afraid he may cause us some trouble," said one.

John didn't recognize the voice.

"Why do you think so?" the second man asked.

John did recognize that man. It was Donald Malloy, about as unpleasant a man as John had ever met.

"He's been askin' questions, plus he's been talkin' to Prescott's wife. We need you to take care of him. We tried to get Harrigan to take care of him, and the dumb idiot wound up gettin' hisself killed. So we thought we would give you a try."

"What's it worth for me to take care of 'im?"

"A hundred dollars."

"A hundred dollars? Hell I wouldn't even pull my gun for that much. You was goin' to give Harrigan fifteen hunnert dollars."

"How do you know that?"

"Word gets around."

"Yes, well, that was because Harrigan had two other men with him."

"And he couldn't get the job done, could he?" Malloy said.

"No, he didn't."

"So you was out fifteen hunnert dollars."

"No, he wasn't going to get the money until after the job was done, and since he failed, he didn't get anything."

"You know, they's actually four of 'em. There's MacCallister, the woman, the old coot, and the Chinaman. You're goin' to need all four of 'em kilt."

"Yeah, you're right. Maybe you had better take care of all of 'em, including the woman. Would you have any problem with that?"

"You mean 'cause she's a woman?"

"Yes."

"Hell no, that don't make no difference to me," Malloy said. "But if I'm goin' to do all four of 'em, it's goin' to cost you more than fifteen hunnert dollars. It's goin' to cost you at least two thousand dollars, 'n I want five hunnert dollars up front, on account I'm goin' to need someone with me."

"I suppose, since he was ready to do fifteen hundred dollars for Haggerty, that I can get the same for you."

"Two thousand," Malloy insisted.

"All right, two thousand, but you don't get the money until after the job is done."

"Five hundred up front."

"And five hundred up front."

"Good, but don't tell nobody how much you're givin' me, 'cause I plan to give whoever I get to help me only one hunnert dollars apiece, without tellin' how much I'm actual gettin'."

"Do you have someone in mind?"

"Yeah, don't worry. I'll find someone."

John had not made a sound while the two men were there, and he maintained his silence in the stall until he was sure Malloy and the other man were gone. Emerging from the stall, John hurried to find MacCallister. He had to tell him what he had just heard.

Since it was nearly lunchtime, John went to the restaurant in the Interocean Hotel and, as he had before, decided to wait till he saw Duff. The dining room began to fill up, but he hadn't seen or Meagan yet, but he did see Elmer come in and take a seat. John went over to talk to him.

"Well, hello, John. I heard about your new job," Elmer said. "When do you get started?"

"Tomorrow morning," John replied, almost dismissively. "Will Mr. MacCallister and Miss Parker be coming here for lunch?"

"Lunch? Oh, yeah, you're talking about dinner, ain't you? No, they ain't comin' here. They was goin' to go to the Trivoli Restaurant. They asked me 'n Wang to go, but Wang found 'im a Chinese restaurant to go to, 'n I figured the Trivoli was too highfalutin for me," Elmer said. "It's on—"

"The corner of Sixteenth and Carey, yes, I know. Thank you, Elmer."

As he walked through the morning commerce toward the Trivoli, John felt a renewed sense of worth and couldn't help but think of his situation just a couple of days ago. Then, his clothes were old, and though he was free of any of the horse droppings, his work, which was primarily shoveling feces, had infused his clothes with a lingering odor. He had also almost always needed a bath, a shave, and a haircut. The way he looked then, he was sure that he would not have been allowed to even enter the Trivoli. But he had new clothes, as well as a recent bath, haircut, and shave, and a respectable job, so it was with confidence that he stepped into the dining room at Trivoli's.

John stood just inside the door, perusing the dining room, and saw Duff and Meagan sitting across the table from each other. Because they were engaged in conversation, they had not yet noticed him.

"Duff, do you have even the slightest idea as to what happened?" Meagan asked. "I mean, are you getting any closer?"

"I've nae a clue."

"Are the police being helpful at all?"

Duff shook his head. "Nae, but to be honest with you, lass, I'll not be for wanting their help. 'Tis more helpful if they'll just stay out of my way."

"You've lost a lot of money in this, haven't you?"

"Aye, but I'm nae the only one. When a bank fails like this, many people are hurt."

"Poor Nettie," Meagan said. "Not only has she lost her husband, but I'm sure she is practically destitute now. Any money they had in the bank was taken along with all the other money."

"Aye, 'n 'tis all the more reason why I dinnae think that Joel Prescott took all the money. If he did take it, where is it? And if he had regrets, why would he kill himself, instead of just returning it?"

"That's a good question," Meagan said then looking up, she saw John and her face brightened. "Oh, there's John."

"Aye, 'n he seems to be looking for us," Duff suggested. He raised his hand and John came toward them.

"Have you had your lunch, John?" Meagan asked.

"No, not yet."

"Then please join us," she invited.

He pulled out a chair and sat down. "I will, thank you. But that isn't why I have come."

"Oh?"

"Mr. MacCallister . . ."

"Haven't we been for knowing each other long enough to use first names?" Duff asked.

John smiled. "Yes

"How did your job interview go?" Meagan asked.

John smiled broadly. "I got the job."

"So, you are to be a newspaper mon, are you?" Duff asked.

John looked at Meagan before he replied.

"I told him what you were going to do," Meagan said.

"Good. I'm glad you did. Starting tomorrow morning, I will be a reporter for the *Cheyenne Leader*. But that isn't why I've come to interrupt your meal."

"Oh?" Meagan said.

"Your lives are in danger," John said. "And not only your lives, but the lives of Elmer and Wang as well."

"Why do you say that?" Meagan asked.

"A man named Donald Malloy is being paid to kill you."

"One man against the four of us?" Duff replied.

"No, more than one man, though I don't know how many more. I know that Malloy is being given two thousand dollars, enough for him to hire some others to kill you."

"Two thousand dollars? That means we are only worth five hundred dollars apiece," Meagan said. "And here I thought I was worth more than that."

"Malloy?"

"Donald Malloy."

"You say he is being paid. Who is paying him?" Duff asked.

"That, I don't know," John said. "I was rubbing down some horses for one last time this morning, and I overheard

Malloy and another man talking about this. They were on the other side of the stall, so I couldn't see them. I recognized Malloy by his voice, but I have no idea who the other man was. I thought about trying to sneak a look, but decided against it. If they had seen me and realized I had just overheard a plot to murder, they may have killed me as well."

"There is nae 'may have' to it, lad. They would have killed you for sure," Duff said.

"Have you found a place to live, yet?" Meagan asked.

"Yes," John replied.

"John, what is your story?" Meagan asked.

"What do you mean, what is my story?"

"Oh, come, John, you know exactly what I mean."

John sighed before he replied. "I'm not sure I know where to start."

"Suppose you start with how you met Joel."

John smiled. "Well now, that much I have told Nettie. John and I met and became friends when we both lived in St. Louis."

"But there is much more to it than that," Meagan said.

John nodded. "There is considerably more to it than that."

Chapter Twenty-three

John had been working at the livery a short time when Joel Prescott came to rent a horse and surrey. John recognized his old friend right away, and was surprised to see him in Cheyenne, and a civilian. Fortunately, Prescott didn't recognize him, but then, how could he? Who would have ever thought the John Jacob Cunningham that Prescott knew in St. Louis would be the Lonesome John who was working in a livery in Cheyenne, Wyoming?

Joel had come to the livery two more times. The second and third time he stared at John, with recognition just below the surface. "This may sound crazy, but I would swear that I know you."

"If you've come to rent horses before, it's quite possible that you may have seen me."

"No, I'm not talking about that. I'm talking about somewhere else, Ft. Laramie perhaps, or maybe—"

John realized his old friend had just remembered.

"My God," Prescott said. "You're John Cunningham! We used to sit together at Sportsman's Park in St. Louis for the baseball games. That is you, isn't it?"

"I'm afraid you have me confused with someone else," John said.

Prescott shook his head. "No, as soon as you began talking, I knew who you were. I don't have you confused. I know who you are. What does confuse me is I don't understand is what brought you to this state of—" He stopped talking, unable to complete his sentence.

John sighed. "Hello, Joel," he said quietly.

"So, I'm right. It is you."

John nodded once.

"John, what happened? How did you wind up here?"

"It's too long a story to share here. Meet me in the Red Bull Saloon after six o'clock. I'll tell you then."

It was rare for John to sit at a table in the Red Bull, but it was also rare for him to be washed up and wearing clothes that didn't smell like the droppings he shoveled every day. He was nursing a beer, beginning to believe that Prescott wasn't going to show. But then, why should he? John had no friends in Cheyenne, and most of his contacts were brief encounters with people who wanted to get away from him as quickly as possible. He was about to leave when Joel Prescott come through the swinging batwing doors.

John started to raise his hand but it wasn't necessary. Prescott saw him, and with a smile started toward his table. Shortly after he sat down a percentage girl approached them.

"I'll have a whiskey, my dear," Prescott said. "And you, John?"

John put his hand over the top of his glass. "I'm good."

The girl seemed a little disappointed that John didn't order another drink, but when she returned with Joel's whiskey, he tipped her more than the percentage would have been from another drink, and she flashed him a grateful smile.

After the girl left, Joel pointed to John's beer. "I don't mean to pry, but was that your problem?"

"It wasn't at the beginning, but it became so," John replied. "The one fortuitous side of my situation is that I quit being an alcoholic, because I could no longer afford to drink."

Joel took a swallow of his drink and looked at John but didn't say anything. He didn't need to. Both men knew why he was there.

"John, you were not just my friend. You were someone I very much admired," Joel said. "You have a PhD in English, and you had a full professorship at Washington University. With all that going for you, what in the world made you leave St. Louis?"

John was quiet for a long moment, but Joel didn't press him to continue. He and this man had once been friends, and Joel knew he would continue his story when ready.

"Cynthia Louise," John said.

"Cynthia Louise? I don't believe I know her."

"You wouldn't. She arrived after you left Jefferson Barracks." Again, John was quiet for a long moment. "Cynthia was a prostitute who worked the Southern Hotel. At first our relationship was strictly business. She was a beautiful young woman, and considerably more cultured than you would expect a prostitute to be."

Two years earlier

Professor John Jacob Cunningham stepped down from the hired carriage, then held his hand out to help Cynthia down. They were at the St. Louis Country Club, where Washington University was holding its annual honors dinner.

John had just sold his book, *Business Communication and Writing*, and in the scholastic atmosphere that honored its faculty for being published, Washington University was holding a reception for him.

Cynthia Louise was already very pretty, and in that setting, she was clearly the most beautiful woman present. She was a delightful guest with the staff, faculty, and with the other women present.

John was smiling as he watched her interact with others, when he was tapped on the shoulder by one of the club employees. "Yes?" John said.

"Dr. Elliot wants to see you."

William Greenleaf Elliot was not only chancellor of the university, he was its founder. He also held a Doctor of Divinity degree and had founded a church. He wasn't a very tall man, but he stood out because of his gray hair and very long, bushy chin whiskers.

John assumed Elliot wanted to see him to discuss something about the award for having published the book, but that wasn't the reason the chancellor wanted to talk to him.

"Dr. Cunningham, about the young lady you brought with you," Elliot started.

"Yes, I'm glad you noticed. She is quite a beautiful woman, isn't she?"

"How well do you know her?"

Something in the back of John's mind told him where this was going, and he decided to push it to the extreme. "I know her very well, Chancellor. I brought her tonight so she could see what my world is like. You see, I plan to ask her to marry me."

"No!" Chancellor Elliot said, speaking the word so loudly that a few who were close turned toward him. "Dr. Cunningham, don't you know?" This question was asked sotto voce.

"Know what?" John replied innocently, though he knew full well where this was going.

"I have it on very good authority that the young woman you have introduced to our cloistered society is a, uh, well there's no other way to say it. She is a prostitute."

John gasped. "No! I had no idea!"

"I suggest that you find some way to leave without causing any further disruption."

"Yes, right away."

As they were in the carriage on their way back to Cynthia Louise's apartment, John proposed to her.

"John, you can't be serious," she said. "Oh, don't get me wrong, I would like nothing better than to marry you, but you saw how it was tonight. I could never fit into your society."

"We can leave St. Louis and go somewhere else," he said. "I am well enough qualified to get a position at any of a dozen more schools."

"But you love it here."

"Yes, but I love you more."

"John, no, I could never do something like this to you."

"Sweetheart, don't you understand? You wouldn't be doing it *to* me, you would be doing it *for* me."

When John left Cynthia Louise that night, the issue was still unresolved, but he fully intended to get an answer from her the next day.

John decided that he would have breakfast with her and remind her that if she would marry him, they could have breakfast together every morning. Then, because he didn't want to put her out by asking her to cook breakfast for him, he stopped at a restaurant they both used and bought a breakfast of fruit, ham, eggs, and biscuits.

John had a key to her apartment and let himself in, smiling because he had gotten there before she awoke. Moving quietly so as not to disturb her, he set the table and lit the candles in the candelabra. Heading in to awaken her, he saw an envelope with his name on it on the counter. Curious as to what it was about, he pulled out the letter.

My dearest John,

I have thought long and hard about your proposal, and how I wish I could say yes, but there are two reasons I cannot. The first reason, and I'm sorry that I have kept this from you all this time, is that I am already married. My husband lives in Chicago. Because I could not stay any longer in a loveless marriage, I asked him for a divorce. He said no, so I left anyway.

The second reason is because I know how much you love teaching, and how right you are for what you do. I could never take that away from you, and they would never let you marry me, even if I could get a divorce.

Please forgive me for what I have done, and for what I'm about to do. My love for you will be eternal, now.

Your
Cynthia Louise

"Your love is eternal now?" John said. Suddenly, he got a sickening feeling in the pit of his stomach, and he tossed the letter aside. "Cynthia!" he shouted at the top of his voice. Running into her bedroom, he stopped when he saw her lying in bed. She was still wearing the same evening dress she'd worn the night before. One arm hung over the side of the bed, and there was a gun on the floor beneath her lifeless hand. Her pillow was soaked with blood.

For the first time since he had been a child, John wept aloud.

When John finished telling his story, Meagan wiped a tear from her eye.

"My name is John Jacob Cunningham, and I have a doctorate in English. As to whether or not I am educated, that would depend upon one's understanding of the word 'education.' Apparently, I lacked either the education, or the strength of character, to prevent myself from falling into the state of disrepute I came to occupy."

"I knew from the moment we met that you were neither an outlaw nor someone who had always mucked stalls," Meagan said.

John was quiet for a moment.

"Please excuse me for prying into your life. I'm afraid I have more curiosity than compassion," Meagan said.

"No, that's quite all right. Until I met you two, I had lost all sense of shame. I can't believe I had fallen so low that I actually attempted to rob you. I'm glad I was unsuccessful. For a while a part of me actually wished you had killed me, rather than just nicking me in the hand."

Meagan stuck out her hand and put it lightly on his. "I'm sorry. I had no right to pry."

John smiled ruefully. "My dear, thanks to the two of you, I believe I have had an epiphany."

"John, would you be for tellin' me what you know about Donald Malloy?" Duff asked a few minutes later as John was enjoying his lamb chops.

"Donald Malloy used to be a policeman, but he was kicked off the force for excessive brutality. He isn't someone you would want to cross."

"What does he look like? It might be helpful to me to recognize him."

John chuckled. "I suppose it would. Malloy is a man of average height, though he is quite muscular in appearance. He has a pronounced brow ridge, bushy eyebrows, prominent cheekbones, and a receding chin."

"'Tis useful information, 'n I thank you for it."

Chapter Twenty-four

The attempt on the lives of Duff and the others took place that night as they were returning to the hotel from the Red Bull Saloon. At the corner of Sixteenth and Capitol three men stepped out from behind the Phoenix Block Building. All had guns in their hands, and they began shooting immediately.

With a sharp cry of pain, Meagan went down.

“Meagan!” Duff shouted in alarm, his concern for her preventing him from drawing his pistol.

Elmer drew his pistol and shot two times, both bullets finding their marks. As the two men were going down, the third attacker went down with a throwing star protruding from his forehead.

Meagan gave Duff a weak smile. “I seem to have gotten in the way,” she said.

Drawn by the shooting, more than a few people were beginning to congregate.

One of the arrivals was a policeman who had been making his rounds.

“What happened here?” he asked.

“Them three fellers there come out a-shootin’,” Elmer

said, pointing to the three bodies not more than thirty feet away.

"He's right, Mickey. I saw the whole thing," said one of the citizens.

"We need to get her to the doctor," Duff said anxiously.

"She'd get quicker attention at the hospital," the policeman replied.

"My buckboard is still hooked up," one of the bystanders said. "We can take her there in that. It's parked just across the street."

Duff scooped Meagan up in his arms and hurried across the street. After putting her in the back, he climbed in beside her and cushioned her head in his lap. The front of her dress, from her stomach down, was covered with blood.

Duff couldn't help but think back to his time in Scotland when Skye was murdered. "Please, Lord, not again," he prayed.

The driver of the buckboard slapped the reins against his team, and though they had never been put to a gallop before, they responded to his urging, and the buckboard began moving rapidly down the street.

"Uhhh," Meagan groaned at the rough ride as the buckboard hurried over the cobblestones.

"Hold on, Meagan," Duff said. "'Tis necessary to go fast for to get you to the doctor."

"I'm all right," Meagan said in a weak voice.

Duff reached out to hold her hand and was relieved to feel the strength with which she returned his grip.

The driver stopped in front of the hospital and Duff jumped out, then reached down into the back of the buckboard and swept Meagan up into his arms. He hurried toward the front of the hospital and thanked the buckboard driver for holding the door open.

"I need a doctor!" Duff shouted. "The lass has been shot!"

"Come with me," a nurse called and Duff followed her into a room that had what appeared to be an elevated bed. Three lanterns hung around the table, all with highly polished cones surrounding the lanterns to direct a bright beam of light down onto the patient.

As one of the nurses turned up the lanterns, another had gone to get the doctor.

Duff was standing beside Meagan. Though her eyes were closed, she still gripped his hand tightly.

A doctor in a white coat came into the room then. "What have we here?" he asked.

"A gunshot wound, Doctor Urban," the nurse said.

"Nurse, cut away her clothing," the doctor ordered.

She cut away Meagan's dress and the "combination" underwear so that Meagan was lying nude on the table. Her lower stomach was covered with blood and the nurse began to gently wash it away. Rather than Meagan's body, Duff saw the bullet hole in the lower left side, just over the hip.

"Well, this is good," Dr. Taylor said. "It doesn't appear to be in position to have involved any of the vital organs. It looks as if the only damage is to the muscle tissue, but I'm going to have to get the bullet out."

"Don't worry, my dear," he said to Meagan. "We'll use ether, and you won't feel a thing." He looked over at Duff. "You probably should wait outside."

"No," Meagan said. "Doctor, let him stay, please. I want him to hold my hand."

Dr. Taylor nodded. "That will be all right."

Meagan held Duff's hand, squeezing it very hard until the ether took effect, then she would have dropped her hand if Duff hadn't held on to it.

The doctor used a probe, sticking it into the wound until he found the bullet, then working it up and out as blood continued to ooze, though not as hard as it was at the beginning. He dropped the bullet into a pan of water, where it made a clinking sound, then little bubbles of blood curled up from it. He cleaned the wound, then treated it with alcohol.

"Close the wound, nurse," he said, turned, and left the operating room.

"Yes, sir."

She poured alcohol over a piece of cotton, stuffed it into the bullet hole, and wrapped a bandage around all the way around Meagan's abdomen, then tied it in place. "She'll come to in a few minutes," the nurse said to Duff as she pulled a sheet over Meagan's nude body, then left, as well.

Duff stood there, holding Meagan's hand until she woke up.

"Duff?"

"I'm here, darlin'," he said, squeezing her hand.

"How are Elmer and Wang? Are they all right?"

"Ha. You must be doing fairly well for to be worryin' about Elmer and Wang. They're doing well, 'n 'twas the two of them who took care of the black'ards that shot you."

"My dress?"

"I'll have to be getting you another one," Duff said. "You'll nae be for wearing the one you came in here with."

"The green one. Bring the green dress."

"Oh, heavens, dear, you'll not be needing a dress today," the nurse said, coming back into the room at that moment. "The doctor wants you to stay here for a few days to make certain infection doesn't set in."

"I'll be able to come see her?" Duff asked

"Yes, of course."

"Duff, I think you should go see Elmer and Wang now. You know they are probably worrying about me."

"Aye. I'll be back in a while."

"It would be best if you didn't come back until tomorrow morning," the nurse said. "It's late, and she needs to sleep."

"All right," Duff agreed, squeezing Meagan's hand. "I'll be back to see you in the morning."

"With the green dress. Oh and also some . . . uh . . ."

"I know what you want and need," Duff said, smiling at her embarrassment over asking that he bring her some undergarments.

"You can bring Elmer and Wang with you if they want to come. But not until I'm dressed."

"It's a good thing that the bullet didn't do no more damage than it done," Emer said. "Me 'n Wang has been worryin' some about it. I'm glad she's goin' to be all right."

"I'll be going back to see her tomorrow morning. I

think she would like to see the two of you, if you would like to come with me."

"Are you sure she wants to see the heathen?" Elmer said.

"Better a young heathen than an old, wrinkled man," Wang said.

"Why dinnae I just take both of you?" Duff asked with a little chuckle.

Elmer reached out to put his hand on Duff's shoulder. "It's good to see that you can still laugh, my friend."

"Could you give me some information on the condition of Miss Meagan Parker?" John asked that evening.

"Are you family?" asked the nurse at the desk of the hospital.

"No, I'm a newspaper reporter, and I'm inquiring for the *Cheyenne Leader*."

"Oh, well, in that case I'm happy to tell you that she came through the operation to remove the bullet just fine. She is resting now, and should be doing quite well by tomorrow."

"Thank you."

Leaving the hospital, he went to the police station to find out who the attackers were. The night clerk was playing solitaire when John stepped up to his desk.

"I'm John Cunningham, reporter for the *Cheyenne Leader*. I would like to ask about the shooting that took place earlier this evening."

"There ain't nothin' to tell," the desk sergeant said as he held an eight of hearts, looking for place to play it. "They was one woman shot, 'n she warn't kilt, 'n the three what shot her was kilt. They're over at the undertakers now."

"Have you been able to identify them?"

"Yeah, just a minute, here." The desk sergeant laid down the eight of hearts, then turned the police log around so John could see it.

Taking a pencil and paper from his pocket, he wrote the names down, not at all surprised to see that one of the names was Donald Malloy.

"Oh, my goodness! You mean one of those shot today was Meagan Parker?" Nettie asked in alarm, after John took a chance that she would still be up after he left the police station.

"Yes, but before you get too upset, I'm happy to say that I visited the hospital to check on her and was told that she would be just fine."

"Oh, thank God for that," Nettie said. "But why in the world would someone target it her?"

"I don't think she was the target," John replied. "At least not specifically. Though she, Elmer, and Wang were certainly ancillary targets."

John told Nettie how, while he was closing up the livery, he'd overheard Donald Malloy and another man plotting the shooting, with Duff being the specific target. "I'm glad I was able to tell Duff about it beforehand, or the shooting may have been worse."

"Yes, I'm glad as well," Nettie said.

"You know what this means, don't you?" John asked.

"I imagine it means that Duff has made a few enemies in his past."

"Yes, but this time he is an enemy for a specific reason. Nettie, I think this is proof positive, if any proof was needed, that Joel did not commit suicide. When they were talking, I heard one of them specifically say that Duff was asking too many questions. And what is he questioning? He's questioning the circumstances surrounding Joel's death. Whoever killed him, he or they are afraid Duff will find answers they won't like."

"You said Donald Malloy was talking to another man," Nettie said. "Who was he talking with?"

John shook his head. "That, I'm afraid, I don't know. But I do know this. As long as that other man is alive, Duff, and all his friends, are still in danger."

"Oh, heavens, John, do you think—?"

"Yes, you may very well be in danger, as well," John said.

"Oh! What should I do?"

"I've taken a room in the Cannady Boarding House. I think you should take a room there, as well, at least until all this blows over. It's clean, comfortable, and most of all, it will be safe."

"But what about Jimmie Mae?" Nettie asked, speaking of her maid. "I can't leave her here alone. What if someone comes after me, and she is the only one here?"

"Get her a room there as well. Look on the bright side," John said with a broad smile. "She won't have to cook."

Nettie chuckled. "If I know Jimmie Mae, she'll wind up cooking in the kitchen of the Cannady House."

"I'm going to be writing an article tomorrow that might shake things up, but before it comes out, I'll come over to get you. Pack a bag as if you were going on a trip. As you need more things, you can come back for them from time to time."

"I don't know, John. That sounds pretty drastic to me."

"Please, Nettie. I would worry about you if you remained in this house. I know it won't be as comfortable in the boardinghouse as it is here, but it would make me feel a lot better. And"—he smiled—"we would be closer to each other." Realizing he might have just overstepped his bounds, he added, "Uh, so I could keep an eye on you."

That evening Eli Kendrick called upon Nettie.

"Eli, it's so nice of you to call on me," she said after Jimmie Mae brought him into the parlor.

"I've been thinking a lot about you, Nettie," he said. "How are you getting along?"

"Under the circumstances, I'm doing well. Of course, I still miss Joel terribly. Sometimes I'll be sitting here in the parlor, reading a book, and I'll look over in that chair, Joel's chair, and I'll see him reading a book, as well. Or sometimes, he'll just be sitting there, smoking his pipe." She gave a short chuckle, heavy with sorrow. "As you can see, his pipe is—" her voice broke and she paused for a moment before she could continue. "His pipe is still there in the ashtray. I've not found the strength to remove it."

As her eyes welled with tears, Eli took her hand in his. "Nettie, if you need anything, anything at all, please call on me."

She allowed herself to be embraced. "Thank you, Eli. That is so sweet of you."

"Do you feel all right? I mean, being in this house, all alone?"

"Why wouldn't I be all right?"

"I'm just thinking of the memories it must hold for you. You did mention Joel's pipe, after all."

"Oh, but you don't understand, Eli. I hold those memories to be very dear. And I'm not alone, Jimmie Mae is here with me."

"Yes, well, I was just asking. I must go, but I did want to call on you, and check up on you."

"Thank you, Eli."

After he left, Nettie wondered why she hadn't told him she would be moving into the same boardinghouse where John was staying.

She didn't wonder long. She knew she was developing feelings for John, and she didn't want to share those feelings with anyone, not even with Eli Kendrick, who had been a friend for so long.

Chapter Twenty-five

In the office of the *Cheyenne Leader* the next morning, John submitted his first story.

Shoot-out on Sixteenth Street

by

John Cunningham

Let me introduce myself to the readers of this newspaper. My name is John Jacob Cunningham, and I am happy and proud to say I have been hired by Messrs. Morrow and Sullivan to be reporter and columnist for this wonderful journal.

My very first report deals with an incident that happened in our city last evening. As it developed, that was the last night on earth for Donald Malloy, Dusty Roberts, and Newly Dawkins. Before you show pity on these three men, you should know their demise was brought about by their own evil doings.

Malloy, Roberts, and Dawkins were waiting in ambuscade behind the Phoenix

Block Building on Sixteenth Street when suddenly and without provocation, these despicable dregs of humanity, stepped out in front of Duff MacCallister, Meagan Parker, Elmer Gleason, and Wang Chow, and began shooting.

One of the first bullets fired struck Miss Meagan Parker, and that fair lady went down with her wound. As Duff MacCallister tended to her, Elmer Gleason and Wang Chow responded to the attack, and in less time than it takes to tell, the three villains lay dead on the street.

One of the bystanders, Mark Worley, had a buckboard nearby, his team already in harness. He rushed Miss Parker and Mr. MacCallister to the hospital, where the bullet was removed. A check with the hospital this morning elicited the fact that Miss Parker's wound was not as serious as first feared, and she is expected to recover without any further complications.

This writer has it on very good authority that the attack on Duff MacCallister was planned as a result of "asking too many questions," about the supposed suicide of the banker, Joel Prescott. If, in fact, Prescott actually did commit suicide, one must wonder why asking too many questions is of concern, and to whom?

If one wonders why Mr. MacCallister is asking so many questions, let it be known that he has every right to do so, as he holds a governor's warrant to investigate the

> conditions that brought about the death of Joel Prescott.
>
> My readers have my promise that I will continue to investigate the demise of Joel Prescott and see if, as I believe, it was not a suicide, but was murder.

Four citizens of the town were gathered around a table in Red Bull Saloon, drinking beer and discussing the newspaper article.

"Who wrote that story, anyhow?" Mel Warner asked.

"He give his name in that self-same article we're a-talkin' about. Didn't you read it? It's some new feller that come to work for the paper. A feller by the name of John Cunningham," Al Blanton said.

"Who is Cunningham?" Harold Deal asked. "I've never heard of him."

"Morrow said he used to work for the *St. Louis Post-Dispatch*, a-fore he come here," Blanton said.

"That's a big newspaper. Makes you wonder why he come here to work on the *Leader*," Frank Condon said.

"No, I'll tell you what it makes you wonder," Blanton said. "I mean after readin' that story, don't it make you wonder whether or not Prescott really did commit suicide?"

"Yeah, I been thinking about that, too," said Warner, owner of the Yes I Have It store. "I tell you the truth. If it warn't for Prescott, I would have gone out of business long ago. When I needed a lot of new things for my store, Prescott gave me a loan."

"Yeah, Prescott helped me, too," Condon said.

"You know what? Now I'm sorry that I jumped on the

bandwagon with a lot of others, and thought Prescott took all the money from the bank, and killed himself," Blanton said.

"All right then, if Prescott didn't kill hisself, who did? 'N what happened to the money?" Condon asked.

"Yeah, well, that's a question I ain't got no answer to," Blanton said.

"If you ask me, the police ain't got no answer to it neither," Warner said.

"Maybe this feller MacCallister will find out," Deal said.

"Yeah, iffen they don't kill 'im first," Condon said.

"If who don't kill 'im first?" Warner asked.

"Whoever it was that actual kilt Prescott, then took all the money," Condon said.

"That was quite an article you wrote," Nettie said to John. They were in her new room as he had helped her and Jimmie Mae move into the boardinghouse. "And thank you for believing in Joel."

John smiled. "Well, don't forget, I knew Joel a lot longer than you did."

Nettie chuckled. "That's true, isn't it?"

"I knew him for two years before he transferred to Ft. Laramie."

"John, what is your story? What did you do before you, uh, began working in a livery?"

John was quiet for a moment. "I was a professor and head of the English department at Washington University in St. Louis."

"I knew it had to be something like that," she said. "Why did you leave?"

John told her the same story he had told Duff and Meagan. He told of Cynthia Louise Robbins, hiding nothing from Nettie as to who and what Cynthia Louise was. He told her of the disaster of taking her to a faculty gathering, then, of finding Cynthia Louise dead by a self-inflicted wound the next day.

"Oh, John," Nettie said, her voice full of compassion. "I'm so sorry. And I'm sorry that I brought such an awful memory back to you." She reached out to put her hand on his.

"That's all right," John said. "I owe it to Cynthia Louise to remember her, and if you and I are going to be close . . . uh, friends, then you have every right to know."

"Thank you. Thank you for telling me." Nettie let her hand linger on John's.

The atmosphere between them was charged for a long moment, then John cleared his throat. "I have to get back to the newspaper office."

The publishers Morrow and Sullivan met John as he stepped back into the office. For a moment he was concerned, but then both men smiled and applauded.

"Here he is," Morrow said. "Our man of the hour!"

"Mr. Cunningham, you have no way of knowing, of course, but the article you wrote has generated more response than any article we have ever run in the *Cheyenne Leader*," Sullivan said.

"And a significant portion of them have been persuaded

by your article. People are beginning to believe that Joel Prescott didn't commit suicide," Morrow said.

"But of course, that raises the question," Sullivan said, "if he didn't commit suicide, who did kill him?"

"I have a feeling Duff MacCallister will find out," John replied.

It was an angry Lieutenant Kirby who slapped the paper down on Chief Peach's desk. "Have you read the paper today?"

"Yes, I read it."

"Well, what are we going to do about it?" Kirby asked.

"What do you mean, what are we going to do about it?" Chief Peach replied.

"I mean we already have that fool MacCallister interfering with our investigation," Kirby said. "And now we have this newspaper writer, John Cunningham, whoever the hell he is, peddling his nonsense. We've got to stop this foolishness."

"How do you propose that we stop it, Lieutenant?"

"What do you mean, how do we stop it? We're the police. We could just go down there and threaten Morrow and Sullivan with closing their newspaper."

"We can't do that, Kirby," Chief Peach said with a sigh.

"Why the hell not? They're interfering with an investigation."

"In the first place there is a little thing called the First Amendment to the United States Constitution, which guarantees freedom of speech and freedom of the press. In the second place, what investigation are you talking about? I thought we had concluded that Prescott committed suicide."

"Yeah, we did. But this damn article in the newspaper is goin' to get people all hepped up over it."

"Leave it alone, Kirby. There's nothing we can do about it."

Lieutenant Kirby stared at Chief Peach for a long moment as a vein in his temple throbbed with anger. "What do you mean, there ain't nothin' we can do about it? We're the police, ain't we?"

"Yes but, as of now, our position on this case is subordinate to the investigation of Duff MacCallister. Don't forget, he holds the governor's warrant."

"Yeah, I know he does, 'n I also know there ain't nothin' right about that. Chief, what you ought to do is go see the governor, 'n talk to 'im. He didn't have no right givin' that warrant to MacCallister."

"What does it matter to you, Kirby? You said yourself that Joel Prescott committed suicide. And if that's true, MacCallister can investigate all he wants, but he'll still come up with the same answer. And if it isn't true, if Prescott didn't commit suicide and MacCallister can find who did kill him, and what happened to the money, then justice would be served. Don't you think? After all, isn't justice what we all want?"

"If you say so. We'll leave it alone," Kirby said, "but it ain't right. He ain't goin' to find nothin' different from what we already found. There ain't nothin' at all about this bein' right."

* * *

As Chief Peach and Lieutenant Kirby were having their discussion, just down the street from the police station, Eli Kendrick was sitting at his desk in a bank that was empty of customers or any other employees.

"Nettie, how good to see you," he said when she stepped into the bank. He put his hand to his mouth. "Oh, excuse me, now that Joel is deceased, I have no right to address you by your Christian name."

"Nonsense, Eli. We are still the same people."

Kendrick gave an uneasy smile. "You are most gracious." He held his hand out toward an empty chair. "Please, uh, Nettie, have a seat."

"Thank you." She took the proffered chair.

"To what do I owe the honor of your visit?" Kendrick asked.

"I thought I should tell you that I have temporarily moved out of the house. Jimmie Mae and I have taken quarters in the Cannady Boarding House." She chuckled. "I'm quite sure I am the only resident with my own personal maid. Anyway, I know that Joel always kept us six months ahead on the mortgage, so there is no immediate problem, but, as the bank does hold the mortgage, I thought it would be information you should know."

"Yes, thank you. If your house stood empty for some time with no explanation, I would be concerned, both as your friend and as your banker. But if you don't mind my asking, why have you moved out? I'm sure you know I wouldn't foreclose on you, even if you did become delinquent in your mortgage payments."

"John was afraid that, after the article he wrote in the *Leader*, my life might be put in some danger if I remained virtually alone in that big house. He suggested that, for the time being at least, I should take a room at the boardnghouse."

"Who is John, and what article are you talking about?"

"John Cunningham. Eli, you know him. You met him at Joel's funeral, then afterward in my house. Are you saying you know nothing of about the shooting last night?"

"Only what I've heard. Three men and one woman were killed. Apparently the three men were targeting Duff MacCallister. There's very little surprise there. MacCallister is well known to be a man with a violent past. I'm quite sure the attack on him had to do with that."

Nettie shook her head. "No, not at all. First of all, the woman, Meagan Parker, isn't dead. She was only wounded, and not dangerously so. And the reason Duff MacCallister was targeted was because he has a warrant from the governor to investigate the real cause of Joel's death. Eli, don't you understand? This is almost positive proof that Joel didn't commit suicide. Somehow, those men who attacked Meagan and the others yesterday were afraid the truth would come out."

"Oh, Nettie, I know how badly you and I both want it not to be true that Joel embezzled the bank's money, then committed suicide. It has to be a hard blow to you, as it is to me. And while I have questioned whether or not that's what happened, I'm afraid, my dear, that is exactly what did happen. Don't forget, I'm the one who discovered his body. The gun was in his hand when I saw him lying on the floor. Please don't get your hopes up that it was anything but suicide, for I am certain that is exactly what it was."

Nettie shook her head. "No, Eli, I don't believe that,

not for one moment. Joel would not have taken all the money from the bank, and he certainly would not have committed suicide. You knew him well enough to know that can't be so. And," she added with a smile, "I'm happy to say that, because of the newspaper article, many others are coming around to the same belief."

"I'll, uh, have to read the article." Eli smiled at her. "Who knows? Perhaps it will be as convincing to me as it is to you, and apparently, to others. How I would like to believe that."

Chapter Twenty-six

"Did you read this damn newspaper article?" Bart Jenkins asked.

"What article?" Lou Martell replied.

"The article that says Malloy and the other two were killed."

"Yeah, Bart, we already knew that," Lou replied.

"Yeah, but this same article also says that Joel Prescott didn't commit suicide."

Lou chuckled. "Well, hell, Bart, we already knew that, too."

The two men were in the hideout cabin, and Lou walked over to the stove to pour himself a cup of coffee.

"Have you read the article?" Bart asked.

"No, I haven't read it."

Bart slid it across the table. "I think you had better read it," he suggested.

Lou read the article, then lay it back down on the table. "Who wrote this? Who is this John Jacob Cunningham?"

"I don't know, but we need to find a way to make him

change his tune. He needs to write an article that says Prescott did commit suicide."

"How are we goin' to do that?" Lou asked.

"We're goin' to have to find out a little more about him," Bart said.

"Are you sure you're up to going down to the dining room?" Duff asked. "I can bring your dinner up to you. 'Tis not a problem."

"I'm sure," Meagan replied. "And ask Elmer and Wang to eat with us, if they don't mind."

"I'm sure they be for wanting to do that."

"This will give me a chance to wear the lavender dress."

"Oh? I thought you brought that dress for special occasions, such as when we had dinner with Joel and Nettie Prescott."

"This is a special occasion," Meagan said. "I'll be with you, Elmer, and Wang. Who could be better company than that?"

Duff smiled. "Aye, lass, that is true."

Elmer and Wang were sitting at a table for four, waiting for Duff and Meagan to join them, when they saw the two of them coming down the stairs. They were walking side by side with Duff holding Meagan's arm, helping her down the stairs.

Elmer and Wang both stood as the two approached them.

"It's good to see that you feel well enough to come down to have supper with us," Elmer said.

"I had to, Elmer. I've been cooped up in that room for a week. It was like being in jail."

Elmer laughed. "No ma'am, it warn't nothin' at all like bein' in jail. I've slept behind the iron a few times."

"You know where I would like to go after this?" Meagan asked.

"Where?" Duff asked.

"I would like to go the Red Bull. I admit that it isn't quite like Fiddler's Green, but it is suitable for women, and I would like to have a drink in a somewhat more dynamic atmosphere than one can find here in the dining room of the Interocean Hotel."

"Now, you're talkin'," Elmer said, grinning broadly and rubbing his hands together with glee.

"Are you sure you want to go to the Red Bull, wearing that dress?" Duff asked, nodding toward the dress with the low-cut neckline that exposed Meagan's shoulders and dipped low enough to show a slight cleavage.

Meagan chuckled. "You may have a point there. If you will help me get back upstairs after we eat, I'll change into something more appropriate."

As Meagan was changing her dress in the Interocean Hotel, John and Nettie were having dinner together in the Cannady Boarding House dining room. He had brought copies of the *Cheyenne Leader,* which he distributed free of charge to the other residents of the boardinghouse.

"Well, that was very sweet of you," Nettie said.

"There is a reason to my madness," John said. With

a smile, he pointed to an article on the first page. "I wrote this."

The Naming

by

JOHN CUNNINGHAM

There is a woman in Denver, who five years previously, gave birth to twin girls. She named the first daughter Bedalia, but unable to come with a name for the second twin, called her, simply "The Other One" and the child answered to that, and indeed, identified herself by that name.

When Bedalia and The Other One were five years old, her mother took them on a train to Missouri. It was when the train passed through Sedalia, Missouri that the twin's mother had a sudden epiphany, and as did Archimedes who ran through the street naked shouting "Eureka" she called in joy and excitement. "I've got it! I shall call the child Sedalia," she announced loudly.

And so, since that day, The Other One has been so named.

"Oh, John, you are teasing," Nettie said with a little laugh after she read the article. "You made that up."

John held his hand up as if taking an oath. "Upon my word, that is a true story. I did not make it up."

"Oh, that poor little girl, being known only as The Other One until she was five years old."

"Yes, but now she has a grand name," John said. "And you know what they say. All is well that ends well."

"Let's hope so. Bless her little heart," Nettie said.

During the meal several of the other residents of the boardinghouse stopped by their table to tell John how much they appreciated the free newspaper and how much they enjoyed the article.

"My, you certainly seem to be popular with everyone," Nettie said as they were finishing their meal.

"And why not?" John replied. "It's my winning personality. I seem to draw people to me."

"Oh, I'm sure that's it. In fact I'm enjoying myself so much that I hate to see our evening come to an end."

"It needn't come to an end," John said.

Nettie caught her breath. "I . . . uh, I'm not sure what you mean by that."

"I mean why don't you come to the Red Bull Saloon with me and have a drink?"

"I don't know as I should."

"You need have no concerns about the Red Bull. It is a very elegant establishment, and ladies need not fear as to any negative reaction about them being there. Many ladies do go there."

"No, you miss the point," Nettie said. "What I'm talking about is that it is too soon after Joel's death."

"Too soon?" John reached across the table to lay his hand on hers. "Nettie, Joel is the only one you should be concerned about. And right now, to Joel, time is meaningless. One day, one month, one thousand years, it is all the same to him."

Nettie was quiet for a moment, then she allowed a pensive smile to reach her lips. "You're right. And I would love to have a drink with you, John."

* * *

Duff, Meagan, and Wang were sitting at a table in the Red Bull, being entertained by Elmer, who was telling stories.

"I spent me some time in Arizona oncet, right soon after I left the sea it was. I thought maybe I might settle down there, start me a farm, then commence lookin' aroun' for a woman 'n make her my wife. I figured she could help me run the chicken farm.

"I was goin' to sell eggs, I was, 'n use what money I got from that to start buildin' up my farm. Only it didn't work."

"You mean the chickens wouldn't lay eggs?" Meagan asked.

"No ma'am, they laid eggs, all right. They laid plenty of 'em. Onliest thang there is that it was so hot all the eggs what was laid come out hard-boiled."

The other three at the table laughed, and they were still laughing when John and Nettie came in.

"Oh, look, it's John and Nettie," Meagan said. "Duff, you men move another table over here, and let's invite them over.

"There's Meagan and the others, inviting us over. Let's join them," Nettie said, pleased to encounter her friends.

"All right," John agreed, though he wasn't particularly happy about the unexpected meeting with the others. He had planned on some time alone with her.

* * *

Willard had been keeping an eye on the Interocean Hotel, but when he saw Duff and a woman leave the hotel and go to the Red Bull, he followed, staying far enough back not to be noticed. He had been told to keep an eye on MacCallister. He wasn't sure who the woman was, but it seemed obvious that she was important to him.

Standing at the bar drinking a beer, he had no idea who the man and woman were who joined them a few minutes later, either, but he thought it might be a good idea to find out.

"Hey, Arnie," he said to the bartender, using as friendly a tone as he could. "Who are those people who just went over to the MacCallister table?"

"Why, don't you know? The man is John Cunningham. He's a new reporter the *Cheyenne Leader* hired. I don't have any idea where he came from, but ever since he started workin' for the paper, he sure does have lots of folks readin' his stories."

"Oh, yeah, I think I've heard of him. He's the one who wrote the article sayin' Prescott didn't commit suicide, ain't he?"

"That's the one."

"And who's the woman with him?"

"Ha, now that's real interestin'," Arnie replied. He leaned across the bar so he could speak a little more quietly. "That there woman is Prescott's widow. I mean, he ain't hardly in his grave, but here she is goin' out with Cunningham. There's some folks as might think that ain't proper."

"You don't think there's nothin' betwixt 'em, do you?" Willard asked.

"I don't know. I have heard rumors."

"'N here they are in here together. It's sure enough to make a feller think."

"So, tell me, Nettie. How are you getting along?" Meagan asked.

"I'm doing as well as can be expected, I guess." Nettie smiled at John. "But I must say, John has been most helpful in seeing me through these difficult times. I mean, I know some people might talk, might think it isn't fitting for me to be out so early after Joel was killed."

"If so, think nothing of it," Meagan said. "You've been through a tragic event, and it's good to have someone who can bring you comfort."

Nettie seemed to take some solace from Meagan's words, and she reached out to put her hand on John's hand. "Thank you for those words," she said to Meagan. "Your opinion means a lot to me."

"Tell me, Miss Parker—"

"Please, it's all first names at this table. It's Meagan."

John cleared his throat before he spoke again. "Meagan, I was about to ask how you are getting along from your gunshot wound."

"I'm doing quite well, thank you." She smiled. "As you can see, I'm out and about."

"Yes, and you've no idea how happy I am to see that, seeing as I feel responsible for you getting shot."

"What?" Meagan asked, clearly surprised by John's comment. "Well, why on earth would you say such a thing?"

"Because the attack on Duff, you, and the others came

too quickly after that article for it not to have been the cause."

"You have nothing to apologize for," Meagan said.

"Anyhow, me 'n Wang took care of 'em," Elmer said.

"Yes, you did indeed," John replied. "Wang, what do you call that weapon you used?"

"It is called, *toe zhì xīng*," Wang replied.

"I beg your pardon?"

Elmer laughed. "What he's tellin' you in that heathen language of his, is that the thing he throwed that stuck in the forehead of that feller is called a throwing star."

"Do you carry one on you all the time?" John asked Wang.'

"No."

"I guess you were just lucky you were carrying it when you were attacked."

"I carry six," Wang said.

John started to laugh, thinking perhaps that Wang was teasing, but he saw not a hint of smile on Wang's face, so he looked down at the table.

"I'm told that you're from Missouri," Elmer said.

"Yes, I'm from St. Louis."

"I'm from Missouri, too," Elmer said. "From Taney County."

"That's in the southwest part of the state, I believe," John said.

"That's right," Elmer said. "Was you in the war?"

"I was."

"Most of you folks up there in St. Louis was Yankees, warn't you?"

"If you are asking if I fought for the Union, I did," John replied.

"I fought for the South." Elmer chuckled. "Well, you could say I fought for the South but, truth is, I was with Quantrill, 'n sometimes Quantrill fought for his ownself."

"So I have heard," John said. "I thank God the war is over. It wasn't right for Americans to be fighting against Americans."

Elmer nodded. "Me 'n you sure do agree on that."

John smiled. "I'm also glad to say I was never in any engagement with Quantrill, so that means you and I never faced each other as belligerents."

"As what?" Elmer asked, confused by the word.

Meagan chuckled. "He means that you and he never faced each other across a battlefield."

"Oh, yeah," Elmer said. "Yeah, that is good, ain't it? Let's shake on that." He extended his hand across the table, and with a broad smile, John took it.

"Ain't no need for you to be shakin' hands with Duff or the heathen, on account of neither one of 'em warn't even here when the war was fought. But I don't hold that agin' 'em none,' cause they's been times when both of 'em have pulled my ashes outta the fire."

Chapter Twenty-seven

The next morning, John gave his story to the typesetter then watched as his skilled hands moved the lead type with exceptional speed from the letter drawers to the composing sticks. This was another story that should raise some attention and further modify the hostility that had been directed toward Joel, and by extension to Nettie, since some were directing their anger toward her after her husband's death and the disappearance of all the money.

John was doing the stories to clear Joel's name. He was doing them because Joel had been a good friend, but also because he wanted to reduce the pressure Nettie was under.

He was developing feelings for Nettie but didn't feel that he was betraying his friend. No such feeling had manifested itself prior to Joel's demise. Some might think it was too soon, but it was as John had told her—time was meaningless to Joel.

John realized it was more than just developing feelings for Nettie. He was actually falling in love with her. He knew that, realistically, it was a star-crossed romance. She had been raised the daughter of an army officer. Her father was a colonel when she married Joel. And certainly, after she'd married him, she'd lived a comfortable life because Joel had been able to give her anything she had ever wanted.

What could John give her? Perhaps when he had been a college professor his income and position would have been economically and socially acceptable. Yes, his current occupation as a newspaper reporter was certainly respectable, but he had no doubt but that his recent history of working in the livery stable would be discovered. He was making more money, but he wasn't making nearly enough to support Nettie in the way she was accustomed.

He wouldn't speak of his love for her. If he did, it would put pressure on her and might destroy the warm relationship they were currently enjoying, and a warm relationship was better than nothing. It would seem that his love for Nettie would remain unrequited. He thought of Charlotte Brontë's story of unrequited love, wherein she apparently fell hopelessly in love with an older, married professor. He had taught Brontë when he was a professor, and considering the relationship he'd had with Cynthia Louise Robbins, that story had always been meaningful to him. A relationship between him and Cynthia Louise had been unattainable because his position was so much higher than hers. Thinking about it, he realized, the current situation was reversed.

"Here it is, Mr. Cunningham," the typesetter said, his words interrupting John's reverie. "Do you want to proofread it?"

John laughed. "Oh, heavens, Abe, I'm not like you. I

can't read the copy when all the words are backward like that. I'll just have to depend upon you."

"Well, it's exactly what you wrote," Abe said.

John nodded and made a chopping motion with his hand. "Then it's ready to go." He watched as Abe set the sticks of print into the bed, lay on the sheet of paper, used the roller, then brought down the ink plate to make the impression. When he lifted the plate, John reached out to pick up the first finished sheet and read it with a proprietary feeling.

The Mystery Deepens

by

JOHN CUNNINGHAM

What happened to Joel Prescott? Prior to the banker's demise, the Cattleman's Bank of Cheyenne boasted over two hundred thousand dollars of depositors' money on hand. These funds disappeared from the bank at the same time as Prescott's death.

That Joel Prescott did not commit suicide is no longer debatable. And proof of this assertion lies in the many attempts that have been made on Duff MacCallister's life. Duff MacCallister holds a commission from the governor to explore this case, and he is conducting his investigation based upon the premise of Prescott's innocence. Is he getting too close? He must be, otherwise there would not have been multiple attempts to kill him.

I have a question for Chief Peach and the Cheyenne Police Department. Why are you not investigating these attacks? If you would

> find out who is behind the attacks on Duff MacCallister, you will not only solve the mystery of Joel Prescott's untimely death, you will also discover what happened to the money.

Across town, Eli Kendrick stepped down from the cab he had hired. "Wait here," he ordered the driver. "The lady and I will be going to lunch together."

"Yes, sir," the driver said, keeping the team still.

Eli felt a sense of excitement as he climbed the steps to the Prescott house. It was a house he had always admired, just as he had always admired Nettie Prescott. During the time Joel was alive, Eli had always observed the most proper decorum. He had kept his admiration to himself, but with Joel gone, he no longer felt such a restraint.

Eli would start gently, offering Nettie only his support to help her through the grief of losing her husband. He would explain to her that Joel was his best friend, and who better to comfort a grieving widow than her husband's best friend?

Eli started to knock, but was stopped by a note pinned to the door.

Mr. Bowman,

Please suspend all delivery of mail to this address until further notice. I am now a resident of the Cannady Boarding House, and will be receiving all mail there.

Thank you,
Nettie Prescott

Cannady Boarding House? Eli thought. *Wait a minute. That's where that meddling reporter lives.*

Eli felt a flash of anger which he repressed before walking back to the cab. "Take me to the Cannady Boarding House," he ordered.

"Yes, sir," the driver replied.

Ten minutes later, the driver pulled up in front of a large house with a wraparound front porch.

"You can go," Eli said, paying the driver.

As the cab pulled away Eli started toward the front door. A couple of women occupied two chairs on the front porch. Nearest the front door, they were rocking back and forth as they carried on a conversation. Two men sat farther away and across from each other at a table, engaged in a game of checkers.

"Miz Cannady ain't here right now," one of the women said.

"That's all right. I'm not here to see Mrs. Cannady. I'm here to see Mrs. Prescott."

"The widow woman?" the other old ladies asked.

"Yes, I was her husband's business partner."

"Oh, well, you'll find her in unit seven. It's at the back of the hall, last door on the left."

"Thank you," Eli said with an acknowledging nod.

He went inside. Then following the directions given him by the old lady in the porch rocking chair, he walked down the hallway until reaching the door marked "7" and knocked on the door.

"John, is that you?" Nettie called from behind the shut door.

"No, Nettie, it's me, Eli," he replied, trying to keep the irritation out of his voice.

Nettie opened the door and smiled at him. "Eli, how nice of you to stop by. Won't you come in?"

He stepped inside and looked around at the small apartment, which consisted only of a bedroom and a living room. "Nettie, what are you doing here? You have one of the most beautiful homes in Cheyenne, and I know you aren't behind on the mortgage, so why have you chosen to live here? Why, you don't even have a kitchen."

"Oh, I don't need a kitchen," Nettie replied. "The meals come with the apartment. We all gather to eat in the dining room."

"You haven't answered my question. Why have you abandoned your home?"

"Oh, John thought it might be safer for me here."

"Safer? What do you mean, safer?"

"I'm sure you've read some of the articles he has written about Joel, and how he is sure Joel didn't commit suicide. Apparently, some of the other people in town are beginning to think that as well. John fears that the same people who are after Mr. MacCallister might also come after me."

"That's ridiculous," Eli said. "The people who are coming after MacCallister have nothing to do with Joel or the bank. You must know that Duff MacCallister has lived a life of violence ever since he arrived in this country. And the two others with him? Elmer Gleason rode with Quantrill during the war and with Jesse James after the war. That should certainly tell you something about him. And the Chinaman is wanted for murder in China. None of that has anything to do with you."

"That may be so, but John thinks it would be better to

be safe than sorry. That's why I moved here, into this house with him."

"What?" Eli said with a gasp. "You mean Cunningham lives here with you?"

Nettie chuckled. "I didn't say that right, did I? No, John has his own apartment here."

"I . . . uh, yes, of course. I'm sorry I misunderstood."

"Well, I appreciate the visit, Eli, but, why are you here? Is there some leftover business with Joel and the bank?"

"No, everything is fine there. I've come to ask you if you would have lunch with me. I stopped by Trivoli to reserve a table for us. I mean, I'm sure the meals they serve here are very good, but wouldn't you like to get out, once?"

Nettie hesitated for a moment, then nodded. "Yes, thank you, I would be happy to have lunch with you."

"Good afternoon, Mr. Kendrick," the maître d' greeted with an obsequious smile. "Your table is ready, sir."

"Thank you."

Eli and Nettie followed the maître d' through the restaurant to a table set back into a small alcove, thus providing them with a degree of privacy.

"Your waiter will be here right away," the maître d' said after they were seated.

"Thank you, Darren," Eli said.

"It is so nice here," Nettie said after Darren left. "Joel and I used to come here often. Thank you for inviting me. Eli, you don't think Joel killed himself, do you?"

"Nettie, you know how close Joel and I were. I certainly

want to believe that he didn't, and I hope MacCallister can prove that he didn't. But it pains me to say this"—he reached across the table to lay his hand on hers—"the evidence that he did seems to be overwhelming."

"Well, I don't believe he did it, and neither does John."

"You're talking about Cunningham?"

"Yes, John Cunningham. Not many people realize this, but John and Joel were very good friends."

"Because Joel was nice to him when he encountered him at the livery stable? That hardly qualifies as good friends. Joel was nice to everyone."

"At the livery stable?" Nettie said in a small voice.

"Believe me, Nettie, I take no pleasure in telling you this, but John Cunningham, the reporter who is writing all those stories for the *Leader*, is the same man everyone in town knew as Lonesome John. If he has convinced you that he and Joel were very good friends, I'm afraid you have been taken in by a lie."

"I know he worked in the livery stable, but before he came to Cheyenne, he lived in St. Louis. I'm sure you know that when Joel was in the army, he was posted to Jefferson Barracks in St. Louis. It was there the two men became friends."

"Joel told you that, did ne?"

"No, John did."

"Nettie, I have no right to tell you who you should accept as friends. But there is something very fishy about this whole thing. You know how close Joel and I were, but Joel never said a word about a friendship with Cunningham. However, it does raise a question."

"What question?"

"If Joel did not commit suicide, as you believe, then someone had to kill him. Working on that premise, I would say your friend John Cunningham would be a prime suspect."

Nettie shook her head. "I don't believe it."

"I know this may come as a shock to you, especially since he has engaged upon a campaign to win your affection, if not your trust, but whether you believe Lonesome John was involved or not, all I ask is that you be very careful around him."

"I have no reason to believe John is involved," Nettie said. "If he were involved, wouldn't it be to his advantage to have people believe that Joel committed suicide? And yet his stories say otherwise."

"You may have a point, my dear." Eli smiled across the table at her. "But, let's not talk about Cunningham anymore. Let's talk about us."

"Us?"

"Yes, us. I want you to know that I am always here for you, as a friend. Who knows? Perhaps, in time, our relationship will grow to something more than mere friendship."

Chapter Twenty-eight

Lieutenant Kirby slapped the newspaper down on his desk. "Damn."

"What is it, Lieutenant? What's in the paper that's got you upset?" Sergeant Creech asked.

"It's that reporter, Cunningham," Kirby said. "Who the hell is he to attack the police department for not investigating the Joel Prescott case?"

"What case would that be, Lieutenant? I thought ever'body was sayin' that he committed suicide, just like his note says."

"But what if he didn't?" Kirby replied. "What if someone did kill him? Wouldn't you think that would be something we should investigate?"

"Yeah, well, that could be. So, why ain't we investigatin' it?"

"Because Chief Peach doesn't want to investigate it," Kirby said.

"Why do you reckon it is that he don't want to?"

"I don't know why Peach won't look into it," Kirby said, stroking his chin. "That's a good question."

"Good lord, Lieutenant, you ain't sayin' that you think the chief had anything to do with it, are you?"

"No," Kirby said. "I'm not making any such suggestion. I'm just sayin' that we are the police department, and it isn't right that we should just let MacCallister do it all, even if he does have a commission from the governor. If there really is something to it, if Prescott didn't commit suicide, why should MacCallister get credit for solving the case?"

"Yeah, you've got a point, there," Sergeant Creech agreed.

Eli had stepped into the police office just in time to overhear some of the conversation between Kirby and Creech.

"Yes, sir, Mr. Kendrick, what can we do for you?" Sergeant Creech asked.

"It isn't what you can do for me, it's what I might be able to do for you."

"What is that?" Kirby asked.

Eli smiled at Kirby. "Have you considered that the newspaper articles may be right? Have you considered that Joel might not have killed himself?"

"What?" The word exploded from Kirby's mouth.

"Perhaps Joel didn't kill himself, and if that's the case, someone had to kill him. I have reason to believe that someone might be Lonesome John."

"Lonesome John? Are you kidding me? You mean the one who works and lives at the stable?"

"He did work at the stable," Eli said. "Now, John Cunningham works for the newspaper."

"Wait a minute," Kirby said. "Are you telling me that Lonesome John is John Cunningham?"

"That's exactly what I'm telling you," Eli said with a triumphant smile."

The cabin

"What needs to be done, is you need to abduct MacCallister's woman. If you have her, you can use her as bait to lure in MacCallister. Then it will be easy to kill him."

"I need to what?" Bart asked. "What does abduct mean?"

"You need to snatch her."

"You keep givin' me these orders," Bart said, "but you ain't puttin' yerself on the line. So far I've got six men kilt, 'n you ain't lost nothin'. Before I do anything else, you goin' to have to come up with some money."

"I can't come up with any money, because I don't have any."

"What the hell you talkin' about? They's been over two hunnert thousand dollars stoled, 'n you say you ain't got no money?"

"You don't understand. The money has been deposited in a bank in Denver. As long as it is there, the money, and we, are safe. But we can't take out the money till all this blows over. 'N it's not goin' to blow over until we get rid of Duff MacCallister."

"'N you think snatchin' up his woman will take care of it?"

"Yes. I don't know why we didn't think of this before."

"How are we sposed to do it? She has a room in the hotel right next to his. There's no way we're goin' to be able to get her, what with him that close."

"You'll just have to keep an eye on her, and get her sometime when she is alone."

"She ain't hardly never alone," Bart insisted.

"She does a lot of shopping. I'm sure the opportunity will present itself."

"What's our cut of the two hunnert thousand dollars?" Bart asked. "It better be a hunnert thousand."

"It won't be a hundred thousand, but it will be a lot of money."

"How much is a lot of money, and why won't it be a hunnert thousand?"

"It will be a little over sixty-five thousand dollars, and the reason it isn't half the money is because someone else is involved in this."

"Why the hell did you get someone else in it? Hell, that just cuts down on the money we'll be getting."

"You don't understand, Jenkins. We didn't get him involved. He got us involved. This whole thing was his idea."

"All right. We'll snatch the woman," Bart agreed.

"That's absolutely necessary, and it is good to know that you will do it."

"But we're also goin' to take care of who's writin' all them articles, too."

"That might not be a bad idea. But first things first."

Washington University, St. Louis

"Dr. Elliot, John Cunningham just got another royalty check from Paddington House for Business Communication and Writing," Dr. Walter Wilkerson said, carrying an envelope into the college chancellor's office. "They keep sending them to the English Department. I guess they think he's still the head of the department, instead of me."

"What is the amount this time?" Elliot asked.

"Seven thousand, six hundred, and seventy-two dollars," Wilkerson said.

"My oh my. Who would have ever thought that book would sell so well?" Elliot paused as he removed the check from the envelope. "It seems as if every college and university in the country has adopted it as a textbook for their English and their business classes."

"How much is there so far?" Wilkerson asked.

"I have been depositing all the money to his account at Boatman's Bank. Let me see how much is there." Dr. Elliot took out a ledger book and examined it. "Once this check is deposited there will be twenty-eight thousand and eighty-six dollars in his account."

"That's a lot of money. Why don't we just use it for the university? Hell, we don't even know if the dumb man is still alive," Wilkerson said.

"Dr. Cunningham is anything but dumb. And we have no access to his bank account unless we have proof of his death. After he's been missing for five years, we can have him legally declared dead," Dr. Elliot said.

"You liked him, didn't you?" Wilkerson asked.

Dr. Elliot was silent for a moment before he replied. "As a matter of fact, I did like him. And I feel responsible for him running away as he did. Worse, I have a strong sense of guilt over the death of his young lady friend, Cynthia Louise."

"I never actually knew Cunningham since I arrived to

take over the department after he left. But I've heard a lot of stories about him. This woman you're talking about, the one that committed suicide. Is it true that she was a prostitute, and he brought her to a faculty event?"

"That's true," Dr. Elliot replied.

"And you asked him to leave the gathering and take her with him?"

"Yes. And that's the last time I've seen him."

"You didn't do anything wrong, Dr. Elliot."

"I tell myself that, but the young woman committed suicide, and Dr. Cunningham left for who knows where, as a result of my actions. You are right that I didn't do anything wrong, but I can't convince my conscience of that."

Cheyenne

Moe Conyers was in The Eagle Bar. He had been sent into town by Bart and told to recruit someone to help him snatch Meagan Parker. Unlike the Red Bull, the Cheyenne Cattleman's Club, or any of the other saloons, the Eagle Bar catered to the men of the lowest means. Moe had visited the bar before because it was cheap. During his previous visits he had met two or three men he thought he could hire to help him. He had been given one hundred dollars to use as payment to whoever he selected.

Smiling, he saw just the man. Moe picked up his beer and walked over to the end of the bar where Jeb was standing. Not sure about Jeb's last name, he thought it was something like Harris, or Harley, or Hogan, or something like that, but he didn't need the man's whole name for what he had in mind.

"Hello, Jeb," he said.

Jeb turned toward him. "Moe, what are you doin' in here? I ain't seen you in a coon's age."

"I had some business to take care of. How are you doin'?"

Jeb laughed. "Well, I ain't got no business to take care of, that's for sure. I mean I'll get a job here 'n there, but I ain't had me no regular job since I quit hauling freight for McKnight and Keaton. 'N them caught me sellin' some of the freight I was haulin' 'n fired me."

"How would you like to make a hunnert dollars?"

"What do I have to do?"

"Help me snatch up a woman is all."

"Is she a good-lookin' woman?"

"Yeah, she is, but that don't matter none."

"Are we plannin' on killin' 'er? Because if we are, we ought to have a little fun with 'er first."

"No, we ain't goin' to kill 'er, on account of we need 'er to do what we got to do. We got to take her to a feller I'm runnin' with, 'cause he wants to use her to get Duff MacCallister, who is her man, to come after her. This feller Duff MacCallister is the one that we're actual plannin' on killin'."

"Moe, you're part of an outlaw gang, ain't you?"

"That ain't somethin' you ought to ask someone, 'special since me 'n you don't really know each other all that well. I mean, I don't even know your last name."

"It's Jaco, Jeb Jaco."

"Huh. When I was thinkin' 'bout your last name, I warn't even close."

"You do belong to an outlaw gang, don't you?" Jeb asked.

"Why do you ask?"

"Because if you are, I'd like to join up with you."

"I ain't the one that decides on things like that. But if you'll help me snatch up this woman 'n take 'er where I got to take 'er, I'm pretty sure you'll be able to join up with us."

At the Interocean Hotel, Meagan was getting ready to go to The Elite Shop to see if Kathy had gotten in the new batch of material. It was a bolt of light blue satin, and in her mind's eye, she was already picturing the dress she would make from it.

Stepping out into the hall, she tapped lightly on the door to Duff's room. "Duff?" she called. "Duff, it's me. Meagan."

"Meagan who?"

"What?" Meagan called back, her voice increased in tone and volume.

Duff opened the door, then without breaking a smile he said, "Oh, this Meagan."

"Duff MacCallister, have you gone daft?"

Duff laughed. "Ah, lass, it was but a bit of fun I was having with you."

"How do I know you aren't keeping company with another Meagan?" she teased.

Duff pulled her into his room, shut the door, then embraced and kissed her. "Sure, lass, 'n one Meagan is enough for me," he said after the kiss. "'N would you be for telling me why 'tis that you came knocking on my door?"

"I'm going to The Elite Shop to see if the fabric I ordered has come in yet. I'll be back in time for lunch. That is, unless you want to go with me."

"'Twas thinking I was, that I might go to the newspaper office 'n have bit of a conversation with John."

"All right. I'll see you at lunch," Megan said, and with a quick kiss, she left.

Moe and Jeb were waiting across the street from the Interocean, watching the hotel where they knew that MacCallister and his woman were staying. They were about to give up when Moe saw the woman, whose name he had heard was Meagan, come out of the hotel.

"There she is," Moe said. "Go grab her."

"What do you mean, go grab her?"

"You're wantin' to join up with us, ain't you? Iffen you're the one that does the grabbin', I'll tell Bart it was you, 'n he'll for sure let you in."

"How do I grab her? If she puts up a fight, ever'one will see what's goin' on."

"That's easy," Moe said. "Put a gun to her head and invite her, real nice, to come with you. I'll stay here 'n keep watch."

"All right," Jeb agreed, starting across the street to confront the woman. "Miss?" he called out as he approached her. "Can you help me?"

"I don't know if I can or not," Meagan replied. "What do you need?"

Jeb pulled his pistol and pointed it at her. "I need you to come with me."

At that moment Duff came out of the hotel.

"Duff, I'm being taken!" Meagan called out.

Moving quickly, Jeb stepped behind Meagan and put his pistol to her head, just as Duff pulled his own pistol.

"I don't know who you are, mister, but this ain't none of your concern," Jeb said. "Now, put your gun away, or I'll blow this woman's brains out." He kept Meagan between himself and Duff, to deny Duff a shot. Jeb peeked around so that only one eye was showing. "I'm not bluffing. I will shoot this woman."

"*Gabh do dhealbh*, Duff," Meagan said in a very calm voice.

"What?" Jeb said, confused by the words. "What the hell did you just say?"

"The lass was speaking in Gaelic, 'n she told me to take my shot," Duff said as he pulled the trigger. The bullet hit Jeb in the eye, and he dropped without a sound.

"Damn," Moe said aloud, but quietly, from his position across the street. "There ain't no way I'm goin' to mess with MacCallister by myself."

Even as the shooting had drawn the curious to the scene, Moe walked away.

Chapter Twenty-nine

"I told you to do it, not hire someone else," Bart said angrily, when Moe reported what had happened.

"If I had done it myself, I would be lying dead on Sixteenth Street," Moe replied. "And look at it this way. There's no way they can trace Jeb back to us."

"He's got a point," Lou Martell said.

"MacCallister has to be stopped," Bart insisted.

"I'll do it," Black Lib offered.

"How the hell are you going to be able to do it, when nobody else has?" Lou asked.

"I'll make certain than when I go to snatch up the woman, Duff MacCallister won't be anywhere about."

"What makes you think you can get close enough to her to do it?" Moe asked.

"I'm a colored man."

Lou chuckled. "Well now, tell us somethin' we don't know."

"Colored men are invisible," Black Lib said.

"What the hell do you mean, you are invisible?"

"We are invisible because whites don't even see us. We are like a piece of furniture to them. We can move into a situation, and if we don't call attention to ourselves, a white man will never even see us do whatever it is that we have to do."

"Yeah," Bart said. "Yeah, now that I think about it, you are more 'n likely right. So, what do you have in mind?"

"I'm going to snatch MacCallister's woman, just like we planned."

"I didn't pick up my material yet," Meagan said. "I'm able to get around pretty well now, so I'm going to The Elite Shop again this morning."

"I would go with you, but I've got a meeting with Chief Peach this morning," Duff said.

"You mean I won't get another chance to practice my Gaelic?"

Duff laughed. "Sure, lass, 'n you had the chance to put your hobby to use. *Ha thu nad bhoireannach às deidh mo chridhe fhèin.*"

"I'm not just after your heart, Duff MacCallister," Meagan replied to the Gaelic with a seductive smile. "I've already captured it. You go on with your meeting. I'll be just fine."

Meagan gave Duff a quick kiss. "Now, off with you."

Black Liberty was standing in front of the hotel, leaning against a lamppost when MacCallister left the building. As Black Lib had pointed out to the others, Duff took no notice of the black man leaning against the post, no more than five feet away.

"You don't see me because I'm black and I'm not a

part of your world," Black Lib said so quietly that he couldn't be heard.

Moe had told the others how Duff MacCallister had broken up the plan by shooting Jeb, even as Jeb was holding his gun on the woman. But that wasn't about to happen again.

At the police station, Duff didn't even ask if he could see the chief. He went right to Chief Peach's office and knocked on the door.

"Here, you can't do that!" Sergeant Creech called out, just as the door to the office was opened.

"That's all right, Creech. Mr. MacCallister and I have an appointment," Then to Duff, Chief Peach added, "Come on in, Mr. MacCallister. I've been expecting you. Coffee?" He pointed to a coffeepot on a very small stove.

"Aye, coffee would be good, 'n I'm for thanking you for your generosity."

The chief poured a cup for Duff, then added to his own cup.

"His name was Jaco, Jeb Jaco," the chief said as he sat down. "I'm surprised that he got involved in this. He's been in jail a few times, but it's always been for some sort of petty crime. If he was trying to take Miss Parker, it was, no doubt, an effort to get to you. Perhaps to force you to quit looking into the matter."

"And would you be for telling me, Sheriff, why they would want me to stop my investigation?"

"The answer seems clear enough," Chief Peach said. "It's obvious Prescott wasn't alone in the embezzlement.

He had people with him, and they are afraid that if you continue the investigation, you'll find out who they are."

"Or that the ones after me not only stole from the bank, but shot Joel."

Chief Peach shook his head. "You aren't giving up on that, are you?"

"I'm not the only one who thinks that. Several in town are beginning to believe the same way I do."

"Yes, no doubt because of the inflammatory articles that new reporter is writing for the *Leader*."

"I don't consider them inflammatory, Chief. I consider them to be reasoned articles."

"Yes, well, when you are finished with your investigation, and you find nothing to change our finding of suicide, I fear you are going to be embarrassed."

Down the street from the police station, Black Lib, who was still slouched against the lamp pole, straightened up when he saw a very pretty blonde exit the hotel. He had never seen the woman before, but she fit the description.

"Miss Parker?" he called out to her.

"Yes?" Meagan said looking toward the black man who had addressed her.

He smiled, then raised his pistol and pointed it at her. "I just wanted to make sure it was you. I didn't want to snatch up the wrong woman."

"Why do you want to 'snatch me up'?"

"Bart and the others figure if we've got you, we can get to your man," Black Lib replied.

"You say 'we can get to your man.' Who would *we* be?"

"It don't matter who we is. You only got two choices, lady. You can see that I got a gun pointed toward you, so you'll either come with me alive or come with me dead."

"No, I have a third choice." She had never exhibited the slightest degree of fear, and the calm way she was speaking under those circumstances, somewhat unnerved Black Lib.

"Oh yeah? Tell me, lady, what would your third choice be?"

"I could kill you."

"Are you crazy? I'm holding a gun!"

"I'm holding a gun, too," Meagan said, producing a gun from the folds of her dress.

"Where the hell—?" That was as far as Black Lib got before he pulled back the hammer of his gun to shoot. He was too late.

Meagan had cocked the pistol even as she brought it up, and she pulled the trigger, putting a bullet in Black Lib's heart.

As the black man who had made his attempt on her collapsed, Meagan stood there a moment, holding the smoking pistol.

"We seen ever'thing, lady," a man called out from a wagon that pulled to a stop beside her. A woman was also in the wagon. "We'll stay here. When the police come, we'll tell 'em what happened, so's you don't need to worry none about being arrested."

"Thank you, sir," Meagan replied.

The sound of the pistol shot brought others to the scene, mostly animated by curiosity, but also two police officers.

"What happened?" one of the officers asked.

"I'll tell you exactly what happened," the wagon driver said. "Me 'n my wife seen it all. This here colored fella tried to attack the lady, like maybe he was goin' to rape her or somethin', 'n she fit 'im off by pullin' her own gun 'n shootin' 'im."

"Is that how it was, miss?" asked the other police officer.

Meagan started to say that it wasn't an attempted rape, but decided it would be easier to just validate the wagon driver's comment. "Yes," she answered.

"Lady, I'm goin' to need you to come on down to the police station so's we can get a statement from you."

Meagan knew that Duff was at the police station, and she could think of nowhere she would rather go. "Yes, I'll be glad to."

Duff was just getting ready to leave the police station when he saw Meagan come in. At first he thought she had come to look for him, but he learned very quickly that she had shot an assailant, and was there to answer to it.

"What do we have here, Marvin?" Sergeant Creech said.

"This here woman shot 'n kilt someone who was goin' to try 'n have his way with her," the policeman replied.

"Meagan!" Duff said, hurrying to her side. "Are you all right."

"My would-be assailant had no intention of 'having his way with me,' unless his way was to abduct me. Duff, he said Bart and the others figured if they could get me, they could get my man. It's obvious now, that they are after you any way they can."

"Did he tell you who Bart was?"

"No, we didn't have much conversation after that. He was holding a gun on me and didn't realize I also had one. By the time he did realize it, it was too late. I shot him."

"Look here, lady, you didn't say nothin' 'bout that when me 'n Tony come upon you while ago," Marvin said.

"I thought I would wait until I got here to make my statement," Megan replied.

Duff turned to Chief Peach, who had accompanied him to the desk sergeant's area. "That should prove to you that they are after me, any way they can get to me."

Chief Peach shook his head. "Oh, I don't doubt that there's folks tryin' to get to you. But you're pretty well known in this area, 'n they could be one of a dozen reasons why someone would be after you. It isn't necessarily because of your investigation into whether or not Prescott embezzled the bank, then killed himself."

"You said one of a dozen reasons. You will be for conceding that one of the reasons could be to stop my investigation, will you not?"

Chief Peach nodded. "Yes, I'll admit that could be a reason. I don't believe it is, but I'll not close my mind to it."

"You're sure he wasn't just trying to rob you, or, uh, have his way with you, as the quaint phrase goes?"

"Oh, I'm quite sure what his purpose was. He was most explicit in telling me what his plans were. He said 'I just wanted to make sure it was you. I didn't want to snatch up the wrong woman.'

"I asked why did he want to snatch me up, and he said Bart and the others figured that if they could get me, they could get my man. That seems a pretty definite motive to me," Meagan said.

Peach nodded. "I reckon I believe you, only there ain't nothin' that needs to be done now, on account of you already killed him."

At that moment John came through the front door of the police station. He had heard about the shooting, and like a good newspaperman, was following up on it to get the story. He took notes as Meagan told him the same thing she had told Chief Peach.

From the *Leader*:

Second Attempt on Miss Parker Thwarted

by

JOHN CUNNINGHAM

Once again, an attempt has been made to take Miss Meagan Parker as hostage. And while the first attempt was broken up by Duff MacCallister, Miss Parker saved herself this time by drawing a pistol and energizing a bullet that entered the heart of the perpetrator with the effect of instant death.

Why these repeated attempts to abduct Miss Parker? There can be but one reason. Those behind the attempts believe that they can use Miss Parker as leverage against Duff MacCallister, who has a personal interest in the safety of Miss Parker. The perpetrators, no doubt, believe that if they have her as their prisoner, they can affect some influence over

> MacCallister's actions. No doubt, they reason, the threat of harm to MacCallister's close friend, could force him to suspend the investigation into the alleged suicide of Joel Prescott.
>
> Any why, you may ask, does it matter to someone whether or not Joel Prescott committed suicide? If Prescott did not commit suicide, it stands to reason that neither did he embezzle the money. And if he didn't, who did? The answer is quite simple. Those who are attempting to stop Duff MacCallister's investigation, are the same people who murdered Joel Prescott, and stole the money from the bank.

By the time Meagan and Duff returned to the Interocean Hotel, Elmer and Wang had heard of the incident and were waiting in the lobby.

"Are you all right?" Elmer asked anxiously.

"Yes, Elmer, I'm fine."

"She's a lot better than the brigand she shot," Duff said with a little chuckle.

"That's the second time they've come after you," Elmer said. "No, it's the third time, seein' as how you was already shot one time before. 'N that time they nearly done it, on account of they shot you."

"They weren't after me then, Elmer. They were after Duff."

"Yeah, well it don't make no never mind whether they was after you or not. You was the one what got shot. 'N now we know they're after you now, 'cause that's what the feller said a-fore you shot 'im."

"That's true," Meagan agreed.

"So, here's the thing," Elmer said. "You've showed us you can handle yourself just real good. But if they's goin' to be people what keeps on a-comin' for you, seems to me like one of us should be with you all the time, from now on."

"Nonsense. I don't need to be watched over like a week-old calf," Meagan replied. "You three have others things to do. You're investigating what happened to Joel Prescott."

"Aye, but if you're to be believing John's newspaper articles, the people who are comin' after you are connected to what happened to Joel," Duff said.

"So what you are saying is, you want to use me as bait," Meagan replied.

Duff held up his hand and shook his head. "Nae, now, lass, I dinnae say anything like that, I was just—"

"I'll do it," Meagan interrupted Duff's response with a laugh. "I'll let one of you be my escort everywhere I go. Why, I'll be the most popular female in town."

Chapter Thirty

Outlaw cabin

"I told you it was a waste of time sendin' a colored boy to do a man's job," Lou Martell said.

"Do you have a better idea?" Bart asked.

"Yeah, I do. If you really want that woman took, send someone who can do it."

"You, perhaps?" Bart replied.

"Yeah, me."

"You know she don't go nowhere now without someone with her. If it ain't MacCallister hisself, it's that old man or the Chinaman."

"That's why I won't be goin' by myself. I'll be takin' Willard with me."

"You can try it by yourself, but you better look out for the Chinaman. He's real tricky," Bart said.

"You don't need to tell me nothin' 'bout him," Lou said. "We done run into him oncet. He fights real good, 'n does things I ain't never seen before. But all the fighting he does won't stop a bullet."

"All right," Bart said. "If you think you can do it, go bring the woman in."

* * *

Standing in the lobby of the Interocean Hotel, Duff said to Meagan, Elmer, and Wang, "I'm going down to the courthouse this morning. I would like to get a warrant from the judge that would give me access to the bank's accounts."

"Are you sure you want to do that?" Meagan asked.

"Aye. Why would I nae want to be lookin' at the books?"

"Duff, you are so convinced that Joel didn't commit suicide and didn't embezzle from the bank. What if you find out that he did do it?"

"Tell me, lass, and are you for thinking he did it?"

"No, I'm convinced that he didn't do it, but at this point, if he actually did do it, I'm not sure I would like to know. It would be . . . hard to discover we were wrong about him."

"The truth is the truth, Meagan, and I'll be for finding it, one way or another."

"Yes," she replied. "I suppose that's right."

"Why dinnae you wait in your room until I get back?"

"Duff MacCallister, would you be for tellin' me now, how is it I can be bait unless I walk around town with a target on m' back?" Meagan asked, mimicking, as she so often did, Duff's Scottish brogue.

"You don't need to worry none about her," Elmer said. "Me 'n the heathen will look out for her."

"And don't forget, I can look out for myself pretty well," Meagan added.

* * *

Fifteen minutes later, Duff was in the courthouse requesting an audience with Judge Jerry Heckemeyer.

"Your name, sir?" the clerk asked.

"MacCallister. Duff MacCallister."

The clerk smiled. "Would you be the same MacCallister that the *Leader* reporter has been talking about?"

"Aye, that would be me."

"Ha, I bet you want to talk about Prescott committing suicide, don't you? Well, it wasn't the judge who made the decision. It was the coroner. He's the one you should see."

"Would you be for telling the judge I'd like to talk to him?"

"All right, all right. Hold your horses. I'll tell him." The clerk tapped lightly on a closed door, stepped inside, and a moment later came back out. "His Honor will see you now."

"Thank you."

Judge Heckemeyer was a large man with rolls on his neck and a face so fat that his eyes looked out from sunken pools of flesh.

"Mr. MacCallister, I'm sure my clerk told you that I have nothing to do with declaring the death of Joel Prescott to be by suicide. That decision was made by the coroner, Tom Goff, although I must say that I agree with him."

"Your Honor, I would not be for trying to get you to override the coroner without enough evidence to present to you so you could make such a decision."

"And you think you have enough evidence, do you?

"I dinnae think so. But I am working on it, 'n I'll need a warrant from you."

"A warrant? What kind of warrant?"

"A search warrant."

"A search warrant?" Judge Heckemeyer said. "I don't understand. What do you want to search?"

"I want to examine the accounts at the Cattleman's Bank of Cheyenne."

"What? No, impossible. Why on earth would you want such a warrant?"

"Since I dinnae believe Joel killed himself, I also dinnae believe that he embezzled the bank's money. 'Tis hoping I am, that I might be able to prove that by examining the books."

"Mr. MacCallister, even if I thought there might be some validity to your argument, I can't just grant a search warrant to a private citizen. Now, if Chief Peach were to come to me with such a request, I might be predisposed to honoring it."

"I'll nae for being asking this as a private citizen."

"Then pray tell what are you, Mr. MacCallister, if not a private citizen?"

Duff showed Judge Heckemeyer the governor's warrant, appointing him as a territorial marshal.

"Oh," Judge Heckemeyer said after examining the document. "In that case, I suppose I can grant you a warrant."

The cabin

Moe Conyers had taken a chair out onto the front porch and was sitting there, watching a couple of squirrels cavorting in a limber pine tree. Actually, he was caught up in deep thought. Moe knew that Lou Martell had volunteered himself and Emmet Willard to go into town to snatch up MacCallister's woman, but Moe didn't give them much chance for success. So far everyone who had tried had been killed. If Martell and Willard wound up getting themselves kilt, there wouldn't be but two of 'em left, him 'n Bart Jenkins.

Moe's ruminations were interrupted by what he saw out on the road. It was frightening enough that he hurried back into the cabin. "Bart, they's a bunch o' riders comin' toward us," he said anxiously.

"A bunch of riders? What does that mean? How many are there?"

"I counted seven," Moe said.

"Get your rifle," Bart ordered. "Better get some extra shells, too."

"Lord a'mighty, Bart, you ain't a-plannin' on fightin' 'em, are you?" Moe asked. "I just told you they's seven o' them. 'N case you ain't took a count of how many of us there is in this cabin, I'll tell you. They's only two of us."

"I don't care. I ain't goin' to just—" Bart halted in midsentence. "Hold on. I know that feller that's in front, 'n he ain't likely to be ridin' with no lawmen."

"So what are we goin' to do?" Moe asked.

"We'll step out on the front porch 'n see what they want."

"Are you sure that's a good idea? I mean seein' as they's so many of 'em, 'n you only know that one feller."

Bart laughed. "Damn, Moe, it warn't two minutes ago, that you was ready to surrender."

Moe chuckled. "Yeah. Yeah, you're right."

The two men stepped out onto the front porch.

* * *

"That's them," LeRoy Semmes said to the others as he and the six other riders approached the cabin.

"You think they'll take us on?" Craig Lawton asked.

Semmes snickered. "They don't have no say-so in the matter."

Semmes knew Jenkins, but he didn't know the man with him. Both were standing on the front porch, and neither of them were armed. The situation put Semmes in control.

"Hello, Semmes," Bart greeted a little apprehensively. "What brings you to this neck of the woods?"

"We come to join up with you," Semmes said.

"Join up with us for what?"

"You know for what," Semmes said. "Maybe you better read this." He held down a letter for Bart.

He took it, then read it. "Looks like I don't have no choice. I have to take you on."

Semmes look around. "Jenkins, looks to me like you been whittled down right good. I was told they was once eight of you. Now they's only you two?"

"There are four of us. The other two is in town to take care of some business for us."

"You can do better 'n that," Semmes said.

"What do you mean, better 'n that?" Bart asked with a look of confusion.

Semmes chuckled. "Me 'n you is all partners now. So you can tell me why you sent two men into town. Who'd you send inter town, 'n why are they there?"

"I sent Lou Martell 'n Emmet Willard into town to

snatch up MacCallister's wife," Bart said. "We figure that once we've got her, he'll come after her, then we'll have 'im just where we want 'im."

"I know Martell. He's a good man, 'n might be able to get the woman you're a-wantin'. Onliest thing is, that woman what's with MacCallister all the time ain't his wife. She's just his girlfriend."

"Girlfriend?"

"Yes."

Jenkins chuckled. "That might be even better. Ain't no man who won't go after his girlfriend, but they's more 'n likely lots of men that'd just as soon leave their wife there."

Semmes and the other men laughed.

"All right. We'll take you on. I know you, Semmes, 'n if you say these men with you are good men, why, I'm willin' to take your word for it. But I don't know none of 'em."

"You fellers all line up, so's I can point you out," Semmes said.

As if forming up in an army detail, the six men stood in a straight line. Semmes started down the line and Bart went with him as if an officer of the guard and the sergeant of the guard were inspecting the guard relief.

"This here is Craig Lawton. He's 'bout the best shot I ever seen." Semmes went on to the rest of the men, naming them one by one as he pointed to them. "This here is Frank Sweeny, Billy Ogden, Frank McCain, Gus Hagen, and this little feller here is Stump Waters."

The others laughed at Semmes calling Stump Waters a "little feller," as he was at least six foot four, and with a very muscular build.

* * *

Unaware of the new additions to their gang, Lou Martell and Emmet Willard had come into town in a wagon expecting to be considered by all who saw them as just a couple of workingmen. Also, once they got the woman they had come for, the wagon would be the easiest way to get her out of town.

They parked the wagon just around the corner from the hotel on Capitol Street, but close enough to Sixteenth Street that they could see the front door of the hotel.

"They say she's a purty woman," Willard said.

"Yeah, she is a pretty woman. I've seen her."

"Bein' as she is a purty woman, 'n we ain't got no women out in the cabin with us, do you think maybe we could, uh, you know, have a little fun with her oncet we've got her?"

"Here she comes," Lou said, not answering Willard's question.

Meagan had just stepped out of the hotel.

"I see her," Willard replied. "How are we going to work this?"

"You pull the wagon right up beside her." Lou said. "As soon as I jump out, I'll grab her and put a handkerchief soaked in chloroform over her nose. That'll make her pass out before she can struggle or even call out. Then we can throw her in the back of the wagon and get her out of town quickly, before anyone is the wiser."

"All right," Willard said as slapped the reins against the team, then hauled back on them to cause the wagon to turn to the right.

They had just made the turn when Elmer and Wang stepped out of the hotel behind Meagan.

"Oh, hell no," Lou said. "I ain't goin' to deal with them two again."

"Wait, ain't that the Chinaman we tried to grab up in Chugwater?" Emmet asked.

"Yeah. Let's get of here."

Emmet slapped the reins against the back of the team of horses, and they broke into a trot.

"Hey, Wang, did you see them two men in the wagon?" Elmer asked as the wagon moved quickly down the street.

"They were the same men," Wang said.

"Ha, you know what I think?"

"They were after *Xiǎojiě* Meagan."

"You damn right they was after Miss Meagan, 'n we scairt 'em off. What do you think of that?" he asked Meagan. "Me 'n Wang scairt 'em off."

"Oh, I feel so safe being protected by such strong men," Meagan teased.

"Yeah," Elmer replied sheepishly. "I guess I was sort of tootin' my own horn there."

"Toot away, Elmer. I'm glad to have the two of you with me," she said in a tone that apologized for her joke at Elmer's expense.

"What are we going to tell Bart?" Willard asked as the two men returned to the outlaw cabin.

"Hell, we'll just tell him that if he wants that woman

so bad, he can go get her his ownself. As long as she has them two with her, it ain't likely that no one, two, or hell even three or four, will be able to get her."

"He prob'ly ain't goin' to like that," Willard suggested.

"Hell, it don't make me no never mind whether he likes it or not," Lou replied. "That's just the way it is."

Chapter Thirty-one

As the two men came in sight of the cabin, Lou, who was driving, called out to the team. "Whoa."

The wagon stopped.

"What you stoppin' for?" Willard asked.

"Look there in the corral. How many horses do you see?" Lou asked.

"I see eight. No, I see nine."

"They's only four of us 'n our two horses is makin' up this team. Where'd all them extra horses come from?"

"Damn, you think it's a sheriff's posse?" Willard asked.

Lou looked glanced at Willard with an expression of condescending expression on his face. "Willard, do you really think a posse would unsaddle their horses, then turn 'em loose in the corral?"

"Uh, no. But I wonder who all them other fellers is?"

Lou snapped the reins over the team, and the wagon started forward again. "Well, I reckon we are about to find out."

When the confused Lou and Willard stepped into the

cabin, they saw nine men. They had left only two men behind.

"Fellers," Bart said to them, "Meet our new partners."

Howell, Wyoming Territory

Howell was a small town, existing only to serve the nearby ranch owners, their families, and the cowboys who worked the ranches. Howell had one church, one doctor, one blacksmith, one general store, and four saloons. The man standing at the bar in the Spur and Saddle Saloon looked no different from any of the other cowboys. He was wearing denim trousers, a blue shirt, and scuffed boots. However, two things separated him from the other cowboys. He wore a low-crowned black hat with a flat top and wore his pistol holster low and tied down.

"Another beer, mister?" the bartender asked, stepping up to see if he could bring the customer another beer. When the man looked up from his beer, the bartender gasped and stepped back.

The man's eyes were technically brown, but the shade of the brown made the irises look yellow. Some said that looking into the eyes of James Hill was like staring into the very bowels of Hell, and the oversized pupils made it look as if the devil himself was staring back.

"I am looking for Roy Mason." Hill's voice had all the resonant quality of a hissing snake.

"He's . . . he's not here," the bartender said nervously.

"I'm going to look around this room. If I find him, I will kill him, then I'll kill you for lying to me."

"He's over there at the table with those three other men. He's the only one wearing a hat."

"You just saved your life," the man called Evil hissed. He stepped away from the bar, then looked over toward the table. "Mason," he called.

The man in the hat looked up toward him. "What do you want?"

"I've come to kill you," Hill said.

At those words all the other patrons within the saloon got up and rushed to the walls to be out of harm's way. Notably, the three men with Mason did not move.

"You're the one they call Evil?" Mason asked.

"I've been called that."

"Well, Evil, I don't know how much education you have, or even if you can count to four, but if you can, you'll see there are four of us here. Four to your one."

Mason and the three men at the table stood up, and spread out a bit before they all turned to face him.

"So, if you're goin' to do it, boy, commence a-shootin'."

With that shouted challenge, Mason and the three men made desperate grabs for their pistols.

Evil's fanning method of shooting his gun sounded, not like individual shots, but as one sustained roar. When it was over, Mason and all three of the men lay dead on the floor. Not one had of them had been able to extract their pistol from the holster.

Stunned silence filled the saloon.

Finally, the bartender spoke. "Mister, what did you kill Mason for?"

"Because I was paid to kill him."

"But what about them other three boys?"

"I threw them in for free," Hill said.

"Mr. Hill?" A young boy was standing just inside the

door of the saloon, wide-eyed over what he had just seen. He was wearing a Western Union cap.

"Yeah," Hill said.

The boy held out a telegram with a trembling hand. "This is for you.

At the Cheyenne Leader

At about the same time Lou and Willard were getting acquainted with the new men, Duff was standing just before the counter, and the smell of ink and freshly cut newsprint drifted out from the composing and printing room.

"Yes, sir, would you like to place an advertisement with us?" an attractive young woman asked, greeting him with a broad smile.

"Nae, I would like to be for seeing Mr. Cunningham."

"Ah, yes, John Cunningham is quickly becoming our most popular reporter. He's here. May I ask who you are?"

"The name is Duff MacCallister."

"Oh, my, Duff MacCallister, is it? Yes, Mr. Cunningham has written about you. Please, wait here, and I will summon him." The young woman disappeared into the back of the office then returned a moment later with John right beside her.

"Duff," John said with a big smile. He extended his hand. "What brings you here?"

"Tell me John, in all your education, would you be for understanding how to read a bank's account books?"

"Well, I suppose I can," John said. "I did write a book about business, but I don't know how it's been received because I haven't heard anything about it since," John replied. "What's this all about?"

"I've got a warrant from Judge Heckemeyer to allow me to examine the Cattleman's Bank accounts, 'n 'tis thinking I am, that it would be a good thing if I had someone with me who would be for knowing what he was looking for. Would you come look at the books with me?"

"I'd be glad to." John turned to the young woman. "Marjane, if Mr. Morrow or Mr. Sullivan asks about me, tell them I am researching a story with Duff MacCallister."

"Yes, sir, Mr. Cunningham," Marjane said respectfully.

"Nice young lady," Duff said as they left the newspaper office.

"Yes, she is," John agreed. "You have no idea what it feels like, not only to regain my self-respect, but the respect of others." He chuckled. "And it all started when you shot the gun out of my hand."

Duff chuckled as well. "'N 'tis glad I am to have been of service."

The CLOSED FOR BUSINESS sign was still on the door of the Cattlemen's Bank of Cheyenne when Duff and John arrived. The door was locked, so Duff banged on it hard enough to be heard if anyone was in the bank. His knocking on the door was awarded by the appearance of Eli Kendrick.

"Mr. MacCallister, Mr. Cunningham," Eli said. "What brings you here?"

"We'd like to take a look at your books," Duff said.

"Oh, I'm afraid I couldn't let just anyone off the street examine the books. That wouldn't be fitting," Eli replied.

"I'm not just anyone off the street. As you already know, I'm a marshal of the territory."

"You, yes, but what about him?" Eli asked with a disapproving glance at John.

"I have appointed Mr. Cunningham as my deputy," Duff replied.

"Yes, well, even so, I still can't let you examine the books without a—"

"Warrant," Duff said, completing Eli's sentence. "Here is a warrant from Judge Heckemeyer, authorizing us to look at your books. Would you be for providing them, please?" Duff nodded toward what he knew had been Joel Prescott's office. "We'll be waiting in Joel's office."

Eli cleared his throat. "That's my office now."

"Then I'm sure you can find us a suitable place," John said.

A few minutes later, with Duff and John ensconced in what was once Eli Kendrick's office, the former vice president presented them with the bank accounting books. "I'm sure you will be able to see for yourselves what happened to the money."

Immediately, John began to examine them. "Oh, my," he said after a few moments.

"What is it?" Duff asked.

"There have been several large transfers over the last few months. Fifty thousand dollars to Savings and Trust Bank in Laramie, fifty thousand dollars to the Bank of Boise, and one hundred and twenty-five thousand dollars to Deseret Bank in Salt Lake City.

Duff got a confused look on his face. "Why would such a thing be done?"

John looked up. "It isn't unusual for banks to disburse funds with other banks. That provides them with a type of insurance so that if one bank would be robbed or destroyed by fire, they wouldn't lose all their money. However, when they do this, they also maintain enough cash on hand so as to be able to do business. It just isn't feasible for a bank to be totally devoid of all funds.

"Mr. Kendrick, have you contacted these banks to inquire about the deposits?" John asked.

"Yes, I have."

"Then I don't understand. Why haven't you brought some of it back to this bank, so that you can continue to operate?"

"Because despite what these books say, there are no funds in any of the banks listed there. I'm afraid this was all a front to cover up what Joel was actually doing."

"And what was he actually doing?" Duff asked.

"Why, isn't it obvious? He was stealing the money."

When John told Marjane that he was researching a story, it was actually no more than a throwaway line. But a story did develop from his visit with Duff to the Cattleman's Bank, and it ran in the very next issue of the paper.

Unanswered Questions

by

JOHN CUNNINGHAM

It is well known that the Cattleman's Bank of Cheyenne failed. But where, exactly, did the money go? A thorough examination of the bank records suggests that every cent of deposit in the Cattlemen's Bank of Cheyenne, totaling $201,659.82, was withdrawn and redeposited in other banks. While spreading out the bank's assets is a common practice in order to protect its depositors from some catastrophe, natural or otherwise, no bank would willingly redeposit every dollar, leaving its own accounts empty.

In this case however, the bank account books show that is exactly what happened. However, telegraphic inquiries with the banks where the money was supposed to be indicated that the money had been withdrawn, with no specific determination of where the funds went. If the money isn't where the bank records say it is, where is it? And if, as was initially believed, Joel Prescott took that money, he would have had to make some disposition of it, such as redepositing it in another bank or banks. That doesn't seem to be the case.

It seems quite unlikely that having so much money secreted away from prying eyes, he would leave it untouched, then in a final act of remorse, take his own life. Would not a remorseful person simply return the money to the bank's coffers?

The note found on the body was suspect from the very beginning, and examination of the wounds on Joel Prescott's body showed them to be inconsistent with wounds which are self-inflicted.

I think all evidence thus far uncovered suggests most strongly that Joel Prescott did not take his own life, but was indeed, murdered. Duff MacCallister, following that same reasoning and working under a commission from Governor Warren, is investigating this matter and, I am proud to say, I have been deputized to help with the investigation. I shall do so under the banner of the First Amendment, which guarantees a free press. With that protection, I will continue to act in the role of investigative reporter, as it is called in journalism. And while I will not write anything that may compromise the investigation, I will share with you, my readers, the latest news in the progress of the investigation.

Chapter Thirty-two

After John lifted the very first sheet of newsprint off the press, he hurried back to the Cannady Boarding House, then went upstairs to knock on the door to Nettie's apartment.

"Yes?" she called from the other side of the door.

"Nettie, it's me, John."

The door opened. "Come in, John, please come in. I've just made some coffee. Would you like a cup?"

Although the small apartment didn't have a kitchen, it did have a small coal-oil burner.

"Yes, thank you. I would love a cup of coffee."

"What brings you here?" Nettie called back over her shoulder as she lifted the coffeepot from the brazier.

"I wanted to give you this," John said, holding up the proof sheet.

"Oh, what is it?"

"It is, or rather it will be, today's edition of the paper, and this is the very first page of the print run."

Nettie brought the coffee cup to John, then took the page from him. As he drank his coffee, he studied her face while she was reading, trying to discern her reaction to it by the expression on her face.

When she finished reading the article, she looked toward him and smiled. "John, this is a wonderful story. Not only is it beautifully written, I think it is just provocative enough even the most entrenched in the belief that Joel killed himself might begin to have second thoughts."

"I certainly hope so."

As they were engaged in conversation, there was a knock on the door, and a man's voice called out. "Nettie, are you here?"

"Yes, Eli, the door is unlocked. Please come in."

Eli Kendrick stepped into Nettie's apartment, carrying a box of Whitman Chocolates. He had a big grin on his face. "Hello, Nettie, I brought you some—" He stopped in midsentence, and the smile left his face when he saw John sitting there holding a cup of coffee. "Oh, uh, I didn't know that you had company."

"John just brought me an advanced copy of today's newspaper," Nettie said. "Wait until you read it. It's beautifully written and will, I'm certain, cause a lot of people to rethink their ideas on what happened. Won't you join us? I've coffee ready."

Eli stared at John. "No, I . . . under the circumstances, I don't think it would be appropriate."

The expression on Nettie's face reflected her confusion over Eli's strange remark. "Under the circumstances? I don't understand. What do you mean?"

"I must go," Eli said as he set the box down, then started toward the door.

"Thanks for the chocolates," Nettie called out to him.

Without an answer or a response of any kind, Eli stepped through the door and pulled it shut behind him.

"What do you suppose that was about?" Nettie asked.

"Nettie, do you really not know?"

"No, I don't have the slightest—" she stopped in mid-sentence, gasped, and put her hand over her mouth. "Oh, my. Do you think he might have been jealous?"

John chuckled and nodded. "Oh yes. You might say the Green Monster came upon him. That's exactly what he was."

"But why would he be jealous? I've never given him any reason to think that I would consider him as a"—she paused, looking for the words—"romantic interest. I have known him for five years, and our relationship has never been anything other than Joel's friend, and the vice president of the bank."

"You are an exceptionally attractive woman, Nettie. And you are a widow. There will be men like Eli . . . and me," he added, "who might seek to gain your attention and perhaps win your affection."

Nettie put her hand on his and smiled at him, but she didn't speak.

The cabin

"Are you telling me that you didn't even try?" Bart asked, after Lou gave him his report.

"We would have been killed," Lou said. "And what good would it do me to be dead, even if we did wind up getting the money? I would be as broke then as I am now, and worse, I would be dead."

"Lou's right, Bart," Moe said. "Look how many men we have lost so far. Yes, not all of them were with our original group, but there sure have been a lot of 'em kilt, enough that we should have learned by now that it's dangerous to mess with Duff MacCallister."

"All right," Bart said. "Stop trying to snatch MacCallister's woman."

"I thought you said that taking MacCallister's woman would mean he would come after her and we could set up an ambush," Lou said.

"Our friend is sending us someone who deals in situations just like this. I'm quite sure he will be able to handle the situation for us," Bart said.

"Our friend?"

"Our silent partner, you might say."

"Who is he sending?"

"He'll be here in a couple of days. Then you can see for yourself."

Two days later the person who had been sent by the silent partner arrived. Because they had been told he would be coming, they were on the lookout for him, and as the rider approached, all eleven men were on the front porch to greet him. The rider who dismounted was a most unprepossessing man who wouldn't warrant a second look, unless someone saw his eyes. His eyes were yellow, and the pupils so large, black, and intense, that it made one think that he could see all the way don't to your soul.

"Boys, this is James Hill," Bart said.

"James Hill? You mean the one they call Evil?"

Hill smiled. "Yeah, I've been called that," he said in a sibilant voice.

"How many men have you kilt, Evil?" Moe asked.

"Do you mean how many have I been paid to kill? Or just how many I've killed?"

"That isn't any of our business," Bart said, interrupting a discussion he feared might become troublesome. "What's important is the man he is going to kill next."

"Duff MacCallister," Willard said.

Bart nodded. "I've been thinkin' about this, 'n I believe it's the best way to go."

"How much is it costin' us?" Lou asked.

"Five hundred dollars now, 'n two thousand more when it's done."

"Twenty-five hundred dollars? That's a lot of money," Lou said.

"Yes," Bart agreed. "It is a lot of money, but we have no choice. MacCallister needs to be stopped."

"We ain't hardly even got two thousand dollars, have we?" Moe asked.

"No, we don't," Bart replied. "But Hill has agreed to wait until we get our money before he gets the rest of his payment."

"When are you goin' to do it?" Lou asked.

The man sometimes called "Evil" didn't answer Lou. He just looked at Lou for a few, brief seconds, and Lou felt a little shiver, as if someone had stepped on his grave.

"I will go now," Evil said.

"Moe, you know what MacCallister looks like. Go with Hill so you can point out MacCallister. You'll probably find him in the Red Bull. I've learned that he spends a lot of time there."

"All right," Moe answered, though it was obvious he wasn't too pleased with the assignment.

Duff and Meagan were having a drink in the Red Bull. She had invited Nettie to join them, and he had invited John. It wasn't particularly designed to put them together since Duff was unaware of their growing relationship.

Nettie arrived first, and she and Meagan were in a spirited conversation when John approached the table. He stopped and stood for a moment as if hesitant to approach any closer.

"Would you be for having a seat, John?" Duff asked.

John looked directly at Nettie. "Do you mind if I . . ." He finished his question with a wave of his hand toward the empty chair.

"Of course I don't mind," Nettie replied. "Why should I mind?"

"The Whitman chocolates?"

"What?" Meagan asked, confused by the cryptic response.

"I was there when Mr. Kendrick came calling on you, carrying a box of chocolates. I just thought that maybe . . ."

"John, Eli Kendrick was my husband's executive officer when they were in the army, and now he is the vice president of the bank. Though now, I expect he is the president of the bank. And that is the extent of our relationship. Now, please join us."

"You're wrong," Duff said as John was taking his seat.

"What?" John asked. "Why do you say I'm wrong?"

"I'm nae talking about you, John. 'Tis the lass who is wrong."

"Duff, whatever are you talking about?" Meagan asked, voicing the question that the surprised look on the faces of John and Nettie were posing.

"Kendrick is nae the president of the bank." Duff nodded toward Nettie. "Joel owned the bank, 'n now the lass here, owns it. 'N because she owns the bank, that means she is the one who is president of the bank."

"Oh," Nettie said, putting her hand to her mouth. "Oh, I suppose I am president of the bank, aren't I? I never thought about that."

"Yes, but unfortunately, it is a bank that is insolvent, thanks to the man who murdered Joel," John said.

"This is why I wanted to meet with you," Duff said to John. "'Tis thinking, I am, that if you would do a story about the lass here being the new president of the bank, that it might stir up a bit of interest."

"Duff, I can't believe I'm hearing this," Meagan said. "It's enough that you're using me as bait. Now you're planning on using Nettie as well?"

"I'll do it," Nettie said quickly. "I'll do anything that will help prove my husband's innocence and find the man who killed him."

"All right. In that case I'll do the article," John said resolutely.

As John was agreeing to do the article, James Hill stepped through the swinging batwing doors of the Cowboy's Haven saloon, and as had been directed by Bart Jenkins, Moe Conyers was with him.

A couple of the bar girls came toward them wearing practiced smiles and not much more.

"Hello, boys," one of them said, then looking into James Hill's eyes, the smile left, to be replaced by facial expressions of absolute terror.

"Get out of my way," Hill hissed.

The two girls hurried back to the far side of the room.

"It's Evil," one of the saloon patrons said.

"He's killed more 'n thirty people."

"What's he doin' here?"

"Anybody seen MacCallister?" Moe asked.

"I just seen 'im over to the Red Bull," said one of the men standing at the bar. "What are you lookin' for him for?"

Evil glared with such intensity at the man who had just asked a question, that, frightened, he turned away and stared into his beer.

"Let's go," Evil said, heading toward the door without another word.

Moe, who thought they might have a drink and visit for a few minutes, had to hurry to catch up with him.

"Where is the Red Bull?" Evil asked.

"This here is Fifteenth Street. The Bull is over on Sixteenth," Moe replied.

Evil stepped right out into the street without regard to the wagon that was approaching.

The driver hauled back on his team. "Hey, why don't you watch where you're goin', you damn fool?" the driver shouted.

Instead of hurrying to get out of the way of the team, Evil stopped and stared at the driver.

The driver, facing the intense glare, had second thoughts about what he had intended to add to his earlier outburst. "Uh, my fault. I was going too fast. Go ahead and cross."

Moe, who had waited for the wagon, hurried to cross with Evil.

"That's the Red Bull," Moe said a few minutes later as they approached the saloon. It was a larger, and obviously much nicer, establishment than the Cowboy Haven, and was easily identified by the large red bull above the sign.

James Hill pushed through the batwing doors with Moe just behind. "Do you see him?"

Moe looked around for a moment then nodded. "Yeah, that's him." He pointed to the table where Duff and Meagan were sitting with John and Nettie. "He's back there at the table with three others. He's the big guy with the blue shirt, sittin' back against the wall. How are you going to do this? Call 'im out, or what?"

"I'm goin' to kill 'im, 'n how I do it ain't your problem," Evil said.

"All right, but you need know that he is very fast."

"I'm going to kill him," Evil repeated, almost as if it were a mantra. He walked over to the table.

When Duff and the others looked up, they saw that he had already drawn his pistol.

"You're MacCallister?" Evil asked, looking at the man Moe had pointed out.

"Aye, I'm MacCallister."

"The rest of you, leave the table," Evil ordered.

John and Nettie got up, but Meagan remained.

"Girlie, I'm goin' to kill MacCallister 'n if you're still sitting there, like as not, I'll kill you, too."

"Leave the table, Meagan," Duff said.

"Duff, I—"

"Please, lass, I would nae want for anything to happen to you."

"All right," Meagan said as she reluctantly got up from the table and walked over to join Nettie. John had disappeared somewhere.

"You're planning on killing me?" Duff asked, his voice as calm as if he were ordering a glass of Scotch.

Evil smiled, but somehow the smile made his features look even more grotesque. "I'm getting paid a lot of money to kill you."

"All right. But let's have our fight out in the street," Duff suggested. "That way 'tis less chance some innocent person will be hit."

"What fight?" Evil replied.

"Dinnae you just challenge me?" Duff asked.

"I ain't bein' paid to fight you. I'm bein' paid to kill you," Evil said. He raised his pistol, pointed it toward Duff, then cocked it.

The roar of the gunshot filled the saloon, and bounced off the walls. But the sound did not come from Evil's gun. Half of James Hill's head was blown off as blood, bits of bone, and brain matter erupted from the wound.

Duff looked over toward John, who was holding the double-barrel, ten-gauge shotgun as a little wisp of smoke was still curling up from the muzzle of the gun.

"I saw you take the gun from behind the bar, 'n 'twas my hope that you would have time to use it," Duff said.

Moe Conyers, who had not moved from the door, was shocked by what he had just witnessed. He stood there for no more than a moment longer, watching the reaction of the others. Then he left the saloon.

"Bart sure as hell ain't goin' to like this." Moe didn't know if he spoke the words aloud, or just thought them.

Chapter Thirty-three

John considered writing an article about the death of James Hill, aka Evil. It certainly was newsworthy. James Hill was one of the most noted and feared gunfighters in the entire West. But because John was the one who had killed Hill, he wasn't comfortable writing the story, so he asked Morrow, one of the publishers, if he would write it.

"I suppose I can," Morrow said. "After all, I was doing most of the writing before we hired you. But the truth is, I'm a little hesitant to write anything now. I'm afraid our readers will compare me to you, and I won't come out all that well by comparison."

"You are a very good writer, Mr. Morrow."

Morrow smiled. "There's no need to butter me up, John. Your job is secure. I'll write the article."

"Thanks. I have another article I want to write," John replied. "And if you don't mind, I would like for the article I write to be front page, above the fold."

"Are you kidding? What could be a bigger story than

the killing of one of the top gunfighters in the entire West?"

"That may be a bigger story than the one I'm going to write, that's true. But that's not the kind of attention I want for myself."

Morrow nodded. "All right, John. I can see your point. If you are going for front page, top of the page, make it a good one." Morrow paused, then chuckled. "Listen to me telling you to write a good story."

New President of Cattleman's Bank of Cheyenne

by JOHN CUNNINGHAM

Many of the readers, perhaps even most readers who have been following the articles printed in this newspaper about an alleged suicide and embezzlement of the funds from the bank have, by now, come to the conclusion that Joel Prescott did not commit suicide. That is certainly the belief of this scribe.

Regardless of cause of the demise of Mr. Prescott, his death did leave a vacancy in the administration of the bank. One might suppose the position of president of the bank would be filled by the current vice-president, Eli Kendrick. But one would be wrong. You may well ask if not Kendrick, who then, will occupy the chair of president of the bank?

Before the name of the new president is revealed, it is incumbent upon this newspaper to provide its readers with some background information. When Joel Prescott arrived in this fair city five years ago, he was accompanied by his wife, Nettie Lindell Prescott, and his closest friend, Eli Kendrick. Shortly after Joel arrived, he started the Cattleman's Bank with borrowed funds. He subsequently paid off the loans, and became the sole owner of the bank. As the sole owner, he was also president of the bank.

Upon the death of Joel Prescott, his wife, Nettie, became the sole owner of the bank. Therefore, it stands to reason that as owner of the bank, Mrs. Prescott has assumed the position of president of the bank.

You may wonder what difference it makes as to who might be president of a defunct bank, but those who know Mrs. Prescott know her to be a woman of tenacity, ingenuity, honesty, and resolve. With Mrs. Prescott bringing all those qualities to the position of president, don't give up on the resurrection of the Cattleman's Bank of Cheyenne.

Noted Gunman Killed

by J. B. MORROW, *Publisher*

James Hill met his just end on the 7th instant. Hill was a gunman who killed so frequently and with such lack of compunction, that he was known by the sobriquet "Evil." One could say that he was a man in name only, for he was possessed of less redemptive tissue than an outhouse cockroach.

Of recent, there have been frequent

> attempts upon the life of Duff MacCallister, as well as his lady friend, Meagan Parker. Hill was known as a man who sold his gun for money, and it requires no stretch of the imagination to believe that he was employed by a person, or persons, unknown to kill Mr. MacCallister, and that supposition is borne by the fact that he was heard to say, "I'm getting paid a lot of money to kill you." But as he raised his cocked pistol to carry out his nefarious mission, the roar of the gunshot that filled the Red Bull Saloon came not from his gun, but from one being wielded by our own John Cunningham.
>
> The weapon in the hands of Mr. Cunningham was so employed as to energize eight large missiles of double aught buckshot from the barrel of a 10-gauge shotgun. The damage thus rendered upon James Hill's body was substantial and fatal.

After reading the newspaper, Lou Martell dropped it on the table in disgust. "Hell and damnation," he said, his words little more than a growl.

"What's the matter now?" Bart asked.

"Cunningham. It's not enough that he's been writing all those articles, he's also the one that killed Hill."

"If Hill couldn't get the job done, he may as well be dead. Besides, 'im getting' kilt has saved us twenty-five hunnert dollars."

"Yeah, but MacCallister is still alive, and we ain't been able to snatch up his woman."

"Maybe we're goin' after the wrong man," Lou suggested. "Maybe we should be goin' after Cunningham.

He ain't no gunman like MacCallister, 'n he don't have any people around him like that old guy and the Celestial that's allus around MacCallister."

"Before we come to such a decision, let me see what our friend wants us to do," Bart suggested.

"How come you ain't never told me who our friend is?" Lou asked.

"There's no need for you to know. Besides, I had to swear that I'd never tell."

"What if somethin' happened to you? Then all this would be for nothin'."

"You don't need to worry none 'bout that. If somethin' happened to me before all this was done, our friend would get in touch with you."

So far, in all the failed attempts against MacCallister and Meagan, resulting in the assailants being killed, only one, Black Liberty, was of Bart's original gang. As a result, Bart was able to go to town and spend some time looking around without danger of being recognized.

"Bart, what are you doing in town? It's dangerous for you to be here, isn't it?" asked Norman Sweeney, the middleman in all of this craziness.

"Nah, it ain't dangerous at all. I ain't hardly even been in town before, so they don't nobody even know me." Bart went on to explain how he and Lou Martell had come to the conclusion that they were after the wrong man.

"Well, you're right. We have been going after the wrong person. I suppose you have been reading the newspaper stories in the *Leader*?"

"Oh yeah, I've been readin' 'em. That's how come I come into town in the first place to see iffen you want 'nything done about Cunningham."

"Absolutely. Those articles he has been writing are as dangerous, or perhaps even more dangerous than the investigation MacCallister has been conducting."

"Ha! So we are going after him. That shouldn't be no problem. Cunningham will be a lot easier to kill than MacCallister."

"No, don't kill him."

"What do you mean, don't kill him? How are we goin' to stop all them articles he's a-writin' if we don't kill 'im?"

"That's just it. We don't want him to stop writing articles. We just want him to change them, to make them more favorable to us."

"How are we goin' to do that?"

"We are going after the woman."

"You may not have noticed it," Bart said, "but we've done had five men kilt tryin' to snatch her up."

"No, I'm not talking about her. I'm talking about Cunningham's woman."

"Who is his woman?" Bart asked.

"Joel Prescott's widow."

"Wait a minute. Her husband was just kilt, 'n you're sayin' that she's Cunningham's woman? That's kinda fast, ain't it? Are you sure she's his woman?"

"I'm quite sure. Her name is Nettie, and as you may have read, she's the new president of the bank.

"Yeah, I read that. But what can she do to hurt us? The money has already been redeposited."

"It's as I told you. She is Cunningham's woman, and if we take her, it will give us leverage with him."

"You mean set up an ambush for him, like the one we was goin' to do for MacCallister."

"You're thinking small. Remember, I said it would give us leverage. If we have Mrs. Prescott, we can use that to force Cunningham to write any anything we want. For example, he has been looking into the situation, and has come to the conclusion that Prescott committed suicide after all."

"Yeah, well how are we goin' to snatch her up? We sure ain't had a lot of success goin' after MacCallister's woman."

"MacCallister, that old man whose name is Elmer, and the Chinaman, Wang, are always around the Parker woman. They are used to living in danger so they are always alert for it, as you can well attest, since you have lost several men in previous attempts."

"Only one of them was my man," Bart said.

"Nine men have died either trying to capture Miss Parker or kill MacCallister. And one of those was James Hill."

"Onliest thing is, it warn't MacCallister who kilt Evil," Bart pointed out.

"Nevertheless, Hill, who I considered our best opportunity to kill MacCallister, failed, and is dead. It is time to change our tactics, and that means we will take Nettie Prescott."

Cabin hideout

"What did you find out?" Lou Martell asked after Bart returned from his sojourn into town.

"I found out we been goin' after the wrong woman," Bart said.

"Well, who the hell are we supposed to go after?"

"Nettie Prescott.

"Nettie Prescott? Hell, I don't even know who that is."

"She's the president of the bank."

"Yeah, well, what good will it do to get her? The bank ain't got no money."

"Trust me. She will be helpful," Bart insisted.

John and Nettie were having their dinner in the Canady House dining room.

"That was a beautiful article you wrote about me," Nettie said.

John smiled. "Well, when you have a good subject, it's rather easy to write well about that subject."

"But what good will it do?" Nettie asked.

"What good will what do? What do you mean?"

"I am president of a bank that has no money," Nettie said. "You have to admit that, under those circumstances, it is a useless position."

"I will admit nothing of the kind," John said. "Duff is the one who came up with the idea, and he must have a reason for it. He is one of the most intelligent men I have ever known."

Nettie chuckled. "Well, seeing as you were once a college professor, and spent a lot of time around a lot of other college professors, saying that Duff MacCallister is one of the most intelligent men you have ever known is quite a comment."

"Nettie, don't confuse education with intelligence.

Many people have made that mistake, to their own detriment."

After dinner they walked up the stairs together, she to go to her room, which was number 7, and he to number 3, which was his room.

Nettie couldn't explain what she was feeling. Whatever it was, it came with a sense of guilt. There was a lightness in her head, and an emptiness to her stomach, even though she had just eaten. She took the door key from her reticule, but her hands were trembling so that she was having difficulty putting the key in the lock.

"Let me help you," John offered, and taking the key from her, he opened the door.

"John, would you like to . . . uh . . . come in for a few minutes?" Nettie invited.

"I would like nothing better," he said as he followed her into her room and closed the door behind him.

Turning to Nettie, John put his hands on her shoulders, holding her in such a way that she was looking at him. Though she knew she felt a strong attraction toward him, she had been able to suppress those feelings. But in the confines of her room with his hands on her shoulders, she felt a charge of excitement.

"John, I think that we . . . should . . ." The words of her unfinished sentence were much huskier than her normal voice.

"I think we should, too." With a seductive smile, he leaned down to touch his lips against hers as gently as a drifting floret from a puffy dandelion head.

"John, no, I . . . it's too soon," Nettie said, but even as she mouthed the words, he took her head in his hands and she kissed him passionately.

The kiss deepened, then she felt John pull back, and she looked at him with an injured gaze. "John?"

"Not yet, Nettie. It is, as you said, too early. Let's let it build of its own volition."

"Yes. Yes, that's as it should be."

Chapter Thirty-four

They arrived in a wagon in the middle of the night, and as they passed the courthouse, Lou Martell glanced up at the clock tower.

"It's lacking twelve minutes of three, if that clock is right."

Billy Ogden was driving the wagon and he chuckled. "This is the first time I've ever been out this late unless I was passed out drunk on the saloon floor or upstairs in a saloon girl's bed."

"You was most likely passed out in the bed, too," Gus Hagen said, and the others laughed.

"Quit your laughin'," Semmes said. "You want to wake up the whole dang town?"

It didn't seem likely that the town would be waking up anytime soon, so with shushes and silence they continued through town until they turned down the alley behind the Cannady Boarding House.

Semmes, Ogden, and Hagen stayed with the wagon. Bart, Lou, and Stump Waters went in through the back door, then upstairs.

"She's in room seven," Bart said in a low but authoritative voice.

When they reached the door to room number 7, Bart produced a skeleton key, which he used in the keyhole. Pushing the door open, they went inside quietly.

Nettie awakened just as the three men reached the side of her bed. Looking up, she saw them and drew a breath to scream, but one of then held a cloth over her mouth and nose. There was a sweet, cloying smell, then nothing.

"Coffee, Mr. Cunningham?" the Cannady House server asked John the next morning."

"Yes, thank you, but hold the breakfast until Mrs. Prescott joins me."

"Very good sir," the server answered.

John drank his coffee and watched the others eat their breakfast as he waited on Nettie. It was strange that she would be late. He knew she wanted to go to the bank the first thing and to assume her role as president. She didn't think she would have any trouble with Eli, but at dinner last night she had asked John to go with her.

The other breakfast diners began to leave until, finally, John decided to go up to her room to see what was keeping her. When he reached her room, he saw her door was slightly ajar, and that concerned him a little.

"Nettie?" he called quietly. When he received no response, he pushed the door open. "Nettie?" he called again.

John stepped inside and saw that her bed was still mussed. That was very unlike her and, concerned, he stepped deeper into the room for closer examination. That was when he saw the note on the bed.

Cunningham—

We have took yer woman. Rite a story and say that you changed yer mind and now you know that Prescott kilt his ownself. If you do that we'll let her go. If you don't do it we'll kill her.

"Of course we will look for her," Chief Peach told a distraught John when he went to the police with the note. "But if they have taken her out of the city, we won't have any jurisdiction."

"MacCallister," Sergeant Creech said. "He's the one you should see. He's got that warrant from the governor that will let him go anywhere."

"Yes! Yes, I'll go see Duff."

John found Duff and the others just finishing their breakfast in the dining room of the Interocean Hotel, and he showed them the note. "They've taken Nettie somewhere," John said, distraught.

"Have you seen Chief Peach?" Duff asked.

"Yes, and he says if they are somewhere in the city he will find them, but if they aren't in the city, he has no authorization to look for them."

"Gardner," Elmer said.

"Gardner?"

"Don't you 'member that he talked about this feller named Bart, 'n so did the black man who tried to take Meagan."

"Aye, I do remember," Duff said. "Come on, I think we should be for paying a visit to the jail."

* * *

"I don't know nothin' 'bout nobody named Bart," Gardner said a short time later when Duff and the others visited with him through the jail cell.

"That ain't what you said when we took you," Elmer said.

"Mr. Gardner, would you be for calling yourself a smart man?" Duff asked.

"Yeah, I'm smart enough."

"And yet you have been here in the jail for several days, but your friend, Bart has made nae attempt to get you out."

"What . . . what does that have to do with me bein' smart?" Gardner asked.

"If you were a smart man, you'd be for making yourself a deal now."

"A deal? What kind of deal?"

"A trade, you might say. If you would tell us what you know about this man called Bart, and where to find him, I'll see that you are let out of jail," Duff said.

"What do you mean you'll see that I'm let out of jail? You ain't a policeman."

"He's more than that, Gardner," John said, speaking for the first time. "He is a territorial marshal with authority over the police. If he says he can get you out of jail, he can do it."

Gardner was quiet for a moment. "I don't know nothin' about tryin' to kill MacCallister or tryin' to grab up the women. So there ain't nothin' I can say to help you there."

"You mentioned a man by the name of Bart, and so did the black man who tried to take Miss Parker."

"Black Lib got hisself kilt, didn't he?" Gardner asked.

"Black Lib?" John asked.

"Yeah, he called hisself Black Liberty, but most just called him Black Lib. There didn't nobody knows his real name." Gardner said

"When you say 'most,' would you be talking about men who are part of Bart's gang?"

Gardner was quiet for a moment before he answered. "Yeah."

"And you were also part of this man Bart's gang?" John asked.

"Yeah."

"Tell me what you can about him." Duff asked now.

"This will be part of the deal?" Gardner asked.

"If you give us enough information to help us find Mrs. Prescott," Duff replied.

"What do you want to know?"

"Who is this man, Bart, and why has he been after me, and now after Mr. Cunningham?"

"His name is Bart Jenkins, 'n he's got some deal goin' with the money that was took from the bank. Onliest thang is, he ain't actual got the money yet. There don't nobody but him know who it was that took the money or where the money is at now."

"Where can we find him?"

"When I was runnin' with him 'n the others, they was holed up 'n a cabin 'bout five miles west of here."

"I appreciate the information," Duff said as he and the others turned away.

"Hey, wait a minute!" Gardner called. "Ain't you goin' to let me go, now?"

"Not until we ken the information you gave us is correct."

"What if you go out there 'n you get killed?"

"You'll still be in jail," Duff said.

Outlaw cabin

When Nettie awakened, she had a headache and a total sense of confusion. The last thing she remembered was going to bed in her own apartment at the Cannady Boarding House. She didn't know where she was, but she knew she wasn't at the boardinghouse.

Was she dreaming? If this was a dream, it was certainly the most realistic dream she had ever had.

Her nose itched and she tried to scratch it, only to learn that she was tied to the bed. "What?" she said aloud and knew it was no dream. "Hello? Where am I?"

"Well, well, look who is awake," someone said.

Nettie felt a sense of panic. "Who are you?"

"The name is Jenkins. Bart Jenkins, but we're all friends here, so you can just call me Bart. Hey, fellers, she's awake in here. She didn't die."

Several other men came into the little room and looked down at her on the bed.

"We was worried maybe we done too much chloroform. I hear tell that too much of that can kill a person. But, here you are, alive 'n breathin'," said one of the other men.

"This here feller is Lou Martell," Bart said, the introduction all the more bizarre, under the circumstances.

"What am I doing here, and how did I get here?"

"We brought you here, girly, my men and me. 'N the

reason you're here is so's we can make your boyfriend put in the paper whatever it is that we want him to write."

"My boyfriend?" Nettie asked.

"Ain't that feller that's been writin' all them stories in the newspaper your boyfriend?" Bart asked.

"No," she said. "I mean, I don't know. Yes, yes I suppose you could say that he is my boyfriend. But how did you know?"

"Oh, you don't need to worry your purty head none about that. We got ways of knowin'. 'N if he really is your boyfriend, he'll do what we asked him to do to get you free."

"I hope he doesn't," Nettie said.

"What do you mean you hope he don't? Don't you want to get turned loose of here?" Bart asked.

"I figure that I'll be kept alive only as long as I can be used as a bargaining chip. Once you get what you want, there will be no need for you to keep me alive any longer."

Bart chuckled. "Damn, Martell, what do you think about that? Turns out Miz Prescott is smarter 'n we thought."

"Yeah, I reckon she is. You want some breakfast?" Lou asked.

Breakfast, Nettie thought. She had planned to have breakfast with John, yet here she was, God only knows where, and she was being offered breakfast. It was the last thing she wanted, and she started to say no, but she stopped.

"How do you propose I eat breakfast when I am tied up, hand, and foot?"

"Untie her, Semmes," Bart said him. "It ain't like she's goin' to run away. She don't know where she is, 'n she ain't hardly wearin' no clothes."

Nettie gasped. It wasn't until that moment that she realized she was still in her nightgown. That meant she was taken from her bed. But how were they able to do that?

She thought about John asking her to move out of the house because she would be safer in the boardinghouse. She couldn't help but wonder if she wouldn't have been safer had she stayed home.

Chapter Thirty-five

"I'm going with you," John said.

Duff shook his head. "Nae, I dinnae think that would be such a good idea."

"Why not? I'm the reason Nettie was taken, aren't I? And there is no way I plan to just stay back and let others do the work."

Duff, John, Elmer, Wang, and Meagan were holding the discussion in a corner of the lobby of the Interocean Hotel that provided them with some privacy.

"John, they are not just going to turn her over to us. We're going to have to take her, 'n that means 'tis likely to be some shooting, a lot of shooting. 'N that would be nae place for an English professor, nor a newspaperman."

"You say I can't go, but Miss Parker is going?"

"Aye, for 'tis thinking I am that having another woman around when we find Mrs. Prescott would be comforting for the lass."

"And you think I won't be of some comfort to Nettie?"

"Aye, but it's like I said, there's going to be some shooting, and Meagan has been in such a situation before."

"I was a soldier under fire during the war, and you may

recall that I was able to handle a gun all right to save you from being killed," John said with resolve.

Meagan chuckled. "He has you there, Duff."

Duff sighed. "Aye, 'tis reason I suppose for me to be having second thoughts. All right, John. You can go with us, and we'll be happy to have you."

"The post office," John said with a big grin.

"What? What do you mean, the post office?"

"Were we not, just a few minutes ago, lamenting the fact that we had no real knowledge of the location of the cabin, other than approximately five miles west of Cheyenne? The post office might know."

"Duff, yes. That is a brilliant idea!" Meagan said.

"Walter Bizzell," the postmaster said. "He's drawn up a map of every house and cabin within ten miles of the city."

"Do you know where we can find Mr. Bizzell?" John asked.

The postmaster smiled. "He's here, in the back room."

A few minutes later, after Bizzell was told what they were looking for, and why, the old postman stroked his chin, and nodded. "The Underhill cabin."

"I beg your pardon." John asked.

Bizzell led them over to the wall where a map of the region was displayed. "Right here on Silver Creek there's a cabin that used to belong to Earl Ray Underhill, but he moved away several years ago, and nobody has moved in since. At least, nobody as far as we know. But if there's a bunch of outlaws looking for a cabin that's out of the way in this area"—Bizzell took in a part of the map with a sweep of his hand—"that is exactly where they would be."

"Are there any landmarks we can use as a guide?" John asked.

"I'm afraid not," Bizzell said. "That area right through there is as flat and open as the sea."

Elmer chuckled. "The sea, huh? We don't need no landmarks." He went over to examine the map. "I used to do this at sea, and I make it a heading of about 280 degrees. If we follow that, we'll find the cabin.

John was carrying a double-barrel 10-gauge shotgun; Duff, Meagan, and Elmer were armed with pistols on their hips and Winchesters stuck down in the saddle sheaths. Wang, as always, was unarmed. Elmer led the way by taking compass settings, and when they left Cheyenne, they were following a course that was slightly north of due west. After a couple of miles, Wang dismounted, gave the reins of his horse to Meagan, then began scouting ahead on foot. No more than half an hour after Wang had begun his dismounted scout, he came running back. "I have found the cabin," he reported. "It is one mile."

"We'll leave the horses here and go the rest of the way on foot," Duff said.

The others dismounted, snaked the rifles out of the saddle holsters, ground hobbled the horses, then continued on foot.

Although the terrain was flat, Silver Creek was flanked on each side by a berm that was high enough to provide some concealment as they approached the cabin and some cover if and when it was needed.

As they came even with the cabin, Wang broke away from the other four.

Duff waited until Wang was gone, then he called out, "Jenkins, if you want to live, send the woman out!"

"What the hell?" Jenkins called out in alarm. "Where did that come from?"

"Lawton, get up on the roof and see if you can see anything," Semmes said.

Responding to Semmes's order, Craig Lawton went out the back door, then using the ladder which was there just for that purpose, he climbed up onto the roof. Using the three-foot-high lip at the front of the cabin, he crawled up to have a look around and saw three men and a woman just behind the bank of Silver Creek. "Damn," he said with a laugh. "Is that all you've got?"

Lawton hurried back down. "They's only three of 'em. Well, four if you count the woman that's with 'em."

"Woman?" Bart asked. "Let me take a look."

As Lawton had a moment earlier, Bart climbed up onto the roof of the cabin, the crawled forward to have a look. "I'll be damned," he said aloud, though speaking quietly.

Bart hurried back into the cabin with a wide grin on his face. "Boys, we have hit it lucky. Not only is MacCallister one of the men out there, his woman is with him. And"—the grin growing even broader—"they's only four of 'em, countin' the woman, to eleven of us. This couldn't have worked out better."

"What are we goin' to do, Bart?" Moe Conyers asked.

"We got 'em outnumbered by three to one," Bart said. "McCain, Hagen, you two stay in here 'n keep an eye on the Prescott woman. The rest of you come with me. Once we take care of the business outside, there won't be nothin' standin' between us and the money." Bart chuckled. "Damn, they fell right into our laps."

"You mean there won't be nothin' standin' between us 'n half the money, don't you?" Martell asked.

Bart's smile grew larger. "I'm thinkin' we can take care o' that, too, when the time comes. But first, we've got a little business here to deal with."

Duff was keeping his eyes on the front door, and he didn't realize he was in any danger until a bullet popped right over his head. Surprised by the shot that was so close, he poked his head up to see where it came from, and saw a wisp of smoke drifting away from a corner of the house. Jacking a round into his Winchester, he kept his eye on the spot and when just the sliver of a head appeared a few seconds later, he fired. Whoever it was that had been shooting at him from the corner of the house fell to the ground and didn't move. Since the only part of him that had presented as a target was his head, Duff knew that the bullet strike was fatal.

There was a shooter at the opposite corner, too, and Elmer killed him. Meagan got one who was shooting from the roof of the cabin.

"Put up your hands!" someone shouted, and looking toward the sound, Duff saw that two men had entered the creek some distance from him and the others, then worked their way down the stream unseen until they announced their presence to Duff and the three with him.

"Do it now!" the second of the two armed men shouted. "Or the first one to die will be the woman."

"Bart!" one of the men shouted. "Come on down, we've got 'em . . ."

That was as far as they got before the roar of the shotgun in John's hands took both of them down.

Duff nodded toward John, who was holding the shotgun as wisps of smoke curled up from the muzzles of the twin barrels.

"'Tis thankful I am now, that we brought you along," Duff said.

They heard a shout from the direction of the cabin. "What was that? Semmes, Waters, did you get 'em?" Bart shouted.

"Is that what their names was?" Elmer shouted back. "You'll need to remember them when you start carving out the tombstones." He giggled manically. "Onliest thang is, there ain't none of you goin' to be around to be carvin' no tombstones. They'll be someone else carvin' 'em out for you."

"Damn, Bart, they've done kilt Semmes 'n Waters, 'n Conyers 'n Martell. I figure they'll be turning on us, next!" Duff heard someone shout.

"'N Billy Ogden was kilt, too, don't forget," another shouted.

"We gotta take 'em out," Bart shouted. "We ain't got no other choice. Spread out 'n keep shootin'!"

From Nettie's position inside the little cabin, the shooting outside sounded like a full-scale war. The glass windows had been broken long ago, and the window openings had been covered with wood. Hagen and McCain were looking between a few of the gaps and holes, hoping to see what was going on outside.

"Do you see anythin'?" McCain asked.

"I tell you what, McCain, it don't look none too good," Hagen replied.

"What the hell? They's only four of 'em. We still got 'em outnumbered," McCain replied. "Maybe we ought to go out there 'n help 'em."

"You want to get kilt, do you? As least in here we ain't gettin' shot," Hagen said.

"But what if ever'one gets 'emselves kilt?" McCain asked. "We sure as hell cain't stand 'em off by our ownselves."

"We'll bargain," Hagen replied. "We'll still have the woman, so we'll bargain."

"Yeah," McCain said with a satisfied smile. "We'll bargain."

The back door opened.

"Some of you fellers comin' back in here, now, are you?" McCain asked as he and Hagen turned to see who had entered.

"It's a damn Chinaman!" Hagen shouted.

"What? Who the hell are you?" McCain asked.

"I am called Wang," he replied in a calm, conversational voice.

"Shoot 'im! Shoot the damn chink!" Hagen shouted.

Wang stepped toward them. Before either could draw their weapons, he drove the heel of his hands against the bottoms of their noses. Bones were splintered and driven into their brains, instantly killing both men.

"Come," Wang said. "We will go now."

Nettie followed him out through the back door of the house, then over to some nearby boulders. From there they could see the battle in progress. Nettie saw two of the men that she could identify.

One was Emmet Willard and the other was Bart Jenkins. The exchange of gunfire continued, and she saw first Jenkins, then Willard go down.

The gunfire stopped, and an acrid-smelling white cloud drifted over what had been a battlefield. The battlefield was strewn with the bodies of Bart Jenkins's gang members.

After a prolonged moment of silence, Wang and Nettie stood up and started walking toward the creek.

"Nettie!" John shouted. Abandoning his position of cover and concealment, he started running toward her. There, without shame or embarrassment, they shared a warm, thankful embrace.

"Take me home, John," Nettie said. "And when I say home, I mean my real home, my house, not the boardinghouse."

Nettie Prescott Rescued

by

JOHN CUNNINGHAM

King Richard III was a despot who murdered and threatened his way to the throne. Entrusted to look after his nephews in preparation for his brother's coronation as king, the boys were murdered, and Richard claimed the throne for himself.

No less a figure than Shakespeare wrote of King Richard's tyranny, and if the Bard walked among us today, he might be persuaded to write a story about the evil machinations of Bart Jenkins and the others who followed him.

In a deed most foul, and striking in the middle of the night, men of Bart Jenkins gang took Mrs. Prescott, the widow of the murdered banker, Joel Prescott, from her own bed and held her as hostage, hoping thereby to halt the investigation of, and the articles about the perfidious operations of Bart Jenkins and his gang

But, as the famous Scottish poet, Robert Burns so aptly put it, "The best laid schemes o' mice an' men Gang aft a-gley." Bart Jenkins's intention to hold Nettie Prescott was thwarted and Jenkins, and those who rode with him, paid the ultimate price.

Chapter Thirty-six

"What a lovely article John wrote," Meagan said. It's lyrical in its poetic references to such things as the writing of Shakespeare and Burns."

"Aye, the lad has a touch of the great writers of the past about him," Duff agreed.

The conversation was taking part on the depot platform as Meagan, Elmer, and Wang were waiting for the train that would take them back to Chugwater. Duff had made the decision to stay in Cheyenne just a little longer. Yes, Jenkins and his gang had all been killed, and though he knew that, somehow, they were involved in the disappearance of the money, a thorough search of the cabin had turned up nothing.

"That money has to be somewhere," Duff said, "and you have to admit that I have a sixty-five-thousand-dollar interest in finding it."

Meagan smiled. "I can't argue with you over that, but it will be good to see you when you get back home."

* * *

Nettie was performing the sad duty of making the final disposition of Joel's clothes, coin collection, papers, and books, when she saw something wrapped in cloth, then tied shut with strips of cloth. She had never seen this before and was intrigued by it. Unwrapping it, she saw that it was a book like the account books. What was even more intriguing was her name was on an envelope taped to the book. She opened it and read a letter to her. Even before she finished reading, tears began to flow down her cheeks.

She decided to take the letter to John.

After having seen Meagan and the others off on the train, Duff returned to the room he had sublet in Judge Heckemeyer's office suite. Surprised to see John and Nettie waiting for him, he asked, "What is it?"

"I think you should read this letter," John invited, holding it out toward him.

Duff was curious, not only because of the mysterious envelope, but also because of the serious expressions on their faces.

My darling Nettie,

If you are reading this letter, then I am probably dead.

Duff glanced up at the two of them, then continued to read.

For some time now, I have suspected Eli of some sort of chicanery. It hurts me to say this, as our friendship goes back to our time together in the army. We were "brothers in arms," and outside of immediate family, there are no closer relationships.

It started out innocently enough, a mistake in the books of fifty dollars here, or one hundred dollars there, which after questioning and searching, would eventually turn up somewhere else as having been improperly posted.

As you know, we divide the bulk of our funds among three other banks, the purpose being to act as an insurance plan against a total catastrophe. Six days ago I received a receipt from the First Mountain Bank and Trust in Denver. The receipt acknowledged establishing a new account in the name of the Cattlemen's Bank of Cheyenne. The account was begun by the transfer of fifty thousand dollars from Savings and Trust in Laramie, fifty thousand dollars from the Bank of Boise, and one hundred and twenty-five thousand dollars from Deseret Bank in Salt Lake City. The primary signatory would be Eli Kendrick, and I would be the secondary. Having a secondary signatory was necessary to establish the account, but I knew nothing about the account.

I'm concerned about this, and I'm going to look into it. But in the meantime, I have taken a bold move on my own. I have transferred every cent of that account to the finance office at Ft. Laramie. Nettie, I have made you, not Eli, the secondary signatory. If anything happens to me, you will have access to the funds and will be able to continue the operation of the bank.

Before the bank opens tomorrow morning, I intend to discuss this matter with Eli. And though I would be upset with him for making this transfer of funds without my knowledge, I would be most eager and relieved to hear a reasonable explanation. The account book to which this letter is attached represents the true and accurate state of the accounts of the Cattlemen's Bank of Cheyenne.

And know, Nettie, as you read this letter, I have always loved you.

Your loving husband,
Joel

"Judge Heckemeyer, Your Honor, I wonder if you could come in here for a moment, please?" Duff called.

The judge, who was rotund and bald headed, stepped into Duff's office. Duff showed the letter to the judge.

"My word," the judge said after he finished reading the letter. "It wasn't suicide."

"No, sir, it wasn't. I wanted you to see the letter, because the three of us are going to call on Kendrick now and confront him with this new knowledge."

The bank was open again and operating at a very reduced level on borrowed funds. The staff was also reduced to one teller and Eli. When the three went into the bank, Nettie stepped up to the teller's cage.

"Hello, Mrs. Prescott," the teller greeted with a warm smile.

"Mr. Grant, take the rest of the day off, please," Nettie said. "And post the 'closed' sign."

"Yes, ma'am," Grant said, without question.

"Kendrick, come out here," Duff called. "We have some business to discuss."

"I will not be summoned out of my office like some servant. If you want to talk to me, you can come in here. I am the president of this bank."

"No, Eli, you aren't the president," Nettie said. "I am."

"Nettie, you're out there as well? What is this about?"

"Kendrick, come out of there now, or I will come in there and drag you out," Duff said.

Showing resentment, curiosity, and some fright, Eli went out. "You," he said, seeing for the first time that John was there. "What do you want?"

"Eli, when is the last time you checked your account in the bank at Denver?" Nettie asked.

His face reflected shock and a lot of fear. "Bank account in Denver?"

"Without notifying anyone, you took every cent from every ancillary bank we were using, and you opened a new deposit in Denver." She held up the account book. "And right here is the proof."

"I . . . I was going to tell Joel about it."

"You mean just before you killed him?" Duff asked.

"I didn't kill him."

"Come along, Kendrick. You're going to jail, but you

dinnae need to worry too much about it. I expect they'll hang you in a week or so," Duff said.

"I-I did embezzle the money, but I wasn't alone, and I didn't kill Joel. He was my friend."

"It's rather dangerous being your friend, isn't it, Kendrick?" John said.

Ten minutes later they were standing in the police department with Chief Peach, Lieutenant Kirby, and Sergeant Creech.

"Joel did not steal the money," Nettie said. "In fact, the money isn't gone. We have just learned that the money has been redeposited in another place, and I have access to it. We can have the bank fully operational within a day."

Chief Peach smiled. "There are going to be a lot of happy folks when they hear that. Now, what about him?" he nodded toward Eli.

"Kendrick stole the money, then killed Joel when he found out about it," John said.

"I did not kill Joel," Eli insisted. He paused for a moment, then pointed to Lieutenant Kirby. "We were in this together, and he's the one who killed Joel!"

"Damn you!" Kirby shouted, and drawing his pistol, he shot Eli.

Almost immediately, Chief Peach shot Kirby.

Two months later

Unlike the few who had attended Joel Prescott's funeral, so many of the townspeople had turned out for the wedding of John Cunningham and Nettie Lindell Prescott, that St. Mark's Episcopal Church couldn't hold all of them. Although neither John nor Nettie were in the cattle business, the Cheyenne Cattlemen's Club made their facility available for the wedding reception. "After all," the president of the club said, "how could any cattleman do business without a bank?"

"Or any cattlewoman," Meagan added, and with a laugh, the president accepted her contribution to the conversation.

Elmer and Wang had come to Cheyenne with Duff and Meagan to help John and Nettie celebrate their nuptials. At the moment, John and Nettie were with Meagan and Duff, accepting their congratulations.

"Who would have thought it?" Meagan asked.

"I beg your pardon?" John asked.

"I can't help but think that poorly dressed man with scraggly hair, a long beard, and a gun in his hand could be the same person I'm looking at now."

"It all started with you two, you know," John said. "You could have taken me right to jail, or you could have killed me. You had every right to do either one, but the way you reacted, helpful instead of condemning, turned my whole life around." He took Nettie's hands in his, and the two looked at each other with love in their eyes. "Now I'm married to a beautiful woman, and I am doing work that I love to do, writing for the newspaper. How could I possibly want more?"

At that very moment a rather small, nattily dressed man wearing horn-rimmed glasses stepped up to the four of them. "Professor Cunningham?"

"I'm not a professor. I am a newspaperman."

"Yes, I know. It was one of your columns that was picked up by the Associated Press that led me to you. I don't think I would have been able to find you, otherwise."

"Find me for what reason?"

"First, I need to ascertain if you are the author of *Business Communication and Writing*."

John chuckled. "How in the world did you ever find that book? Yes, I wrote it, but it just disappeared somewhere. I don't even have a copy of it."

"I can take care of that."

"What do you mean, you can take care of that?"

It was the small man's time to chuckle. "Dr. Cunningham, do you mean you don't know?"

"Don't know what?"

"My name is Gary Tobin, and I'm from Paddington House. Your book has become a standard business textbook at colleges and universities all over America. When I left New York last week, it was the number three best-selling textbook of all textbooks."

"Oh, John!" Nettie said. "That's wonderful!"

"You say you are from Paddington House. Did you come all the way here just to bring me a copy of my book?"

"I did indeed."

"Well, I thank you for that," John said.

"I brought something else as well," Tobin said. Reaching into the inside pocket of his jacket, he took out an envelope. "I brought you a draft royalty payment in the amount of thirty-three thousand two hundred and seventeen dollars. All you have to do is find a bank that will handle an instrument that large."

John and Nettie smiled at each other.

"I think I know just the bank," he said.

Keep reading for a special excerpt!

National Bestselling Authors
William W. Johnstone
and J. A. Johnstone

RED RIVER VENGEANCE

A PERLEY GATES WESTERN

**JOHNSTONE COUNTRY.
VENGEANCE IS HERE.**

A good man like Perley Gates knows that when you race with the devil, you'd better cross the finish line first—or you won't finish at all . . .

They rode into town like the Four Horsemen of the Apocalypse. Four armed outlaws bringing their own brand of hell to Paris, Texas. First they rob the First National Bank. Then they take a woman hostage as insurance. When Perley Gates learns that local waitress Becky Morris is in the hands of these tough customers, he joins a posse with the Triple-G ranch hands to get her back. Problem is, the outlaws are heading toward Red River—straight into Indian territory. That's where the ranch hands draw the line. But Perley won't give up. He manages to rescue the girl, but not before killing the gang's leader. Now he's incurred the wrath of the other three . . .

The race is on. Come hell or high water, Perley has to get Becky across the Red River—before three vengeful devils make it flow with their blood . . .

Chapter One

"Reckon we'll find out if Beulah's cookin' tastes as good as it did when she called her place the Paris Diner," Sonny Rice announced as he drove the wagon carrying supplies behind Perley, who was riding the bay gelding named Buck.

"How do you know that?" young Link Drew asked. "He just said he wanted to see the new hotel."

"I know 'cause he always eats at Beulah's place when he comes to town for supplies," Sonny replied. "Why do ya think I volunteered to drive the wagon in?"

"I bet the food won't be a whole lot better'n what Ollie cooks," Link said. It was his honest opinion. The gangly orphan had never eaten as well as he did now, ever since Perley brought him to live at the Triple-G after his parents were killed. Although most of the crew at the Triple-G complained good-naturedly about Ollie Dinkler's lack of compassion, they had to admit that he had taken a special interest in the welfare of the young lad.

"It'll be a whole lot fancier," Sonny said, "and it'll look better comin' from a pretty woman, instead of an old man with tobacco juice in his whiskers."

Ahead of the wagon, Perley reined Buck back to a halt and waited for Sonny and Link to come up beside him. "They built it right next to the railroad tracks," Perley stated the obvious. "That'll be handy, won't it? Get off the train and you can walk to the hotel." He nudged his horse and rode up to the rail in front of the hotel and stepped down to wait for the wagon. "Park it on the side, Sonny," he directed. "You and Link go on in and get us a table. I'm just gonna walk through the hotel and take a look." The hotel had been completed while Perley and Possum Smith were down in Bison Gap, and he was curious to see what kind of place it was going to be. According to what his brother Rubin told him, the fellow who built it made his money in cotton. Amos Johnson was his name, and he thought the little town of Paris was ready for a first-class hotel. Rubin said he had talked Beulah Walsh into moving her business into the hotel. Perley figured what Rubin had told him must have been right, because the little Paris Diner building was vacant when they had ridden past.

When Sonny drove the wagon around to the side where the outside entrance was located, Perley walked in the front door. He was greeted by a desk clerk, smartly dressed in a coat and vest. "Can I help you, sir?"

"Howdy," Perley replied. "I'm on my way to your dinin' room and I just wanted to get a look at the hotel. My name's Perley Gates. I work at the Triple-G, and your hotel opened while I was outta town."

"Pleased to meet you," the young man said. "I'm David Smith. If you're looking to see the owner, that's Mr. Johnson. He's in the dining room eating his dinner."

"Oh no," Perley quickly responded. "I don't need to

bother him. I just wanted to see what the hotel looked like on the inside. It looks like a first-class hotel."

"Would you like to see what the rooms look like?" David asked. "I'd be glad to show you one."

"No, no thanks," Perley replied. "I won't have much occasion to rent one, anyway. I'll just go on to the dinin' room, but I thank you for offerin'." He pointed to the entrance to a hallway. "That way?" David nodded. "Much obliged," Perley said, and headed down the hall.

The first door he came to wore a sign that said it was the entrance to the dining room. Perley stepped inside and stood there a moment to look the room over. Still looking and smelling new, it was about half again bigger than Beulah's original establishment. Unlike Beulah's original location, there was no long table in the center of the room, only little tables with four chairs at each one. He saw Sonny and Link sitting at one of them over against the outside wall. He started toward them but stopped when Sonny waved his arm and pointed to a table beside the outside entrance, holding several weapons. Perley nodded and unbuckled his gun belt, looking toward the kitchen door as he walked over to leave his weapon with the others.

He was curious to see if Becky and Lucy had come to the hotel with Beulah, but if they had, they must all be in the kitchen right now. He rolled his holster up in his gun belt, and when he put it on the table, he noticed there were three others there. One he recognized as Sonny's six-gun. It was easy to guess who the other two belonged to. He glanced at a table near the center of the room where two men were attacking the food in front of them as if they were afraid someone might try to take it away from them.

One of the holsters caught his eye. It was a well-oiled fast-draw holster. He glanced again at the two strangers and tried to guess which one belonged to that holster before going over to join his friends. "I thought you would already be eatin'," he said when he sat down at the table.

"It's on the way," Sonny replied, and nodded toward the kitchen just as Lucy Tate, carrying two plates, came out the door. "We're havin' the pork chops, since we don't get much pork at the ranch. It's either that or stew beef today. You don't usually have a choice at the midday meal, but Lucy said today you do because it's Beulah's birthday."

"Well, how 'bout that?" Perley replied. "Don't reckon she said how old she is today."

"Nope, and I sure ain't gonna ask her," Sonny responded. Perley had to laugh at his response. Beulah had reached the age where she was no longer young, but she didn't consider herself old. And only she knew how many notches she had actually acquired.

"Well, there you are," Lucy Tate greeted him. "You haven't been to see us in so long, I figured you'd found someplace else to eat."

Before Perley had time to answer, one of the men at the table in the center of the room blurted, "Hey, Red, where the hell's that coffeepot?"

"Keep your shirt on, cowboy," Lucy yelled back at him. "Got a fresh pot workin' and it'll be ready in a minute." Back to Perley, she said, "I heard you had been gone for a while. You back to stay?"

"Far as I know," he answered. "At least I ain't plannin' to go anywhere right now." He looked at Link and winked.

"I expect my brothers are thinkin' it's about time I did my share of the chores at the ranch." Back to Lucy, he said, "Those pork chops look pretty good, I expect I'll try 'em, too."

"Right," Lucy replied, "I'll tell Becky to bring you a cup of coffee." He hadn't asked, but she figured he was wondering where Becky was.

As she walked past the table with the two strangers, one of them stated loudly, "The coffee, Red."

"I told you," she replied, "it's making. And don't call me Red. I don't have red hair, and my name's not Red."

"I reckon she told you what's what," Leonard Watts japed, and reached over to give his partner a playful jab on his shoulder.

Not to be put down by the cocky waitress, Jesse Sage called after Lucy as she continued on to the kitchen. "What is your name, Sassy Britches?"

There were only a few other patrons in the dining room, but Lucy didn't respond to Jesse's last attempt to rile her, sensing an air of discomfort among those diners already. When she went into the kitchen, she met Becky Morris on her way out with a cup of coffee for Perley. She knew the young waitress must have recognized Perley's voice when he joined Sonny and Link. "He wants the chops," Lucy said.

"I heard," Becky said, "but I thought I'd take him some coffee while Beulah's fixing up his plate."

Lucy chuckled, unable to resist teasing her. "You do have good ears," she japed. "I could have waited on him."

Accustomed to her friend's joking, Becky didn't respond while she went out the door, hurried over to Perley's table, and placed the cup of coffee down before him. "I know how you like your coffee," she said, "so I brought it right out. It's the first cup out of a new pot. Beulah's fixing your plate right now."

The warm smile she always caused to form on Perley's face blossomed into a beaming grin of embarrassment as he tried to think of something intelligent to say. Failing to come up with anything, he settled for, "Howdy, Becky."

His response was not loud, but it was enough to be heard at the table several feet away. "Yeah, howdy, Becky," Jesse demanded, "where the hell's my coffee? If anybody got the first cup, it oughta been me. Hell, he just walked in."

Leonard chuckled. "I swear, Jesse, you sure are feelin' ornery today, ain'tcha?"

"Damn right I am," Jesse said. Then to Becky, he ordered, "Tell that other gal, Miss Sassy Britches, I want some fresh coffee right now."

It had already gone too far. Perley was not happy with the obvious disrespect shown the two women, and now he could see that same resentment building in Sonny's eyes. Afraid Sonny might get into an altercation with the two drifters, he thought he'd better try to see if he could defuse the situation before it blew up. "Hey, there ain't no problem, friend," he called out to Jesse. "Becky, here, didn't know you were supposed to get the first cup. You can take this one and I'll wait for the next one. We don't talk to the ladies here in the dinin' room like you might talk to the ladies in the saloon, so it doesn't set too well with 'em. Whaddaya say? You want this cup of coffee?"

Both drifters looked at Perley in disbelief for a long moment before Jesse responded. "Mister, in the first place, I ain't your friend, and it ain't none of your business how I talk to a woman anywhere. So you'd best keep your mouth shut and mind your own business. I don't want your damn cup of coffee. If I did, I woulda already come over there and took it. Whaddaya say about that?"

Remaining unruffled, Perley paused and shrugged. "Well, I'd say that wouldn'ta been necessary, since I offered to give it to you, anyway."

Jesse looked at Leonard and asked, "Do you believe this mealymouthed jasper?" Looking back at Perley then, he warned, "Like I told you, keep your nose in your own business and stay the hell outta mine."

"Don't fret yourself, Perley," Becky said. "I'll run get the man some more coffee. There's no reason to have any trouble."

Jesse didn't miss hearing the name. "*Pearly*, is that what your name is?" When Perley nodded, Jesse declared, "Well, it sure as hell suits you. *Pearly*," he repeated, laughing. "What's your last name? Gates?" He looked over at Leonard and gave him a playful punch on the shoulder.

"Matter of fact, it is," Perley said.

That caused Jesse to pause for a moment. He was so surprised to find he had guessed right when he thought he had made a joke of the fellow's name. He looked at Leonard again, then they both howled with laughter. "Pearly Gates," he repeated a couple more times. "If that ain't a perfect name for a jasper like you, I don't know what is." He paused then when it occurred to him that the innocent-looking cowhand might be japing him. "Or maybe that ain't really your name and you're thinkin' you're pretty funny." He was about to threaten Perley but was interrupted by Lucy, who came from the kitchen at that point, carrying two fresh cups of coffee.

"Sorry to make you boys wait," she said. "I had to clear my throat first." She glanced at Becky and winked. "Now, I hope you two will settle down and act like you've been around decent folks before."

Having caught Lucy's quick wink at Becky, Jesse was at once suspicious. "I don't reckon there's anything in that cup but coffee, right?"

"Of course, that's right," Lucy answered. "Did you want something else in it?"

He looked at his friend and gave him a wink. "Then I don't reckon you'd mind takin' a little drink of it first," Jesse said.

Lucy shrugged and without hesitating, picked up the cup and took a couple of sips of coffee. Then she graced him with a broad smile as she placed the cup back on the table. "Fresh out of the pot," she said. "Satisfied?" She turned to Becky then and said, "Come on, Becky, let's let 'em eat so they can get outta here. Perley's plate is ready now, anyway."

Becky started to follow her to the kitchen, but Jesse grabbed her wrist and pulled her back. "To hell with Perley's plate. You can stay here and keep company with me and Leonard."

That was as much as Perley could abide. "I reckon you've gone far enough to make it my business now," he said as he got up from his chair. "We don't stand for that kinda treatment to the ladies in this town. Let her go and we won't send for the sheriff. You can just finish your dinner and get on outta here and let decent people eat in peace."

Jesse gave him a big smile as he released Becky's wrist. She shot one worried look in Perley's direction before running out the door to find the sheriff. "Well, well," Jesse asked Leonard, "did you hear what he called me?"

"He called you a dirty name I can't repeat in front of these citizens settin' in here eatin'. And he said you was a yellow-bellied, scum-eatin' dog," the simple man answered, knowing what Jesse was fixing to do. Judging by the foolish grin on his face, it was easy to guess he possessed mere childlike intelligence.

"I'm thinkin' a man ain't no man a-tall, if he don't stand up to a yellow snivelin' dog callin' him names like that. Whaddaya think I oughta do about it?"

"I reckon you ain't got no choice," Leonard said. "A man's got a right to stand up for his honor. If he don't, he ain't got no honor. Ain't that what Micah always says?" They both got to their feet and stood grinning at Perley. "Maybe if he said he was sorry and admitted he was a yellow dog and crawled outta here on his hands and knees, you could let him get by with what he said," Leonard added, excitedly.

Perley patiently watched their little parody for a few minutes before responding. "You two fellows are puttin' on a good little show over one cup of coffee. If you think I'm gonna participate in a gunfight with you, you're mistaken. I came in here to eat my dinner, just like the rest of these folks. So why don't you sit back down and finish your dinner? Then you can go to Patton's Saloon and tell everybody there how you backed me down. That way, nobody gets shot, and we can eat in peace."

Since it was fairly obvious that Perley was not inclined to answer his challenge, Jesse was determined to force him to face him in the street or acknowledge his cowardice. He was about to issue his ultimatum when Sheriff

Paul McQueen walked in with Becky right behind him. "What's the trouble here?" McQueen asked as he walked up to face the two strangers still standing.

"Ain't no trouble, Sheriff," Jesse answered. "I ain't got no idea why that young lady thought there was and went and got you for nothin'. Me and my friend, here, was just tryin' to enjoy us a nice dinner. Then this feller"—he nodded toward Perley—"came in and started bellyachin' about a cup of coffee."

"That ain't exactly the way I heard it," McQueen replied. "I heard you two were disturbin' the peace. We don't stand for any rough treatment of the women who work in this dinin' room, or any rough language, either." He looked at Perley then, knowing he hadn't started any trouble. "Perley, you got anything to say?"

"Not much, Sheriff," Perley replied. "I think these fellows just forgot their manners. They're new in town and don't know how to act in a peaceful place of business. But there ain't any need to lock 'em up, if they'll just finish their dinner and get on outta here. That oughta be all right, wouldn't it, Beulah?"

Beulah Walsh, who was witnessing the confrontation from the kitchen door, shrugged and answered. "I reckon, if they agree not to cause no more trouble."

"Seems to me you ain't hearin' but one side of this argument," Leonard Watts declared. "That feller, there, is the one oughta go to jail. He as much as called Jesse out, but we'll finish up and get on outta here, anyway. Ain't no need to put us in jail."

"Leonard's right," Jesse added. "We ain't gonna start nothin', but I ain't gonna back down if he calls me out."

McQueen couldn't suppress a little smile. "Well, that

would be a different matter. If Perley called you out, you'd have a right to defend yourself." He looked at Beulah to see if she was satisfied to let them remain.

She nodded and asked, "You wanna sit down and have a cup of coffee or something, Sheriff?" He had already eaten there earlier, but she figured it would ensure the peace if he stayed awhile.

"As long as I'm here, I might as well," McQueen said. "I'll just sit down over here." He walked over and sat down at a table near the one that held the weapons. "I'll make sure Perley don't call one of your customers out," he couldn't resist saying.

"I'll get you some coffee," Lucy sang out, and went into the kitchen with Beulah and Becky.

Beulah fixed up a fresh plate for Perley, since the first one had begun to cool off. While she dished it out, Becky stopped Lucy on her way out with the sheriff's coffee to ask a question. "I thought I knew why you winked when you said you had to clear your throat. Why did you take a gulp of that coffee when that man dared you to?"

Lucy laughed. "'Cause it was just my spit in it. I was just glad he didn't want me to taste the other fellow's coffee. Beulah spit in his."

"That fellow was really puttin' the challenge out on you," Sonny said to Perley, his voice low so as not to be overheard at the table where the two strangers were rapidly finishing up their meal.

"It's just mostly big talk," Perley said. "He probably owns that gun on the table in the fast-draw holster, so he's always lookin' for some excuse to shoot somebody. I didn't want it to be one of us."

"I reckon it was a good thing Becky went to fetch the sheriff," Sonny said. "You mighta had to meet him out in the middle of the street."

"I wasn't gonna meet anybody out in the middle of the street," Perley insisted. "That's one of the dumbest things a man can do."

"I reckon you're right," Sonny allowed. He had heard rumors of how fast Perley was with a six-gun, although he had never witnessed it, himself. And he once overheard Perley's brother John telling Fred Farmer about an incident he had witnessed. Fred was older than the rest of the hands at the Triple-G and had been with the Gateses the longest of any of the men. John told him that Perley was like chain lightning when backed into a corner. He said Perley didn't know why he was so fast, something just fired in his brain when he had to act. John figured because he didn't understand that "gift," he was reluctant to use it. Thinking about that now, Sonny thought he would surely like to have been there with John to see for himself.

"Ain't you afraid they might go braggin' around town that you were too scared to face that bigmouth?" Link asked. Perley was his hero, and he didn't like to think there was a flaw in his hero. The man called Jesse had openly laid down a challenge to Perley, and Perley just tried to talk his way out of it.

"Doesn't make any difference to me what they say," Perley told him. "It's just words, and words get blown away by the first little breeze that comes along. Sometimes you might get caught where you ain't got no choice. There ain't much you can do then but try to do the best you can. Anyway, it ain't nothin' but tomfools that pull a gun on another fellow just to see if he can get his out quicker. The folks that count are the folks you see and work with every day. And they know who you are, so it doesn't matter what some stranger passin' through town thinks about you. You understand that, don'tcha?"

"Yeah, I reckon so," Link answered, but he was still thinking he would have liked to have seen how fast Perley really was.

Chapter Two

When the two drifters finished eating, they left money on the table and walked toward the door. As they passed by the table where the three Triple-G hands were eating, Jesse reached down and knocked Perley's coffee cup over, causing him to jump backward to keep from getting his lap filled. He just managed to catch himself from going over backward with his chair. "Damn, Perley," Jesse mumbled. "Sorry 'bout that. That was kinda clumsy of me, weren't it? I'll be down at the saloon if you wanna do somethin' about it."

Perley reached over and grabbed Sonny's elbow when he started to jump to his feet. "No need to get excited," he said. "I didn't get any on me, and it needed warmin' up, anyway." He looked at McQueen and shook his head when the sheriff got to his feet.

As a precaution, the sheriff walked over to stand beside the weapons table while Jesse and Leonard picked up their guns. "You two are gettin' close to spendin' the night in my jail. You're damn lucky the man you been pickin' away at is a peaceful man or you mighta been sleepin' in the boneyard up on the hill."

"We ain't gonna cause no more trouble, Sheriff," Leonard was quick to assure him. "Come on, Jesse, we don't wanna spend the night in jail." They went out the door and McQueen followed them to watch them as they walked away.

When the two troublemakers reached Patton's Saloon and went inside, McQueen returned to the dining room. He was met at the door by Becky Morris. "You should have put them in jail," she said, "especially when that dirty-looking one knocked Perley's cup over."

"Perley's after the same thing I am," the sheriff told her. "And that's to keep from havin' gunfights in our street and endangerin' the good folks in this town. I'm beholden to him for not answerin' that saddle tramp's challenge." He glanced at Perley and nodded his thanks. He was well aware of Perley's skill with a six-shooter, but he also knew that the young man's lightning-like reflexes were not something Perley liked to display. He slowly shook his head when he thought about Perley's dilemma. McQueen had never met a more peaceful man than Perley Gates. His father had placed a tremendous burden on his youngest son's shoulders when he named him for the boy's grandfather. McQueen could only assume that God, in His mercy, compensated for the name by endowing the boy with reflexes akin to those of a striking rattlesnake.

When he realized Becky was still standing there, as if waiting for him to say more, he thanked her for the coffee. "I'd best get back to shoein' that horse," he said, referring to the job he was in the middle of when Becky came to find him. It brought to mind a subject that had been in his thoughts a lot lately. The town was growing so fast that he felt it already called for a full-time sheriff, instead of one who was also a part-time blacksmith.

"Thanks for coming, Sheriff," Becky said, turned, and went back to the table where Lucy and Beulah were already warning Perley to be careful when he left the dining room. "They're right, Perley," Becky said. "Those two are just looking for trouble."

And like John and Rubin like to say, if there ain't but one cow pie in the whole state of Texas, Perley will most likely step in it, was the thought in Perley's mind. To Becky, however, he said, "Nothin' to worry about. We've already got the wagon loaded with the supplies we came after, so we'll be headin' straight to the ranch when we leave here. Besides, I've got Sonny and Link to take care of me. Ain't that right, Link?" Link looked undecided. Perley continued, "So, I'm gonna take my time to enjoy this fine meal Beulah cooked. By the time I'm finished, those fellows probably won't even remember me."

"I hope you're right," Becky said, and turned her attention to some of the other customers, who were waiting for coffee refills. The room returned to its usual atmosphere of peaceful dining.

Just as he said he would, Perley took his time to enjoy his dinner and some idle conversation with Becky and Lucy, plus a pause to stick his head inside the kitchen door to wish Beulah a happy birthday. Unfortunately, it provided enough time for his two antagonists to think of another way to entertain themselves at his expense. "We saw them two fellers ol' Perley met with when they drove that wagon around to the side of the buildin',"

Jesse recalled as he and Leonard walked out on the porch of the saloon. "But he came from that inside door from the hotel."

"Yeah, he did," Leonard replied, wondering what that had to do with anything.

"Look yonder at that bay horse tied out front of the hotel," Jesse said, a grin slowly spreading across his unshaven face. "I'm thinkin' that's ol' Perley's horse. I bet you he ain't got a room in the hotel. He just tied his horse out there."

Still not quite sure what his friend was driving at, Leonard asked, "Maybe, so what about it?"

"I'm thinkin' about borrowin' his horse for a little ride," Jesse answered, his grin spreading from ear to ear now. "See if that don't get his dander up enough to make him do somethin' about it."

"Damned if you ain't got the itch awful bad to shoot somebody, ain't you? How do you know how fast he is?"

"I know he ain't faster'n me," Jesse crowed. "I just don't like his attitude—like he's too good to have to stand up like a man." He continued to grin at Leonard, waiting for him to show some enthusiasm for the caper. When Leonard remained indifferent, Jesse announced, "Well, I'm gonna take that bay for a little ride up and down this street a few times, till ol' Perley shows his yellow self."

"What if it ain't his horse?" Leonard asked.

"Then I'll just say, *Beg your pardon, sir,* and if whoever owns him don't like it, we can settle it with six-guns." Jesse didn't wait for more discussion but headed straight for the hotel. Thinking it was bound to provide some entertainment, no matter who owned the horse, Leonard followed along behind him. He didn't think it was a good idea, and Jesse's brothers wouldn't like for him to draw any more attention to them. But he knew better than to tell Jesse not to do something.

When he walked up to the hitching rail, Jesse took a quick look toward the front door of the hotel. Seeing no one, he untied Buck's reins from the rail and turned the bay gelding toward the street. "You're a good-lookin' horse for a jasper like that to be ridin'. It's time to let you feel a man on your back." He put a foot in the stirrup and climbed up. While he was throwing his right leg over, Buck lowered his head toward the ground and reared up on his front legs, causing the unsuspecting Jesse to do a somersault in midair and land hard on the ground in front of the horse. "Damn you!" Jesse spat as he tried to gather himself. "You like to broke my back!"

It only made matters worse when Leonard whooped and hollered, "Hot damn, Jesse! You never said nothin' about flyin'. Looks to me like that horse don't wanna be rode."

"Well, he's gonna be," Jesse announced emphatically and got back up on his feet. "C'mere, you hardheaded plug." Buck didn't move but stood watching the strange man as he advanced cautiously toward him. "You fooled me with that trick, but I ain't gonna be fooled this time." The horse remained stone still as Jesse walked slowly up to him and took the reins again.

Leonard bit his lip to keep from laughing, urging Jesse on. "Watch him, Jesse, he's waitin' to give you another flip."

"He does and I'll shoot the fool crowbait," Jesse said. "He ain't as ornery as he thinks he is." Buck continued to watch Jesse with a wary eye, but he remained as still as a statue. Trying again to approach the stone-still horse, Jesse kept talking calmly. "You just hold still, ol' boy, till I get settled in the saddle. Then I'll run some of the steam outta you." With his foot in the stirrup again, he took a good grip on the saddle horn, then stood there on one leg before attempting to climb into the saddle. Still he paused, waiting to catch the horse by surprise. When he was ready, he suddenly pulled himself up to land squarely in the saddle. Buck did not flinch. He remained still as a statue. "Now, you're showin' some sense, horse." He looked over at Leonard and grinned. "All he needed was for . . ." That was as far as he got before the big bay gelding exploded. With all four legs stiff as poles, the horse bounced around and around in a circle while Jesse held on for dear life. When that didn't rid him of his rider, the incensed gelding started a series of bucks that ended when Jesse was finally thrown, landing on the hotel porch to slide up against a corner post.

With the fuse on his temper burning brightly now, Jesse rolled over on the rough boards of the porch, his hands and knees skinned under his clothes. He scrambled on all fours to recover his .44, which had been knocked out of his holster when he landed on the porch. When he had the pistol in hand, he turned to level it at the offending horse. "Damn you, you four-legged devil, I'm sendin' you back to hell where you came from!" He cocked the pistol at almost the same time his hand was smashed by the .44 slug that knocked the weapon free.

Jesse screamed with the pain in his hand as he turned to see Perley standing in the doorway, his six-gun trained on him. "I'm willin' to ignore your childish behavior when it ain't doin' any harm," Perley said. "But you're goin' too far when you mess with my horse." He glanced over at Leonard, standing in the street, to make sure he wasn't showing any signs of retaliation. He wasn't, after having witnessed the swiftness of the shot just fired. Perley looked back at Jesse. "I'm sure Sheriff McQueen heard that shot and he'll be up here pretty quick to find out who did the shootin'. My advice to both of you is to get on your horses and get outta town before he gets here. If you do, I'll tell him it was just an accidental discharge of a weapon. If you don't, you're goin' to jail. So, what's it gonna be?"

"We're gettin' outta town," Leonard said at once. "We don't want no more trouble." He hurried over to the edge of the porch. "Come on, Jesse, he's right, it's best we get outta town. You can't go to jail right now."

Jesse was in too much pain to argue. He picked up his pistol with his left hand and let Leonard help him off the porch. "I might be seein' you again, Perley," he had to threaten as he went down the one step to the street.

"Come on," Leonard urged him. "Let's get outta here and find a place to take a look at that hand."

Perley stepped out into the street to watch them hurry to the saloon, where their horses were tied. They galloped past the blacksmith's forge just as Paul McQueen came walking out to the street. He paused to take a look at the two departing riders. Then, when he saw Perley standing out in front of the hotel, he headed that way. By the time he walked up there, Sonny and Link were there as well. "Wasn't that those two in the dinin' room before?" the sheriff asked.

"Yep," Perley answered. "They decided it best to leave

town before they wound up in your jailhouse." When McQueen asked about the shot he heard, Perley told him he fired it and why. "I did the best I could to avoid trouble with those two, but that one that kept pickin' at me was fixin' to shoot my horse. So I had to keep him from doin' that."

"You shot him?" McQueen asked.

"Just in the hand," Perley replied. "I told 'em you'd be on your way to most likely put 'em in jail, so they decided to leave town."

"Good," the sheriff said, "'cause it don't look like I'm ever gonna get done shoein' Luther Rains's horse."

"Sorry you were bothered," Perley said. "If you do get called out again, it won't be on account of me. We're fixin' to head back to the Triple-G right now."

"I know it ain't your fault, Perley. You don't ever cause any trouble," the sheriff said. To himself, he thought, *but damned if trouble doesn't have a way of finding you*. He turned away and went back to finish his work at his forge. He had put his wife and son on the train the day before for a trip to visit her family in Kansas City. So he was trying to take advantage of the opportunity to catch up with some of his work as a blacksmith. Maybe if Perley stayed out of town for a while, he could get more done. As soon as he thought it, he scolded himself for thinking anything negative about Perley.

"He was gonna shoot Buck, so you had to shoot that feller, right, Perley?" Link was eager to confirm. His admiration for Perley had wavered a bit after having witnessed

Perley's reluctance to fight before. But now his faith was restored.

"That's right, Link. There wasn't any time to talk him out of it. It's too bad it takes a gun to talk somebody outta doin' something stupid." He glanced down the street to see a few people coming out into the street, curious to see what the gunshot was about, so he climbed up into the saddle. "Let's go home before Rubin sends somebody after us."

When they reached a small stream approximately five miles south of Paris, Leonard Watts said, "Let's pull up here and take a look at your hand." He dismounted and waited for Jesse to pull up beside him. "Is it still bleedin' pretty bad?"

"Hell, yeah, it's still bleedin'," Jesse complained painfully. "I think it broke all the bones in my hand." He had bound his bandanna around the wounded hand as tightly as he could, but the bandanna was thoroughly soaked.

"Come on," Leonard said, "let's wash some of the blood off and see how bad it is." He helped Jesse down from his horse and they knelt beside the stream to clean the hand. After he had cleared some of the blood away, he said, "The bullet went all the way through."

"Hell, I know that," Jesse retorted, "you can see the mark on the grip of my Colt. And I can't move my fingers."

"Well, quit tryin' to move 'em. That just makes it bleed more. Lemme get a rag outta my saddlebag and I'll try to bind it tight enough to hold it till we get back to camp. Micah can take a look at it and see what we gotta do. You might have to ride down to Sulphur Springs. They got a doctor there."

"That sneakin' egg-suckin' dog," Jesse muttered. "I oughta go back and call him out with my left hand."

Leonard shook his head. "I don't know, Jesse, that was a helluva shot that feller made, comin' outta the doorway when he done it. You weren't lookin' at him when he shot you, but I was lookin' right at him when he opened the door. And his gun was in the holster when he started to step out. I don't know," he repeated.

"I reckon that was the reason you never thought about pullin' your gun," Jesse grunted sarcastically. "He was just lucky as hell," he insisted. "He was tryin' to shoot me anywhere and just happened to hit my hand."

"I don't know," Leonard said once again, thinking he had seen what he had seen, and knowing he had never seen anyone faster. Finished with his bandaging then, he said, "Maybe that'll hold you till we get back to the others." Jesse's two brothers were waiting at a camp on the Sulphur River and that was fully ten or eleven miles from where they now stood. Leonard didn't raise the subject with Jesse, but he was thinking Micah and Lucas were not going to be very happy to learn of the attention he and Jesse had called upon themselves in Paris. Their purpose for visiting the town was to take a look at the recently opened bank while Micah and Lucas rode down to Sulphur Springs to look at that bank. Their camp was halfway between the two towns and the plan had been to go to the towns in the morning, look them over, and meet back at the river that afternoon. It was easy for Leonard to forget his part in encouraging Jesse's behavior and then blame him for causing them to be one man short in the planned robbery. *I reckon he can at least hold the horses while we do the real business,* he thought. "We'd best get goin'," he said to Jesse.

Leonard was right on the mark when he figured that Jesse's older brothers were not going to be happy to hear the cause for his wounded hand. "What the hell were you two thinkin'?" Lucas demanded. "We told you to lay low while you were up there and not attract any attention. So you decided to challenge somebody to have a gunfight out in the middle of the street? I swear, no wonder Ma and Pa decided not to have no more young 'uns after you popped out." He looked at the eldest brother, who was busy examining Jesse's hand. "Whaddaya think, Micah? Think we just oughta hit that bank in Sulphur Springs? It's been there a lot longer than the one they looked at, but there is a damn guard."

"Yeah, and they got a pretty tough sheriff, too," Micah replied. He turned to Leonard and asked, "Tell me what you did find out when you weren't tryin' to get everybody to notice you."

"I swear, Micah," Leonard responded, "we did look the town over. It didn't take long. It ain't a big town, not as big as Sulphur Springs. The bank's new, and they ain't got no guards workin' there. It'd be easy to knock it over. They got a sheriff, but he's just part-time. Most of the time he works in a blacksmith shop. I don't think they'd be able to get up a posse to amount to much. And there weren't but a few people that got a look at me and Jesse. Besides, we'd be wearin' bandannas over our faces, anyway."

"Right," Lucas scoffed, "and one of the bandannas

would be blood soaked on the feller with a bandaged-up hand. How 'bout it, Micah? Is he gonna have to go see a doctor about that hand?"

"Well, it ain't good, but it coulda been busted up a lot worse. Just feelin' around on it, I think it mighta broke one of them little bones in there but not all of 'em. It just went straight through. If he can stand it, I think a doctor can wait till we get the hell outta Texas." He turned to Jesse then. "What do you say, Jesse? Can you make it?"

Jesse took a look at his bandaged right hand and cursed. "Yeah," he decided. "I can wait till we get our business done here and get gone."

Micah studied him for a long moment before deciding Jesse was not just blowing smoke. Considering what he now knew about the two possible targets for bank robbery, he made his thoughts known to the others. "Right now, I'm thinkin' that Paris bank is the smartest move, especially since we're short a man. It's smaller, not well guarded, and they've got a part-time sheriff. There's one other thing I like about it, it's a lot closer to the Red River, only about sixteen miles and we'd be in Indian Territory. I'm thinkin' that right there would discourage any posse they might get up to come after us. Sulphur Springs is more like fifty miles before we could slip into Oklahoma Indian Territory. It's been a while since we were up that way, but ol' Doc O'Shea is most likely still over at Durant Station. If your hand don't show signs of healin', we can let him take a look at it."

"If the old fool ain't drank hisself to death by now," Lucas said. Dr. Oliver O'Shea was a competent physician when he was sober, so it was said. They knew that he was adequate even when drunk, since that was the only state in which they had ever seen him.

There was no disagreement on the plan from any of the four after they discussed it a little further. They decided Micah was right in his opinion that there was less of a gamble on their part if they struck the smaller town. "All right, then," Lucas declared, "I reckon we'll ride on up to Paris tomorrow, camp outside of town tomorrow night, so the horses will be rested up good. Then we can go to the bank the next mornin' to make a withdrawal. That'll be a Friday. That's a good day to go to the bank."

Visit us online at

KensingtonBooks.com

to read more from your favorite authors, see books by series, view reading group guides, and more.

Join us on social media

for sneak peeks, chances to win books and prize packs, and to share your thoughts with other readers.

facebook.com/kensingtonpublishing
twitter.com/kensingtonbooks

Tell us what you think!

To share your thoughts, submit a review, or sign up for our eNewsletters, please visit: **KensingtonBooks.com/TellUs.**